Caribe

Caribe by Evangeline Blanco was the 1995 first-prize winner of the twenty-first Chicano/Latino Literary Contest of the University of California, Irvine, in the category of the novel. *Caribe* was lauded for its historical dimension, meticulous investigation, and handling of characters.

Caribe

A Novel of Puerto Rico

Evangeline Blanco

Doubleday

New York

London

Toronto

Sydney

Auckland

PUBLISHED BY DOUBLEDAY

a division of Bantam Doubleday Dell Publishing Group, Inc.

1540 Broadway, New York, New York 10036

DOUBLEDAY and the portrayal of an anchor with a dolphin
are trademarks of Doubleday, a division of
Bantam Doubleday Dell Publishing Group, Inc.

Book design by Chris Welch

This is a work of fiction. Major and minor characters are all figments of the
author's imagination, and any resemblance they may have to actual persons, living
or dead, is purely coincidental. Historical places, individuals, and statistics are
included strictly for verisimilitude from the reading matter acknowledged in the
bibliography. Because some sources disagreed on dates and/or contained opposing
viewpoints, the material and statistics chosen fit the purpose of placing the
imaginary events depicted within the realm of possibility.

Library of Congress Cataloging-in-Publication Data

Blanco, Evangeline.

Caribe: a novel of Puerto Rico / by Evangeline Blanco. — 1st ed.

p.   cm.

Includes bibliographical references.

1. Puerto Rico—History—Fiction. I. Title.

PS3552.L36525C37   1998

813'.54—DC21   97-26596

CIP

ISBN 0-385-58650-2

All Rights Reserved

Printed in the United States of America

January 1998

First Edition

1   3   5   7   9   10   8   6   4   2

For Esther

Acknowledgments

While it is difficult to remember every person behind a writer's work of fiction, my heartfelt thank you to all who encouraged me: María Trujillo Timmis, Esther Parra, Myra Fonseca, Norma and Charlie Bonilla, Gerry Storch, Richard L. DeJesús, Saiyed Abbas, Rose Ann Tack, Ángel L. Parra, Ivonne M. Parra de Torech, Cano Torech, and Francesca Dadea.

I feel a debt to readers, teachers, and novelists for their input and enthusiasm: Georgia Bender, Peter Bricklebank, Robert G. Dunn, Sarah Schulman, Doug Schaff, and John E. Thompson, Jr.

My gratitude and best wishes to the judges and staff at the Department of Spanish and Portuguese of the University of California, Irvine: José Agustín, Juan Bruce-Novoa, Alejandro Morales, and Ruth M. Gratzer.

For reference material I thank Mr. Pedro Domínguez Collazo, director of the Cataño library, for providing photocopies of historical information and to that special *Mujer al Servicio de su Pueblo*, Felisa Rincón de Gautier, for her gracious interview.

Last but not least a very special thanks to Janet Hill and Victoria Sanders who not only read and encouraged but who also worked hard to make publication possible.

Characters

From San Juan

Dr. Rafael Rodríguez, benefactor of the poor and separatist
Josefa Rodríguez, Dr. Rodríguez' adoptive aunt
Félix Cienfuegos, Sr., disinherited poet
Félix Cienfuegos, Jr., son of Félix, Sr.
Jorge Bartolomeo, lawyer and partner of Diego Toledo

From Cataño

Dr. Rafael Figueroa, respected physician and family man
Josie Figueroa, Dr. Figueroa's wife
Rafaela Moya, friend of the Figueroas
Doña Antonia Moya, Rafaela's mother
América Moya, Rafaela's sister
Europa Moya, Rafaela's sister
Asia and África Moya, twin sisters of Rafaela
Ana Betancourt, Rafaela's friend
Edelmira Betancourt, Ana's daughter raised by Rafaela
Darío Ferrer, Spaniard and pharmacist

Characters

Francisca Ferrer, Darío's spinster sister
Diego Toledo, lawyer and partner to Jorge Bartolomeo
Waldemar Toledo, Diego's younger brother
Miguelito, Rafaela's friend and servant to Félix Cienfuegos
Tomasa, flower seller and Miguelito's mother

From Caguas and Comerío

Pedro Cienfuegos, landowner and granduncle of Félix, Jr.
Doña Marta, governess and housekeeper for Pedro Cienfuegos
Julián, servant of Pedro Cienfuegos
Ciriaco, servant of Pedro Cienfuegos
Jacinto, foreman of Pedro Cienfuegos

From Loíza Aldea

Socorro Peña, known as Mamá Tumba and Mamá Abuela
Juan Peña, spiritualist and grave digger
Paula Meléndez, cousin of Juan Peña

From Manatí

Luis Arriesgo, beggar with deformed spine
Tomás Arriesgo, Luis's younger brother
Luisa Arriesgo, Luis and Tomás's mother

Chronology

Chronology

1897   Yauco rebellion

Spain grants autonomy to Puerto Rico through efforts of Luis Muñoz Rivera and Spain's Práxedes Mateo Sagasta

1898   Autonomy inaugurated in Puerto Rico

Warship Maine explodes in Cuba

McKinley declares war on Spain

North Americans invade Puerto Rico

Félix Cienfuegos born

Dr. Betances dies in France

1899   San Ciriaco hurricane

United States renames island Porto Rico. An entire generation grows to call itself "Porto Rican" and to affectionally call the island "Portorro"

1900   Senator Bate opposes statehood for Puerto Rico, implies it contains savages, cannibals, and head hunters

Paula Meléndez born

1903   Rafael Figueroa returns to Cataño with wife Josie

Josie Figueroa works to help Rafael obtain medical degree

Juan Peña born

Rafaela Moya born

1910   Luis Arriesgo born

América Moya born

1911   Europa Moya born

1912   Asia and África Moya born

1913   Tomás Arriesgo born

1916   Luis Muñoz Rivera dies

Pedro Cienfuegos dies

1917   Jones Act grants U.S. citizenship to Puerto Rico

1918   Puerto Ricans volunteer to help fight World War I

1920   Rafaela and Félix meet

Edelmira Betancourt born

1922   *Independentistas* form the Nationalist Party to protest the formula of a "Free Associated State" with the United States

Chronology

1924   Paula Meléndez, Luis and Tomás Arriesgo move from Manatí to Cataño

1925   Rafaela meets with movie director

1927   Cataño becomes a municipality

1928   San Felipe hurricane

1929   Luis blackmails Félix

1930   Under President Albizu Campos, the Nationalist Party adopts a militant policy and realizes revolutionary acts of armed insurrection against colonial rule

1932   San Ciprián hurricane

Island takes back its name of Puerto Rico

Tomás Arriesgo leaves Puerto Rico

1936   Nationalists kill Coronel E. Francis Riggs

Albizu Campos is blamed and jailed in Georgia along with poet Clemente Soto Vélez

1937   Massacre of nationalists in Ponce

1940   Tri-party union

Popular Democratic Party headed by Luis Muñoz Marín, son of Luis Muñoz Rivera

Casino of Puerto Rico turned over to American forces

1943   Albizu Campos released from federal penitentiary due to heart problems and partial paralysis of left side

Migration of Puerto Ricans in search of employment

1946   Felisa Rincón de Gautier first woman mayor of San Juan

1949   Luis Muñoz Marín, first Puerto Rican since 1898 to become governor

1952   Inauguration of Puerto Rico as "Free Associated State"

1960   An attempt to unite nine nationalist organizations fails

The U.N. General Assembly adopts a resolution for the abolition of all colonialism

The U.S. Congress prohibits Puerto Rican constitution from amending regulations of the federal government

1990   A family reunion in New York's Marriott Marquis hotel

Caribe

Folktale 1

Juan Bobo cuida su casa

Simple Simon takes care of his home

Once, many, many years ago on a mountain in Puerto Rico four hungry people lived in a shack: Juan Bobo, his parents, and his infant brother.

"Praying to God for enough food is good," his father said to his mother. "But leaving the house and baby alone with Juan Bobo while I am at work is a bad idea."

"How do you feel?" his mother asked, turning to her son.

"I touch very well," Juan Bobo replied. He flexed his fingers.

"No child. Can you feed apples to the pig, kernels of corn to the chicken, milk the goat, guard the baby, and watch the house while I go to church?"

"Pigs apples, chicken corn, goat milk, guard house, watch baby."

Juan Bobo's father went to work and his mother made Juan Bobo repeat it again. "Apple pigs, corn chicken, milk goat, house guard, baby watch."

"If you do a good job, I will return with crackers for you."

After she left, Juan Bobo opened all the doors and windows in their shack and stood in the doorway, unmoving and open mouthed, to stare at butterflies, sunlight glinting on green hills, and at fat white clouds that turned gray until it began to rain. Then he scratched his head.

"Did mamá say baby pigs, milk watch, goat guard, chicken house, corn apples?"

He gave apples to the chicken, corn to the baby, and kept his eyes on the goat while he tried to milk the pig. The baby coughed a few times, turned a lovely shade of blue, and became quiet, which made Juan Bobo very happy. The chicken pecked at the apples

1

rolling around the floor until rats appeared. The pig ran away, and the goat brayed so much it gave him a headache. Afraid the goat might wake his sleeping baby brother, he hit it on the head with a piece of wood and, tired, fell asleep.

His mother returned to find the earthen floor of their shack flooded from the thunderstorm, the baby cold, rats eating the chicken, the goat covered with flies, the pig gone, and their shack filled with sparrows flying and whistling. Awakened, Juan Bobo said, "I did a very good job. Give me my crackers."

Juan Bobo's father did not say a word when he learned what had happened. His parents looked at their son, swallowed their sadness, and wondered what to tell their neighbors.

Part
One

"The great are only great because we are on our knees. Let us rise."—Ramón Emeterio Betances

I

Dr. Rafael Rodríguez

When he began his 1890s excursions, heart-stopping blackness covered the mountains of the Central Cordillera on crescent moon nights. To carry out his master plan of helping his downtrodden compatriots, Dr. Rodríguez made an annual three-month trip throughout Puerto Rico giving free treatment to the poor. His travels also allowed him to keep track of the growing legion of his offspring and to look for children with particular attributes to lead an army of revolutionaries. At night his pupils dilated in his widened eyes to no avail. Blinded, he felt unanchored as if he floated without direction in an inky limbo of threatening sounds and earthy scents. The cool, dark void disoriented his mind and confused his senses so that wind rushing through coconut palms sounded like drops of fanciful rain. He attached cowbells to mules loaded down with his medical supplies, rode slowly through narrow mountain passes, and held a lantern high in his black right hand. It shed light only a few feet in front of his donkey, and many times his uncanny instincts alone—inherited from some unknown ancestor—tingled with fear and danger and made him halt to save himself and his animals from plummeting down dark ravines that bordered dirt roads. Giant ferns, bamboo trees, and other luxuriant foliage grew up the sides of steep inclines and gave bottomless drop-offs the treacherous illusion of gradual down slopes.

In the dark, buzzing flies sounded like mosquitoes, squawking parrots like dangerous birds ready to swoop and attack. In the croaking of tree frogs he imagined that bandits signaled each other, and in the gurgle of streams he heard footsteps. Calming his heartbeat with his own voice and fearful the Spanish militia might shoot him with their rifles for the revolutionary he was, the black doctor shouted his mission.

"Free treatment for the poor! Medicine for the sick!"

Gradually he relied on his lantern, the clang of the cowbells, and the clop, clop of his donkey to identify and protect him from attack by bandits, grateful that the sting of iodine on an open cut might save their fingers or hands, but mainly to attract the peasants who awaited his care and who called to him.

"Over here, Dr. Rodríguez. Watch your left side. Rainfall has swollen the stream."

His lip curled at the lisp of their Spanish accents as it did at his inability to segregate the various noises of the mountains. When he could discern the direction of the caller, Rodríguez drove his tired, stumbling animals toward the voice and asked, "What's the problem here?"

"My child has a fever," some answered.

Children were his favorite patients. Redeeming an otherwise unproductive trip was the saving of a child's life or the grateful smile that rewarded his soothing the hot itch of chicken pox with camphor. The comfort shining through their feverish eyes filled him with a joy that lifted his usual gloom.

One or two of his patients yelled, "My wife bleeds too much." In some of those cases he looked around the small, shabby dwelling with its central dining table, which had held food for meager meals, fabric for sewing dresses, patterns cut from plain brown paper, as well as, on sad occasions, the overripe corpse of a beloved child, skin turned magenta in death. Parents, loathe to bury the lost child, often waited too long, until the tiny body burst forth its internal liquids. Then, fearing unsanitary surfaces, Rodríguez had little choice except to set up a makeshift clinic with tent poles and sheets outside in the open air, pray it would not rain, operate to remove tumors or cancerous intestines, and pray again that he have no further use for his now bloody and contaminated surgical instruments until his next trip. Sometimes he arrived too late after the woman, anxious for the well-being of her needy family, continued to work without complaining and lost so much blood that she was beyond saving. On those occasions his tongue tasted the rotted fruit of defeat, which soured his entire rounds.

Often, some of his patients hung their heads in shame for troubling him with mundane matters and said, "My chickens are dying." When this happened, he treated those too without protest or judgment because he knew it meant the difference between life and slow starvation.

This night he heard a squeaky, apologetic voice.

"My hand hurts."

In the paltry arc of his lantern, Dr. Rodríguez stared at a short, stick-thin peasant wearing ragged pants shrunken to midshin, looked at the straw-covered roof of his single-room hut resting on stilts, and glanced around for one of the barefoot children of the household.

While he led his mules to the front of the home, dismounted, and climbed the steps to enter, the family lit candles so he could see to examine them. Inside the hut, he spoke only to the husband without glancing at his wife, a woman Rodríguez knew too well.

"Was this an accident or a knife fight?" he asked the peasant, Miguel, who unwrapped a ragged, blood-stained cloth from his left hand.

"Accident. Cutting coconuts with my machete."

"Had you been drinking?"

Miguel hesitated as his eyes flew to those of his wife. "Just a little," he replied.

"I'll teach *that* child," he said, pointing to this household's mulatto.

Rubbing his eyes, this particular sleepy boy, with skin a deeply burnished copper and hair standing upright, approached haltingly.

"Here I am," he said, standing barefoot.

"Pay attention," the doctor commanded. "We have to help your father become well."

"What needs to be done?" the wife asked, smiling. She walked toward him in her nightgown without an effort to cover herself and brushed her fingers on his arm.

Rodríguez stared stonily at her brazen behavior in front of her husband for a half-minute without replying until her mouth opened in mystification over his rudeness. Then he turned to her injured husband who had been watching the interchange so intently he sat as if forgetting his pain.

"Have your son bring me boiled water if he knows how."

Year after year his tactics quieted the families, protected unfaithful wives as their mates, confused by the formal manners of the black doctor, doubted the truth of nasty rumors and regretted any suspicions they harbored against their wives and against Rodríguez.

Between the boy's running trips to gather wood, start a fire, and fill a pot with stream water, Rodríguez barked orders at him.

"Faster! You're too slow and sloppy. Bring me some moonshine. Here, bring it closer. Stop your laziness."

Close to tears, the harried boy watched Rodríguez as he poured mountain-made white lightning on a red, open gash splitting his father's left palm.

"I have no iodine left. See what I'm doing?"

"Wasting good moonshine?"

"Wrong!" Both father and son startled at the doctor's forceful voice. "Sterilization is all it's good for. Drink it and you might as well poison yourself and throw yourself off a cliff. This rotgut blinds you and makes you stupid." Rodríguez glanced at Miguel then back at the boy. "Understand?"

"*Sí señor.*"

"Boy, go wash your filthy hands," Rodríguez said. "Don't you know enough to keep yourself clean?"

Rodríguez knew such comments further confused the men of the house. They reasoned it made sense for the doctor to dote over a child that was his instead of treating the boy or girl like a trained insect. He ventured that those thoughts filled many a humble stepfather with an urge to protect the child who was obviously not his. That along with their fervent desire to believe in their wives' fidelity led white men to accept the possibility that a mulatto child could really be theirs.

Supervising, he watched the boy wash his father's injury with soap and rinse thoroughly with boiled water. He took over with another application of moonshine before stitching the wound with a large needle and thick black thread. Miguel whimpered and shook. Then his son applied a salve and a bandage as he was instructed.

"Now, open your palm and look at these two white powders. See the difference?"

The boy nodded. "One is thinner than the other."

"Show me how much of each you can pinch with your thumb and index finger." The boy did so. "Good. This one is for pain. With boiled water allowed to cool, give some to your father every five hours. This other is quinine for fever. No matter how hungry you feel, you must not eat any or you will become very sick. Understand?"

"Yes, sir."

"Are you in school?"

"My son is a good boy," Miguel said, with an edge creeping into his voice.

"I know he is. But good is not enough. We have to be smart and fast, very fast."

"He is."

Noting the child's obvious surprise at his father's support, Rodríguez smiled and ignored both as he repacked his tools and powders, closed his medical bag, and approached the doorway.

"I'll try to return," he said over his shoulder, "in a couple of days to check on the healing. Let me give your son a few last instructions."

Shaking, the boy followed him into the darkness outside.

Hiding behind his mules from the prying eyes of the child's parents, Rodríguez whispered.

"How do your brothers and sisters treat you?"

The boy lowered his head and did not answer.

"I'll return to check if you're learning to read and write. The Spanish will never allow a mulatto like you to enjoy your life if you're ignorant.

When Puerto Rico is free of them, you can do whatever you like, as I do, but only if you have an education. Will you do that?"

"Yes, sir."

"Don't tell your family because they're white and will not understand." He paused, heartbroken that his parents did not know how to handle the boy's hair. "Have your mother cut your hair very close to your scalp instead of brushing it up like that."

"Yes, sir."

Rodríguez allowed the boy to go back home confident that it never occurred to the children's ignorant fathers, not familiar with the intricacies of manipulation, that he did not always scold the children, that in his own way he loved them because he had great plans for them.

Spending blinding, sunny days in the open burned his brown skin to almost charcoal. During chilly nights along the mountain roads he followed, biting winds stung his sensitized face and hands. Dr. Rodríguez ground his teeth in frustration, not finding the children he sought.

Men who labored in fields for twelve-hour days and worried about their livelihood the rest of the time neglected the niceties women craved, and their wives, starved of nourishment for their emotions as well as their bodies, turned to a solicitous, educated man willing to listen, to pet them, and to feed their inner hunger.

He carefully allowed himself to be approached only by milk-white women for his "little mothers" as he called them. The doctor encountered them everywhere on the island, in the cities among the educated and in the hills among the illiterate, young and old, rich and poor. He thought them all flirtatious and greedy and took advantage of their willingness to claw for attention, affection, and sexual fulfillment to feed their vanity and petty carnal needs at the expense of their hard-working husbands. If not him, he felt sure, it would be some other man, perhaps one of the many Puerto Ricans forced to become migrants in their own country by constantly moving between sugarcane fields and coffee and tobacco plantations in their search for work or food. The women fit his agenda although he hated them because they reminded him of two Spanish sisters, his adoptive "aunts."

In his memory it began with his beloved Tata, the chubby housemaid who took time from her kitchen chores to brush fleshy lips on his forehead and call him *negrito lindo*, an endearment the two "aunts" never used. That, or any other. Tata taught him to play a game called the wheel. He jumped up to grab the waist of her apron while she held it fast and twirled around and around, lifting him off his feet causing him to fly in a circle. Josefa, the eldest of his adoptive "aunts", pursed her thin lips at the laughter in the kitchen, stood in the doorway, and watched, arms crossed, until her disapproval silenced them.

"Go to your aunt now," Tata said, almost whispering. "I have scrubbing to do and will talk to you later."

"No, you will not." Josefa commanded. "And you stay, boy. One is never too young to learn so there will be no further mischief in the future." Josefa placed him in front of herself by holding his shoulders and turning him around to face Tata. "We bought him and he belongs to us, not to you. We told you when he first arrived that you were to teach him to take over your duties if you wanted your freedom. Did you not understand?"

"Doña Pepa, he is still too young to do so much work. The house is so big I can hardly do it all myself."

"That's because you spend too much time playing with him. Do not think we will easily grant you permission to marry."

"I'll help Tata," he said, worried about the fear demonstrated on his friend's face.

Josefa punched him. The force of the blow on his cheek swiveled his small face and neck so violently to the left he thought himself unable to move his head. Numbed with pain, his eyes watered but he did not cry. In shock, he stared, open mouthed.

"Us. You help us, not her. She is our servant."

The unspoken, "and so are you," filled him with a sense of otherness, his color.

After that he and Tata settled into a damaged relationship, quiet and aloof except for a dry explanation about how her job was her livelihood and she could not afford to lose it—and that in the future he would make new friends. Although he understood the anxiety his nearness caused her, he still sought her out only to be pushed away. By the year Tata went away, leaving him with the household chores, the boy had accepted and lived with the pain of separation, the loss of kind, loving banter for a long time.

No matter how much he begged, his "aunts" refused to allow him to attend school with other children by saying they did not want him among ruffians and individuals with strange ideas although they did not say specifically what these strange ideas were. They educated him at home with tutors.

"That way we can watch you ourselves," they said.

The first of the soon to be many contracted teachers looked from the "aunts" to him and asked, "What exactly do you require?"

"We want to know if you can teach him anything," they answered.

In one of his rare impetuous moments the growing child spoke with pride. "I can learn anything."

Like something out of a dream, he felt the blows before his eye registered long rustling skirts coming at him so quickly that their feet did not seem to touch the floor.

"Speak only when spoken to," Josefa screamed. Shame burned his face as he hung his head in front of the stranger.

"No hitting!" the teacher said, a bit too loud. "I don't teach that way." The indignant young man straightened and stuck out his chin. "Besides, the boy is right. Why shouldn't he be able to learn?"

His other "aunt," Isabel, more controlled and businesslike, answered him.

"Thank you for coming but we will not need your services."

When he recovered from his stunned silence, the tutor said, "My references are impeccable."

As the young scholar kept his eyes locked on Rodríguez, the "aunts" showed him the door without reply and continued to interview.

Although he was present during subsequent interchanges, the boy heard nothing as his thoughts filled with the difference yet similarity between Tata and the teacher. Although white, creole, educated, and outspoken enough to try to defend him, the teacher had been just as powerless to help as his former friend.

Finally after several teachers were hired, Rodríguez, damned if he would let himself fail, toiled through his lessons while the small white women listened, sat side by side and waved their fans.

"Excellent student," his tutors reported. "He learns everything the first time it is taught to him. You may want to consider an additional, more advanced teacher."

"We will."

"Also, I want to enter one of his essays in a competition."

"No, we don't wish to become a laughingstock in case he wins. We forbid it."

"But he's brilliant!"

Yet, listening behind doors, Rodríguez also heard those same thin, immaculately groomed scholars say, "I would never have thought a Negro could be that intelligent." Often the spinsters reminded him of fat hens fluffing their feathers in front of a rooster as they fanned themselves and cooed through tight, smug smiles.

"It is, no doubt, our influence."

They taught him proper manners and educated him but he hated their control. Wrapped inside the cloak of adoptive caring maidens, their grasping fingers and greedy hands stroked him intimately when he was long past proper age. If he objected, "Stop. What are you doing?", he was punished, made to stand in the patio where midday sun roasted his skin and scalded him until he felt faint.

During those times he stood erect, closed his eyes against the dazzle of sun ghosts dancing in the air. He allowed perspiration to drip down his temples past his lips, soak his chin and continue all the way to wet his socks and shoes. Rodríguez let the streams trickle without once wiping himself off, every thought focused on not allowing his knees to buckle in a faint before one tutor or another arrived to rescue him.

Sometimes his "aunts" gave in out of fear they might kill him and rushed to him in the patio carrying water or a *pava,* a straw hat.

"You are very lucky and must respect our affection," they said, "without making improper insinuations." Calmly, they fitted their white lace gloves on each stubby finger. "We consider you our own even though you aren't. Even though you're black, we are very grateful to do so much for you." They flounced away to church fanning themselves.

As he watched their mantilla-clad heads retreat, his hatred for Spanish domination grew strong as did his desire to understand how he could be considered lucky. Inherited lands and money did not come free.

A slave is a slave.

Why had the white spinsters adopted him? If, as they said, he had been born out of wedlock to a poor family from Loíza Aldea, had they started out with good intentions that deteriorated through time and circumstance? Rodríguez thought not, or else his "aunts" would have accepted one of the many white or mixed-race babies offered daily by distressed parents who could not bear to watch their children starve.

Fueled by the conviction that his fate decreed great accomplishments because he believed himself more logical than others, he often promised himself that someday Negroes from Loíza Aldea including the natural parents who gave him up would have the same opportunities to make a good living as the ruling class and would never have to forfeit their children again.

Obsessed with freedom, Rodríguez studied history to find out why the Cuban revolution against the Spanish succeeded while the Puerto Rican cry of independence organized the same year of 1868 by his exiled idol Betances had been aborted in its infancy. He read pamphlets detailing Puerto Rican lack of armaments, traitorous informers, and about patriots jailed together and abandoned to yellow fever.

"So what?" he thought. No fight for freedom ever lacked these same elements. He found nothing in the records to provide an answer to the question, "Why did the revolution just stop?"

On the eve of his sixteenth birthday, Rodríguez formulated a theory.

As he sat in a large metal tub full of heated water, he watched the two women with amusement as they soaped and sponged his penis and testicles. He had gotten too old for this ritual and knew this had to be the last bath they gave him. As determined as they looked to make the most of it, he also determined not to get an erection they could laughingly chide him about. Rodríguez watched their flushed faces concentrate on keeping their composure while they stuttered and stammered.

"Get more water."

"No you get it. I'll continue scrubbing."

Both refused to leave and Rodríguez thought.

One I can strangle. Two . . . "The numbers!" he said, raising a soapy index finger.

"W-What?"

"Nothing."

He found his answer. In contrast to Puerto Rico, Cuba's population had been numerous with many more mistreated slaves motivated to fight for freedom. Less simple minded in their acceptance of fate and better educated, Cubans even had Negro generals to lead their revolt.

Rodríguez despaired for his fellow Puerto Ricans and began to think of them as Simple Simons.

He did not object to giving his "aunts" a rare, farewell kiss on the hand as he packed his suitcase in preparation for his studies abroad.

"Make us proud," they said. "Keep your attention on your studies and not on inappropriate women."

Pausing from stuffing shirts into his soft leather satchel, he turned to face them.

"Who is inappropriate?"

"Those neither educated nor virtuous."

How many Negro women will have my schooling?

Elated to be rid of the short, square women, Rodríguez looked forward to studying in France—possibly meeting with the exiled patriot Betances. He expected to practice medicine in Spain and obtain freedom in the middle of his enemies.

$\mathcal{D}uring$ his education in Europe, the French and Spanish of the late 1880s greeted Rodríguez with comments like, "Isn't it wonderful that someone from the colonies can also have all the opportunities."

"Someone like you," is what he heard and dove into his textbooks.

Beautiful Spanish women from large cities had many wealthy suitors and no interest in Rodríguez once they satisfied their curiosity about his studies, his travels, and his homeland, marveling over the generosity of his "aunts", so Rodríguez sought the company of the less attractive. He first found the "little mothers" in Spain's countryside, small white women with slivers of lips stretching from one ear to the other and square jaws atop square bodies. They lived for one compliment after another on their "good looks." Loving to be called *guapa*, the women flirted shamelessly to hear it.

He found them all amusingly similar until he met La Mercedes, a younger, more charming woman who did not avert her large, black eyes to speak to him and laughed easily about her gypsy blood, offering to read his palm for a gold coin.

"Aha!" she said. "A very long life line." He laughed. "But my goodness, look at this. No love line, yet many wrinkles at the side where children are supposed to be numbered." He laughed again, more loudly.

"Señorita, children are the furthest thing from my mind. If you plan to make your living from palmistry I fear you will miss a few meals."

"Speaking of which," she said. "Dinner is served."

With that, she took his arm and escorted him to the dining room. There he repeated his often-told tales of France and Puerto Rico to her parents and her brother each of whom invited him to return.

Fooled by their polite hospitality, he thought her family found him intelligent and attractive enough for serious consideration as a marriage mate to Mercedes especially since the recent death of his "aunts" had made him a wealthy man. But when he returned her attentions in a self-deceptive need for real love, her horrified expression at his overtures for a formal relationship convinced him otherwise. She shunned him politely with an insipid excuse.

"You're an educated man," she said slowly, suddenly averting her entire face, "but I'm already engaged to one of my brother's colleagues and I never thought of you as anything but a friend."

Knowing otherwise, that obvious, unsubstantiated lie was a bigger blow to his ego than if she had simply said, "No, I don't love you nor do I want to marry a Negro." He might have understood such an explanation since he had a first-hand understanding of prejudice. He cursed his stupidity over misinterpreting what he meant to Mercedes as real feeling rather than as simple entertainment. *What can be more pathetic than a needy person?*

"Forgive my imprudence," he said, kissing her hand. When he had taken his leave, vowing to sever the friendship, he mourned his situation. Too dark-skinned for educated white women and too educated for dark-skinned women working as domestics, he would have to search far and wide for a soul mate.

After obtaining his second medical degree, he practiced in Spain for almost two years until a poor country couple came to see him.

An elderly farmer who had not bothered to change out of his stable-scented work clothes pushed a thin, very young woman toward him.

"I've buried three wives," Pepe Soto said, without looking at him. "Now this one won't give me sons either."

Milk white, the girl's skin paled further as she kept her eyes on her fingers. His patients fell into two categories. The first came to stare at his dark face and the second, too poor to afford another doctor, averted their eyes.

"How old is your wife?"

"Fifteen."

"Does she menstruate regularly?"

"That's the trouble." Pepe struck a blow on her arm. She lost her balance, almost fell. "She bleeds every month."

"It might be her youth. Suppose I examine you first."

"Not me. There's nothing wrong with my functions."

"What a dumb fool," Rodríguez thought. In spite of four supposedly infertile wives, it had not occurred to the old cretin that it might be his own infertility keeping him from having children. Knowing he could do very little, he put a bottle of tarlike tonic in the hand of each.

"These will take time," he said. "Please return in three months."

After the allotted time, she returned by herself. Assailed by her husband's complaints and distressed by his sexual demands, the unattractive young wife begged Rodríguez for help.

"Look what he did to me," she said, uncovering her back. "Every time I menstruate, he beats me."

As he applied salve to raised, red welts on her white skin, Rodríguez moved to pity, identified with her predicament.

"Ignorance is a terrible enslavement," he said. "In my country, life is so hard that many accept themselves as Juan Bobos, content with a despicable and unexamined existence."

With eyes blank and mouth open, she stared. "Sr. Doctor, your words are too difficult for me."

Unconsciously, he reached out and patted her hand. "What I mean . . ." He paused when she squirmed at his touch and withdrew her hand. As he looked straight into her small, close-set eyes, he could hardly believe her presumption that he was trying to make an improper overture. Still in love with Mercedes, he found her with her large nose ugly by comparison. This had happened once too often and it awoke his sleeping fury of rejection, of being considered inferior. "You're a beautiful woman," he lied, "and your husband is a very stupid man. If this happens again, I will talk to him."

The next time the homely young woman visited him, he gave her a bouquet of flowers and some perfumed soaps he ordered from Madrid.

"Perhaps, aided by your natural beauty, these will help," he said and waited to see if she told her husband. She did not. If she had, he might have reconsidered his resolve to rid his heart of the last vestiges of a Puerto Rican inclination toward sympathy. On hearing of an enemy's downfall, most reacted with *"bendito,"* poor thing.

On subsequent visits she offered him a whiff of the perfume lingering from her bath and listened to his Simple Simon tales. Then she found excuses to see him for headaches, indigestion, and broken fingernails, laughed that her husband Pepe might be Juan Bobo, and did not with-draw her hand. Squashing any idea of hope that she might be sincere, he hardened himself against feeling sorry for her.

In time he felt confident enough to recite erotic poems and declare his passion until he believed her to be so impressed that he could safely graduate to greater intimacies.

When she began to avoid him, her growing abdomen and her new formality told him what to expect.

"Sr. Doctor, your services are not needed. The town midwife will attend to the birth of my husband's child, not you."

Rodríguez found that the old farmer proved not so stupid after all. Pepe did not accept the possibility that he had moorish blood to explain the brown infant whose hair, unlike the dead straight hair of his parents, turned wiry after his third month.

"I'm from León," Pepe said, as if that explained everything. "We killed all the Moors. Watch out for yourself Moor." Old Pepe shook his rake at Rodríguez and added, "Watch out you're not skewered on a night as dark as your soul and your testicles fed to my pigs."

That incident alone did not chase Rodríguez from Spain but news from Puerto Rico did. He heard about a growing movement advocating auton-omy from Spain and learned of both the establishment of the Puerto Rican Autonomy Party, begun by Román Baldorioty de Castro's "Auton-omy Credo," and of a secret organization called "The Old Man's Tower," which was to give economic preference to creoles by boycotting Span-ish-owned businesses. Given the political upheaval occurring in Spain between monarchists and nonmonarchists, he believed in the possibility that Puerto Rico might be freed. Patriotism surfaced in him with the idea that his grand purpose in life ordained his return to the island to take part in the struggle against Spanish colonial rule, and he quickly made plans to return home at once.

Time abroad had dulled his memory of his homeland's tropical beauty. Shortly before his ship sighted land, the air changed. Breezes carried the scent of mangoes, rose apples, and guava. Pineapples mixed with coconut oils and acerola, wet earth with tuberose to form a unique aura, the unmistakable bouquet of Puerto Rico, hot, sweet, and sad. Through flared nostrils and open mouth, he took deep gulping breaths of the scent as if he had been drowning.

His eyes watered at the sight of giant coconut palms towering near white sand beaches bathed by a multicolored Caribbean Sea. Brilliantly hued royal poincianas, *flamboyán*, along with poinsettias decorated the countryside. *Cucubanos*, large relatives of the common firefly lit up bread-fruit trees, *guanábanas*, papayas, and sea grapes.

At home Rodríguez also became reacquainted with ignorance. Illiterate because of the lack of schools or the necessity to work at a very young age, few among the lower class could read, write, or even reason logically whereas the well-off still lived regally, traveled, and produced a genera-tion of lawyer and journalist poets and painters. Lack of sanitation, proper housing, and nourishment resulted in short, painful life spans. He felt newly offended at a rigid class system where only appointees of the Spanish court reigned supreme over politics and the economy, perpetuat-ing the unlivable conditions.

He considered Luis Muñoz Rivera, white descendant of Spaniards and leader of the autonomists, totally incompetent, a man who ran his politics on the self-interest of safeguarding his own class power while maintaining the illusion that he was really striving for independence on the sly.

To Rodríguez, the problem remained numbers, education, and coward-ice, and he thought about the child in Spain. If he had many children in many different parts of the island and educated them, they could make a difference. As the legal, light-skinned offspring of white parents, the Church could not include the names of those children in the secret documents they kept to record all of mixed heritage, denying them op-portunities. Startled, he remembered Mercedes' fortune-telling and began to make himself available to his "little mothers."

When he started his amours in Puerto Rico he found most of the creole parents isolated and ignorant of history, easier to persuade than the old Spanish farmer, Pepe Soto, that no matter how fair skinned, few could argue positively that they had no Indian or black blood unless they were newly arrived from Europe.

Simple Simons!

In a country of people filled with deep-seated bias in favor of good looks, money, intelligence, and above all light skin, Rodríguez believed only those who fit that description had a chance at being accepted or voted into positions of leadership, and he wanted his children to be among those leaders. Remembering a lonely Betances abandoned by former compatriots after the mysterious death of Segundo Ruiz Belvis, Rodríguez decided not just one or two but many generals were needed for the fight. In order to break future generations of their genetic passivity, his task required that he create those generals and teach them to hate a yoke of any kind until that hatred boiled up in them like a bubbling tar pit.

Then what? He weighed the consequences of violent revolution against the possibility of insidious infiltration and takeover. Without being able to choose between the two, he decided on a combination of both to ensure continuity of rebellion. "No matter," he thought. "My sperm, my tar pit will know what to do."

Over the years he rejected many of his children as leaders because he did not see the right combination. Two or three turned out good-looking, either with light skin, his hair, and negroid features or very dark with straight hair but in the illumination of his lantern showed the dull eyes of the mentally slow. He did not abandon those he considered his infantry. He visited them whenever possible to speak to them and leave gifts of money and food, but he accelerated his adventures going so far as to initiate encounters with reluctant women to continue his quest for the leaders he wanted to produce.

II

Félix Cienfuegos

The boy, mummified inside the mosquito nets' gauzy layers, realized his mistake too late. During his first moments of panic and ensuing terror, he had spread three nets out on the rough floorboards in his bedroom, clutched his precious string of pearls tightly to his chest, and lay down lengthwise along one side of the nets' edges. He grabbed the edges with his free hand and rolled over and over inside the nets, gathering momentum until he banged against one side of the oversized bed he shared with his father. Two of the termite-eaten legs collapsed on impact and it fell on top of him. He ended face down tightly cocooned in a white ball wedged between the floor and one of the bed's heavy sideboards. Weakened by hunger and unable to free his arms and legs from the filmy fabric, now steel-like against his panicky struggles, he bumped his head against the bed's crushing sideboard whenever he fought his cloth shroud.

Sweating from his exertions in the torrid room, Félix Cienfuegos panted to catch his breath. It bounced back from the net covering his face, hot and sour. Remorse grieved him more than the netting that obscured his vision and inhibited his breathing. His face throbbed hot and ran with perspiration and tears. He wiped them off by pressing his cheek against the imprisoning mosquito nets and rubbing his face up and down, but the cloth grated and irritated his skin. He tried prayer using the pearls as a rosary, but unable to move his clamped right arm, he could only finger two of the smooth warm pearls as beads. Whenever he thought of his father's death, Félix worked to free himself. Help might never arrive. Guilt and fear pounded his heart at the thought that if he were rescued, he would have to explain the dead body in the living room. "Stupid," he thought. *Why did I do this to myself?* Félix groaned in desperate sadness at the loss of his only parent and at the absurdity of his entrapment.

"Oh, God," he prayed. "If only I could go back to do the day over."

Earlier, father and son had patiently waited for the doctor's arrival. They stood awkwardly in their tiny balcony, careful not to lean against the low black railing lest they trip and plunge down to the cobblestones below.

His father's large, bony hand on his shoulder felt a comfortable weight. Expectantly, he looked up at his father while Félix, Sr., peered through the growing twilight over the pastel blue and pink shops of San Juan toward the distant waters of the bay.

"Dr. Figueroa should be arriving soon, Félix. A ferry just docked."

"What does he look like Papá?"

"Short and thin with an olive complexion. Better this new doctor than the other one."

"Dr. Rodríguez?"

"Who else?"

"Papá, why do you shake your fist at Rodríguez?"

Félix straightened as he always did when he expected an explanation but this time he was disappointed. His father looked down at him without answering. Félix learned no moral, no lesson from enigmatic silence. He watched his father slap himself in the face, smash a mosquito, and stare at the blood on his hand. Félix, Sr., absently rubbed the remains of the mosquito off his sunken cheek, lowered his eyes, and sighed wearily.

"It's getting late," he said. "Let's go inside."

Confused by his father's unusual distraction and thinking it too early, Félix reluctantly allowed himself to be led back into the steamy apartment's small parlor.

"You know what to do before he gets here," his father said.

Félix lit three hurricane lamps, placed them near his father's favorite metal chair, and concealed all the price tags on their furniture. Together they closed the balcony doors and hoisted wood blocks into the hooks and into the window latches to seal them. Dying pink traces of the setting sun filtered through warps in the wooden shutters.

"Why are we closing up like this?"

"If it's hot and dark," his father said, "he won't stay long."

They sat on a scrubbed floor to wait for the doctor. A few moments later, the young man knocked on their door and entered smiling. Dr. Rafael Figueroa shook hands with both and looked down at his shoes when father and son stared at his feet.

"Tell me your complaint," he said, still smiling.

"My bones hurt," the father said. "But that's not the problem. I'm so exhausted, I can hardly move."

"Can you remove your shirt, please?" The doctor lifted out his stethoscope and looked back into his medical bag when he noticed the boy peering inside.

Accustomed to his father's acquaintances who treated him like an equal, Félix grabbed at the examination as an opportunity to interrogate the doctor.

"What interesting cases have you handled, Dr. Figueroa?" He ignored Rafael's annoyed look.

"Do you want to be a doctor?"

"That depends on your answer."

Before answering, Rafael smiled at the large-eyed boy and his father. From the moment he met the emaciated duo, Dr. Figueroa had his own questions. Father and son, both too thin, dressed in the rough clothing of sugarcane workers including the bandannas. Rafael knew that San Juan merchants never wore the typical garb of impoverished workers except for masquerade balls or festivals, and then it was with the sarcastic, superior attitude of people who believe life's ill fortune can never touch them.

The constant exchange of glances between father and son as their eyes roamed over Rafael's hatless head and brown pin-striped suit irritated him as did their probing about his wife and his medical cases. He was the doctor, not they, and he wanted to draw them out, elicit something other than emotional rigor mortis from their unexpressive faces.

"Bad diets and genetics interest me," he replied. "Puerto Rican diets are grimly deficient. Ninety percent of all deaths are anemia related." Dr. Figueroa warmed to his subject. "So much so that country people refer to cardiac failure and natural causes as death by anemia." Uninterested hooded eyes stared at him. "Surely among your workers, you encounter early deaths?"

He believed their blank look meant they did not care about the health and well-being of laborers and changed the subject.

"I'm worried about my friend, Luisa Arriesgo. She's pregnant and a congenital defect runs in her family."

"What kind of a defect?" the elder asked, his voice a high whine.

"So!" Rafael thought. *They are not immune to common, morbid curiosity.* "Odd bone fusions, paralysis, and spine problems."

The young doctor expected the usual questions such as "did cousins marry?" or, "what does the deformity look like?" Instead he felt personal affront as the father turned abruptly to his twelve-year-old.

"You see how important it is to marry well? You must be very careful whom you choose or you and your children will suffer."

Rafael took the comment as criticism directed at him. Everyone knew he had married an American Negro. Suddenly, he needed to escape the stiff twosome, the airless, oddly sanitized room. He stood, feeling his shirt sticking to him. As Félix also rose to his feet, Rafael spied a white price tag dangle out from beneath the boy's chair. All the furniture was tagged. Not mahogany and wicker but metal patio furniture with a too-new look, as if for sale or borrowed from a showroom or a warehouse, no overhead lights or fans, just common country lamps. Rafael understood what had disturbed him. These two were out of place in San Juan, living as bare as paupers from Amparo Street in his hometown of Cataño.

"Sr. Cienfuegos, you're not tubercular but you are undernourished and your blood pressure is very low. Eat more red meat and drink a glass of red wine from time to time."

"Yes, doctor. Thank you for coming." The elder Cienfuegos removed some coins from a leather bag tied to his waist, weighed them in his long thin palm as if afraid to lose them, and closed his fist on them. "Can you bill me later?"

"Yes, of course," Dr. Figueroa replied, glad to escape the muggy apartment. Outside, the humid night felt cool by comparison.

Rafael left with the uneasy feeling he did not do or say enough. *Why didn't I tell him his heart's weak?* Instantly, the answer reached him. How could he tell poor people to rest? What good would a doctor accomplish with that advice in Puerto Rico? He remembered telling Félix, Sr., to eat more meat and drink wine and groaned at how much he had to learn. Better to have brought them some beef.

All the way back to his own home across the bay he brooded about this strange family. He decided to return very soon on the pretext of a follow-up visit, catch them off guard, and learn more about them. Then, too, they owed their bill and it would not be the first time a patient tried to take advantage of his newness, his desperation for clients in the face of competition from an older, more established Dr. Rodríguez.

Rafael found it beyond his powers of reason that women continued to consult Rodríguez when all over the island everyone gossiped that he impregnated his patients. Many a jealous husband had threatened Rodríguez's life and some had tried to ambush him, unsuccessfully. Frustration that patients still favored Rodríguez while shunning him, imperiling his livelihood, made him angry.

"Too bad they didn't kill him," he thought. When apprehended, the would-be assassins pointed to Rodríguez and whined to authorities, saying *"Este hombre."* Despite their fury, the strength of the doctor's education, formality, and money prevented them from daring to call him *negro sucio*, that ugly expression frequently flung from the lips of the biased and ignorant against black men who most times were cleaner and smelled better than they did. That Rafael wished they had insulted Rodríguez in that manner, whether he considered the man immoral or not, startled him and made him feel soiled.

Shamed by his failing that it even occurred to him, Rafael thought of his beloved Josie. Although she had light eyes, his wife had skin almost as dark as Rodríguez's. Then he remembered that regardless of his infamy, Rodríguez, year after year, was the only doctor on the island who constantly provided free treatment to the abject poor, refusing to accept even a single plantain or chicken egg in payment. Rafael also recalled the embarrassing incident of the twins.

Rafael heard the story while he was still studying for general practice. The two doctors involved with the case had been too stupid to keep quiet and had spread the news themselves.

A thirty-five-year-old woman giving birth for the first time experienced a long, difficult labor. The two doctors breathed a sigh of relief when she finally gave birth to a boy but they could not stop the woman's distress nor her bleeding although they packed her with gauze in a desperate attempt to hold back the red flow. She continued gasping, panting and thrashing about in bed. Her screams pierced the streets all night and into the next day while she bled through the packing, staining the sheets. One of her neighbors could take no more and sent for Dr. Rodríguez.

Eyewitnesses said that the tall, thin Rodríguez walked in slowly, back straight and hard as rock, to survey his domain as calm as a wise judge. He did not touch the woman. He merely looked, thought for a minute while the woman's husband, pale and panic stricken held his breath, and turned to the doctors.

"You really are incompetent fools," he said.

"How can we stop the bleeding?"

"Unplug her you idiots. She's having a baby."

The doctors looked at each other. "She already had the child," they said, in unison.

"Twins," Rodríguez said, trembling with rage. His face became blue black. "Have you never heard of twins?"

Rodríguez calmed the woman with a look and turned to her frightened husband.

"Your wife is a strong, healthy woman. These two failures almost killed her and the babies. Next time call a real doctor or use a midwife."

With that he had left, head high and reciting, "Simple Simon knows not how, to properly milk a cow."

Rafael bristled that Rodríguez, who studied in France and Spain, had no equal as a gynecologist and diagnostician and felt free to continue to do whatever he pleased.

He sighed, resigning himself to his competition. "At least," he thought, "I have two new patients I can count on until I build my practice."

As glad to escape the Cienfuegos as Dr. Figueroa had been, they had been just as happy to lock the door behind the young doctor. Chuckling, father and son moved all the furniture to one side of their living room.

"Eat red meat," Félix, Sr., mimicked.

"Puerto Rican diets are dismal," Félix said, looking at his father for approval.

The elder nodded. "He looked at everything. If he's as smart as I think he is, he knows how little we have to eat. I'm sorry Félix but soon it'll all be worth the sacrifice."

Félix hoped so. He felt tired of drinking water to quiet his hunger cramps and to dilute the acidity burning his stomach.

"Are you proposing to the widow Sánchez?"

"Yes. The final softening will be when I show her the pearls."

"Won't she be angry when she finds out Fernández only lets us live here so we can sell his furniture?"

"It'll be too late. Once we're married, her property will be considered mine also."

"Then we'll have everything?" Both their stomachs growled.

"Yes, Félix," his father said, hugging him. "Then you can go to a real school and amount to something, become a lawyer or go into politics like our friends."

"L.M.R.," Félix said. As a private understanding they sometimes used initials for the movers and shakers of the island instead of fully naming them. "When I grow up, I'll be a great man, just like Luis Muñoz Rivera."

"When we have enough for food and schooling from my rich widow's money. But right now, I'll drink some of that sugarcane rotgut. It's all we have."

As Félix, Sr., sipped moonshine out of a battered metal cup, Félix, Jr., apprehensive, moved into a far corner. Strong drink turned his father silly. Félix hated being hugged too much, kissed on the mouth.

"Bring me the machete from under the bed. It's important you understand the difficult life you'll have if you stay poor."

Félix pressed the palm of his hand to the walls to feel his way into their darkened bedroom, reached under the double bed, and pulled out their machete by its handle. He dragged it behind him letting its blade tip screech on the wood floor as he returned slowly into the living room. He sat far away on the cleared floorboards to listen to his father's often-repeated lecture.

"Four hundred years of rape by the Spaniards left Puerto Rico a swamp. Now, this American colonization is going to finish sucking our bones." He sipped the moonshine and grimaced as the lukewarm liquid numbed his tongue and burned his throat. "What hope is there to get out from under a concubinage? Every man has to fend for himself."

After too many quick gulps of alcohol, his father brandished the machete, began a familiar demonstration on the horrors of hard labor.

"This is how to hold a machete. Oomph, it's heavy." He huffed with effort and stopped to set the pearls near Félix, wobbling slightly as he did.

A thought, like the appearance of an earthworm after a cleansing rainfall, popped up at the back of Félix's mind. He opened his mouth to admonish Félix, Sr., then closed it.

"But the cane is hard," his father continued. "Chopping is like this."

Cutting through the air, the sharpened blade created a breeze with an unnerving swishing sound. Félix rolled up his knees away from it.

"One chop is not enough. Splinters fly, sap gushes out at you, sticky, attracting flies and mosquitoes. Rats charge out of the fields, attack you for ruining their nest." He paused, swallowed more rum. "After you finish straining your back and arms under a roasting sun and finally get your product to market, you barely break even, still don't have enough to eat. So you get more credit for food and labor, start planting, nurturing, and harvesting. Now you are heavily in debt again. The cycle begins anew." A drop of blood oozed out of the mosquito bite on his cheek and ran down his face.

Swish, whoosh. The blade glinted as it rose high and blurred as it fell to slice viciously at the bottom of imaginary stalks. Félix, Sr., hopped on one leg with the other raised, lost his balance and laughed.

"Be careful!" Félix spoke loudly and trembled at his father's antics.

He became bold, switched hands to chop left handed. The machete flew out of his hands. Félix ducked. It banged against a wall, clattered to the floor.

"Stop," Félix cried. "You've already taught me." He rose, ran to reach it first, but his father moved faster. Uneasiness crawled down into his stomach.

"Cursed cane has no end," he said. He retrieved the machete, sliced to the right, to the left, straight in front. Félix dipped his head, ran back and forth to avoid his father's swaying.

He twirled the machete like a lasso, brought it down just when his right leg rose as he lost his balance again. It crashed down hard below his knee, sliced through his leg to crack his shin bone. The machete fell with a plunk. Félix opened his eyes wide, thought, "This can't be!"

Gushing blood quickly soaked through the light cloth of his father's pants and streamed along the dangling leg.

Looking down at himself, the elder's face mirrored the astonishment of his son's. Félix, Sr., breathlessly gripped his chest, and collapsed. He opened his mouth, looked beseechingly at the boy. Pain and regret fused in his saddened eyes.

"*Las perlas,*" his father gasped, unmoving. "Never sell them for food. It's the only thing you have."

Félix scooped up the strand, first clutching then looking at it as if it could make his father whole again. Blood-splattered, Félix screamed. He and his father had wanted so much for themselves. Years of using the pearls to deceive outsiders into thinking they were well-off, going hungry, milking the minds of anyone who knew anything which might prove useful, and the constant grooming for a better future, all now dissolved as time wasted in vain sacrifices and gagged him with despair. He stared helplessly at his father, grimaced with pain, and his frustration grew into anger. The intense love he previously felt became loathing.

He raced for a coverlet to stop his father's convulsions but when he returned, Félix, Sr., had died, mouth open, eyes wide, hand tearing at his chest.

"Don't leave me you dumb, you dumb . . ." Enraged, Félix leapt upon his father, pummeling him. "What did you do, stupid? What am I going to do now?" There was no answer except the frozen impotence of death. Ashamed, Félix stepped back, eyes and nose streaming, ears hot and steamy.

Félix wailed, stomped his feet, and sobbed. He trembled, hugged himself on the floor, rocked back and forth on his haunches until he could hardly breathe. Why hadn't he done something?

"Oh, God. I'm sorry, so sorry, Papá."

A dark flutter soared past and frightened him. It was a giant water bug flying to the wounded corpse. Félix jumped back, startled at the sound of a stray dog howling outside. His hair stood on end and it was then that, to escape the sight and smell of the blood and to escape the pangs of his conscience, he had foolishly rolled himself in the mosquito nets and then caused the bed to topple on him, trapping him beneath. His every decision agony, he did not forgive his failure easily.

Recalling the mutilated leg and his punching his helpless father convinced Félix, encased now in the white cloth, that he too deserved to die trapped in heat and thirst. He could have done so much: thrown open a window, yelled for help, bound his father's leg. In his right mind he would have taken a drink of water. His mouth felt dry yet his bladder full.

Mosquitoes buzzed and whizzed becoming louder in protest when daylight seeped through his boarded windows. He heard banging outside and thought to explain away his predicament by saying robbers had attacked him and his father but no one responded to his muffled calls for help. No longer able to hold back, Félix felt a hot stream of urine on his thighs. He struggled weakly with his wrappings and bumped his head anew. His tongue, heavy, stuck to his throat.

While he yearned for water and begged God for forgiveness, blackness covered the room once more. He wondered how much wretched time he had survived. Minutes punctuated with tiny, gaseous explosions emitted by the corpse, how many suffocating hours enduring the stench of death and decay while his lips cracked and swelled, his skin burned. Félix dozed on and off through thirst, fevers, hallucinations of ghosts, and despair until the beginning of the third day not sure whether he was alive or dead but hoping dead rather than to be found soiled and trapped. He chuckled at the thought of death by shame and wept without tears.

Noises filtered through his cotton-filled ears. Squeaks like hinges? Clicking heels, harder, louder, calls and curses. Suddenly, he was free of the bed's weight. Something, no, somebody overturned it. Glazed, vision fuzzy at the edges, he tried to focus on the ghost but it was not his father. It was young Dr. Figueroa. Félix fainted.

"Good God!" Dr. Figueroa exclaimed aloud. Rafael unwrapped the senseless, dehydrated boy who moaned through lips wrinkled white and blistered.

Gagging more from the stench of the corpse than from the smell of the boy's days-old urine and defecation, he dragged Félix down a narrow hallway into a bathroom. After pulling him over to a small tiled area with a floor drain in the middle, Rafael released him gently and looked for a water source. A hose dangled loosely through a hole in the ceiling and high up, almost beyond his reach, a valve. He stretched up on his toes and turned it. The first brown splatters smelled rusty.

"Unfiltered rain water," Rafael noted, stepping away from the meager stream. As he watched tepid water cascade over Félix, he wondered how this happened. The boy, shocked, hesitated then turned his trembling face up, opened his mouth, and gulped.

Confident Félix would not move, Rafael returned to the living room and threw open all the shutters, inhaling deeply of the fragrant, sunny air. Carefully avoiding the stagnant corpse blackened with insects, he unlocked the balcony doors, opened them, and stepped out. He leaned over the fragile black railing and called down into the street to the neighbors who helped him break into the apartment.

"Call the authorities," he shouted. "And find some relatives."

A gathering crowd looked up at him with blank faces. No one moved. A few of the women, turning their parasols aside, asked, "What happened?" "Is someone dead?" They called him Señor Doctor.

"Call the relatives," he repeated. "The boy's father died of a heart attack."

Rafael quickly retraced his steps into the bathroom. Passed out, Félix lay face up atop the drain like an island in a deep puddle of water surrounding his long, skinny body. Rafael turned off the valve. Then he pulled and tugged off the boy's soiled and smelly clothes and loosened the pearls from his grip.

Félix's rib cage protruded and the bones of his shoulders and knees poked out unpleasantly. Dr. Figueroa dragged him into the bedroom, wrapped him in a clean white sheet he found in a trunk on the floor, and opened the apartment door to the waiting busybodies.

"Help me get him to my home," he said.

Raúl Ángel, a fisherman from La Perla offered his rowboat.

"I'll take you to Cataño," he said, craning his neck back and forth to see past Rafael into the living room. "Stinks like mountain skunk weed in there," he added. Rafael did not think Raúl smelled too fresh himself.

"The boy's father died of a heart attack a while ago. Let's get out of here."

Both carried semiconscious Félix down the cobbled streets of San Juan, past ragged children begging, to the dock. Raúl, pale and scaly as dried codfish, dropped Félix's legs into the rowboat with a thump.

"They kept to themselves but sometimes they entertained important visitors." He looked around for someone listening, whispered, "Politicians, conspirators, know who I mean?"

"No, I don't. Where are these people now?"

Raúl shrugged his bony shoulders. "I sold them fish but they never paid on time."

Rafael did not know to whom Raúl referred. "The friends or the boy and his father?"

"Are you a doctor or a comic?"

"Are you a fisherman or a journalist?"

The fisherman's boat, bleached and rickety, did not inspire Rafael's confidence especially after their sarcastic interchange, but aside from the sea spray from a few rolls and wobbles on the blue-green waters of San Juan Bay, Raúl's smooth, wide oar strokes delivered them safely to Cataño.

Thanking Raúl, Rafael pressed a quarter into his hand.

"Spread the word along the coast that the son of Félix Cienfuegos needs his family."

"Will I get another quarter?"

Rafael did not have any quarters to spare and feared the appearance of a sudden onslaught of false relatives, each looking for a reward.

"Do you want responsibility for adding one more to the many orphans roaming the countryside?"

Félix awoke on a cot in a small white room. When his vision cleared he focused on Dr. Figueroa and, behind him, a brown-skinned woman with green eyes.

"Water," he begged, voice sandy.

Dr. Figueroa helped him hold up his head, gave him a glass of water. Lukewarm liquid soothed his parched throat deliciously until his stomach heaved. Rafael took the glass away, wiped drippings off his chin with a crisp white cloth. It was not enough, he still felt thirsty. Félix fisted his hand. It was empty.

"Where are my pearls?" he asked, struggling to get up.

"They're safe, Félix, and will be returned to you when you're better. Now, where did you get them and what happened to your father?"

"It was an accident." Félix struggled against sobs wracking his frail body. "He injured himself."

"Why didn't you go for help?"

"I didn't know what to do." He wailed. "I was scared." He stammered, "Can, can I have my pearls now, please?" Félix almost regretted asking when he noted the frown on the doctor's face, but the black woman opened a roll-top desk in a corner, removed the pearls, and held them up for him to see. They reflected lavender from the woman's dark hand and cream from her cotton dress.

"Hello, Félix," she said, smiling. "My name is Josie and I'm Mrs. Figueroa. See, no one has stolen them and you can have them back after you eat something. All right?"

Félix thought her Spanish sounded strange but he did not care. He felt starved and she intended to give him food.

"Yes, thank you," he replied, keeping an anxious eye on the resting place of his pearls.

On a large plate, she served him a banquet of freshly sliced pineapple, mangoes, and papaya. He was about to tell her the pearls had belonged to his mother but changed his mind. Félix wanted to keep an unhappy good-bye to himself, a vague recollection of a man throwing him a string of pearls, saying, "This is for the loss of your mother." Then his mother disappeared into the night, going away with the stranger as his father looked on, passively.

For the three days the Figueroas tended him, Félix drank, ate, slept, and said very little except to inquire politely after his pearls. Alone during quiet times, he stuck his fist in his mouth and stifled tears as he felt his heart break from loneliness for his father until the kindness of the Figueroas dared him to hope that they might adopt him. That dream quieted his soul and allowed him to attempt a smile.

The Figueroas

Just when Josie and Rafael despaired of finding any friend or relative to care for Félix they received a visit from a huge, mustachioed man identifying himself as Pedro Cienfuegos, uncle of Félix, Sr., the deceased.

At eight in the evening swarms of mosquitoes from the nearby swamp in search of their evening meal prepared to attack. Josie and Rafael began to move their rocking chairs from the balcony to seek safety indoors, behind the screens of their house. The clip-clop of horse's hooves they had been hearing became louder and a cloud of dust rounded the corner at the far end of their street. The rider looked almost the same size as the horse he rode, and the Figueroas thought that the horse looked relieved when the man dismounted. He kicked dust off his boots and thundered up the few steps of their balcony.

They saw both a pistol in a holster and a large knife hanging from his belt. His suit was dusty black, wrinkled and speckled with bits of grass as if he had slept in it on some mountain road. He wore a weathered hat with a large warped brim.

"We are very glad you came, Señor," Rafael said, extending his hand. Pedro Cienfuegos looked down at it curiously, hesitated, and dwarfed it with his own, shaking Rafael's hand lightly and briefly. Uneasiness overwhelmed Rafael. He had expected grief or dismay, anything except an expression of "Who the hell are you?" showing on the face of this armed colossus.

Rafael, rarely intimidated or impressed, began, "We accompany your grief in the loss of your nephew." He stopped, chagrined by the lameness he heard in his own voice.

Without waiting for an invitation, Pedro Cienfuegos removed his hat, looked around for a chair, sat heavily on Rafael's favorite rocker, and demanded, "Who killed my nephew?"

"He accidentally injured his leg and died of a heart attack before help arrived." Not totally the truth but Rafael sensed this was not a man who forgave a scared young boy's foggy thinking no matter what the circumstances.

The big man nodded thoughtfully, pursed his lips, and said, "I doubt it was a real accident. My nephew was stupid. And unlucky."

Baffled by what seemed a genetic lack of emotion, Rafael associated this man with a wild dog he had known during his boyhood in Bayamón. The dog approached slowly neither barking nor growling until he was close enough to chomp down on a leg or an arm with gusto and then calmly strode away as if he had just been patted on the head. No one ever shot the dog. People simply learned to walk as far from it as they could.

"A tragedy," Rafael continued. He tried to put iron in his voice. "But now there is his son to care for."

"That's the real reason I'm here." Pedro struggled with his sizeable midriff to lean forward. As he did so his shirt, yellowed by too much laundering, strained its buttons and parted to reveal a hairy white chest. "What is all this about a son? Who is this boy?"

"Your grandnephew Félix."

Harsh, sarcastic laughter erupted from the big man. "Who says my nephew had a son, and what is the boy to you?"

"To me a patient and nothing more." Rafael could not keep irritation out of his voice. "I had never seen either your nephew or the boy before last week's tragedy."

"Then why have you taken him in?"

Rafael would never give Pedro the satisfaction of knowing that Félix was presently his only patient. Livid, he kept quiet. Large protruding eyes from Pedro's red and bloated face blazed at Rafael but he said nothing until Rafael burst.

"All the neighbors in San Juan know of the son and, and," Rafael stammered in anger, "the boy cries for his father."

"My nephew," Pedro growled, "lost his inheritance twenty years ago. There can be no son for him nor a nephew for me."

"Aha!" Rafael thought. So that was it. A disinheritance explained the comportment of class and power without the trappings, not even enough to eat. With a vengeance the father had been grooming the boy to regain his lost status, and now this uncle no doubt accustomed to having all the money was reluctant to share it with Félix Junior.

Both men faced off, silent, each thinking private thoughts. The invisible force of their growing anger and impatience sizzled into the air and wafted over to where Josie, ignored by them, stood listening. Seconds ticked by. Reacting to the hostility in the air, her green eyes darkened.

Josie disliked the ignorant, selfish uncle. She assessed him as she did some white men from her country, the United States, men who although poor and uneducated thought themselves superior because of their color. To those who remained furious as late as 1910 over the loss of their slaves, she and her family were nothing more than "uppity niggers" for seeking to improve their situation through hard work and education.

Josie thought she had left that world behind when she met an aspiring foreign doctor at Howard University and married him. Gladly, she had moved to Rafael Figueroa's homeland of Puerto Rico when his money ran out and helped him complete his studies in his own country with her meager schoolteacher's salary. Yet, she continued to struggle for acceptance as the *negra americana*. She knew that although many young women of color held secondary positions as instructors, her well-paying teaching position in one of the few good schools on the island was due first to her status as an American and second to her university degree. Without both, Josie would have been consigned to struggle in a lower-paying position. *Can't the mind go beyond the black skin that the eye sees?* Even her favorite students laughed behind her back because she spoke Spanish with an American accent.

"Don't you at least want to see the boy?" she asked harshly. Startled by the tone of her voice, both men turned to face her. She glared at Pedro Cienfuegos and saw his confused eyes soften.

"I don't know what for," he said. "But all right, why not? I don't understand any of this."

Josie and Rafael exchanged glances, shrugged simultaneously. They did not understand either but together they led the big man to the sick room. His frame filled the doorway, casting a large shadow into the lamp-lit infirmary.

Félix, barely awake, heard the murmuring and footsteps, opened his eyes, and screamed as dark shadows draped his cot.

"Papá, I'm sorry," he cried.

They saddened at the realization that the boy expected his father's ghost.

Josie and Rafael watched Pedro's sudden interest. At this moment they noted the strong resemblance and wondered if laws against marriage between blood relatives had been violated.

Both Cienfuegos had milk white skin framed by incongruous black hair, large, glossy brown eyes with thick, feminine lashes. Both possessed a talent for showing no facial expression.

"Who is your father?" Pedro asked.

"Félix Cienfuegos. He's gone now." No tears streamed down the boy's rigid face.

"Do you know who I am?"

"Yes. You are Uncle Pedro. Papá told me you and he looked alike except for, for . . ." Here Félix let his eyes roam openly over Pedro's ample girth, as if wondering how much food his uncle had to eat.

Ignoring the boy, Pedro asked, "Who is your mother?"

"She went away when I was five years old. Papá said she was not suitable and that we were better off without her, but after she left, I, we, were hungry all the time. I missed her. Papá did not."

A smile transformed Pedro Cienfuegos. He grabbed Josie's delicate hand, kissed it, and pounded Rafael on the back almost knocking him over.

"*Muchas gracias*," he said. "Another chance. This one will be watched, supervised with utmost care. No mistakes." To Félix he said, "As soon as you're well enough to travel you will come home with me. Rest now."

With that, Pedro stepped out of the infirmary, closed its door and smiled at Josie and Rafael, a frightening grin which scared them both into holding hands and stepping back. They were stumped until Pedro said, "There are certain family affairs that one might tell a doctor but which perhaps are too strong for a lady?"

Josie understood two things. That she had just been dismissed and that she had been wrong. The man was not prejudiced. He had something to hide, something which had perplexed him as much as it did them, and he was now going to share whatever it was with her husband. Coughing into her hand, she mentioned duties to attend to in the kitchen, excused herself, and left them alone.

The two men sat in Dr. Figueroa's unused receiving room. "I never thought my nephew would take a woman and have children. During his youth, while studying away from home, he picked up some bad habits." Pedro peered anxiously at Rafael. "Do you understand?"

"No, not precisely." Rafael could not imagine although he suddenly thought about a male cousin of his who had run away to Spain to dance flamenco. He stifled the urge to smile.

Pedro sighed. "Everywhere in the country, in the sugarcane fields, the tobacco and coffee plantations, boys grow up around animals, see them copulate, and themselves begin to feel urges for which there is no outlet except animals or other boys. They outgrow these things, usually. My nephew studied in San Germán and in Spain. He returned with big ideas, became mixed up with that autonomy movement leader from Barranquitas." He paused. They both listened to the lapping of the nearby waters of the bay.

Josie's loud knock on the door interrupted their reverie. She entered with a service for two of strong coffee and soft bread, diced cheese, and slivers of guava paste. They thanked her, waited until she left and then continued their conversation.

"Félix fell in love with intellectuals, mostly poets and journalists who wanted to move away from our mother country. He returned with good-for-nothing men who criticized my business methods as stupid and ignorant. They thought to insult me by calling me a Spaniard. Me, a third-generation Puerto Rican." Pedro thumped his chest.

"My nephew wanted to write political poetry all day instead of working or looking for a wife. We fought." The large man stood up, raised his voice, and waved his arms, scaring Rafael. "In front of my workers he shamed me by saying he preferred to sleep with men, not women!" Pedro put his hand on his pistol. "How is that for repaying my kindness in taking him in after his parents died?"

Rafael discreetly pressed for specific details but Pedro Cienfuegos volunteered no more except to repeat that he had kicked his nephew out, disinherited him, and promised to watch Félix, Jr., every moment of every day for the rest of his natural life. He paid Dr. Figueroa insisting he would return for the boy.

"Where do you live?" Rafael asked as he and Josie bid the big man good-bye.

"None of your business. I've only said so much because of your kindness." He thundered out of the house, mounted his horse, and galloped away.

Josie and Rafael chuckled over his line the next morning.

"What's for breakfast?" Rafael asked, peering over her shoulder at the stove.

"None of your business. Ask me more and I'll shoot you."

They spent their day watching Félix eat and drink nonstop as he continued to make up for twelve years of starvation, and their evening hours in private puzzling over whether or not the boy had been mistreated, and wondered where he obtained the pearls and if the uncle truly intended to return.

"Was his father really a homosexual?" Josie asked.

"I only spoke to him briefly about his father, but I don't think so." Rafael pursed his lips, turned to look at her suspiciously.

"What?"

"His father told Félix, Jr., to marry a woman who was beautiful, strong, wealthy, and stupid. He said intelligent women put horns on their husbands." He narrowed his eyes at Josie.

She burst into laughter.

"Let's go to bed."

Three days later a mule load of supplies arrived with mangoes, green bananas, coffee, and clothing. They relaxed. Félix was not forgotten and they felt free to stop worrying.

Rafael's practice picked up, due mostly to a little girl. Their pet, Rafaela, was named after Dr. Figueroa. He had delivered her when he first returned to Puerto Rico under the shame of not having completed his studies in the States and before he obtained his medical certification. The girl's unmarried mother was too poor to pay a midwife, and none of her neighbors wanted any part of a woman who, they believed, had secret liaisons with all their husbands.

Though spoiled, outspoken, and precocious, seven-year-old Rafaela was also the best-loved child in the entire town because she was beautiful, intelligent, and affectionate. To Josie and Rafael, still childless because of financial necessity, Rafaela could do no wrong even when she burst in on them unannounced, screaming.

"My mother's giving birth!" She cried uncontrollably and would not release her choke hold on Josie's waist.

"Calm down, Rafaela," Josie pleaded. "We can't understand what you're saying if you don't stop crying."

She sobbed, wiping her nose with her bare arm. Her tear-filled eyes were the color of light oak.

"Now more people will make fun of me."

"Who makes fun of you?"

"Everybody. Because I have no father. Dr. Rodríguez told me." She shook her head up and down.

"What did he tell you?"

"He said nobody wants me as a daughter just like the United States didn't want Puerto Rico as a state."

Josie's mouth dropped open. Furious, she could not think for a moment and watched Rafaela cry until her husband spoke.

"Stay away from that liar and don't ever speak to him again," Rafael said. He and Josie looked at each other astonished.

"He's not a liar," Rafaela protested. "He said it's in old records from 1900 and he promised me a nickel if I remembered that."

Startled, Josie recalled her family's concern for her well-being when she met Rafael because Tennessee Senator Bate had once compared the people of Puerto Rico to cannibals and head-hunting savages. She had forgotten that and wondered how Rodríguez had obtained the congressional records.

"Forget about him," she said. "Tell us what's wrong."

Josie sat Rafaela on her lap, hugged and stroked her until Rafaela hiccupped out that her mother was giving birth and needed help.

"Stay here until I return," Rafael said, rushing around for his medical bag. "How long has she been in labor?"

"She's been telling me she has cramps from something she ate, but I finally saw her stomach this morning. She's been moaning in bed for two days."

"What? Two days? Why didn't you come sooner?"

"I told you. I didn't know." Rafaela lowered her eyes.

"Rafaela? You've seen pregnant women before and we discussed where babies come from."

"All right, I thought she may be having a baby, but I was angry because I didn't want her to have another so I didn't care if she didn't feel good. Now I'm scared; her face looks wet and green."

Rafael ran out of the house while Josie took Rafaela into the infirmary. "You should be ashamed," she said. "You have a mother who loves you and soon you'll have a brother or a sister as family. Look at this poor boy who has no mother or father or brothers or sisters."

When they opened the door, Félix sat up as though in a trance.

Rafaela stared. "He's the most beautiful boy I've ever seen," she whispered. "His eyes are like a calf's and he looks sad, so sad. Can I kiss him?"

"No. Let him go back to sleep."

"He's not a poor boy," she said, eyeing Josie suspiciously. "What is he doing in your house?"

Afraid Rafaela might throw a jealous tantrum, Josie pushed her back to the living room. "We are waiting for a long-lost greatuncle, who doesn't really want him, to come pick him up when he's better."

Looking pacified, Rafaela paged through some books Josie gave her to teach her English. She glanced occasionally at the infirmary door until Dr. Figueroa returned to tell her she had a sister.

"I hate that," she said. "Now I'm not the only girl. I much prefer a beautiful boy like the poor sick one in there." She pointed a long delicate finger.

"Come on, time to go home. I'll take you."

Days later pregnant women crowded Rafael Figueroa's receiving room saying that when their time came they too wanted a painless birth and a guaranteed healthy delivery. Rumor circulated that Dr. Figueroa had not only saved the life of Rafaela's mother, miraculously doing away with all pain, but had also revived a stillborn baby. Immediately, Rafael and Josie knew the source of this story and said, "Rafaela!"

At the end of two weeks, Pedro Cienfuegos, at night and on horseback, arrived. He ordered Félix to gather his belongings, sat him on a mule roped behind his horse, and led him away.

Swaying atop the animal, Félix, fleshed out and no longer a skeleton, stared inquiringly at Dr. Figueroa and Josie. He looked back at them over his mule's rump until he rounded a corner, cut off from their sight. The townspeople of Cataño who lived on the Figueroas' street followed uncle and nephew with their eyes until the entourage disappeared. When their neighbors threatened to approach with questions, Josie and Rafael quickly waved goodnight, backed into their home, and bolted the doors.

Embracing the woman he married and loved ferociously, Rafael Figueroa said a silent prayer for Félix Cienfuegos, a child he expected never to see or hear from again. Then, as he continued to think about the young boy, Rafael went from room to room extinguishing all the lanterns, leaving a trail of darkness behind him.

IV

Félix

Far from Cataño, both day and night, Félix prickled at the feel of many eyes watching him. It had begun the instant the old man led him away from the Figueroa home. Pedro Cienfuegos constantly turned around on his horse to stare back at him, trailing behind on a mule.

"Sir, where are we going?"

"Call me Uncle Pedro and don't ask questions."

Accustomed to the narrow, peopled streets of San Juan and the even smaller apartment he had shared with his father, Félix felt awed by the openness of the dark countryside, deserted of humans but crowded with hills bursting with flaming bushes, mango and breadfruit trees, wild grass, and multicolored violets. The smell of damp earth, the call of unfamiliar plumed birds filled his senses, and he felt lost in a leafy primeval world.

When they stopped along the dirt road to relieve their bladders, Pedro handed Félix a canteen.

"Wash your hands before you eat, or didn't your father teach you such things?"

"Yes, sir, he did!" Félix replied emphatically.

The old man drew his pistol and checked the bullets.

"Watch your tone and remember I told you to call me Uncle Pedro."

Trembling, Félix stood up straight and closed his eyes.

46

"What the hell are you doing?"

Félix realized his foolishness. He was not getting shot. He rubbed his painful backside. "I've never been on a mule before."

"Nor on a horse?"

"No, Uncle Pedro."

"Too bad. You'll have to learn fast. Men ride horses."

Finally arriving at a big house, which sat on stilts a few feet off the ground, Félix, sore and tired, met Ciriaco, the house servant, Doña Marta, the woman who would be his governess, Jacinto, the foreman of the tobacco plantation, and Julián, who worked the sugarcane fields. His future watchers all. Uncle Pedro introduced them.

"Doña Marta will sleep in your room with you. I know you're tired, but Julián will wake you tomorrow early. Be ready by daybreak." Uncle Pedro strode away, calling, "Good night," over his shoulder.

Alarmed to think a woman might see him naked, Félix refused to allow Doña Marta to remove his clothes, insisted on towel washing himself, and plunked into his soft, cool bed, falling asleep immediately.

He awoke to candlelight. Julián shook him saying, "Wake up boy. Get up and hurry."

Félix rubbed his eyes thinking something was wrong. He and his father did not rise before daylight.

"It's too early," he said.

"No, you're going to be late." The older boy pinched him. Félix felt the chill of hard fast pain along with a knot of fear and said nothing.

"Stop that." Doña Marta scolded.

"Why do I have to help him?" Julián threw Félix a venomous look. "He's taller than I am."

"Take him for his shower."

Félix hurried outdoors after Julián to a three-sided partition made of old wood. A huge ladle hung on its side just below a rain barrel. Tugging on a rope attached to the rain barrel a latch freed a cascade of frigid water that splashed on Félix's head. Julián handed him a piece of coarse soap and said, "Toss me your underwear." He paused to spit on the ground. "And I'll give you a towel when you finish."

Naked, Félix shivered in the early morning cold of the mountains but lathered and rinsed himself vigorously, keeping a wary glance on the older boy. Julián gave him his towel and clean underwear.

Back in his bedroom, he put on the soft cotton work clothes Doña Marta prepared for him and followed her into the kitchen. He attacked the breakfast she served him of bread, cheese, and milk fresh from the cow, still frothy and lukewarm. He finished with a small cup of hot black coffee.

Julián, sullen, ate his breakfast slowly. "When was the last time you ate?" he asked. Félix felt a flush on his cheeks.

"Leave him alone," Doña Marta said. "He'll learn." Still, she shook her head.

"Félix!"

"There's your uncle," she said, hustling him to his feet. "Hurry."

He barely had time to brush his teeth.

"This won't work," Uncle Pedro said. "Too slow and too disorganized."

They spent the entire day traveling. First they rode on horseback to acres of sugarcane fields, then they followed a small path to a sugar mill and, finally, to a coffee plantation while his uncle explained what he eventually expected of Félix.

Nothing about agricultural life was totally new because his father had told him many times what to expect. Still, he found it interesting to see the size of the hacienda, watch skinny, sad-eyed peasants standing in midday sunlight wearing bonnets and long cotton dresses as they picked coffee beans and the glistening brown workers hacking away at the light green sugarcane fields.

"Tonight, you go to bed earlier."

"Yes, Uncle Pedro."

"So you can get up earlier, understand?"

Félix nodded.

"Answer, don't gesture like an animal."

"Yes, Uncle Pedro."

When his uncle left, saying, "I have to attend to a personal matter,"

Jacinto, a handsome young man, despite a smile lacking a front tooth, took over.

"I'm showing you the place where we clean tobacco leaves."

Félix sighed. "Yes, sir."

"Are you tired yet?" Jacinto's brown skin gleamed with rivulets of perspiration.

"No, sir."

Jacinto laughed, showing a mouthful of missing molars. "Yes, you are. Your uncle's a slave driver." He laughed again. "I was white when I started working here. Look at me now."

Neither Félix's father nor his father's friends ever ridiculed themselves just to make someone laugh. More often than not, they directed their malicious humor at others. As a result, Félix did not know how to react and so he said nothing although his face reddened with the effort of not laughing.

"You've got the right attitude," Jacinto said. "Be quiet and tough. It's your uncle's idea of a man." He patted Félix's head, added, "Poor little hair mite."

Near a barnlike shed, Jacinto called out, interrupting a man hired by the workers to read aloud to them from classic novels and poetry.

"Caution, ladies. Here comes the future owner." The women stripping stems glanced at Félix quickly, smiled, and looked back to what they were doing. "Yes, you'll have to wait until he grows up before you throw him your pantalets." Their laughter burned Félix's cheeks. He and Jacinto watched the women work for a while, drank strong black coffee out of a coconut shell, and listened to part of the *declamador* and his rendition of Victor Hugo's *Les Miserables* before they returned to the house.

"Ciriaco takes over inside. He'll follow you around." Jacinto laughed. "See you on the days you work with me."

Ciriaco helped him climb up into the house. "I'll show you all the rooms," he said, watching Félix drag his feet. Ciriaco was hunched over, walked quickly on bowed legs with a falling forward motion. "You're a good boy, you don't complain." He looked at Félix with small, kindly eyes. "Don't say anything to anybody. We all have to report to your uncle." He pressed a finger, gnarled by arthritis, to his lips. "Especially to Doña Marta. She must be a witch because normal people have to sleep."

Ciriaco was right. That night, after tucking him into his bed, she sat down in her rocking chair with a book. On a table near her, she lit two candles, something Félix had been too tired to notice the night before.

"Will the light bother you?" she asked.

"No." He did not care about flickering candlelight and trusted the cool mountain air to drug him to sleep.

"Don't fall asleep without saying your prayers. Loud enough for me to hear."

Félix yawned his way to "Amen" and fell asleep. During the night, he dreamed he saw his father's pale, thin face and pleading eyes reach out to him. Félix opened his eyes and sat up, gasping. Doña Marta stood near his bed and followed his gaze into a dark corner where his father's ghost dispersed like fog blown away by a gust of wind.

"I was about to wake you," she said. "What were you dreaming?"

Félix lay down again, closed his eyes and muttered, "Nightmare." He began sinking into sleep when she lifted his mosquito net insisting he tell her the dream. Ciriaco's warning came to his mind. "I don't remember. I'm sleepy."

"Well, next time remember and tell me."

"Don't you sleep?"

"Only for minutes at a time. It's all I need."

Ciriaco warned him again two days later. "Tomorrow, your uncle expects you to start working."

The next morning, Uncle Pedro said, "Today, I'll teach you to chop down sugarcane." He stared at Félix as if he expected protests but received none. "Can you lift a heavy machete?"

"Yes, Uncle Pedro." The boy politely endured both his uncle's clumsy fingers while he tied a bandanna around Félix's forehead to absorb perspiration and the ridicule of the workers, whose bare chests already gleamed with sweat. They gambled aloud that Félix would not last one hour before he fainted.

"I bet he can't even lift it," one cutter said.

"From *patrón* to baby sitter of little gentlemen," another worker added, laughing.

Pedro pushed Félix to an edge of the field away from the workers and began to demonstrate the use of the machete but before he could continue, Félix, wanting to prove his father trained him right, asked, "May I try it please?"

The surprisingly strong fat man noted Félix's girlish eyes and flaccid arms, smaller than some of his other twelve-year-old worker's muscles, and could not contain his amusement, especially when one of the workers howled.

"Ay, Don Pedro step away or you'll get your head chopped off." He stopped smiling when the boy's eyes blackened and suddenly turned into furnaces of hatred that shot pure ill will toward the speaker of those words. Recalling the death of the boy's father suffused Pedro with a strange mingling of fear and shame.

"All right, you have to learn sometime," he said. "Don't embarrass me boy. No one here had a good opinion of your father." He handed Félix the machete and stepped away.

Expertly, Félix hacked away for the next several hours, chopping each stalk with a single blow until he felled three stalks and tossed them aside. Then, bent over, he chopped down the next three and more after that, tossing them into a huge pile until he made an inroad on his edge of the field as large as that by any experienced cutter. The handle of his machete ran with the blood and water of his blistered hands and his sweaty clothes stuck to him, wetly transparent. Stubbornly he continued, although it was obvious to himself as well as to the onlookers that he could no longer lift the machete.

Many times, Pedro tried to get him to stop, rest, bandage his hands, or remove his shirt only to receive that look of disdain. Worry and perplexity further creased Pedro's brow. He didn't want the boy dead.

"It's finished," Pedro insisted. "You've done a good job." Relief flooded him when Félix, huffing, stopped. The other workers stopped too, staring in disbelief.

"Get back to your business," Pedro yelled at them.

"Was I adequate?" Félix asked.

"Not bad." Smiling, Pedro added, "You're almost an expert."

"No, I'm not." Félix looked at his damaged palms. "I did not hold it efficiently." He looked at the workers to make sure they heard. "But I will next time."

Pedro's mouth opened then slammed shut. He peered down at his nephew. "What do I have here," he wondered. This boy looked and sounded like his father but was different. Félix spoke with the same educated words Pedro remembered his nephew had used, but he worked like a slave. He did not complain or flinch when Pedro poured water on his blisters, smeared ointment on them, and wrapped his hands. Félix asked for neither water nor food, nor did he act particularly uncomfortable in his drenched clothing, which were already starting to dry in the hot sun. His face had turned a fiery red.

Pedro Cienfuegos chuckled, put his arm around Félix's shoulders feeling proud of his charge.

"Har, Har," he yelled at the workers. "What do you think now? One Cienfuegos is better than ten of you."

The wiry workers, bronzed by sun, waved and cheered. Félix surprised Pedro by turning his face toward him unsmiling.

"What do we do now?" Félix asked.

"Back to the house for bathing, then your lessons."

"Lessons?" He perked up.

"You must learn to read and write."

"Can't you tell I already know how?"

"Then other things, whatever they teach in schools."

"School?" The boy's enthusiasm annoyed Pedro.

"No need for you to go away. I've hired a teacher to come to you."

"Oh," Félix said in a deflated tone. "A tutor."

"Yes, that's it. Why?"

When Félix did not answer, Pedro, fueled by newly discovered paternal instincts, asked, "Aren't you tired? Don't your hands hurt?"

"Yes."

"Why don't you say so?"

Félix shrugged. "Everybody's tired and everyone's hands hurt."

Pedro mulled that over until they reached the house where he entrusted Félix over to Doña Marta and left, his heart filled anew with long lost pride and love. He resolved to learn what the boy was thinking.

Félix liked Doña Marta. She fit his idea of a real lady with her black lace dresses and mantillas. She wore her hair braided across the top of her head and fluttered her fan gently against her chest. It felt wonderful to have a perfumed woman brush his hair, kiss his blisters, and cluck over his meals as if he were a baby chick. From the feel of her hands, he found a depth of softness unrivalled by the gentle poet's touch of his father's hands. She never left him alone in the house even at night when he relied on her semidozing presence should he awaken from a bad dream. And they shared a secret. Doña Marta allowed him to finger his pearls as a rosary when she supervised his prayers before bedtime.

"It will keep them shiny," she said.

What he did not like were lessons from tutors who instructed too slowly, and the constant prickling on his neck and back from all the eyes watching, always looking for some defect he might have inherited from his father, a man he remembered with waves of love and shame.

During his morning showers, Julián tormented him.

"What happened to your father?"

"He died." He hoped to discourage the bully with simple answers.

"Where's your mother?"

"I don't know."

"You're a real little Simple Simon aren't you?" Félix could not answer that without a fight. Julián was illiterate and would not like a lesson on symbolic folk stories from Félix.

Doña Marta asked her share of questions.

"What are you thinking?"

"Nothing." Really, it was none of her business and she might be shocked to know how much he hated country life.

"How do you feel?"

"Fine."

"What did you dream last night?"

"I don't remember."

His sole ally, Ciriaco, didn't ask questions, he issued warnings.

"Don't trust anyone."

"I won't."

"Always play innocent but not dumb."

"I will."

"Look at every woman as if you've never seen one before in your entire life."

"I'll try." Félix laughed.

"Don't just try. Do it. It's what your uncle expects."

His weekly routine consisted of bathing in the morning while Julián watched and warned him not to masturbate or he could become a homosexual; working as a conscripted sugarcane worker three days a week, callouses growing on his hands. The other three days, he harvested plantains, picked coffee beans, and cleaned and dried tobacco leaves. His schedule was lightened only by three distractions: Jacinto's naughty jokes about his Uncle Pedro's "personal business" being visits to prostitutes because he was afraid of losing his money to a wife, by Ciriaco's superstitious fear of Doña Marta, and by the random, skulking presence of Dr. Rodríguez who stared at him from a distance.

Over the years, as his body hardened and his muscles became defined from hard labor, he grew taller than most around him and continued to hear indiscreet whisperings about his parents. "No," he thought. *My father could not have been a homosexual.* He was dainty, a gentleman, though a bit tarnished. Yes, Félix surmised, his mother had been a prostitute supporting him and his father until she received a better offer. But she left him with the pearls! His father also left him something, the overriding need to cast off the yoke of servitude to family and an enduring single-mindedness with which to do it no matter what the sacrifice. All this in spite of Pedro's strict supervision.

"You're about fifteen now," his uncle said. "Doña Marta is going to work for someone else."

Fearful of exhibiting any affection for her or sadness at her leaving lest he be ridiculed as weak, he said, "That's fine. Fifteen is too old for a governess and also to have someone watch me bathe. Get rid of Julián, too." As he expected, Uncle Pedro pursed his lips, nodded his approval, and raised his eyes to stare into the night sky.

V

Juan Peña

Flickering pinpoints of light, delicate and hypnotic against a black velvet sky, dueled for attention with the opaque full moon. Crashing surf pounded the powdery beach of Loíza Aldea.

Monstrous waves assaulted the white sand, thinned and reached out, threatening to swallow up the black boy sitting by himself in the darkness, knees bent to his chest, bony buttocks firmly imbedded in the sand. Fresh night breezes pelted him with sprays of icy salt water and chilled the flesh on his skinny arms.

Nine-year-old Juan Peña, with his hands over his ears against the distracting roar of the sea, focused his eyes on a distance just above the horizon over the ebony water. He peered calmly at the vision forming in the sky in an area devoid of stars. What he saw was small, round and red, strange and ugly with bluish veins. It breathed, pulsated, grew slightly larger, then suddenly deflated from the knife plunged into it. Quickly, the vision changed into thick, bloody drippings and dispersed.

"Paula!" Juan thought, scrambling to his feet and starting to run toward the village. His feet sank into thick sand hampering his speed. Panic and anxiety assailed him. "Too late," he thought. *I waited all day with my premonition and now it's too late to save her.* He slowed down as remnants of dead crabs, pebbles, and sharp edges of discarded coconut shells pricked and stabbed his bare feet. Away from the cool edge of the sea, the steamy humidity of the hot August night bathed him in perspiration. His heart throbbed like the ocean in his ears.

Juan stopped running at the sounds of screaming. Shouts began as screeches of surprise, changed to wails, then to cries and calls for help. Lights went on, one by one at random, in some of the tiny shacks of the village, flaring then settling down as candle flames calmed to a steady, dim source of light. In the distance, tenants opened their doors and held up lighted candles. The flames shed a red glow a few inches outside but no further. Night blackness swallowed the wavering lights before they reached as far as Juan. Juan, with vision accustomed to the dark, caught a movement to his left and turned his head.

Crouching in a stretch of tall grass growing on the periphery between earth and beach, a girl, her black face glistening with iridescent tears, whispered to him.

"Psst, Juan! What are you doing out so late?"

Juan studied his twelve-year-old cousin, who was tall for her age. Cocoa-colored muscles defined her arms and legs. She emanated a strong scent of mucous and musk. He lowered his eyes. Living in a crowded household where adults shared single rooms with children had educated him about sex beyond the necessary for his nine years, and Paula's beauty always pained him in an uncousin-like manner. He walked over to her, squatted alongside surrounded by tall grass.

"What happened?" he asked, fearing the answer.

Paula wiped her tears with her right arm, the one still holding a bloody knife almost as large as the length of her forearm.

"I killed my father," she said. "I hope the pig burns in hell."

"Why did you have to kill him?" he asked, frowning.

Without answering, Paula stood and stared out to sea with large, tear-blurred eyes until her face hardened, sharpening her cheekbones. Juan softened at the sight of her ripped and tacky nightshirt. Blood, shining in the moonlight, ran down her legs.

Anxious for her well-being, he said, "Let me help you, Paula. You know I can." When she said nothing, Juan began to stiffen in a trance. "Step backwards into the ocean, three times to cleanse yourself," he said in a hoarse voice. "Walk without looking behind you. Then pray for forgiveness, both to God and to the spirit of your father. Let the knife float away to sea."

"The hell with both of them."

Astonishment wrenched Juan out of his trance. "Don't talk like that," he said. "You have to beg for forgiveness or you'll be haunted forever." When she did not move, he added, "And the police will get you."

Paula stood up. "You don't know what he did to me, you little lunatic."

Fearing her loud voice would attract the townspeople exiting their doors to investigate the commotion, Juan tried to calm her down.

"Paula, you're in trouble and you need all the help you can get. Please, do what I tell you."

"You're the only one who cares," she said, sighing and putting her hand on his woolly head. "And all you know are the spirits." Reluctantly, she allowed her cousin, who did not reach her shoulder, to lead her across the beach to the water.

She did as she was told, walked into the sea backwards three times up to her ankles to chant Juan's prayer.

> *In the name of powers that impart*
> *blessings to believers who strive*
> *for justice, let evil forever depart*
> *and goodness quickly arrive.*

Rough waves rose high, almost rolling over her head and back. Sand sucked at her feet as she fought the tug of the fierce Atlantic until the ritual ended. Paula emerged, soaked and smiling, all anger spent in the strenuous effort against the current.

"I hope this works," she said. "I don't want to hang for killing a rapist."

She confirmed Juan's worst suspicion, but he did not have too much time to think about it. The townspeople's voices became louder, and their shuffling footsteps grew closer as did the fire and the acrid smoke rising from the torches they carried.

"Pray," he commanded. "It doesn't matter what you say except to ask forgiveness."

"Dear God," Paula began, "forgive me for killing my father and ask him to forgive me too." She hesitated. "But he was a drunken pig and deserved to die. I should have killed him sooner when he raped my sisters except the idiots accepted it."

Paula's lack of cooperation exasperated Juan as villagers approached with shouts of "There she is!" He pleaded, "Hurry up and finish your prayer!"

"I had to protect myself," she continued, "since my mother would not help me. Maybe I should have hit him on the head hard enough to knock him out. I'm sorry. Thank you. Amen."

Relieved that Paula finished her prayer but troubled by what he learned about his aunt and his other cousins, Juan stopped the villagers by facing them with hands held up and chin lifted towards the heavens. He knew they feared him and his grandmother, the gargantuan Mamá Abuela.

"My poor cousin Paula has suffered an evil," he said. "A white man stole into their house, raped her, and when her father tried to protect her, the white man stabbed my poor naked and defenseless uncle."

Juan did not know which of the spirits who inhabited him inspired these words but the speech felt right. He scanned the crowd for reactions and small bits of logic reached him. Even the strongest cynic, aware of his uncle's drunken debaucheries, was prepared to accept his explanation in spite of Paula's nervous giggle. They felt content not to contradict the grandson of Socorro Peña, or Mamá Tumba as they called her, a well-known witch in an area rich with voodoo traditions. In the crowd Paula's mother and sisters averted their eyes when Paula tried to speak to them. They turned their backs to her and walked away to return to their hovel.

When the crowd dispersed, Tonio, Paula's eldest brother stepped forward. "I suppose," he said, "that's the lie we'll have to tell the police?" Flat-headed Tonio looked fearfully at Juan but approached Paula pointing his finger in her face and whispered, "Black bitch!"

"I may be darker than you," she said, getting closer to him and gritting her teeth. "But at least I'm not an ugly traitor." Before he could move, she chomped her teeth hard on his pointing finger, making him howl. "As our brother you should have protected us."

Paula spent the night at Juan and Mamá Abuela's shack.

The civil police had no interest in pursuing a nonexistent assailant. A white man had somehow entered the poverty-stricken black community of Loíza Aldea without attracting the attention that a clump of white rice in a bowl of black beans merited? A killer who chose the most meager household to rob, then murdered Paula's father and escaped?

The investigating officer, Captain Ojeda, knew Mamá Tumba and Juan Peña's reputations. During the head-bashing orgies he and his men routinely practiced in the community, he had also learned from the itch in his groin that Paula Meléndez, a child of twelve, was already a beautiful, sensuous woman. So he did the sensible thing, ignored the case and never spoke of it except to arrange for a professional grave digger since none of the superstitious villagers wanted to touch the bloody decomposing body.

Despite everything, Paula Meléndez thrived for two years. She grew taller and more athletic. Her breasts became fuller, higher, thrusting through handed-down dresses until Mamá Abuela tore strips of old sheets to bridle her chest. This, after her flat-headed brother Tonio suffered a drunken accident. They found him with a knife imbedded from one side of his throat clear through to the other.

Once again the handsome Captain Ojeda, heavier since his marriage, conducted a cursory investigation. Paula watched him as she leaned, arms crossed, against the side of her shack. He gestured for the grave digger and glanced briefly at her. His look gave her an uneasy feeling but she tried not to think about it. He was white and married, and should present no threat.

As she grew and her cheekbones and jawline refined, Paula lost all semblance of childhood. Meanwhile she contended with another brother, Sancho.

Sancho crabbed at the loss of his father and brother's manpower in the fishing boat as if the family had been deprived of two great providers instead of two drunken troublemakers.

"Who do you think you are?" He barked whenever he spoke to Paula. "Don't think you'll get away forever."

Sancho threw tantrums and stomped his feet if neighbors shared a catch because he returned with empty nets. If anyone spoke of Paula's beauty and especially if anyone mentioned her generosity in giving her free time to help young mothers with their children, he grit his teeth and punched the already shaky walls of their shack threatening its collapse.

"You work for strangers," he said, "but us you kill."

The rest of her family joined Sancho's complaints by slitting their eyes and saying, "He's right. You're nothing without us."

Paula understood her mother and sisters' jealousy. Her beauty dimmed theirs. She also understood her brother's frustration at having to be a major provider for his family without the comradeship of his drinking companions. Her fear was that he wanted to be the one to outwit her, make her submit to his domination as the others had not been able to do, so she worked hard to blend into the landscape, bide her time growing up without giving him cause for complaint. But try as she might, she could not forget his grinning face during her rapes. Neither that nor her mother and sisters' faked snores while she struggled to escape.

For these reasons, she knew, she sometimes ignored Juan's advice and did not try to keep peace quite as hard as she might. Too many times Paula took pleasure in spiting them by accepting gifts of inky squid and green plantains from neighbors and bringing these home to her family as offerings of her own benevolence saying, "I could have kept these for myself but I didn't because you need help."

"Shut up, you murderer," Sancho said. "You needed our help. We kept our mouths shut and you out of jail. You're not better than us and you have to do what I tell you."

"Touch me and you die." She spat at his feet.

"You can't kill everybody. I'll be more careful, you bitch."

Paula turned to her mother and sisters, crowded in the small living room festooned with the hammocks they used as hanging beds.

"You hear that? You better finally speak up and do something. We had to talk about it some day. Now Sancho has brought it up."

Her mother, short and bone thin, said, "Sancho, leave her alone. Haven't you learned enough from what happened to your father and your brother?" She shook her round woolly head. "I just can't choose. She's my child, too."

"What kind of a speech is that?" Paula asked. "You can't choose between your children if one is right and one is wrong just because both are your children?" She crossed her arms. "What kind of an animal are you?"

"You're the animal," Sancho cried. "Oh, don't you talk about right and wrong. Nobody here but you ever killed their own flesh and blood over a disagreement."

"A disagreement!" Paula repeated, hands on hips. She looked at her sisters. "And did you two agree with Papá and Tonio? And what about you, Mamá? Was it an agreement to share your husband with your daughters in bed?"

"Sort of," her mother answered, quietly. She looked at Paula's open mouth and shrugged. "My father did it too. My mother said, 'better your father than a stranger.'"

Speechless, Paula stared at her mother's lipless face, the pale gray color of wet sand, with no chin, and a jutting brow and thought not for the first time that she resembled a small, withered creature.

As if reading Paula's thoughts, her mother continued. "Look at me. Where would I go? Who would want me?"

Her sister Celeste joined in. "I didn't help you because I felt relieved that it was your turn with them, but when you killed them, I was glad." Paula despised them all. Before returning to Mamá Abuela, she gave Sancho a last warning.

"Try to rape me and I'll get you when you least expect it."

"And I'll get you when you least expect it." He laughed.

She uncrossed her arms and walked out distorting her face and voice to mimic his laughter.

$\mathcal{M}am\acute{a}$ Abuela cried at Sancho's funeral. The mammoth woman covered her intimidating girth in numerous yards of white cloth and wore a matching scarf round her head. She glared, through tears, at Paula.

"I can no longer condone these murders," she said. "There must have been another alternative but you chose not to take it."

While the priest talked about the torments of hell awaiting assassins, Juan Peña took an interest in and spoke to the grave digger. The man said, "These poor people are making me rich."

Later that evening, Mamá Abuela spoke to Juan.

"You're getting too old to follow Paula around. Stay away from her." She turned to Paula. "If it happens again, you'll have to leave Loíza Aldea because nobody will keep quiet to protect you."

"But Mamá Abuela, I have no more brothers. I'm safe now."

"You have no more brothers but you're not safe. I see too many men in your future. God help you."

Juan loved Paula, ignored his grandmother, and continued to follow Paula around until his fourth vision about her. A terrible dream about them drowning in a river of blood awakened him. He jumped off his hammock half-asleep and stumbled out of the doorway groping his way in the dark until he found Captain Ojeda face down and unmoving near some crab traps. Bits of gray shells stuck to his uniform.

"How do you do it?" he asked.

This time Paula was crumpled in a heap. "I make believe I like it." Her puffed eyes were purple with bruises.

"You make them think you like beatings?"

"No, estúpido. First I try to reason with them, then I fight but they're too strong. To make them stop beating me, I make believe I like it." She unfolded herself off the ground. "I even kiss them and tell them 'thank you' afterwards. Then I look for them another time. They're stupid and believe I want more sex." She raised her knife and slashed the air. "When they start lowering their pants, I stab them."

"Give me the knife." Juan took it, closed his eyes and stabbed Captain

Ojeda thirty times. Panting, he uttered, "Now it looks different from the other times."

Together they dragged and buried the body under an outhouse. Juan looked at his bloody hands, shivered, and wiped them on the ground.

"You better leave immediately. The spirits say go to Manatí."

"What am I going to do there?"

He averted his eyes. "I'm not sure but go there and you'll be all right, I promise." He kissed her cheek. "Wait right here until I return. I'm going to sneak into your mother's house to bring you something."

"What if they wake up and catch you?"

"We've got to try."

As he stumbled away, he prayed that his aunt and cousins not wake while he stole from them and that, for once, Paula not be so stubborn and strong willed and that she stay where he left her. He had no trouble with the dark or with making any noise above the snoring in the house but his bare feet stepped on a warped nail and he almost cried out. Catching his breath, he unhooked two dresses off a wall, removed two oranges and two mangoes hanging in a bag outside and returned.

"When we grow up we'll meet in Cataño."

"Why there?"

"I don't know. I love you." He gave her a slight shove. "Go with God."

"Manatí now, Cataño later. Is that right?"

Paula left the instant Juan handed her a bundle of fruit, clothing, and some coins to take. Despite his zealous devotion to her, he had admitted defeat. There could be no protecting Paula. Only she could do that. He would miss her, but now at the age of eleven, Juan had important choices to make.

The town priest had been giving him hellfire and brimstone for his spiritualistic powers. Yet Juan, raised in a household where spiritism was natural, remained unconvinced he was the dupe of devils. Padre Hernán wanted Juan to be rebaptized, make his communion and confirmation in the Catholic faith, and give up the spirits. But the spirits had been Juan's friends long before he ever knew the priest, since a time when Juan had been too young to fear visions and manifestations.

His home with Mamá Abuela, a one room shack of sun-grayed planks confusedly hammered together, like all the other homes in the area, stood on stilts a few feet off the ground to keep out stray crabs and occasional floods from heavy rains. They shared a communal outhouse with three other families.

With good organization the large single room served diverse functions. Late afternoons it was living room, family room, and study. Evenings, hammocks were unhooked from one wall and strung across its width to the opposite wall to provide bedding. During the day, it was Mamá Abuela's place of business. Early mornings and weekends she cooked and sold garlicky crab in a red stew, and late mornings she prepared aromatic herbs and reddish powders. By "reading" a client's glass of water, she dispensed advice and cures to the sick and lovelorn, which she had learned to do from her ancestors, runaway slaves from neighboring islands given freedom in Puerto Rico.

Her nickname of Mamá Tumba came about as a result of a mishap when Socorro Peña and her brother were children. Fresh from a beating by another boy, her brother ordered their mother to knock down the bully in retaliation. Their mother did not, of course, but his sister, Socorro, pointed to the bully and insisted he had to pay. The child later fell, suffered a head injury and died.

Juan's earliest recollection was Mamá Abuela's worried face as she woke him. He was three years old, his father was unknown and his mother had died in childbirth. He slept on the floor under the hammocks of his grandfather, Papá Abuelo, and his uncle Moncho, and she slept on the floor next to him since no hammock could support her weight.

"Who are you talking to, Juancito?" she asked.

Sleepy, annoyed by the heat he felt coming from her layers of fat, he pushed her away, mumbled in his baby voice, "Let me sleep . . . the lady."

She shook him. "What lady?"

Mamá Abuela's hands were hot, sweaty, not cold and dry like the lady's. "My friend, the lady in white."

She let him go back to sleep but questioned him in the morning while she sat him on her lap and scrubbed him with a wash cloth.

"You talk and laugh in your sleep," she said. "And your skin gets cold and puckered like a chicken's. Tell me who is with you."

"All my friends," he said. "The lady with the long white dress and the big man dressed in hair and the little man like me except his clothes are grass."

"Does the lady have white skin or is she black like us?"

"I don't know, Mamá Abuela. Sometimes she's white and other times she's darker."

"The spirit of Yemayá," Mamá Abuela said, sitting Juancito, as she called him, back on one of their front stairs. "What do they say?"

"Secrets." He tried to make her understand but he could not find the words to explain that they told him things that would happen later because he usually forgot what they said. She left him alone but he was aware she watched him constantly after that.

By age five, Juancito had found the words.

"Mamá Abuela?"

"Yes?" She mixed and pounded myrrh and sweet smelling anise seed in her wooden mortar and pestle.

"Sometimes I see the father."

"You mean Padre Hernán from the church?" She did not pause her measuring and mixing. Great drops of perspiration poured down her face from the heat of the midday sun. A slight onion smell permeated her.

"No. Like him but not Father Hernán. This one is dark with no hair except on the sides and back of his head. He has pigeons."

"And his clothes?" She stopped moving to stare at him.

"Brown dress with a rope tied around his waist."

"Does he speak?"

"No but the others do. They tell me secrets, like you're going to burn yourself."

"Are you putting the evil eye on me child?"

"What's that?"

"Never mind, just listen. You must always be a good boy to get God's

66

blessing. Don't ever do bad things and don't listen to the spirits if they give you cruel ideas. Do you understand?"

"Yes." Juancito bobbed his little head up and down. "My friends tell me the same thing."

Mamá Abuela's attention encouraged him to tell her more about his invisible friends, the little man in the grass skirt who walked barefoot on hot coals and carried a spear, the giant woman with long red braids and a huge sword in each hand, the big dark man wearing fur, the gypsy girl, and of course, the lady in white with the long black hair.

Mamá Abuela let him ramble more than she ever had before, until she singed her hand with the carbon she used for baking chicken. Then she dismissed her protesting customers, closed shop, and taught him the purification ritual in the ocean.

Juan Peña also remembered accompanying her to seances where he learned to voice his second sight, amazing even Betances Tomaril, a renowned spirit medium, and where he learned to enter trances and semitrances. At first he felt chills, then muscle spasms as he flailed his hands around his head in circles until spirits came into him. As years passed, more and more spirits channeled freely through Juan, spoke in different voices, and he learned from them. Some of these new spirit friends caused dissension as one medium after another accused him of stealing powers from them.

Now, on the verge of manhood, his problems were no longer jealous mediums, fearful townspeople, or Paula's well-being. It was Padre Hernán. The old priest bullied everyone with the fervor of a real zealot, a champion of the true faith. Whenever he had the chance he made Mamá Abuela, whom he called Socorro, and Juan Peña prisoners of his preaching. Mamá Abuela played along by agreeing to everything he said, but Juan argued with Padre Hernán, telling him how similar his lady in white was to the Virgin Mary statuette in the church and how good his spirits were to help people find jobs and mates. Instead of getting discouraged, Padre Hernán rose to the challenge.

Opening his Bible to Leviticus 19:31, he quoted with dramatic intonations, "Do not turn yourselves to the spirit mediums, and do not consult professional foretellers of events, so as to become unclean by them. I am the Lord your God."

Those words riveted Juan. "What?"

Mamá Abuela's eyes bulged, her mouth dropped open.

Triumphant, the priest hurriedly turned pages to read some more. "There should not be found in you anyone who makes his son or his daughter pass through the fire, anyone who employs divination, a practitioner of magic, or anyone who looks for omens or a sorcerer."

As the Spaniard's voice strained to reach heroic emotional proportions, he emitted prideful feelings which buffeted Juan like sharp slaps to his face.

"Or one who binds others with a spell or anyone who consults a spirit medium or a professional foreteller of events or anyone who inquires of the dead. For everybody doing these things is something detestable to the Lord your God, and on account of these detestable things the Lord your God is driving them away from before you." The priest closed his Bible, tapped it, added, "This is the word of God, boy."

"Aieee," Mamá Abuela shrieked. She raised her massive arms, clapping her hands to her ears, thought better of it, crossed herself, and shooed the priest outside the shack. Mouth agape and feet rooted on the wooden planks supported by stones that served as stairs outside his house, Juan stood staring at the priest, his thoughts in turmoil as Mamá Abuela hung a cloth as a door and left him alone in the glaring sunlight with the white priest. Padre Hernán's thoughts screamed at Juan. *Pure white Spaniard I am and defender of the true faith!*

"Come with me to the church," he said. "I'll teach you to read so you can see what God says for yourself."

Disoriented, Juan followed the priest, feeling like a sinner in need of salvation.

True to his word, Padre Hernán began to teach Juan to read. Juan tried very hard even though the spirits distracted him with their nightly whisperings.

"The church doesn't understand," the lady in white said.

"We protect you against your enemies," the Viking woman told him.

68

He repeated all this to the priest who asked, "What enemies do you have that the all-powerful God cannot protect you against? The spirits are your real enemies. They're devils fooling you with their lies."

Faithfully he went to church every day for reading lessons no matter how tired he felt because of lack of rest. The spirits kept him up at night, tried to entrance him in his sleep so that he had to rouse himself, kneel, and recite the prayers the padre taught him sometimes for hours before he could sleep again, and then usually it was time to get up to help Mamá Abuela with her chores. She provided little assistance with his confusion. She continued her herbs and powders, repeating over and over, "I'm not bad, I'm not bad. The priest is wrong."

Finally, he saw pity in her eyes over his exhaustion, and that evening Mamá Abuela stepped out behind the house and returned with a bag of coins.

"These are to find someone." She clinked them in her hands. "In two days you're going to talk to an educated man from San Juan." The next day she made arrangements with the owner of their general store to send for the man.

Dr. Rodríguez arrived on schedule. Mamá Abuela pushed Juan outside while she hid inside their shack and refused to meet with him.

In his black suit, he looked lighter skinned than Juan, more of a dark chocolate than blue-black, but he carried an aura of anger so profound that it emanated pulses of heat. Juan had a brief vision of his own face as he looked at the man and believed he could grow up to resemble this doctor.

In the glaring sunlight, Rodríguez smiled.

"Why is your grandmother afraid of me?"

"Because you're important?"

"I doubt that is the real reason." He chuckled. "Maybe she's afraid I'll put her on a diet." When Juan continued to be solemn, he added, "Never mind, just listen. The spirit mediums in the Bible practiced black magic. They were evil but we are not. There are some spirits who will do evil if their human host tells them to, but if you're careful to do good things only, it won't happen to you."

"But the padre says all the spirits are bad," Juan cried.

"He is mistaken. Are angels bad? Are they not spirits too?"

"Padre Hernán says the age of miracles and communication with angels is over, he read it to me."

"Then why does the church make saints of those who claim to speak with angels?"

"I don't know. I'm confused. I only know I want God to love me and reward me for my good acts like the spirits used to tell me. They're mad at me now."

Dr. Rodríguez took Juan's hands in his own. "Don't listen to the big religions. Their fanaticism causes wars. What you have is a gift the church doesn't understand because not everyone has it. Your spiritualist religion is part of our culture, something Europeans don't respect."

Rodríguez looked into Juan's eyes. "And I'll tell you another secret. There are many fake seers and mediums who practice witchcraft. God will punish them because they try to hurt others. If you think the spirits are angry, it's because you believe you're turning your back on your gift."

"But I don't think I want to be a medium anymore."

"Why not? You haven't done anything bad have you?"

Juan shook his head solemnly.

"There, there." Dr. Rodríguez patted Juan's head. "Always exercise the first freedom. Be yourself, not what others want you to be. How can you be so sure they're right?"

Soothed yet perplexed Juan stared at the doctor's fine suit, his manner, more calm than that of the priest.

"You act white."

"If by white you really mean superior, I am, by virtue of education."

"We're black."

"Is it because the priest is white that you feel you have to listen to him? Without skin everyone is the same color, mostly red. I should know. See this?"

To Juan's surprise, the doctor removed his jacket, folded it neatly in the crook of his left elbow and rolled up his shirt sleeve to show a scar, long healed, on the top of his right forearm.

"As a child, I used a knife to inflict a painful wound on myself hoping that if I had white skin underneath I might please my aunts, but I found only pink flesh, red blood, and blue veins. It's what made me decide to study medicine."

Impressed, Juan said nothing. He had seen that in the wounds on Captain Ojeda, yet he had not thought about it as meaning that everyone was the same.

That night, Juan slept peacefully, had lovely dreams of climbing shimmering white stairs past fluffy clouds. Against the backdrop of a cerulean sky, he received a gold star from a beautiful Indian woman, and he awoke rested and refreshed.

He did not go to church. Instead, he went to the beach and stared out at the blue water watching the waves for hours like he used to before his reading lessons. Oblivious of anyone swimming or lounging in the sun, he meditated.

After a long while, Juan walked towards the church slightly scared of what he had to say to the priest. Padre Hernán was waiting with a big smile on his face and that made things a bit more difficult.

On one of the polished pews lay a white suit.

"A present," he said. "For your communion and confirmation because you have been a good student and have been saved by me." Juan accepted this gift, and remembered it had been in his dream. He was very quiet during his lesson, dry of all questions or protestations. He could read now after many months of study and had memorized his catechism.

Back home Mamá Abuela sat fanning herself, tremendous thighs parted embarrassingly. Juan looked away.

"Mamá Abuela?"

"Yes?"

"We're alone now. Papá Abuelo is gone and so is Uncle Moncho."

"Yes, Juancito. We all die. We can only do our best while we are still alive."

"Why couldn't we save them?"

"It was their time. God called them."

"But we knew it was going to happen. None of our amulets worked."

"I told you it was their time and God called them. We can't fight against that; we can only accept God's will."

"Look what Padre Hernán gave me." He held up the white suit.

"It's elegant," she said, fingering the linen. "You're going to look very handsome." Mamá Abuela gasped, burst into tears and hugged him. "Oh, Juancito, may my sins and sorrows never be yours."

"I'm not going to make my communion and confirmation," he said, in a low voice. "I've been baptized in the ocean. That's enough."

"Have you made a decision then?"

"I didn't have to. I just see that's what will be."

"I don't understand."

Juan turned away and did not utter another word to Mamá Abuela. She was good with spells, prayers, and herbs to cure cramps and infections. She even excelled as a soothsayer of sorts but not as the clairvoyant he was.

Mamá Abuela's gift was not as strong as Juan's. He just knew things, could tell what was going to happen with conviction, predicted the death of her husband and the drowning of his Uncle Moncho, months before they occurred. Mamá Abuela needed to look into water and be near the person she was reading. Juan did not. He could also feel thoughts and those of Padre Hernán still troubled him.

The priest was more concerned with his reputation for saving an igno-rant sinner than with whether or not he was right. The truth was too important an issue to be decided by personal ambition and, if it came to that, Juan had his own future to consider.

He yawned. The day, busy, decisive, was ending.

Early the next morning, Juan put on his new white suit, rolled the trouser legs up to his knees, and carrying his sole pair of shoes in his hands, walked barefoot to the beach. On his way, he watched for scorpi-ons and excrement from scavenger dogs. It was slow careful going. His inky legs grew ashy with salt water and sticky sand. He ran along the edge of the cold water, exhilarated, now that he had squashed the doubts put into his head by the priest. Feeling the heat of Mamá Abuela's eyes on him even at this distance, he threw his shoes and socks up in a wide arc above the crashing waves and turned his back, not allowing himself the satisfaction of watching them bob out to sea.

Resolutely, he moved away from the water, feeling needle pricks of salty spray that bathed him in chills. He called upon his black Congo spirit, waved his arms around his head, and concentrated on his bare feet.

On his way back home, he felt nothing as he crunched mango pits, garbage, and pieces of glass underfoot. He had made his decision and dedicated himself to the spirits. Juan would become a great medium and reap the reward the spirits had promised: salvation for a lifetime of dedication to caring for others. The outward signs of his sacrifice, the bare feet and white suits every day of his life were a small price to pay for the glories of the visions he had seen.

"When are you telling Padre Hernán?" Mamá Abuela asked.

"Now. Give me some money."

"I don't have any."

"Yes you do. It's buried out back. I'll repay you. In the future, I'm going to find a very good job."

Reluctantly, she dug it up, and handed him the money.

Then Juan walked away, toward St. Patrick's.

The doors of the church were open. Strong scents of incense and candle wax wafted out to him. Inside, a few people knelt in various stages of prayer. He looked toward the confessional, walked up to it, whispered, "Padre Hernán?"

"Yes, my child."

"May I speak to you outside?"

"Aren't you here for confession?"

"No, and I won't be here Sunday."

"Sunday's First Holy Communion. You must be here."

"I can't."

"Is there an emergency?"

"I must speak to you outside."

Frowning, the old priest told his waiting parishioners he would return shortly and hurried after Juan outside the church.

"Why are you wearing your communion suit?"

"Here's payment." Juan handed him what he thought it cost.

"It was a gift. We didn't have to come out here for this."

Juan took a deep breath, looked into Padre Hernán's reddening face, and said, "I'm not coming to confession anymore and I'm not making my communion. Thank you for teaching me to read but I'm going with the spirits."

Sputtering, the priest said, "You'll burn in hell. I've saved you, you can't back out and return to the devil." He waved his arms so violently, Juan believed Padre Hernán was about to strike him.

"I'm sorry if I wasted your time but I've made up my mind."

"You little ingrate! You're sinning. I've proved it to you." The priest looked around at his parishioners emerging from the church. "None of you should have anything to do with this boy," he admonished them. "He is excommunicated. Don't go near him!"

Juan backed off, turned, and walked away. "Your salvation is at stake," Padre Hernán called after him. "Come back."

"No," Juan thought. *We each believe in our own brand of salvation and work toward that.* As he walked away Juan understood he would have to wait until he died to find out who was right, him or the priest.

As he headed back to Mamá Abuela's, he thought about becoming a grave digger. What better occupation for a poor boy, as blue black as ink, with no other prospects. People die everyday so he could be sure of always having a job and always being in touch with the dead. He planned to wait awhile before starting his new career, careful not to make an enemy of the church. Let them think him ignorant. He had his whole life ahead of him, a life of placating the spirits as a barefoot grave digger dressed at all times in formal white but first and foremost, as a spirit medium.

Happy with his decision, that afternoon Juan helped Mamá Abuela with her customers by running back and forth to the general store as she ran out of oil or annatto seeds for her famous crab stew until evening when he hung up his suit, hummed softly while he strung out his hammock, and, smiling, said his prayers. Still sniffing incense and candle wax, he fell asleep almost before he lifted his feet off the floor.

VI
Rafaela Moya

An insistent wail from one of the latest of her new baby sisters pierced Rafaela's sleep. She floundered on her narrow bed, pounding her delicate wrists against the pillow to waken from her comalike trance. Beating her slender legs, numb and heavy, she kicked at her mosquito net to get her feet free and over the edge. Light chestnut hair in scruffy braids untidy with escaping strands, shiny with oil and sweat, framed Rafaela's rosy, swollen face.

Rafaela's eyes, pasted shut and sealed together at her eyelashes, refused to open. Behind their closed lids, they felt dry and gritty.

She heard her mother call, "Rafaela! The baby! Get her before she wakes the other children."

She hated the sound of her mother's voice and wished she would be quiet.

"I'm coming," she answered. Then more quietly, *"Cállate la boca."*

Rafaela sat up, rubbed her eyes open, and took a deep breath. She lifted the mosquito net over her head and got up, leaving her three-year-old sister, América, alone in their bed. Listening to the baby's cry both angered and shamed her. For one fleeting moment a terrible idea popped into her head: to smother the screeching infant with a pillow. That thought stabbed guilt wounds in her abdomen and almost moved Rafaela to tears. Almost but not quite. An intelligent child who forgave herself easily, she learned early that she did not like any sensation-causing psychic pain or discomfort. She shook off the guilt.

"I'm so tired," she said, soothingly to the baby in a wicker basket near her bed. "Can't you ever sleep?" She removed the wet diaper's safety pins and threw the yellowed cloth down into a nearby pail of water. It splashed as it joined its ammonia-laden predecessors.

After changing her diaper, she lifted her sister and carried her into the tiny kitchen directly in front of her bedroom. There Rafaela plucked a bottle of milk standing inside a bucket half filled with melted ice water. She tested the lukewarm milk and crammed the nipple into Asia's impatient mouth. Back in the bedroom, the three-month-old child, fatter than her twin, sucked with a desperation that emptied the bottle at an alarming rate and left her gasping for breath after only a few moments. To burp her, Rafaela tried to remove the nipple from those tender lips. As she pulled and tugged against the viselike grip of toothless gums, Asia's small, crimson face angrily protested with loud shrieking. Hearing her mother's shuffling footstep, Rafaela quickly threw the infant over one shoulder as carelessly as she did lifeless dolls and patted Asia's tiny back in whacks and thumps not entirely innocent of malice.

"What are you doing?" her mother Antonia asked.

"Burping this greedy pig," Rafaela said, extending Asia out at arms length.

Hung out in the air with no warm body to lean against, the baby ceased her screaming, her puffy eyes and open mouth suspended in confusion and rejection until her wobbling head and bicycling feet rested on warm flesh once more. Rafaela's. She repositioned Asia on her lap and began to feed her again because Antonia was already on her way to feed África, Asia's twin.

Asia did not take her eyes off Rafaela for the rest of her meal and tensed at every questionable movement her older sister made until the bottle was empty. After strenuous efforts not to do so, desperately blinking her eyes open whenever she began to fall asleep, Asia finally succumbed and nodded off. Rafaela slowly dislodged the warm infant from her comfortable cubby in the crook of her arm and lap and gently returned the baby to her makeshift crib.

"Mamá," she said, going into Antonia's room. "I'm too tired. How can I get good grades if I can't even get enough sleep to stay awake in class?"

"You don't have to go to school tomorrow, if you're too tired." Her mother breast fed África while two-year-old Europa snored softly on a small cot in the corner of the jammed bedroom. The entire house smelled of warm milk and used diapers.

"I want to go to school. I don't want to stay up all night."

Antonia bit her sliver of a bottom lip. She was a small, square woman with close-set glittering eyes and a tiny nose just a bit hooked. She sighed. "All right, Rafaela. Starting tomorrow all the children sleep with me and you can get more rest." Her lips disappeared in an expression familiar to Rafaela. "I know who has your head filled with all this nonsense about school and good grades but just remember, those Figueroas are not your family. We are."

"I'll help you with the chores when I get home. I'll wash, sweep, mop, and go to the store. Anything, I'll do anything but I have to sleep, Mamá. It's not fair."

Rafaela fled to her own room before her mother had time to start an argument. She heeded Josie's advice not to contradict Antonia or else she would end up punished, unable to do the things she liked: go to school, visit the Figueroas for English and piano lessons. Rafaela tried to be very careful how she spoke to Antonia. But her strong temper, impulsive and outspoken, bubbled up and out with everyone else so that her neighbors tread lightly fearing the havoc her precocious ten-year-old, heart-piercing tongue might wreak.

Rafaela lifted the mosquito net and plummeted back into her now cooled spot on the bed next to her sister, América. She kissed the sleeping little blonde on the forehead, put her arm around the child's neck, and snuggled into the pillow they shared. Her eyes closed gratefully.

América was her favorite sister, the one delivered by Rafael Figueroa the evening that Rafaela had seen the beautiful boy who was staying with the Figueroas. América had never cried or awakened Rafaela at night, and

América had pretty hair, shiny and streaked by sun with ribbons of gold. The other children she did not like. They cried too much, ate too much, and took all of her mother's time as well as much of her own.

She remembered how she had felt at each and every one of her mother's pregnancies. With no husband or father around, the burden of shame and disappointment had pierced her stomach and sunk into her abdomen like a heavy rock that splashed into deep water first sinking quickly then more slowly as it settled down into dark depths until some chance rollick of the tides lifted it and delivered it, by a miracle, back up and on to sunlit shores. Feeling the same as a submerged rock at the whim of fate, Rafaela did not like the helplessness of a sensation that involved accepting a fate of less food, clothes, attention, and few of the things she needed to be happy.

With her mouth she imitated bubbling water and resolved to be the tide that moved them all out of poverty and hunger. To do that she needed to go to school, and she wanted desperately to avoid any unpleasant feelings that interfered with her happiness and her clear thinking.

Sleepily, she opened her eyes. América was awake, staring at her intently.

VII
Dr. Rafael Figueroa

Three years from the first time he had set eyes on Félix, Dr. Figueroa received an urgent message from Manatí. He remembered his conviction, long ago, that Luisa Arriesgo should not have children and set off quickly. The trip, faster by boat along the coast than by land, did not end happily. His fear came true when he examined the child who could not walk except on all fours.

It turned out to be a spinal defect beyond Rafael's modest capabilities and beyond the science of 1913. He could do nothing and said so. Rafael examined the hapless child's newly pregnant mother, declared her healthy, and admonished Luisa not to have any more children while he fielded her drunken husband's disturbing questions.

"Why did my wife give me a son who can't walk?" he asked through a whiskey-slurred tongue. "Is it really my boy or did she consort with an animal?" Before the drunk nodded off, he added, "I won't have him named after me. She calls him Luis."

Dr. Figueroa fled the house with the ignorance of the last question hurling around in his head. Troubling intimations Rafael could not answer because puzzles of his own preoccupied him. He knew Luisa Arriesgo to be an educated woman, a schoolteacher from a good family. Why had she married an ignorant country man and why had she insisted on having children when the proof of her genetic shortcomings were demonstrated among many of her family members?

Back home, Josie said, "Loneliness and desperation for love impair logic and fill even the most rational mind with deceptive hope. Surely you know that from the number of unmarried pregnant women who come to you."

"Well, once married why did she have children? One of her brothers was a hunchback and the other had a twisted body. She had to name the boy Luis after herself instead of her husband."

"Listen, she grabbed a good-looking man when she was out there by herself and getting past marriageable age. Who knows what happened behind closed doors? Maybe he refused to use prophylactics or pull out, or maybe he pressured her for children and she put her fate in God's hands. You know how some men are about heirs."

Josie and Rafael examined each other for a moment. They still had no children even though Rafael now made a good livelihood from his practice and they no longer tried to prevent conception.

"I've never complained," Rafael said, quietly. He perched his medical bag on his knees, opened it, and looked inside.

"No," she said. "But God knows I have." She sighed. "Anyway, this isn't about us, it's about a desperate woman and her savage husband." Filled with tears, Josie's lime green eyes glowed like iridescent sea water against her dark skin.

Having children did not define happiness for Rafael as it did for Josie. For him, life felt complete with Josie, so he wanted very much to lighten the mood only he did not know how. Whatever occurred to him to say, he dismissed instantly as frivolity which would make Josie more sad. He regretted discussing Luis Arriesgo and his heart-breaking deformity.

A familiar authoritative knock on the outside door wrenched them both out of their reverie. Grateful, they masked their faces into the selves they presented to the outside world.

"Hello, Rafaela," they said in unison, even before the door was completely opened.

They gazed fondly at the lovely child as they would a savior. She looked rested today. No circles under her eyes, skin smooth, and cheeks rosy again, and her amazing hair, gleaming as if with streaks of liquid silver, braided across the top of her head. The mood broke when the ten-year-old, innocent of what had transpired before she arrived, said, "Hello, my real mother and father."

Josie burst into tears and fled to her bedroom. Rafael sat staring at Rafaela's obvious distress.

"Why did you say that?" he asked, wondering once again if this child was an eavesdropping adult in disguise.

"What did I say wrong, now?" Rafaela asked. She looked close to crying.

Rafael hugged her close, kissed her forehead.

"Nothing, you didn't say anything wrong, darling. We know you love us. Josie doesn't feel well today, that's all."

Not appeased, Rafaela said, "No! I said something wrong." She stared at Rafael, who squirmed under her light brown gaze. Her eyes widened and she slapped her forehead. "I know," she added and ran for the bedroom. She banged on the door, yelling. "Josie, let me in. I didn't mean to make you cry. I love you!"

Josie opened the door. Rafaela went in and shut the door behind her. Two girls against the doctor.

When Josie and Rafaela came out an hour later with their arms wrapped around each other, they were talking and laughing.

After Rafaela went home without her piano and English lessons, Josie and Rafael ate their dinner in silence and then retired. That night Rafael reached out to Josie and they made love slowly, hesitantly, and conceived their son.

When his son was almost three years old, Rafael received another urgent message from Manatí, signed by someone he did not know.

"Luisa!" he thought and wondered if her second child was deformed like the first. He dreaded visiting but there was nothing to do except to go see for himself. Perhaps Luis had died. "God forgive me," Rafael thought. *It might be best for all concerned.*

On his last trip his boat was almost capsized twice by giant sea waves and left him on the coast from where, heart thudding in fear, he had to hike through dark and hilly terrain. Now he felt that making the slower trip by mule on rutted dirt roads, though subject to flooding and fallen trees, was less dangerous and less prone to attack by thieves if he rode quickly under the shade of trees, bushes, and other vegetation. For twenty-four hours he traveled by sun, moon, and starlight too intent on his mission to enjoy the beauty of the countryside bursting with giant, blood-red poppies and white orchids veined by tiny, pink striations.

He arrived late that night, found the second boy perfectly formed and healthy. Tomás only walked on all fours to emulate his older brother, Luis, who despite his severely deformed spine appeared well: a miracle during an age of want and shortages.

It was Luisa who died, murdered by her husband in a drunken fit of ignorant madness. After his arrest but before Dr. Figueroa arrived, Luisa's husband had been shot trying to escape from his makeshift prison.

"Who sent for me?" Rafael asked. The villagers turned to an exceptionally good-looking young black woman standing near the doorway, arms crossed under extraordinary high, round breasts.

"I did," she said, in a smooth, strong voice tinged with authority. Rafael's juices stirred and worry filled him. This young woman's prominent cheekbones, voluptuous breasts, and throaty voice drew an immediate and unwelcome erotic response. Although he resented her annoying sensuality, every pore in his body stood at attention. It was an effort not to fidget.

"Why?" he asked. "Luisa's dead and buried. What can I do now?"

She uncrossed her arms, smiled shyly, said, "I didn't want the other doctor to touch me, Luis, or Tomás."

"You mean Rodríguez?"

"Yes, that's the bastard." She spat into the darkness outside the house. Neighbors flinched, some jumped back slightly but none said a word.

"Why don't you like him?"

"He comes around staring at Tomás, trying to talk to him."

Rafael remembered Dr. Rodríguez's influence on Rafaela and felt alarmed for Tomás.

"Don't let him near the boy," he said.

One of the men concentrated on twirling the rim of his battered straw hat around in his hands and gestured at an old woman with a black lace mantilla over gray braided hair. She approached.

"My name is Doña Marta," she said, extending her hand. "I'm governess to the Sánchez family who owns the property on the hill." She gestured toward the man with the straw hat.

Doña Marta pursed her lips. "And this is our neighbor, Paula Meléndez." She neither pointed nor looked at the young black woman, and Rafael wondered at this strange introduction. "She wants to keep the children."

Confused, Rafael walked toward the door, turned to Paula, said, "Fine, good, but you don't need me for this."

"You don't understand," Paula said, sighing. "They won't let me keep the children unless you say so."

The hat twirler spoke up. "Señor Doctor, we found letters that show you were a good friend of the late Luisa Arriesgo, may she rest in peace." He crossed himself with his thin, pale hand. "If you examine Paula and say she can keep the children, we will agree unless you yourself want to take them."

Paula stepped over to a curtain, pulled it aside, and led Rafael to one of the cots serving as their beds. Luis, the older boy, crawled over on arms and legs to join them. Paula told him to wait with his brother, reclosed the curtain behind herself and Rafael.

"Ask me questions," she said. Lights from lamps held by neighbors outside the home glittered through separations in the boards of the shack.

Understanding, Rafael burst into laughter shocking Paula who opened her eyes wide then smiled showing small, perfect teeth.

"What do you do for a living, young woman?"

Paula straightened like a schoolgirl. "I sew, crochet, cook, take in laundry, and . . ." She looked at him defiantly. "And when there is no money for food, I take in men."

"Just as I thought," he muttered. "Do you have sores anywhere on your body?"

Abruptly, Paula removed her long cotton dress and her bloomers, undressed completely. "See for yourself."

His throat constricted. "Lie down," he said, gently. "And open your legs." He found nothing except velvety, chocolate skin. "Get dressed now." He made a pretense of listening to her heartbeat, strong and steady, and of measuring her pulse, normal. His own felt less so. Rafael removed his glasses, pinched the bridge of his nose, and rubbed his eyes. "Why does Dr. Rodríguez look at Tomás?"

"Who knows? He's a pig and deserves to die." She stared at him as calmly as if she had just recited the alphabet.

"Can you read and write?" he asked.

She lost her arrogance, lowered her head. "No." Then she raised her face, eyes glaring. "I'm young. I can learn. So can the children. Luis already knows how. His mother taught him. We'll all learn together."

Her torrent of words inspired Rafael to rashness. "I can help," he said. "My wife's a schoolteacher."

Ignoring him, Paula continued her flood.

"They won't go hungry. I'm very clean and will take good care of them. I'll protect them. You won't be sorry." She paused to catch her breath, chest heaving with excitement. "You won't be sorry," she repeated. "You'll see. Come back anytime. You and your wife, we'll be waiting." As an afterthought, she added, "We, I'll find pencils, paper, you'll see. You promise to return?" She bit her bottom lip, dimpling her cheeks. Her forehead furrowed with desperation.

Rafael patted her face, already regretting his impulsive offer. He wondered what Josie would say. "Have you no family?"

"A younger cousin named Juan but I don't know where he is or if he works yet."

To the crowd waiting in the black night outside the home, he announced, "I, Dr. Rafael Figueroa of Cataño, approve that Paula Meléndez keep the children unless and until a better home can be found."

"Cataño?" Paula gasped.

Rafael continued. "Any volunteers to take the children?"

Silently, the crowd turned their backs and trudged slowly back to their homes, holding their lanterns high in front of their feet to light their paths. He had counted on such a response just as he counted on the community's habit of sharing their meager income and surplus with Paula and the children. To himself, Rafael said, "May God forgive me. Again."

On the trip back home, Rafael thought of all the children. He thought first of the two boys, Tomás and his brother Luis Arriesgo, whom he had just left behind in the care of a prostitute, of his own son, surprisingly light-skinned, with green eyes, and perfectly healthy, which had been Josie's major worry in an age of crossed eyes and club feet. He thought of beautiful Rafaela who became enraged each time her mother gave birth to another illegitimate daughter, and he thought of Félix Cienfuegos who had escaped orphanage and early death. Rafael calculated that by now Félix would be eighteen, Rafaela he knew was now twelve, the hapless Luis Arriesgo six, and his brother Tomás, two years old.

His own son, Junior, had Rafael and Josie to care for him and, should something happen to them, Junior still had Josie's relatives in the States. Rafaela might fare better to some extent by the preparation he and Josie could give her, but what about the deformed Luis and the other countless orphans and cripples who slipped through his benign grasp and into the hate-filled influence of Rodríguez? He dreaded speaking to Josie about the promise he had just made to a sixteen-year-old prostitute.

He and Josie would have to travel to Manatí at least once a month to teach them, and he saw that drudgery stretch out before him far into the coming years without relief.

VIII

Félix

In the countryside Félix began his strenuous labors under a sadistic sun, each early morning very much like the others. Sunlight glinted harshly against verdant hills softly rolling with lush green plantains, speckled red mangoes, and sweet papaya. He watched small brown birds flit cheerfully and call with loud clear whistles without seeing them. He daydreamed, reimagining his youth with a happier outcome for his father. In his yearned-for reality, the widow Sánchez had married not her country bumpkin cousin with the same last name but his father, and they had all gotten so fat that at sumptuous feasts surrounded by their business partners they joked about the size of their paunches and chattered on about the state of the economy and the usefulness of the latest inventions. That fantasy never bored him.

He hated rainy seasons the most. In clearings, he sat on his horse reining the animal's skittishness against thunder claps. Pelted by wind and rain, he tried to entertain himself by listening and picking out the various sounds of falling water. Zinc roofs clattered like metal washboards, foliage crunched like gypsy moths, and the ground first plunked reluctantly, then splotched, then ran serenely illuminated by flashes of lightning until the sun reappeared. The landscape dried bright, hot, and steamy until the next torrential shower began so that the entire day was divided into still photographs of sharp, wet brightness or hazy mist. Those times he pictured himself captured in sepia prints in a ballroom waltzing with lovely debutantes who spoke knowledgeably about the paintings of El Greco and the literature of Cervantes.

During dry seasons his horse lifted a dusty trail as Félix rode back and forth, straining his eyes while he examined dried brown fields for signs of green life and usually found none.

Evening sunsets striated blue skies pink and turned puffy white clouds smoky, then gray, and finally a red glow disappeared into blackness as night, interspersed with glittering stars, engulfed the vast open spaces around him.

None of these things held any charm for him. Snaky roads with deep ravines on either side and the cool, sweet air of the mountains oppressed him. He yearned for civilization to hedge him in, provide specific goals as discipline. He wanted walls, a smaller space, and he knew exactly what they were: a city house, a city career.

"Félix!" Pedro called. The old man's face reddened. "What are you thinking?"

He looked down at the shredded tobacco leaves in his hands. "The harvest is bad."

"For some time now. I'm giving it up."

"Not planting anymore?" Félix asked hoping it was so.

"No." Pedro's bottom lip curled up. "Selling or leasing the land."

"None of the plantations are doing well. Why sell this one?"

"It's the most difficult. Coffee may be next."

"Can I attend the university then?"

Before answering, Pedro looked at his paunch and then at the ground. He sighed. "How many times and in how many ways do I have to say no."

Félix watched his uncle strain to control his temper. He knew the old man had grown to love and respect him, but he felt that Pedro's arguments did not apply to him.

"My father spent his childhood away at schools," he said. "That's why he didn't want to return. I'm not like that." He paused. "Please, Uncle Pedro, I promise to practice here with you when I finish." Félix knew he had to vow whatever would convince.

"How can I take that risk?" Pedro asked. "You're the last Cienfuegos."

"I love the mountains," he said. "But I want to know more than swinging a scythe. My mind is hungry." He hesitated to search for the words to make his uncle understand his need to exercise more than just his body.

"Come on," Pedro said. "It's time you had a woman."

Félix did not know what to expect and did not like the woman who surprised him later that evening by being small, sun-scorched, and businesslike.

"Take off your clothes," she commanded. "I'll be back to wash you down first." No words of endearment to ease his nervousness, no exotic trappings to excite his senses, no comfort as he looked down at the hard, narrow cot. Nothing to separate his first lovemaking from a lesson in horseback riding. Her boniness, her scent of sun and stale cooking oil combined to lump her with all his uncle's peasants, male and female. Because of his shyness, his erection faded repeatedly until she gave up, called Pedro, and said, "Don't bring him back. He's too slow."

To Félix's relief Pedro misinterpreted and chuckled, saying, "Good. Not like your father. He refused."

"Now can I go to the university?"

"Talk to me next year."

He hoped those words pointed to signs of softening but the waiting proved difficult. To vent his frustrations, he took refuge in the pains of his labors. His father, he felt, had been wrong. Physical work was not to be avoided, rather something Félix used to displace anger with patience. He sometimes comforted himself by picturing his uncle's face as he swung his machete. How long could Uncle Pedro's opposition last? As he chopped and hacked, time did not go faster but it passed more easily.

The promised year went by and then another. Just when he thought his uncle would agree, one of the workers came running over to him.

"Come quick, the patrón broke his neck."

Uncle Pedro died from a fall from his horse. He had tried a jump, which his old horse could not accomplish. With a sense of history repeating itself Félix stared down at his uncle, size undiminished by age, as the old man lay not breathing on the red earth with his neck twisted at an impossible angle. A cold knife of loss stabbed him and Félix wept.

"Always control yourself," Ciriaco said. "Now you can go to school as you wanted." He patted Félix's back. "Old people have to die sometime," he added. "It was now or later."

Félix did not tell Ciriaco how too late he realized he respected his great uncle, that once again he felt not just deserted but somehow responsible for this death also because of his coldness, his preoccupation with his own needs to the exclusion of attending to the old man's welfare. How easily he could have insisted to Pedro that his old horse should retire, no longer be forced to show off. That might have saved both his uncle's pride in his horsemanship and his life.

During the funeral, amid the crowd of mourners, he said nothing. There was no time for his thoughts, the machinery of everyday concerns called to him even before the burial.

"What's going to happen now?" the workers demanded.

To answer instead of staring dumbly at them, he had to take over the business.

The same afternoon that he threw a pinch of earth on his uncle's grave, he returned to the big house to examine his uncle's primitive accounting ledgers. Félix found all future income pledged in advance.

"My uncle," he told the workers, "left no will and too many debts to make a fight worth my efforts."

"You can't mean that," they responded. "Fight for your land."

But Félix thought they really meant he should fight for them and their jobs. As his father had told him, Félix saw a system that rolled around to itself in an interlocking cycle of credit, hard labor, debts, payments, credit, hard labor, and more debts.

No wonder neither my uncle nor my father wanted a wife.

He was left with his beginnings, the pearls he still used as rosary beads. They were translucent and multihued from their contact with his skin but were also a constant source of worry to him. Without his tough uncle as mentor, he imagined thieves, scoundrels, and users everywhere waiting for him to turn his back so that they could steal his pearls in exchange for a pile of self-perpetuating debts.

He thought to grab any cash remaining from the last poor harvests of sugar, coffee, and tobacco, pack his pearls, and set out for a college education, leaving the land to his uncle's creditors. He did not feel sorry to leave. Doña Marta had become another's governess long ago and Ciriaco was well provided for. Félix did not want responsibility for anyone else.

Next to his uncle's name, newspaper obituaries of 1916 included Luis Muñoz Rivera, friend of his father and hero of his boyhood political fantasies. The print blurred as he thought that Muñoz Rivera had died disgraced as a chameleon in the minds of impatient radicals because in 1898 he had sold himself to the United States after having pledged loyalty to Spain in order to obtain autonomy. Sadness at the death of illusions filled him as he remembered the ill-fated night his father died. During that last conversation even his father had begun to lose patience with impossible dreams. All hope for freedom vanished with the disappearance of the brilliant political minds who had lived during his father's childhood. After the death of Ruiz Belvis and Betances, there had been no one to step in to fill the vacuum of courage and self-sacrifice created by their passing. Fear and greed prevented those who might have put aside personal ambition to step up to the front of the line. Félix compared those who failed to do so to the skinny, sunburned peasants, so humble, so ignorant, and then shivered, knowing he would not have done so either.

Time and circumstance change politics!

Félix felt prepared to leave all this behind, never think or sadden himself about it again. He intended to play the game of life as most successful people did. During the years when every minute of every one of his days and nights were supervised, watched as he bathed, ate, slept, and studied, he learned to safeguard impressions as did his uncle and his uncle's friends who had lived with hypocrisy.

At social gatherings he had listened as his uncle lifted a glass of red wine to toast the beauty and fecundity of Don Lorenzo's wife while in private settings Pedro laughed at his creditor's whole family.

"Ugly as sin and just as crooked," Pedro had said. "Every one of the dirty thieves."

For his part Don Lorenzo also played the game well, complimenting Pedro's business acumen while holding secret meetings to raise prices of his supplies and then offering to buy Pedro's land at a fraction of its worth as if he were doing him a favor. It did not matter what a man did, only that he not get caught and so ruin the perception others had of him. When he finished his studies, Félix would not commit errors. He vowed never to do or say anything that might be remembered as a definite stance, something which should it later change could be interpreted as betrayal. Better not to have strong feelings about anything except improving his situation until he could enter politics.

Three days after the funeral, his uncle's main creditor, Don Lorenzo, knocked on his door and asked to speak to him privately before he left or made any decisions.

"I beg your pardon?" Félix asked. He did not believe the job offer.

"We've all watched you grow up here Félix," Don Lorenzo said. "We take care of our own." The gentleman farmer smiled and patted him on the back. "You can keep my books if you like. I believe that's more suitable to your talents."

The position as accounting clerk for Don Lorenzo turned out to be a light charity job because business was off. Félix saved the salary from his bookkeeping job and supplemented his ambitions with sweating out hard labor in the sugarcane fields for half-pennies. He slept in his employer's back room and ate only whatever he got paid in kind for tutoring the local village people, often staying up late into the night preparing the next week's lesson by candlelight. While he saved every cent toward his coveted law career, he spurned all overtures, did not have one friend, nor would he have known what to do with one.

When Don Lorenzo's daughter Carmencita reached marriageable age, he looked askance at Félix and alluded to a dowry.

"She's my only daughter," he said, winking.

Carmencita reached Félix's belt and, at fifteen, had a heavy shadow above her upper lip. As if that were not bad enough she never spoke, devoting herself to crocheting all day. She sat on a chair under mango trees with a big hat on her head as her fingers constantly worked the white thread. She only acknowledged conversation and jokes by interrupting her count of the stitches to say, "One, two, ha, ha, five, six."

Félix thought over the proposition. Now that two years had passed, he understood why he had received Don Lorenzo's job offer in the first place. Had not his father planned on marrying a rich widow? The flaw in his plan was that Carmencita was not a widow. She was the homely daughter of a man who had three sons all older than Carmencita and Félix had first-hand knowledge that Don Lorenzo's businesses were failing.

Still, for lack of anything better to do until he had enough money, he accepted a formal invitation to dine with the family to court Carmencita.

Her mother set a table loaded with an entire pig roasted on a spit, different rice dishes, and served hearty country vegetables such as yuca and *yautía*. But all he concentrated on was that the woman of the house had long straight hair above her upper lip, which rivaled her husband's waxed moustache, and a very high voice that grated Félix's nerves. He wished Carmencita spoke, yelled, or did anything, aside from blushing and hiding behind her fan. Her broad-faced brothers and their dowdy wives sat stiffly at the table as if expecting an announcement.

"Señora, we are out of wine," their servant said. Landed gentry never lacked wine or brandy.

Don Lorenzo's wife began a shrieking so disconcerting that Félix dropped his fork and stared disbelieving. Carmencita stifled a giggle. Then another, then she began a nervous laughter in an alto solo. Mother shrieked and daughter laughed so long and loud it seemed like a bad opera.

When Félix declined to marry Carmencita, he found himself out on the street, his saddle bags thrown after him on to the dusty roadway in front of Don Lorenzo's main house. He picked them up, chagrined at the light weight of his belongings. Carmencita ran after him.

"Is it because I'm so ugly?" she asked, her face filled with a need he could not oblige.

"No," replied Félix, amazed that Carmencita fully expected him to tell her what he really felt. *How sad, to suspect the truth yet still want desperately to be told a lie.* "It's because we are both too young."

"What?" Carmencita looked surprised by his answer. "Félix, you're twenty years old."

"I haven't finished my education and I don't have a penny. How can I take care of you when I can't even take care of myself? Look, I'm out on the street now." He stifled the urge to turn out his pants' pockets. The pearls might fall out.

Carmencita clasped her hands in prayer, then reached into a lace bag tied around her wrist and withdrew a wad of cash.

"Will this help for your education?"

The roll of American dollars looked huge to him. As he stared at the green bills, they filled his mind's eye with visions of books, paper, a law degree. He thought about hypocrisy and Don Lorenzo's ulterior motives for hiring him, paying him just enough to keep him around but hungry.

"Yes," Félix answered, grabbing the money. "But what about your father?"

"He doesn't have to know. My mother either." Squinting her eyes, she added, "You will come back won't you?"

"Of course. As soon as I become a lawyer. I'll never forget you." He envisioned kissing her mustachioed lips, thought better of it, and kissed her hand instead. He waved good-bye.

When he had walked a safe distance away, he counted the cash. Yes, coupled with his savings, it was enough for him and his frugal ways to go to the university and become a lawyer, thanks to Carmencita. Involuntarily, he thought of the relationship between his mother and father. An ice-pick stab of recognition, guilt, struck him from behind and quickened his pace down the road away from this reality into, he hoped, a more righteous future.

IX

Rodríguez

Three children in particular fascinated Rodríguez: Rafaela from Cataño, Félix from San Juan, and Tomás Arriesgo from Manatí. He included their towns in his regular route to stare at them in his search for similarities and ignored their Simple Simon parents and guardians. He felt each might belong to him because of past events.

With his help, a sixteen-year-old prostitute from La Perla, near San Juan, had miscarried every child she conceived, paid him with sex until she refused.

"You're the one who has to pay me. If you don't I'll go to the magistrate."

That shamed him. Blackmail had no place in their relationship. "Don't I perform a service important to your business?" he had asked. She was not as poor as the people in the countryside. Did he not deserve some recompense rather than to have to pay on top of helping her? "Go ahead, Marlena, tell anybody you want. Who is going to believe an ignorant prostitute?"

"I'll ruin you," she said, smiling.

"Accept it, you can't. Better people than you have tried." He gathered his medicines. "Who is going to treat your sores? You'll turn into an old witch in no time and rot young." Rodríguez put on his hat, turned to leave.

"You'll go to jail," she said, blocking his exit.

"You'll be right there with me. Then the guards will take you for free. Have you thought of that?"

"Wait." Reluctantly, she recapitulated. "All right, treat my sores but you should know you've aborted your own child twice. That's why I'm so angry with you."

Rodríguez did not know that. How could he have made such mistakes?

"Impossible," he said. "I can't have children. I was injured in Spain."

"What?" She eyed him suspiciously. "You look all right to me."

"It's internal. Where you can't see it. I can't have children though I can have relations."

"And you certainly love to do that," she said.

"So do you. Isn't that why you ran away from a good home?" When she did not answer, he added, "What is it going to be Marlena? I refuse to be taken advantage of. You have to pay me one way or another."

She began to remove her skirt. "How is it you never get sores?"

"I treat myself the same way I do you."

"Then whose children were they?"

"Your customers'," he said indignantly. "I've told you what to do. You don't listen."

"I do listen," she cried. "It's the men, they refuse to pull out." She licked her lips as she laid down on her cot. "You never pull out."

"And I'm not going to," he thought. *You owe me a child.* When she got pregnant again, he would not terminate it. To allay her suspicions he took her longer and harder than he had ever done before savoring every inch of her plump, moist flesh. Gently, he kissed her forehead, her eyes, her lips. He sucked her earlobe, plunged his tongue inside her ear and sucked mildly, making her moan. He nibbled, bit, and sucked her breasts, then her entire body while she writhed and begged for him. Then he plunged and thrust against her, watching her eyes until they glazed in concentration and she climaxed.

"Well," she said, mesmerized.

"Greedy bitch," he thought. But what he said was, "An adventuress only does well in books not real life. Find a man to care for you or remember what I taught you."

"There's only one," she said. "A friend. He hardly ever touches me."

"What's his name?"

"Félix Cienfuegos. He's a patriot and a poet."

"Some poets are useless human beings. They don't eat as well as prostitutes and with few exceptions are patriots only in their verse, their poems. Find someone else but keep him for the forty days you have to stay away from all sex."

Rodríguez left, not planning to see her again until she had given birth to his child, but in early 1897 a secret communique forced him from San Juan to Yauco on the other side of the island.

The badly written message, scratchy and ungrammatical, simply said, "You are needed by the tower builders," and when he arrived and saw the group of rebels he understood why.

For the sake of secrecy, different groups of three or four were supposed to meet on different evenings in various homes, but the same attended for so many weeks that Rodríguez began to recognize them. A sign of poor planning.

"Your numbers are few," he said. "And machetes don't make effective weapons against gunpowder."

"Can you help us?"

"I don't want any part of this." His instinct told him some could not be trusted and had probably either already informed Spanish authorities or had confided their intentions to those who could betray them. He waited a few days until satisfied none had been arrested and sent a deaf mute to deliver a mule loaded with rifles and pistols. An anonymous note accompanied.

"The best strategy," he wrote, "is to take possession of the Civil

Guard's armory. If you can do that the people will feel more secure. They will rally and the region will be yours."

Recalling former times, rife with traitors and spies against their own people, he declined to join them. Instead, Rodríguez watched from a distance as fifty to sixty malnourished patriots armed with machetes and his rifles and pistols marched on Yauco. Close to the cemetery, Spanish authorities surprised them, opened fire, and began their arrests.

As soon as he saw the failure of the intent, he quickly fled to the lower Cordillera range to hide his collaboration. Warned of a search, he endured one night clutching a thick vine while he hung over the side of a ravine, listening to the militia's footsteps and calls as they passed over his head and praying they did not spot him with their torches. The ligaments in his arms never regained their strength and later the Autonomists obtained release of the rebels.

To Rodríguez's surprise, Luis Muñoz Rivera successfully negotiated Puerto Rico's autonomy from Spain on October 6, 1897.

It was a half-way measure of freedom that proved pitifully short-lived when the United States invaded in early 1898. His heartbreak over the failure of Puerto Rican leaders to follow a vision of independence joined with the suffering of Betances in exile upon learning that Puerto Ricans did not greet Americans with firearms and a raised Puerto Rican flag to declare themselves free but meekly accepted the invaders as they would yellow fever, malaria, and hurricanes. Rodríguez bristled that Muñoz Rivera had scurried to declare himself a good North American, thus ingratiating himself when the United States army invaded instead of standing firm for independence. A new yoke had to be thrown off and his solution remained viable.

In 1899, seventy-five-mile-an-hour winds surged on distant San Juan as hurricane San Ciriaco cut an upward diagonal across the middle of Puerto Rico from Aguirre to Aguadilla like a cosmic scythe which flattened most of his lands. Clearing uprooted, splintered trees, reseeding and harvesting kept Rodríguez busy rebuilding his capital base well into the new century.

He did not return to San Juan until 1900. Marlena refused to answer his question and a growing Félix was attached to the poet, a pitiful and penniless failure of a man who shook his bony fist at Rodríguez whenever he caught him staring at little Félix.

Was Félix his or had Marlena disregarded his advice and made love to the poet? Rodríguez regretted not knowing the exact time of the boy's birth since he had been born at home and only had his baptismal record which Rodríguez knew could be months, even years off the correct date.

In 1902, Antonia Moya entered his San Juan office wearing a white cotton blouse and skirt on her short, square body just as Rodríguez prepared for one of his trips. It had been a long time between conquests and he felt hungry. His penis would not stay down so when he saw her, he thought to postpone his travels.

"Good afternoon, Dr. Rodríguez," she said, extending her hand as if to be kissed.

"How do you do?" he replied, shaking her hand. "What is the problem?"

She pursed thin lips and held her hands under her breasts, fingers interlaced in a pose.

"I see little lights and feel warm. Then I faint." She fisted her hand, put it to her forehead and he noticed a film of perspiration above her upper lip.

"Do you feel ill now?"

"Very weak."

He led her to a seat, fanned her but to no avail. Her eyes rolled up into her head and she keeled over.

Rodríguez loosened the buttons on her blouse and skirt, examined her nails and lifted her eyelids. He diagnosed anemia, which was commonplace in the rest of the population.

Antonia awoke with a moan.

"You're anemic but do not cope as well as others. The tonic you need might cause your stomach some distress."

"That won't be a problem, doctor. Thank you and forgive my inconveniencing you." She batted her eyelashes, flirting awkwardly.

He thought her stiff and formal yet a potential little mother and began his seduction.

"My lovely young woman . . ."

"You are mistaken, sir," she interrupted. "I'm a spinster neither young nor lovely. Good day."

Astonished, he stared as she walked out until he collected himself enough to rush after her.

"If this tonic doesn't work for you, please return before two weeks as I might be away after that time."

"Perhaps I won't need to."

"That is to be hoped, however, there is the question of my fee."

"Your fee!" She tightened her lips until they disappeared and then she dug into her purse. "Excuse me. I had understood you gave free treatment."

"Not in my San Juan office. Only for country folk too poor and sick to come to me."

He saw her thinking and wondered what else she had on her mind. Before the allotted two weeks elapsed, a young boy walked into his office with a note requesting assistance in Cataño.

"Smart woman," he said, chuckling. Now she wanted free treatment without asking for it.

When he arrived in her town he almost whistled, fully expecting the homely little woman to succumb gratefully, more so as soon as he saw the tiny, weather-peeled shack she lived in. There she sat crocheting by the doorway, her white skin tinged with green.

"The tonic gives me cramps and makes me throw up," she said, leading him inside.

He looked at the one large bed in the bigger of two small bedrooms, then up at the termite-ridden ceiling and at the bare floors and walls. Why did she live here under these circumstances? Was he mistaken about her being a lady of some means?

"Please lie down so I can examine your abdomen."

Instead of doing so, she put her fisted hand against her forehead and fell to the floor with a soft plop. He picked her up, tossed her on the bed, and struggled to remove her clothes. Half-naked, she awoke.

"How dare you?"

"Madam, I must examine your abdomen."

"Get your hands off my breasts."

"I have to examine them too."

"Please leave."

Enough was really enough. There were so many truly sick people awaiting his services that he had no time to waste being a crazy woman's servant boy until she made up her mind. Reaching into his bag, he withdrew a bottle of chloroform, poured some on a handkerchief.

"This will make you feel better," he said.

"I don't want it!"

Rodríguez forced it over her nose and mouth until she quieted. After examining her and suspecting nothing other than possible low blood sugar in addition to the anemia, he wrote a prescription and a diet. Then he relieved his lust.

Cleaned up and half out of the drugged state, she opened her eyes, stared straight at him, smiled, and called him by the name of an idiotic Spaniard.

What?

"Indeed, madam," Rodríguez said. The crazed fantasies of ugly little Antonia who had not been a virgin after all. Disgusting! New conquests and new children in other parts of the island called to him. He refused to treat her again and occupied himself with mountain women but perked his ears up when he heard she gave birth to Rafaela. Rafaela! That excited Rodríguez. His given name was Rafael, although he never used it. He insisted on being called Dr. Rodríguez as if his first name was Doctor.

In Manatí, Luisa Arriesgo, mother of the deformed Luis, went to Rodríguez shortly after Dr. Figueroa's first visit to her.

"My old friend, Rafael Figueroa admonished me not to have more children. I want to miscarry this child."

"Why?"

"Congenital deformities run in my family."

"Each and every one?"

"Except for me."

"Why doesn't your 'old friend' help you?"

She lowered her head. "He did not think of it."

"Or would not."

Convinced her drunken husband compounded the problem with his alcohol thinned blood, Rodríguez performed her requested abortion and told her to prevent pregnancy. On a follow-up visit days later, her blackened eyes and bruised cheeks told him that Luisa had received a beating from her husband.

"My husband beat me until I confessed about the abortion. He wants to see all subsequent children and accused me of consorting with the devil or with a horse or a bull or whatever his crazed imagination conjures up when he drinks."

"Why don't you leave him?"

"I have a little boy. Where would I go?"

"Surely as a schoolteacher there are jobs for you."

"Then who would care for my child?"

He sighed. What was she trying to tell him? That she loved the beastly drunk? That she wanted him to rescue her? How?

Rodríguez knew that Luisa's husband insisted on sex five and six times a day and knew she would get pregnant again, chancing another deformed child. They stood staring at each other for several minutes as it gradually dawned on him what she might really be asking. Mixed bloodlines showed in the flare of her nostrils, in the friz of her curly hair. Just when he was about to remove the chloroform from his bag and say, "Let's try a three-day series of treatments," in case he was wrong about her intentions, she moved closer to him. Gently, she embraced him, pressed her face against his chest and wept.

"Please forgive me," she said. "And help me."

A long forgotten sensation of sympathy welled up in him at her desperation and tempered his anger at her refusal to help herself. He complied, expecting her next child to be born perfect and to be his.

For that reason he later imagined himself to be the father of Tomás Arriesgo a child who, except for the normalcy of his spine, looked a twin of his older brother Luis whom he followed and imitated. He reasoned that the drunk had shot Luisa because he suspected Rodríguez to be the real father.

After the death of Marlena's poet and as a result of his island wanderings, Rodríguez found Félix sometimes in Caguas and sometimes in Comerío but always under the watchful eyes of a tremendous old man who claimed to be the boy's uncle.

Experimentally, Rodríguez walked on the road in front of the uncle's house, back and forth, carrying his black bag, hoping for a glimmer of interest from the good-looking boy. His biggest reward was that Félix hid behind gardenia bushes to stare back, and when Rodríguez turned to smile at him, shock lit the young boy's face. The boy obviously remembered him, and Rodríguez believed he recognized a smoldering genius in Félix, which the doctor happily attributed to his own genes. Unfortunately, Pedro Cienfuegos accosted him one evening.

"If you're ever so much as seen in this town again, I'll shoot off your testicles." The old man's pistol roared into the sky for emphasis.

Once again he stayed away long enough for passions and memories to cool. When he returned, both the uncle and Félix were gone, but he heard the story of Don Lorenzo's daughter, Carmencita, and laughed at the hypocrisy of the privileged young man.

Meanwhile he stalked Rafaela and Tomás trying to carve out opportunities to talk to them.

Folktale 11

Juan Bobo va a la escuela

Simple Simon goes to school

After his father died, Juan Bobo drove his mother almost to madness because he was always so hungry that he sometimes boiled their shoes and ate them and because he called useless whatever did not fill his stomach. She worried about his future if something happened to her so she decided to send him to school to learn a useful skill.

Warned by the name Juan Bobo, the schoolteacher refused to admit the skinny young man to class by saying that he was too old, although he really meant too stupid, until Juan Bobo's mother spoke to the town mayor. Juan Bobo's mother washed laundry for the mayor, and the mayor paid the teacher's salary.

Teacher wrote the alphabet on a blackboard and saw Juan Bobo scratch his head and tilt his face left until his head was almost upside down.

"Chicken feet make those marks on sand," Juan Bobo said. "You won't catch me wasting time by writing chicken. It is useless."

Teacher recited the alphabet in a loud voice.

"Only foreigners talk like that," Juan Bobo said. "Useless."

For the next few days the instructor tried vowels.

"Repeat after me, A E I O U."

Each time Juan Bobo, carrying his reader upside down, scratched his head and asked, "What do you owe me?"

Teacher shouted, "A E I O U, a burro is smarter than you!"

"A burro is smarter than you," repeated Juan Bobo.

Evangeline Blanco

The other students laughed loudly, and they jumped from their seats to circle the teacher and Juan Bobo. In a chorus, they sang: "A burro is smarter than you."

Suspecting they really meant him, the teacher ordered Juan Bobo to dust, sweep, and clean erasers.

"I know that already," Juan Bobo said. "Useless."

By listening to Juan Bobo's grumbling stomach and noting his sunken midsection, the teacher told Juan Bobo to go outside to the school yard tree to pick mangoes for the class. Juan Bobo stayed out so long the teacher happily taught his lessons with no interruptions, but by nap time he worried that Juan Bobo might be lost inside the school yard. They found him asleep against the base of the tree surrounded by a mountain of discarded mango skins and pits, his midsection swollen from having eaten so much fruit.

At home, Juan Bobo told his mother that school taught him to kill hunger outdoors. She did not know what it meant but smiled, glad she had sent Juan Bobo to school to learn something useful.

Part
Two

"In general, there is no doubt that there is a great deal of fear among our people: fear of all kinds, fear of losing the present wellbeing, fear of bringing suffering and misery to their families, fear of the floggings, of the guns, of El Morro Castle, of the execution,—those fears existing amongst almost all of them."—*Ramón Emeterio Betances*

"To take away our country, they must first take away our lives."—*Pedro Albizu Campos*

Cataño

After the island's discovery by Europeans in 1493, waves of immigrants from Spain, Portugal, Corsica, and the Canary Islands, all brimming with grand ideas, washed over the virgin territory and the patient Indians of Puerto Rico. Fully expecting to find gold in the earth, the immigrants dug every bit of it up, intending to return to their former homes, old, fat, and rich.

To their surprise, what they dug were their own graves and those of the Taíno natives who had always known their land as "Borinquen", a humble island of hurricanes and mosquitoes, which provided a diet of an occasional fish but more likely just coconuts, frogs, herbs, and grasses.

Later, adventurers from France, the Netherlands, England, and Italy arrived to gain whatever they could even if it meant becoming pirates or scavengers roaming the hills. Most thought that this tiny island in the New World had powers to give them talents and opportunities denied them in their own countries. Black Arabs, Berbers, and Jews smuggled to the island to serve as slaves, despite laws against doing so, along with black slaves from Spain and Portugal arrived against their will. They did not believe in the promise of the new land. They simply wanted to be free.

Dr. Hernando de Cataño, contracted by the Spanish crown because

Puerto Rico needed doctors, landed in 1569 to survey his promised property, Cataño Palms.

Shortly afterwards the civil police arrested him for breach of contract. Caught trying to sneak off to Santo Domingo, he said, "How can you want me to stay here when my family is starving to death?"

Not a single home was built in Cataño until three hundred years later, after 1870, when, because it was close to the sugarcane fields of Bayamón and just across a bay of silvery water separating it from the capital, the forgotten area known as Cataño Palms began as an overspill city. Landowners, workers, and freed slaves from Bayamón as well as businessmen from San Juan chopped down fanlike palm trees and built homes, each reflecting the style and means of the owner. Some built stately homes of fine wood, some smaller houses, and others shacks of hay, zinc, and planks, all in a haphazard arrangement meant to keep each group separate from the other.

Landowners graveled narrow dirt roads and, thinking they had accomplished enough, stopped dead all further improvements, leaving the nearby swamp intact and a primitive sewer system running along open troughs carved near the edges of sidewalks so narrow only one person might walk comfortably on them if at all.

Hot and dusty from sun-bleached gravel roads with few palm trees for shade, Cataño dropped the Palms from its name and became a desert masquerading as a bay town. Sunlight bounced off the stark, white ground and rose in heat waves blurring the distance. Between putrid swamp and the smelly, green sewage the inhabitants threw out of buckets into the street troughs, mosquitoes fed and swarmed, spreading malaria.

By the time of the occupation by the United States and the 1903 arrival of Rafael and Josie Figueroa, Cataño was a haphazard stew of about seven thousand rich and poor, but mostly poor as hopes for affluence fell under the weight of duties and tariffs. Despite its overabundance of illiterates, the poverty-stricken town could not be dismissed entirely because of its proximity_to the capital, San Juan, because of some prominent citizens, and because Cataño was renowned for its good-looking women.

Rafaela

Cross-legged, Rafaela sat in the middle of her tiny living-room floor holding a ball of white thread on her lap; she furiously dug the crocheting needle into her index finger with every stitch. She had hoped to bleed all over her half-finished doily to ruin it, but she did not like hurting herself and lost patience.

"I hate this *porquería*," she screamed, and threw everything together against the furthest wall. She wrenched her arm with the effort and struggled to her feet, cursing.

Antonia's long skirt hardly moved when she walked as if on rollers over to the tossed and soiled ball, picked it up, and calmly began to rewind the thread.

"Now I'll have to wash this part before I sew everything together," she said.

"I don't care." Rafaela pulled down on her earlobes painfully to resist the urge to put her hands over both ears.

"How do you expect to earn enough money for your *quinceañera?*"

"I'll sell newspapers," she answered in a sudden burst of inspiration. The idea excited her. She slapped her forehead. "Of course! That's what I'll do."

Her mother sat down on one of their two hard wooden chairs and examined Rafaela's handiwork. "No, you won't."

Exasperated, Rafaela said, "You never let me do anything I like!"

"I let you waste all those years with special lessons from the Figueroas."

Rafaela burned knowing her mother gloated that the birth of the Figueroa's boy, Junior, eliminated Josie's time for Rafaela's private tutoring. She had learned English well but not well enough. Her previous dreams of brilliance and success were now reduced to the feeble hope of being amusing enough to the colonial elite to marry well and in so doing lift herself and her family up from poverty and mediocrity.

"I've got to get out of here. I'm going to the Figueroas' for a while to read the newspaper."

"Ha! They won't let you in."

"We'll see." Rafaela stormed out of the house, wearing her mother's old, cotton dress, refashioned for her thinner, taller frame. Its faded white fabric sagged at her undeveloped bosom and its let-down hem trailed bits of frayed edges.

"Take América with you," her mother called after her. "And don't forget my medicine."

She pretended she did not hear, ran down Amparo Street toward the plaza, unaffected by the sun burning into the top of her head, and kicked up gravel dust along the way to scare off stray dogs.

"Hello." She waved to her sour-faced neighbor. The woman replied, "Bah."

Rafaela giggled glad to be out in the sunshine and rounded a corner. She bumped into the towering figure of Dr. Rodríguez who cast a shadow on her. She listened to his speech for a few minutes, asked a question, and continued on her way.

As she neared Josie's house, she slowed. She felt grateful for their help and knew the Figueroas still loved her, but she visited them infrequently so as not to tire them with her presence. She no longer burst in on them unannounced. Instead, she stood outside their house, in front of their balcony inhaling the fragrance of Josie's prize *azucenas*, the long-stemmed and particularly sweet white flowers she called calla lilies.

"Josie!" she shouted. "It's Rafaela."

Within seconds, Josie appeared in the doorway motioning her to come in.

They kissed hello. Josie asked, "Why haven't you been around? I've missed you very much."

Rafaela felt that was not true. But how could she tell the Figueroas that their son made a fountain of jealousy bubble inside her. She resented Junior Figueroa because he limited the time Josie and Rafael could spend with her.

"My sisters had colds," she lied.

"Bring them to Rafael."

"My brats are better now."

"Rafaela, they're not your daughters."

"They might as well be."

Josie led her past the waiting room into the study. As they went by, Rafaela greeted the patients, mostly sweaty pregnant women who sat fanning themselves.

"Where's the baby?" she asked, even though Junior was almost four years old.

"Napping, thank God." Josie rolled her eyes heavenward.

In the study Rafaela inhaled the fumes of wood polish and said, "I came for *El Tiempo*. Can I read it?"

"It's over here somewhere." Josie reached into her old rolltop desk, rummaged through it, and found the new journal stained with furniture oil. "This is a special issue." She handed it to Rafaela. "It discusses the Jones Act. Puerto Rico is getting United States citizenship."

"I know all about it," she said. "Dr. Rodríguez told me it's an appeasement, an exchange for our country."

"Not him again?"

"He said they only did it in time to draft our young men into the world war." Rafaela laughed loudly. "He said it was a good thing I was a city girl instead of a young country boy. Rodríguez is going to teach the *campesinos*, how to act as if they can't read, write, or speak English. That way they don't have to fight in a war that doesn't concern them."

Josie's mouth opened into a wide, dark tunnel. "Read the paper for yourself before you believe anything he says."

Rafaela looked at the pages not seeing them. She found it difficult to concentrate. "Do you think I can get a job selling these?"

"Boys sell newspapers, not girls." Josie laughed and Rafaela looked up sharply.

"Why not?"

Josie paused. "You can do everything a man can do but some things make no sense. Selling newspapers, except out of desperation for money when all else fails, is one of them."

Rafaela lowered her eyes. She had tried cleaning tobacco but she could not take the silent act of peering into the leaves, fingers working against time to remove dirt and other particles. It made her feel like a bird, cleaning its moist and smelly nest.

"Rafaela, you're so far away. What are you thinking?"

"Can I keep this?" She held up the newspaper.

"Read it. It's important."

"Thank you." She mustered enough excitement and energy to make Josie believe she felt happy and then got up to leave.

Josie grabbed her arm. "Tell me what is bothering you."

"Nothing." She kissed Josie good-bye and skipped out, heading for the pharmacy.

Three people waiting for their medicine filled the storefront pharmacy to capacity. Don Darío, the pharmacist, accepted cash from Tomasa, the recently widowed flower seller, when he noticed Rafaela. The short, fat man's eyes lit up.

"Miss Rafaela!" he said. "A pleasure to see you. How can I serve you?" He ignored the slim, dark woman's outstretched hand and kept holding her change.

Rafaela ignored him in return, suspicious of his constant attentions. "Tomasa, how are you? Not sick I hope?"

Tomasa smiled at her, touched her cheek. "Sweetie. I'm having a baby. See my stomach?" The thin young woman proudly turned sideways to show her abdomen in profile. "I'll have another part of my husband to remember him by with this new baby."

"Do not speak to Miss Rafaela of such things," interrupted Don Darío, trying to put his arm around Rafaela's shoulders. She shook him off. Both women ignored him.

"But how is Miguelito?" Rafaela loved Tomasa's glossy-eyed seven-year-old.

"Sad since his father died but maybe a little brother will help him forget."

"No," Rafaela said, pouting. "Because then he won't be special, but tell him I'll always love him best."

Both Darío and Tomasa stared lovingly at her. Rafaela liked Tomasa. The young woman's dark skin, delicate features, and thick, shiny curls were lovely, as were her large, languid eyes. But the oval face and rosy cheeks of the cloying pharmacist annoyed her. He looked like an old, squat boy doll and reminded her of something or someone she detested but did not know what or who.

The other two customers, thin and pale, began wracking, tubercular coughs and shifted their bodies from one worn shoe to the other.

"Please attend to these people first."

"Yes, Miss Rafaela." Darío rushed his rotund body around his counter hurrying to get rid of them.

"See you soon, Rafaela," Tomasa said. "I'll always have a special *clavel* for you." She winked and left.

"Why a carnation instead of a rose?" Darío asked, dispensing with his last customer. "I would have served you first, you know. I have great regard for you and Doña Antonia." Rafaela shrugged. "Tell her I have something better for her anemia." He held up the same bottle of tarlike tonic she had seen Dr. Rodríguez carrying around for years. "Something new for Doña Antonia."

That too annoyed Rafaela. Mysterious how everyone treated her mother. Following the pharmacist's example, it was Doña Antonia this and Doña Antonia that with the respect afforded a proper lady instead of a woman with five children born outside of marriage, none of whom Rafaela believed looked much like the other. She thought maybe it was possible that a man or woman could do anything frowned upon by society as long as their personality carried it off. She supposed her mother's stiff and regal posture silenced all criticism and Rafaela decided she herself also would do whatever she liked under the immunity of her outspokenness. If anyone bothered her, she told them off.

"In another few months," he said, "You'll be fifteen. Where are you having your party?"

"Why do you ask that when you know our situation?" His question hit a sore spot and infuriated her.

He lowered his bald head and shook it. "All girls deserve special treatment for their *quinceañera.* Reaching womanhood is an important time."

"I can have a beautiful white dress, a big party with a photographer taking pictures if I sell my sisters for the money." Her mind whirled with insults to hurl at his egg-shaped body but she was too choked to utter them. Good thing because her ears prickled at his next words.

"If Doña Antonia permits it, you can work here, helping me sweep up, clean my displays."

Astounded, she stuttered. "Th-Thank you, I'll ask," and ran out clutching the medicine before he changed his mind.

Outside the pharmacy, away from its perfumed soaps and fragrant ointments, she wrinkled her nose at the stench of humid streets and nearby swamp. She skipped and jumped over putrid sewer troughs, barely containing her laughter. She had been so rude and still obtained what she wanted.

She heard, "Hello gorgeous," and turned her head in the direction of the voice. It was Claudio Blanco calling from his second-floor balcony. "I'm dying of love for you."

"Tapeworm! How dare you? Better grow up first." The boy laughed and his head disappeared back into his house.

Rafaela thought herself a good person who told the truth no matter what one wanted to hear. Her honesty was a brutal weapon. In the long run the truth benefited everyone, a cathartic that cleansed the system of illusions, tricks of the senses whereby fat old men, ugly and boring, thought themselves lotharios (she remained cautious and would watch out for Don Darío) and whereby women deluded themselves into thinking against reason that they were admired for their beauty when they were being used. Rafaela girded herself to equip everyone for the rigors of practical reality. Telling the truth was so much easier than telling lies, no need to remember in case of contradictions.

"Mamá, I'm going to work for old, fat Don Darío," she announced. "In the pharmacy."

She hugged her smiling sisters, received a mild shock at seeing her mother, already finishing a new doily with her discarded ball of thread, smile too. It gave her a strange feeling. Not sure why, she asked, "Are you ever going to tell me who my father is?"

"Again with that? He's not here, is he? So it does not concern you."

"Then who the hell does it concern? You alone?"

She left the question hanging in the air and stomped into her tiny bedroom followed by her sisters. They crowded into her bed expecting Rafaela to amuse them. When she did not, Europa jumped off the bed to dance. Europa trembled her shoulders, undulated her hips, shook her backside, and smiled toothily to the tune of a *plena* while her other sisters clapped in time to the imagined music.

Because Rafaela never saw a man spend the night, never knew of a boyfriend who called on her mother, she constantly wondered who fathered her and who fathered her sisters. She looked at Europa's suggestive movements and, wondering how she could find out, slapped her forehead.

"What?" her sisters asked, expectantly.

"I can also work for the Figueroas."

That night she slept soundly with her arm wrapped around América's neck and made her plans early the next morning.

Not caring if she appeared tomboyish, Rafaela hopped, skipped, and jumped down Barbosa Avenue calling after Josie. Josie's grimness as she turned around to face her dampened Rafaela's enthusiasm. She half-smiled. "What's wrong?"

"Come home with me and I'll tell you. Right now I have to rush back because I left Junior with a sitter while I was in San Juan."

"Why didn't you send for me?"

"I had so much on my mind, I didn't even think of it."

Holding Josie's smooth hand the rest of the way, Rafaela told her, breathlessly, that she had been offered an early morning job with Don Darío in the pharmacy.

"Now I'll learn something," she said. Then, experimentally, added, "But not enough."

"What else do you want to learn?"

"Wouldn't it be wonderful if I worked for a doctor in the afternoons?"

Josie burst into laughter. "Your hints are as subtle as firecrackers. Come on, I'll give you my news."

As usual, the Figueroas' waiting room was full of pregnant women, but Dr. Figueroa turned his attention to Josie.

"Well?" Rafael asked.

"Well what?" Rafaela asked.

"The answer is yes," Josie replied.

"This morning you looked unhappy," Rafael said. "What changed?"

"Something this girl suggested." Josie kissed Rafaela.

Pleased with the smiling attention of the Figueroas, Rafaela dug into her pocket, pulled out a *quenepa*, cracked off its green skin, popped it into her mouth to suck on the small slimy fruit, and waited.

"I'm having another baby," Josie announced.

Rafaela's heart leapt. *Now Josie will be too busy to help Dr. Figueroa and I can have the job!*

Josie shook her head. "I don't know why I didn't think of it myself," she said. She looked at Rafaela. "If you work here, I won't be so tired. Between teaching school, keeping house, tending Junior, and handling Rafael's patients, I feel exhausted most of the time."

Excited by the idea, Dr. Figueroa hurriedly gave Rafaela a run-down of what she would do. "Eventually, I'll get you a uniform." He snapped his fingers. "You can become a midwife. After I finish training you, you will be better than the *matasanos*." She smiled as he referred to "the dangerous men," the wealthy, lackluster students who failed their certification examinations but obtained their medical degrees anyway through their political connections and were more likely to kill the healthy than to cure the sick. "Excellent," he said, rubbing his hands together. "We begin tomorrow."

Unable to contain her excitement, Rafaela hitched her dress up at her sides and ran to tell her sisters.

"I've got two jobs," she announced to them. Afternoons, I work for the Figueroas." She turned to her mother and said, "Now Mamá, you can do all the crocheting," and leapt into her bedroom more to avoid her mother than to prepare her three, well-worn dresses.

At the pharmacy Rafaela had to learn how to fill out cards for the clients, hand their prescriptions to Don Darío, and watch for thieves while he turned his back to fill them. Eventually, she graduated to collecting money, giving proper change plus a receipt, and wishing his clients good health. At the end of her day with him, she put the money in a large, black safe, closed it, and dusted and straightened the displays of soaps, powders, and ointments imported from Spain.

After working with Darío a few days, Rafaela realized she had nothing to fear except his homely spinster sister who turned her large nose up at everyone who wasn't rich. The mannish woman carried handkerchiefs soaked in a French perfume called Narcisse Noir, which Rafaela envied but never complimented because Francisca Ferrer pursed her lips and crossed her hands in front of her when spoken to and, instead of answering, stared at her as if she were an insect.

"What are you doing here?" she asked.

Rafaela, who imagined herself jumping up to the level of Francisca's pink face and punching her, weighed the consequences of doing so and swallowed her anger. "Working," she replied, as she strode quickly toward Darío's back room and vowed to never again even look the woman in the face.

The pharmacist behaved affectionately with every male and female who came into his shop and never became fresh with her. She found him lovable once she accepted his paunch and his aversion to diets. She thought him especially lovable when, a few months later, he told her to stay late.

From behind his counter, he brought out a large, rectangular box and opened it. Inside, she saw a white, satin dress. Imported Spanish lace bordered its bodice, sleeves, and hem and seed pearls peppered its skirt.

"You must have," he insisted, "the same things other young ladies have on their fifteenth birthday."

The dress was so beautiful it took her breath away as she held it up.

"It'll be a perfect fit," she said, misty eyed. "How did you know?"

"I asked your mother."

"When?"

"Um, once as she walked on her rounds to sell her doilies."

"Exactly when?"

"I don't remember." He patted her head.

While not nearly as grand an affair as she might have desired, her coming of age birthday party was a success in large part because of the dress.

Afternoons she helped the Figueroas by keeping watch over the appointment book and preparing the patients files for Rafael before he saw them. Her haphazard system got her into trouble with him.

"Sixta complained she arrived earlier," Rafael said. "Why did you let Tomasa in first?"

"Tomasa has to go home to feed Miguelito. This is Sixta's first baby. She can wait."

"I make the decisions, not you."

"All right." She smiled, afraid to alienate Rafael. He patted her cheek.

When Josie miscarried Rafaela worried, briefly, that she might lose her job; nevertheless, she continued to let in first whomever she wanted until the patients stopped complaining to Dr. Figueroa and appealed to her instead.

"Rafaela, please let me in first. My husband is waiting."

"No, me, Rafaela."

"Me. My water is bursting," said still another patient.

It gave Rafaela a feeling of power she refused to relinquish, and, in the end, all were pleased especially Rafaela whose master plan had been not to become a midwife but to study the men and women and their children.

During her three years searching the faces of Rafael's patients, she did not find any clues, but the quest to find her father eventually lost importance. What mattered to her more was that her mother no longer bore children. "Maybe she's stopped giving birth because she ran out of continents," Rafaela thought, laughing aloud. *I better not tell her about Australia.*

Her youngest sisters were eight years old and handled household chores to free Antonia to crochet delicate doilies, tablecloths, and even bedspreads for the rich.

Rafaela's favorite sister, América, was no longer blonde but still pretty, and her other sisters, Europa, Asia, and África changed from squalling, red-faced monsters into small-boned potential beauties. As infants they had not looked alike. Now they had a subtle similarity pointing to one common father. She believed it had to be a tall, slim man with light hair and a peachlike complexion, smooth and rosy, or else of medium height, very white skin and brown, not black, hair. Rafaela imagined all these combinations in her mind's eye as she studied Dr. Figueroa's patients and their offspring, but she did not really care anymore; she felt grateful there were no more sisters and wanted no children of her own.

As she grew older, she forced Josie to repeat the tales of life in Philadelphia, of studying in Washington, and of traveling to New York. The stories never tired her; they filled her with ambition and every time she heard them, she had new questions to ask.

"Do the big cities all look alike? How do the women wear their hair? Do they travel alone? What work do they do?"

Three years into her routine, she spied her friend, Ana Betancourt, motioning to her outside the pharmacy. She turned to Darío but before she could ask permission to meet her outside, he said, "Go on. She's probably going to be a mother."

"She's only been married six months." Rafaela put her hands on her hips. "You know that because I talked about her wedding so much."

"Yes," he laughed, belly rolling. "You told me how beautiful you looked in your pink bridesmaid's dress and how the boys all wanted to waltz with only you, none of the other bridesmaids."

"I was maid of honor." She corrected then blushed, remembering she had said nothing about Ana's lovely bridal gown or what a handsome couple the two blonds made. She rushed outside.

"Ana!" she said, hugging her friend. "How's married life?"

"I'm trying to have a baby," the demure blonde replied. "When I do I want you as the godmother."

Chagrined, Rafaela smiled. Being a *madrina* was an honor she did not relish but what could she say?

"Stupendous. I hope it's a little boy."

They both laughed. Rafaela had told Ana many times how she had wanted to be an only child or at least have a brother.

"Are you healthy enough?"

"I don't know."

"Go to Dr. Figueroa."

"That's what I intend to do but I wanted to tell you first so you wouldn't be surprised when you saw me there."

"Come on Tuesday. It's not a busy day."

"I will," Ana replied, "but now I better rush off to shop for my husband's dinner. He's been in a bad mood lately and I don't know why."

Rafaela waved after Ana and then walked slowly back into the pharmacy.

"Was I right?" Darío asked.

"No, but she wants to."

"And what do you think about that?"

"You know what I think." She snapped at him. The pharmacist lowered his head.

"You've been working with me a long time. Have you thought of learning English shorthand so you can work with the Americans?"

She widened her eyes. "You don't want me here anymore?"

"Of course, I do. It's just that you've told me you want to do big things. Without university, you're better off working with politicians."

She thought it over. *Yes, working with powerful people. It can rub off on me.* Those options thrilled her. She looked at Darío with new respect.

"No early marriage for me," she thought. *I want to work, travel, and be interesting like Josie before I commit myself.*

Juan

Padre Hernán's gift, the white linen suit, which Juan handled so lovingly that he washed his hands before he removed it from its special padded hanger and which he lovingly brushed and ironed before and after wearing, finally became too small. At first he hardly noticed he did not have to roll up its cuffs as many times as before in order to keep them at midshin, but later, when he no longer had to roll them up at all and the sleeves of the suit's jacket crept up his forearm, he worried about its replacement. He had to have another just like it. Nothing else would suffice as his growing clientele identified him with bare feet and white linen suit. Loathe to charge his poor neighbors for remedies that barely succeeded in staving off their illnesses, he began to follow the grave digger wherever he went. The old man complained.

"What do you want?" he asked.

"To be your apprentice."

"I don't need one and I don't want you." After turning his head to look at those gathered for a burial, he stopped digging, thrust his spade into the ground, and leaned on it. "There's not enough work for both of us. Get away from here."

"I'm just watching, that's all."

"You make me nervous." They stared at each other as Juan tried to read his emanations and the old man resisted. "I'll give you my old shovel if you promise to leave me alone."

Juan looked up into an overcast sky and then toward the sandy beach. Instead of the small shacks and tall grass, which bordered the thick, rutted sand and instead of hearing the breaking waves of the Atlantic, Juan saw two cemeteries, one at each end of a long road and heard bells tolling. He smiled, accepted the grave digger's heavy, rusted shovel, and walked away to dig by the side of his own shack.

"What are you doing?" Mamá Abuela asked, breathless. She looked alarmed and Juan laughed.

"Don't worry, it's not your grave." Mamá Abuela had recently begun to have trouble breathing on particularly hot days in July and August. "I want to practice until I can dig a hole big enough to bury a grown person without stopping to rest like the old grave digger."

The sun burned the top of his head, perspiration soaked him, and particles of flying earth stained his suit making it necessary for him to wash it more often, but eventually he learned to dig a full-size grave in two hours and made it known to his neighbors that, for pay, he would dig graves, foundations for new homes, or latrines.

Grateful neighbors granted him enough work so that in less than one year he not only built Mamá Abuela a new and larger shack with small shelves dotting the interior where she set up her altars with candles, rum, and cigars, but he also earned enough to buy a Panama hat and two new white suits, one for every day and one for special occasions.

Juan first saw her at her mother's funeral, shivering under a parasol in a light drizzle of rain, waiting for him to cover the grave. Her dark and delicate beauty enhanced her vulnerability as she stood surrounded by five men, fat and white, including her father. First love struck him with the force of a tidal wave and he could hardly do his job without glancing at her. After patting the last shovelful of earth on the grave mound, he approached them for his payment and addressed her.

"Señorita, have you a handkerchief I can use to wipe my forehead?"

Innocently, she gave it. Her brothers stared at him sideways and allowed him to accompany Carmela to their waiting carriage.

He cast a spell on the handkerchief and returned it to her, desperate that it work since he considered her too beautiful for him and feared the prejudice of her white relatives. It surprised him that she allowed him close enough to accept a drink of coconut water from him and surprised him even more that she accepted his marriage proposal easily, with no objections from her family. Before her brothers had an opportunity to change their minds and because he now was to become a husband and provider, he felt it imperative to move away, to put his long-term plan into operation.

Resplendent in his white linen suit and Panama hat and accompanied by his bride, Juan Peña, moved into his new house on Flower Street in Cataño. Two strange and striking children, both seventeen, married and set up a home in a town deserted, centuries ago, by the man to whom it owed its name.

To the townspeople, Juan, a barefoot grave digger and spiritualist, and his wife Carmela whose straight black braided hair extended all the way down to the back of her knees, presented a dilemma. How could she of the delicate build and sharp features marry such a blue-black eccentric? More fanatical gossipers among the town's citizens had fun with this puzzle until those particularly more rude, unable to control their curiosity, asked her outright what she was doing with him.

"I love my husband," Carmela replied. "We help each other and never argue." Her skin was the color of cinnamon. As she walked through the steamy air away from them, her braid swayed from one buttock to the other. Before she retreated inside their rented house, she added, "I'm a Catholic but Juan controls a power I've learned to respect because he sees things others do not and because I've witnessed him cure the sick."

"Well done," Juan said, later, when she told him. "I'll never stop you from going to church as long as you don't interfere with my work. A priest taught me a lot of what I know."

That was a little lie but Juan believed it smoothed things over and brought him some peace. He intended to live in that house for a long time and needed to give Carmela some ammunition to use on the neighbors. Since Padre Hernán lived far away and was doubtless unknown here, Juan could use his name with impunity if the occasion arose. Happier than he had ever been, with his luck running strong, Juan felt confident that he could win Carmela over to his religion before it was too late or before she awoke from the love potions and spells he had worked on her.

He had chosen to move Carmela to Cataño because the town was close enough to the San Juan cemetery as well as to a smaller cemetery on the road to Toa Baja to provide a good income, yet far enough from the capital to be affordable, a place to start their family and a place to meet, eventually, with his cousin Paula. He felt the sun shining on his life as only the very young and optimistic can before the dark clouds of disappointment and setback settle a bitter cynicism on dreams.

IV

Félix

The entire island was hot all year round but during the infernal summer of 1920 Cataño, with poor planning and little vegetation, was a furnace operating at capacity, spilling sun-blackened townspeople out of their baking homes and on to its beach and its tree-shaded town square. When fellow classmate Diego Toledo invited Félix to his home in Cataño after graduation, he accepted the opportunity to visit a town he remembered from his childhood. Félix surrendered to bittersweet yearnings to return to the past as if he could capture what he missed the first time around and so realize the impossible things that had existed only in his childish and romantic imagination.

Félix crisscrossed the confusing town, searching. If he saw dilapidated shacks, he turned back, or west or east until he found better areas. During his early morning quests, he passed by house servants as they swept clean the balcony floors of the dust raised by horses and by the trudging feet of migrating workers. Domestics fussing at their fate for being born poor in an intolerant society swept the dust out into the sewer troughs, threw water on the floors, and mopped it out into the streets. The sun later baked the mud into a dry white powder which resettled on the balcony floors the next morning.

"There," thought Félix. Just when he despaired of finding the house and thought he needed to give up his solitary walks because his hosts, the Toledos, showed concern over his aloofness and the secrecy of his morning missions, he saw the brown-skinned woman open her gate and walk briskly toward the ferry road.

"Good day," he called after her, heart thumping. Josie Figueroa turned her head back to look at him over her shoulder. He had forgotten her green eyes.

"Good day," she said, and walked off. Her long black skirt moved primly with her steps.

"She doesn't remember me," Félix said, aloud.

Disappointment pierced him. Then he remembered himself as she had last seen him: a pale skinny boy reluctant to talk for fear of losing his last precious connection to his lost parents, his pearls. Now, over six feet tall, muscular from hard work and sporting a full moustache, there was no resemblance. Rooted in front of her house, Félix had not noticed Diego following him.

"So, there you are," Diego said. "Do you need a doctor? Is that what you're looking for?"

Félix smiled down at his friend. "I thought I saw someone I knew."

"Really? The Figueroas?"

"Yes." Félix stiffened and remained quiet. He forced himself to make friends with Diego and Jorge Bartolomeo before graduation because he needed good contacts, but he shared little of his life story with them. He told them his uncle had lost his land, died penniless, and nothing more.

Félix and Diego Toledo had graduated from law school in the same class as Bartolomeo, the only wealthy one in the group. They had talked about beginning a three-way law practice and arranged to meet in Cataño to discuss it.

"Let's go to San Juan right now," suggested Diego. "I'll show you Bartolomeo's house and the cathedral and after dinner, we'll meet him here in Cataño."

"Why does Bartolomeo prefer to come here?" Félix looked dubiously at the humble facade of the pharmacy they passed.

Diego pretended to curl and twirl his moustache. "The women. We have the best-looking women on the island right here."

Félix smiled again, and as they boarded the ferry to San Juan he asked, "Are all the stories Bartolomeo tells true?"

"Definitely. He makes women laugh while he romances them. The number of his conquests increases daily." Diego paused to look at the white foam created and sliced by the ferry's hull as it broke through silver blue waves. He laughed and added, "Most times anyway, but his latest conquest is difficult."

"Good for her," Félix said, remembering tales of Bartolomeo's father having to pay off the parents of daughters victimized by Bartolomeo's amorous ambitions. "He should marry and stop impregnating. It must be getting expensive."

"Oh, he'll marry all right. But it won't be any of these girls. Wrong class."

Félix looked at the other passengers to see if they had heard. Some had business in the capital but most were dusty, sun-baked countrymen dressed in faded *guayaberas*. If they had heard, they kept their reactions to themselves.

As they disembarked in San Juan, Félix felt a peculiar sinking in his stomach, asked, "What's down that way?" He pointed toward his old street.

"Some of the older stores with apartments above them. Don't worry, we'll see everything but let's walk over to the cathedral first."

With his every step on the cobbled streets, Félix trembled with regret, frustration, and sadness, but he did not allow his eyes to stray to his old neighborhood fearing its power over him, afraid to incite Diego's curiosity. The smell of the salty air, the breezes, the shady parts of the sidewalks and the feel of the cobblestones under his feet, each brought back a shadowed memory. Here he had walked with his father's friends discussing the liberation of the island, there he had spent an afternoon listening enviously to happy cries of children playing while he recited lessons, and here he had caught his foot and fallen on his way to church.

The cathedral! That somber building chilled him with its proud history. Félix went in, dipped his hands into cool holy water, crossed himself, and knelt into one of the pews.

From his pants pocket, he removed his pearls and began to pray, confident that he could explain this peculiarity to Diego's satisfaction.

Diego did not ask and Félix did not volunteer the story he had invented for others who had seen him.

"Yes," he'd say. "An heirloom. The pearls, once two sets of rosaries, began to lose pieces so I had them restrung into a double strand I will give to my wife when I marry. Meanwhile, they keep their luster from contact with my fingers." If anyone expressed disbelief or doubt, he shrugged and ignored them.

Félix had almost lost patience when they finally walked down his old familiar street and he gazed lovingly at the shop, now boarded, and up at the tiny balcony he and his father stood on many a time waiting for visitors. *It looked so small! However had they both fit?*

His stomach rumbled and he suddenly remembered those years with less kindness, thought himself a sentimental fool, and felt grateful to return to Cataño.

Dinner with the Toledo family was informal and good natured. The easy teasing between members impressed Félix but especially the remarks that came from Diego's amiable younger brother, Waldemar, an intelligent ten-year-old.

His own dinners with his uncle had been a study in restraint, no talking while eating, no rushing through dinner, and no leaving the table without reporting the day's events. Félix's recitations were either denied or attested to by his watchers so that if he made the slightest error from a hasty telling, his uncle subjected him to hours of clarifications and explanations as to meaning and intent until Félix, dismissed, left the table exhausted.

The Toledo family came and went according to their own schedules. A simple *"Permiso"* directed at the father suited all manner of requests from "May I eat?" to "May I leave?" Throughout the meal, to the clatter of forks scraping plates and glasses tinkling, the elder Toledo chewed mouthfuls of food while he bobbed his head up and down granting requests, acknowledging interruptions of "Papá, Papá!"

To Félix who reached out for second helpings, ten-year-old Waldemar said, "You certainly have a healthy appetite." The boy laughed. His startling light green eyes reminded Félix of sugarcane fields. Deciding he had eaten enough, Félix pushed away his plate and thanked his hosts.

After dinner Félix and Diego strolled through slightly cooling streets to la plaza, the town square, and central meeting place of lovers and busybodies. They spotted Bartolomeo at the far end. He gestured them over and the young woman standing beside him straightened.

As Félix walked toward them, past slabs of concrete nestled under leafy shade trees on either side of the parklike rectangle, he studied the girls who sat on the benches and fanned themselves languidly. He found them all equally attractive. All had large eyes and full lips but he thought nothing distinguished one beauty from the other except for their diverse coloring and varying sizes.

Bartolomeo introduced Rafaela. She reached Félix's shoulder as did Diego and Bartolomeo.

"It's a pleasure," she said, extending a long-fingered hand. Her light brown eyes and silvery brown hair sparkled. Diego nudged the staring Félix.

"The p-pleasure is mine." He stammered, overwhelmed by visions of mangos, papaya, and pineapples.

"Congratulations," she said, smiling and swaying. "I understand you've just graduated with a law degree."

"Yes." It was all he could muster with his thoughts on her rosy cheeks, the white mantilla on her shoulders, her long cotton skirt. Félix stared at her lips, her hair braided across the top of her head. Rafaela stared back with the same searching concentration reserved for a familiar face not neatly placed in the memory. Diego and Bartolomeo tittered. Heat rose to Félix's face, and in a fit of disorientation he began to brag.

"I'm a lawyer," he said. "Someday I'm going to be the most important lawyer in Puerto Rico. And I'll be rich, very rich." He stopped, feeling like a fool as she eyed his country boy's clothing and laughed.

"Good. You can defend me. Maybe I'll go into politics and, as you know, politicians are always in trouble."

"I like myself in politics, not women."

"Why not?" She pouted a fleshy bottom lip, then smiled. "What if she happens to be your wife?"

"My wife will be too busy taking care of me and my children to run for office. It's ridiculous. Women can't even vote."

"Oh but we will. A friend told me it is only a matter of time for us because women in the States have recently obtained the vote. Besides, if you become as rich as you say, your wife will have plenty of time what with all the cooks, maids, and nannies." She winked and touched his arm.

Her touch exhilarated him. He felt light as if he lost all his body weight and could float away. Félix restrained an urge to move, dance, hop, and ignored Diego and Bartolomeo who laughed, pointed at him, and nudged each other with their elbows.

"Do future politicians eat?" he asked.

"I suspect we do so more than beginning lawyers."

"Well then, will you accompany me to a picnic on Saturday?"

Rafaela smiled, put an index finger on her firm, smooth cheek in thought, and gazed heavenward.

"I don't know," she said.

Félix looked so hopeful, Bartolomeo said, "Oh go, Rafaela. It's only a picnic and I can vouch for Félix."

"You?" Her face changed. "You can't vouch for anyone and you know it."

The words chilled Félix; he feared Rafaela had been one of Bartolomeo's castoffs but he felt taken with her.

"Please, Rafaela," Félix begged. "I would like to talk to you without these two clowns around acting like children." His behavior surprised him but she rewarded him with a yes before they walked her home.

Disappointment washed over him as they reached her slatternly home. Her mother waited on the front steps, arms crossed, and her sisters were barefoot.

"Good night, gentlemen," she said, after introducing them to her mother. "Thanks for seeing me home."

Rafaela hugged her mother.

"I've just met the man I've been waiting for all my life!"

"Ha!" Doña Antonia said. "Keep waiting."

On the way back, Diego pounced on his back and whooped. *"Hombre,* I was beginning to worry about you. No dates, not even female friends. Now your *conquista* has warmed my heart."

"Yes," said Bartolomeo. "Just stare stupidly until they give in out of boredom or pity." He laughed.

"Bad luck," said Diego, soothingly. "This one escaped you."

"I don't care," said Bartolomeo. "There are others whose tongues are not so sharp. Anyway, Rafaela has strange ideas. She thinks she's a man."

Félix wanted to hear details of how Rafaela got away from Bartolomeo. He did not ask though because he never asked too many questions, hoping for the same treatment. Besides, they began to discuss the possibility of a law partnership financed by Bartolomeo's father until they became solvent. Félix felt it had been right to make friends during his final two years at the university. His efforts at forcing himself to be social paid off. If not assured, his future had a chance.

That Saturday, Félix was about to walk out empty-handed when Mrs. Toledo handed him a heavy wicker basket covered with a tablecloth.

"Félix," she said kindly. "Have you never taken a young lady to a picnic before?"

"No, I've always been too busy with my studies to see any girls." He did not tell her that the few female students he met at the university intimidated him. Either they were wealthy girls whose faces changed when they found out he was penniless, or worse, they were more intelligent than he, had traveled, and knew many famous living people. His claims to fame had all died.

"Yes, well." She patted his hand. "Take this food with you or you'll both starve. We all adore Rafaela." Because Félix looked dumbfounded, she added, "Rafaela has very little, you see."

Félix had not thought of taking anything to eat. He believed a picnic simply an excuse to see her, not an idea to be taken literally. Now he realized he did not know even where they should go.

"Can you suggest a good location?" he asked.

"The beach. I've included a blanket to sit on."

He took a longer route, passed by the Figueroas as was his custom, and slowed to peer inside.

From within the darkened living room, Josie called her husband. "Rafael, come quickly. There he is."

Rafael stepped out into the blaring sunlight on the balcony.

"*Buenos días*," he called, squinting. "Are you looking for someone?" Josie, hiding behind a doorway, had told him about the tall young man who habitually stared into their home.

Félix removed his frayed straw hat, held it at his chest, and raising his voice said, "Dr. Figueroa, it's good to see you again. You may not remember me. I'm Félix Cienfuegos. You were once very kind to me."

"Félix Cienfuegos!" they echoed. Josie joined Rafael on the balcony. "How could we forget?" she asked. "You've been the object of endless speculation and failed attempts to track you."

"Come in, please," Rafael said. Félix towered over them. "And how is your greatuncle?"

Félix wanted to impress them, wanted them to know he had survived and amounted to something. "He's passed away. I've recently graduated from law school and intend to begin a practice with Diego Toledo and Jorge Bartolomeo." They looked down at his basket. Embarrassed, he realized they might think it was for them. "Oh, I'm on my way to a picnic with the young lady Rafaela Moya."

"Rafaela?" They looked alarmed.

"Yes, do you know her?"

The Figueroas looked at each other. "Everyone in this town knows everybody else," Rafael said. "How old are you now, Félix?"

"I'm twenty-three."

"We're very glad to see you again, Félix, but since you have an engagement, we don't want to keep you. Please promise to return for a longer visit." Josie smiled. "Rafaela is a good friend of ours, like our own daughter. She's only seventeen."

Félix said good-bye to the Figueroas with their admonition troubling him. Seventeen! An old maid by country standards but clearly a protected child in Cataño. He had to be careful, he was just starting his fledgling legal career and must do nothing to endanger his final goal of obtaining political office as he and his father had often discussed with the movers and shakers of the island.

Her mother and her sisters met him at the door, staring. Doña Antonia kept her arms crossed and her lips thin.

"Just in time to rescue a famished maiden," Rafaela said, whirling him down the street. She skipped all the way to the beach, the walk made further by the heat. He noted the worn heels on her shoes.

On the way, she smiled, waved, and called to everyone.

"Tomasa!" She yelled at a young woman selling flowers. "How's business? Miguelito! How are your grades?" The boy, small for his age, approached her shyly with a white carnation, handed it to her at arm's length and said, "My mother says, 'Thank you' for the notebook." Rafaela hugged him.

On seeing her open affection for the boy, Félix felt jealous, wanted all her attention yet admired her generosity. With a house full of poorly dressed and barefoot sisters, she had still thought to buy a notebook for a school boy even more poor than her family.

"Preparing for public service?" he asked.

Her laughter roared out long and loud, startling him.

"Oh, no, I just like people." Her eyes gleamed mischievously. "You most of all."

Félix forgot to be careful, offered his arm, and continued his stride with a bounce.

After they spread their blanket on the pebbly gray sand, he wanted to hear more about how much she liked him but he did not get another chance. Rafaela inspected the contents of the basket exclaiming over every item of food, wiggled around to make herself more comfortable, and disrupted the blanket so that Félix kept smoothing it out only to have it disordered whenever she waved to anyone, shooed flies, or squashed ants into the sand with her thumb.

"Are you aware I'm anticipating a secretarial job in San Juan?" she asked. "Where did you grow up? Where are your parents? How long have you known Diego and Bartolomeo? Do you know anyone else?" Rafaela tilted her head toward her shoulder and her eyes seemed to turn green, reflecting the waves of the sea. "Somehow I feel like we've met before."

He felt he knew her too but she asked each question before he prepared an answer to the previous one with the result that he did not answer any.

"Oh mysterious, are you? Well, no matter, let's eat. I'm starved. I thought you weren't coming."

Rafaela devoured the fish fries, sweet bananas, avocado slices, and mangoes going from one to the other smacking her lips, licking her fingers, and asking questions with her mouth full. Watching her, fascinated, Félix concluded this was her first picnic too, perhaps her first meal. She sat, unladylike, legs spread wide, with only her long skirt bunched between them to save her modesty. She wiped her fingers on the blanket and burped.

"You forgot napkins," she said. Her lips shone with oil.

"Forgive me," he said.

"Hey, you're not eating. Aren't you hungry?"

"Well, I . . ."

"Eat fast so we'll have time to wet our feet in the ocean. Did you bring a bathing suit?"

"No, I . . ."

"I didn't either but you can roll up your pants."

"Are we in a hurry?" Félix asked, annoyed.

"No but you really did arrive late you know."

"Forgive me."

"You apologize a lot. I like that. Most people make excuses." She yawned noisily without covering her mouth and stretched her arms over her head. Astounded by her breach of good manners, Félix looked around at the others on the beach.

Some of the families sitting on blankets near them covered their mouths and giggled. It shamed and annoyed Félix especially when he spied Waldemar Toledo as unofficial chaperon staring at them from the road that separated the beach from the town's homes. He vowed revenge on Diego and Bartolomeo for letting him get into this predicament. About to plead a previous engagement as a way to escape, he held himself back when she calmed down.

"I'm sorry, too," she said. "You're not having a good time."

"How do you know?"

"Because you look like this." Rafaela made a glum face. It amused him. No matter how she furrowed her forehead or twisted her mouth down at the corners to mimic him, she remained beautiful.

"I'm new at this. It embarrasses me."

"I bet everything embarrasses you."

"Yes." He smiled and looked at his hands sifting the sand. "I don't know why."

"I know why."

"Why?"

"Because, because . . ." She paused and giggled. "I don't really know either. But I'll figure it out. Give me time."

"Take all the time you want," he said, sighing. Félix needed time also, time to refine her a bit or to get rid of her and time to get himself established, so he ended their first date with no promises of seeing her again soon.

"Why not?" she asked.

He shrugged. "Building my practice is very important right now and I'll be too busy doing that to socialize, but I'm sure we will see each other from time to time."

Before he could protest, she kissed his cheek and said, "So long. You won't forget me."

Her words came true. He alternated between feeling close to death if he could not see her and avoiding her every time she embarrassed him, letting weeks go by until he returned for his next injection of public humiliation.

Diego and Bartolomeo sat in their office reading newspapers and smoking cigars until the room became hazy and the air so foul smelling it dizzied Félix.

"Do we have an advertisement in this newspaper?" Félix asked.

"How would you have us behave?" Bartolomeo's cigar almost fell out of his mouth. "Like common notaries?"

"We don't have a single case pending."

"I'm expecting a friend of my father's for a client," Diego said.

"One friend?" Félix rose. "Excuse me but I'm going down to the court-room to try to secure some business." He rose to leave.

"Relax. Everything takes time."

"The rent won't wait."

"Nevertheless, you can't just take anyone as a client or advertise in newspapers. We have to build a reputation slowly."

Félix thought that if they continued like this, the reputation might be that they were lazy, ineffectual at finding new clients, content with the few their families referred. He left for the courtroom.

Through his advertising efforts, some cases began to come in but too few to support his end of the ailing practice, and Félix feared his partners might tell him to pawn his pearls.

"My pearls have been stolen," he announced.

"Where?" they asked, dubiously.

"You don't go anyplace where they can be stolen," Bartolomeo said. "You're so cheap most crooks think they have more than you."

"Right here," he said. Félix slept in the office.

"Here? What do you mean by that?"

"When I woke up this morning, they were gone."

"That's what you get for not living in a real home."

"The custodian, perhaps," Diego said.

"Ask him if you think he'll admit it."

"He's an honest dimwit. It couldn't have been him and you know it." Bartolomeo stared at Félix. "You don't think it was one of us, do you?"

"I have not accused you have I?"

Félix counted on this reaction. He could not have said they were stolen in church nor on the street nor anywhere a description of his assailant might be required. Stolen during his sleep was convenient and cast suspicion on his colleagues, quieting any possible objections they might have to his inability to pay the rent.

Actually he had pawned them several weeks ago, promising to buy them back. With the money, he bought his first piece of property, surreptitiously. Félix had no intention of relying on those two spoiled brats forever. He needed independence from them and sadly, he felt, a divorce from his strange obsession with Rafaela, a beautiful and lively young woman who belonged to a social station beneath his.

V

Luis Arriesgo

Luis Arriesgo lay sprawled on his side in a fetal position atop three large pillows thrown on the sill of his wooden house. He supposed he should properly call it his rich man's outhouse for that was what he bought when he retired from begging.

In the morning light, he stretched his hand away from his face, felt the warmth of sunshine building to a crescendo, but could barely see the outline of his fingernails. Distant rectangles of pink, white, and brown interrupted the blur of blue sky and fuzzy green foliage.

"Ah," he said, taking a deep breath of the pineapple scented air of Manatí. "My eyesight might be short but my memory is long." He spoke aloud as if he had an audience though he knew himself to be alone. Lonely when no letters arrived from Paula and Tomás, he spent the days telling himself the story of his life as if to remind himself that he had indeed lived and done so for much longer than anyone had thought possible.

His earliest, most brutal memory took place when he was three years old.

"Be a good boy, Luisito," his mother had said. "An important man is visiting us today."

The small, thin man wore a dark brown suit and a vest with a pocket from which he produced a watch and showed it to Luis.

"Look," he said. "This tells you the time of day or night."

Luis examined the cool chain and tried to open the round gold face while he lay hung over his mother's lap. The man's fingers kneaded his spine, dug into his hip bones, and tried to force Luis to sit or stand erect. It was impossible and hurt but he would not stop until Luis began to weep.

"Stop crying, Luis," the doctor said. "It's over. Be a strong boy." His mother's face and that of the doctor took on the appearance of someone strangling, and Luis looked from one to the other until his baby mind sensed that it was something about him that saddened them.

"He'll never walk upright, Luisa. You should not have had children and now you're pregnant again." His mother wept.

"But Rafael, maybe a specialist?" Luisa gently placed him on the floor.

"No, he's worse off than your brothers. He'll die young from the strain on his internal organs." Rafael Figueroa paused to blow his nose, clear his throat. "His heart, the gravity. Luisa, I can't do anything. No one can."

From his hunched position on all fours, Luis turned his face completely to his left side to stare at his mother's face. She looked weepy and thin except for her rounded stomach.

"How long do you think?" she asked.

"With the best care eighteen, maybe nineteen, by some miracle perhaps twenty-one, but don't count on it."

"Who was that?" he asked after the doctor left.

"Dr. Rafael Figueroa, an old friend."

"Why did you both cry?"

His mother picked him up, trying to hold him upright which hurt. She hugged him, kissed his hair, forehead, and cheeks.

"Oh, Luis, my baby, I love you so much. You'll always be my baby." He disliked her adding, "It will be so much worse for you because you're intelligent."

In time his mother's stomach disappeared, flattened for a while, but then she got another which did not go away. It became bigger and bigger. After his brother Tomás was born life became difficult for Luis. His schoolteacher mother did not carry him around all day, did not have time for him except to teach him to read.

"I thought I'd always be your baby."

"You are but I must prepare you for the future." She glanced nervously at her husband. Luis followed her gaze to his father who sat on a hard, straight-backed wooden chair behind their table, pouring drinks out of an amber bottle into a very small glass. "If you can't walk you'd better learn to get around, be smarter than anyone else."

"Just what the hell can that thing learn?" his father bellowed.

By concentrating, Luis learned his letters, followed his mother's instructions on how to move around by himself and attend to his toilet. He mastered just how deep a hole to dig so that his urine would not spill over or splash back at him and he defecated on a piece of newspaper, on his side, knees bunched as far as they could go. Using a wet napkin he prepared in advance, he cleaned himself carefully as his mother taught him, not soiling his clothing by wiggling away as the excrement came out. That way, it did not smear up against him. Then he wiggled away further, pulled his pants back up by alternating hands to support his shifting weight, and took the package to the outhouse and dropped it in.

Embarrassed, he once felt like his baby brother as his mother cleaned him, rinsed out his diarrhea-laden pants.

"This is why," Luisa said, "you must avoid getting sick to your stomach. Eat potatoes, yuca, and yautía, starchy vegetables like plantains, and don't drink too much water."

It was a lesson he would not forget, especially when his father dropped his rum bottle, broke it, and, in a fury of alcohol deprivation, menaced both of them with the jagged glass.

"Get me another bottle," he yelled. "Or I'll use this to gut that thing you call a son."

With his father's words echoing inside him, he realized he must eat very little. The enemy, fat, could immobilize him, force him into a bed to await the inevitable, so Luis trained himself to eat just enough to still his hunger cramps.

To forget the hunger and thirst always with him and to alleviate his tired arms, he moved constantly, shifting his weight from one side of his body to the other. Luis forced himself to semikneel and ate his meals in that position, head hovering over his plate, as one hand at all times supported his weight. He became ambidextrous and strong. Just in time too, because his father's belligerence grew and challenged his mother's protestations of, "Nothing! I've done nothing to deserve this."

"Perhaps," Luis thought. *Perhaps not.* She must have done something. After he received Dr. Figueroa's verdict that his first son would never walk normally, something evil behind whiskey-glazed eyes festered in his father's head. More and more often, he remained at home, sipping amber liquid directly from whiskey bottles, and asked repeatedly, "What did you do? What have you done to us?"

Her face grimaced with pain, his mother wrung her hands and replied, "Pity, oh please, have pity on us."

Finally, he stopped working altogether, preferring to spend his days and nights in drunken musings or picking fights with neighbors who stared at Luis. After remaining strangely silent except for muttering to himself for two days, his father finally stumbled out of the house unwashed and unshaven. In the afternoon, while sunlight still blinded and small brown birds twittered happily, he returned with a pistol and fired at Luisa's heart. Neighbors hearing the shot ran in before his father was able to carry Tomás off with him and held him until the police arrived and carted him to jail.

Tomás was two years old, Luis six, old enough to ask himself what *he* had done to deserve this. He thought about what the neighbors called him and tried to understand but he came up with nonsense. If he was an accident of nature, his mother was innocent, but if Tomás who was normal was the accident then she was guilty of doing this to all of them.

The second time Dr. Figueroa arrived, he was exactly as Luis remembered. Same brown suit, glasses, and same tearful manner. This time, though, he did not try to force Luis to sit or stand, merely patted his head, felt his arms.

"You are a good, strong boy," he said. "And handsome too." No one, not even his mother, ever told Luis he was good or strong or handsome so he instantly adored Rafael Figueroa and tried to trot after him when he spoke with Paula but they did not permit him. When they came out of the room where they were talking, he said Paula could stay with him and Tomás.

When she first came to care for Luis and Tomás, Paula fussed over Luis. He did not like it until he realized she did not know all the things he could do for himself.

"Let me try and you'll see," he told her. After a while, they settled into a routine.

Even though the whole of Manatí knew the Arriesgo story, though she had never conceived and she was Negro and they white, Paula insisted she was their real mother. Paula's skin was the color of red sassafras and her face a delicate oval with a deep cleft in her chin. A lump formed in his throat whenever he tried to picture her life if she had been born white. "No doubt," he thought, "she would be living in a grand house with all the privileges of a lady."

Paula was the most beautiful woman in Manatí. She was tall and slim with calves and thighs like the flamenco dancers who performed at festivals. Her breasts were large, round and had big nipples which pointed upwards. Many nervous men visited her. More wrote long letters filled with rambling, romantic poetry, sent anonymously as if afraid to admire her openly. She bundled the letters into a growing pile, unread.

"For when I get old," she said. "Or when I can read."

At age ten, Luis, unhappy with what went on, asked, "How can you sleep with those men? They're disgusting!"

"They pay," she replied, kneeling and staring directly at him. Her large brown eyes with clear whites tilted upwards at the corners. He knew she was not ashamed. "How do you think we eat?"

Luis shifted back and forth from one arm to the other, feeling angry, impotent. Paula played with her long, thick hair, which she straightened with grease and a hot comb and braided, Indian fashion.

"Luis, what could be more disgusting than getting sucked up by a smelly father while your mother pretends to snore her drunken head off?"

"My mother didn't deserve to die," he said hotly. "Yours does."

"We all deserve to die. That's why we're here."

"But you're so good, Paula. So beautiful."

"I'm not good. I've done bad things. Besides, beauty can be a curse. Sometimes I think God hates me."

"The priest hates me," Luis said, wondering what bad things he had done. "Maybe God does too."

Paula smiled, showing pearly teeth all the way back to her molars. Dimples creased her cheeks lengthwise. "Maybe," she said. "Maybe not. You have me don't you?" She stroked his hair. "Luis, don't go to church anymore if you don't want to." Relief flooded him. "But take Tomás," she added. "God doesn't hate him. He's a plain, healthy boy who will lead a plain, healthy life and be successful."

Paula was right. Tomás enjoyed church. He had no questions and as soon as he became old enough went on his own, always came out smiling and talking with the priest who smiled too, until he saw Luis. Then the priest stopped talking, sighed deeply, and made the sign of the cross. Luis surprised himself by laughing. *Very funny, that damned unholy priest.*

True to his word, Dr. Figueroa visited them often, sometimes with his wife, Josie, to teach them to read and to speak English.

Before giving them textbooks Rafael asked Paula, "How are you getting along? Need anything?"

"Yes, more clients, rich ones."

"I can't help you there," he said, clutching himself in mock fear. "I'm poor and I love my wife."

Paula laughed. "No, not you. Impotent husbands or young boys who have problems with girls. Know what I mean?"

Rafael looked from Tomás to Luis. "Hmm, yes," he said, wrinkling his brow.

"No, no." Paula shook her head impatiently. "How can you think such a thing? Nobody touches my children!" She breathed deeply to calm down. "For me. I need money."

Dr. Figueroa examined Paula, left without agreeing to but he must

have referred clients because, later, young men from far away began to
arrive.

Usually their fathers accompanied the boys, sometimes their mothers
or an uncle, while a few came by themselves. They wore matching suits
of brown or black, had faces reddened by shame or fury. Most were shy
or studious, some intense and nervous, others delicate and pretty. Some
of the older boys truly had problems with girls. They arrived alone,
rejected Paula, and turned glittering eyes toward Luis who scooted
around on all fours with his behind forced almost higher than his head by
his long, lean legs. It both shocked and shamed Luis, who liked girls, to
think he could be the object of another male's sexual lust.

Before they had a chance to voice their preference, almost as if she
could read their minds, Paula chased them out of the house with a machete, yelling.

"Criminal! Pervert! He's only a child." Long after they ran away, she
stood in the doorway of their shack screaming curses after them into the
night, letting in the mosquitoes and making Luis chuckle. He wondered
at her peculiar logic of hating the men who rejected her even more than
she hated the ones who slept with her.

Among Paula's clients he saw an old, bowlegged man with a very big
head on which stiff tufts of hair stood facing in all directions.

"Are you the only one here?" he asked Paula. "I like pretty white girls
under fourteen."

"Get out of here, *viejo sucio*, before I split your big old head in two!"

"I am very rich and have rights." He justified himself by telling tales of
rich older women marrying handsome young men.

"But you are ugly and should marry an ugly rich woman as old and
nasty as you are."

"Young woman, in spite of your business, you have no knowledge of the
ways of the world. I do have an ugly rich wife. That's why I'm here." He
swiveled his entire body to turn to Tomás. "That's a good-looking boy. In a
few years, put him to work making love to my wife. She is very generous."
He laughed and walked away on his bowlegs, tapping his cane.

Neighbor women endured beatings from men who satisfied them in bed, and cuckolded husbands stayed with their torrid, unfaithful wives, not knowing where else to go for excitement.

Living with Paula taught Luis that the engine of life runs on the power of looks, sex, and money. Without them a person, no matter how kind, amounted to nothing. So out of the three he chose to pursue money.

Wanting to help out, Luis began to beg but he did not get much because Manatí fell on hard times as one small landowner after the other lost his properties in small pieces and more families found themselves without livelihoods. Many left for larger cities and some migrated to the States, so many that they lost the refuge of the May fiestas, also known as the festivals of the Cross, which they always relied on for food and drink when even the most faithful, Doña Eva, announced she was not hosting the nine days of singing in her home. Friends and neighbors had gathered with her yearly for ten years in remembrance of the death of her husband so that their singing had attained a polished quality other groups envied.

Although the regulars had all the songs memorized, Doña Eva always handed out slips of paper neatly printed with the words so that everyone, including children who could read, would be able to join in. In her mezzo-soprano she would lead, singing slowly.

"The an-gels fo-rm a cho-rus."

Those gathered would repeat some of the lyrics faster.

"Form a chorus."

Afterwards, Doña Eva served food and drink. Now she too was leaving.

Paula began to call the town "Puerto Rico's behind" because she lost clients as they became too poor to afford a woman or moved to the cities for work. Neighbors were no longer as generous as they had been with their offerings of food and discarded clothing, so in 1924, when Luis was fourteen, they packed their few belongings and started on foot for Cataño, hometown of their friend, Dr. Rafael Figueroa and where Paula's cousin Juan lived.

Leaving Manatí, they followed the river a distance and then turned east at the coast preferring to walk close enough to the ocean to obtain its breezes and avoid succumbing to the heat.

A young boy's cries of, "The circus is coming, the circus is coming," beckoned the townspeople of Cataño out of their sweltering rooms and into the blistering midday sun of August. They shaded their eyes to peer through the heat waves blurring the distant trio.

"The freaks are coming first," they exclaimed.

It had been Luis's idea to enter Cataño with Tomás leading him by a rope tied around his neck and accompanied by Paula carrying an empty basket, presumably filled with laundry, on her head. Luis carried his few clothes strapped on his back. Tomás and Paula each toted their belongings in a battered satchel. The wavering nightmare before the eyes of the townspeople appeared to be something half-human and half-horse, a small boy and a tall dark woman with an oversized head. In an age replete with hydrocephalic heads and men with enormous herniated testicles, the only attraction on closer examination was Luis walking on all fours. If they felt foolish for thinking that the laundry basket Paula carried was part of her head, they ignored it, blaming the sun for blinding them.

"Where do you come from?" they asked.

"Manatí," Luis replied.

"The monkey from Manatí!" someone yelled. They stared at Luis's hands tied in bloody rags and scrunched down to get a better look at his face. "Where are you going?"

"To Dr. Figueroa."

"Are you sick?"

"No. Hungry. What can you give a needy traveler?"

They tossed coins, disappointed there was no circus except Luis. The crowd accompanied them to Rafael's house, firing questions at Luis who answered with requests for money. Tomás picked up the pennies and nickels dug from short pockets and thrown into the street by some who shied back, fearful of contamination. He accepted quarters put into his hand by the more generous and adventurous.

"Go back to your homes." Josie reprimanded the crowd outside her home. "And mind your manners." Remembering she was dealing with adults instead of her students, she stopped, said, "Please don't trouble yourselves. We will take care of them now." Her face purple with rage, she muttered under her breath. "Damned nosy bodies."

Luis smiled his horselike smile, showing his full set of oversized teeth, said, "Hello, Josie. How are you?" and laughed.

"Better than you," she said. "You're roasted. Why didn't you wear something on your head?"

"I couldn't find my tuxedo hat," he said, teasing.

"It's not funny. You're as red as a *flamboyán* and look at your hands. Go into the infirmary, right now." Obediently, Luis clambered off but not before winking at Tomás. To Paula Josie said, "How could you allow this?"

"It was his idea," Paula said. "He thought to attract enough attention to get the town in the habit of giving us money to help us." Paula put her head down. "But the roads here are so hard, not like the soft grass in Manatí." She began to cry. "He wouldn't stop." Tomás began to cry too.

From the infirmary they heard, "Hey, are we having a crybaby party?" Then they heard him laughing. "I'm crying too. Can you hear me?" Loud, wailing noises filled the house, then baby imitations. "How am I doing?"

Against her will, Josie laughed. She bathed his hands and tried to remain stern while he howled like a wolf over the alcohol and iodine swabbing.

"At least kiss it to make it better," he complained. "No? Then tell me you've missed my big, brown frog eyes." He batted his eyelashes.

"Be serious Luis. You might have gotten a bad infection."

"My germs are bigger and uglier than all other germs." He paused, smiling. "Besides, only death is serious."

Josie stared lovingly at the best student she and Rafael ever had. He learned everything they taught him, the first time around without taking notes or having to be reminded. "So while you're alive everything is funny?"

"Everything *is* funny. Paula, you, me, especially me. Look, I know a funny song. I'll sing it to you. Ready?

"*Pollo*, chicken, *gallina*, hen,
Lápiz, pencil, and *pluma*, pen.

Like it?"

Josie grabbed his neck, pinning him and showered kisses on his face. He was poking fun at his first English lesson.

"Help, help, Paula! This woman wants me."

Josie whacked him on the head. "Close your mouth and don't talk like that. You're too young."

Grinning, they joined Paula and Tomás whom Luis called "the dusty duo" and waited for Rafael to come home and take them to the house he rented for them on San Alberto Street.

Once moved in, they settled down to a routine. Tomás went to school, Paula took in laundry instead of men, and Luis became a familiar sight in the streets of Cataño and San Juan as he begged full time.

"And I was a rather good beggar."

Luis chuckled into the afternoon humidity of August. He tried to focus his blurred vision inside of his rich man's outhouse but could not. No matter, he knew where to relieve his bladder. Coughing, he crawled six feet to do so. No longer sure he did not splash back on himself, he sniffed his clothes. But then, everything smelled bad to him these days. Not like the days of long ago when he had been fourteen and not particular about the smell of air, land, and water. All things considered, it had been a good time except when that first unthinking child had given him the name, the despicable name which likened him to an animal.

"So many tears," he said. "I shed so many dry, internal tears over being called the 'Monkey Man', yet no one knew."

Luis returned to his place on his sweat-stained pillows to remember.

VI

Juan

Juan and Carmela's fourth child, like their other miscarried
attempts at parenthood, arrived prematurely.

She was hanging laundry in the patio, a narrow alleyway adjacent to
the house with a high fence on one side to keep out the inquiring eyes of
their neighbors and walled on the opposite side by the house itself.
Carmela's sudden cramp accompanied by a burst of water signaled another too-early birth. She cried out for Juan.

Luckily, he was sitting under the only window to the patio, reading his
old Bible, the one given him by Padre Hernán, searching for a flaw in the
rules, a way out of the doubts which still surfaced often, when he heard
Carmela's grunts. He rushed through his living room to the rear, jumped
down the two steps with the grace of a dancer, and led her, bent over and
stumbling, back up into the closest bedroom, the one nearest the kitchen.
He boiled water, took out clean sheets and prepared to deliver his own
child.

Carmela opened her legs. "Can you do it alone?"

"Yes, don't worry."

She screamed as if swords tore her apart.

"Breathe!" he commanded. "And concentrate. Push!"

Carmela passed out. The fetus, five months old, splattered out onto the bed. Juan stared at it in revulsion. No need for water to wipe it off, no need to cut its detached umbilical cord.

From under Carmela's unconscious head, he gently dislodged a pillow and held it suspended in midair over the monster. Covered with sticky, opaque mucous, purple-skinned and striated with bloody residue, an oversized head cleaved from top to chin sucked air from two mouths, two noses, and fluttered one swollen eye. It writhed with need. Nauseated, Juan hesitated to smother it, wondering how Carmela had not aborted it sooner, until the quivering mass stopped pulsating. He wrapped it in one of the soiled sheets and buried it near the old mango tree in the yard. He returned, pushed at Carmela's stomach as the midwives did, cleaned her, and whispered that the child was stillborn.

During the middle of the night, while Carmela slept, he sat cross-legged atop the grave mound with his hands on the fresh dirt, looked up at the moon, and finally let the spirits in.

The spirits had been whispering to him for a long time, while his success as a healer, a medium, and a grave digger allowed him that measure of blindness that only success has a way of bestowing. He believed himself above the petty disasters of everyday living visited on others less talented, less blessed by personal gifts, less able to cope with setbacks. Now, after the death of his fourth child, those whisperings became the roar of the surf pounding in his ear, his consciousness. The ugliness of the revelations could no longer be ignored. He listened to the nudging of his raw, open awareness and looked at the vision of disgust.

"Let me show you something," the lady said. She looked sad, gestured. Juan followed her hand to a large garden, bigger than the El Yunque rain forest. All the trees, beautifully ordered in neat rows and pruned, rose tall and lush. Some labored under the weight of purple fruit and orange berries he did not recognize, and underneath them, in the midst of iridescent grass, naked white men and women worked, lounged, and waited. A huge egg like a black rock striated with swirls of red, yellow, and green hatched a serpent, marked with faces. It approached.

"Ssso," it hissed. "Ssstay with me."

The serpent slithered freely in and out of the women's vaginas while the men busily picked fruit.

"Do you know what this means?" the lady asked. Her dress, light as gossamer, swayed in the breeze.

"No."

"Look closely."

The snake's body shortened, its mouth continued whispering hoarsely. It became thinner, grew legs, stood upright, metamorphosed into a black man consoling women who gave birth to child after monstrous child.

"We told you not to marry, not to have children." The lady shed a large globular tear. It dripped out of her right eye and glistened down her cheek spreading all the colors of a rainbow. "You did not listen."

Wrenched from his trance, Juan heard Carmela calling, but not before he saw the face of Mamá Abuela and the face of the serpent, Dr. Rodríguez.

He picked himself off the mound, sobbed, and prepared to question his wife but he waited until she felt better.

"You seem like your old self again," he lied, three days later.

"Yes," she said, despondent. "Back to not having children." They sat in the dining room between their kitchen and living room. She offered him more coffee: thick, black espresso diluted with boiled milk and sugar. She wore a stained house dress and oily dandruff speckled her long hair.

"We're young enough to have many children," he lied, again. "Let's wait a little."

"You think so?"

"Of course. Don't listen to the midwives. They know nothing." He smiled. "We didn't wait enough between pregnancies, that's all." His lovely Carmela looked so needy, he added, "Strengthen yourself spiritually by devoting nine days to saying the rosary and fortify yourself physically with meat until we're ready."

"I thought you'd be angry with me." She set her coffee cup down, relieved.

"Never. Never angry with you, Carmela. I love you." He remembered the ignored warnings. "If anything, I blame myself. But tell me about your mother. Did she have any problems giving birth?"

"No. You know I have four brothers."

"Yes," he said carefully. "Four, white, older brothers."

"I'm the Indian of the family." Her hand stroked the straight hair that Juan knew made many like Carmela feel closer to the ruling class than those whose skin and hair sang of African purity.

"No," Juan continued, "From the time of the discovery of the island, Indians were very few in number. Your parents and grandparents were white so any Indian blood would already have been too diluted to make a difference in your appearance."

"What are you saying?"

"You're also the youngest," he prompted.

Carmela shrugged. "What of it?"

"There's a big age difference between you and your brothers." She shrugged again. "Carmela, I'm as black as tar, and . . ." He paused. "Different from everyone else. Isn't it odd that your family didn't protest your marrying me?"

"I knew it!" Carmela, agitated, rose from her chair. "You want to leave me." Wrenched with sobs, she whimpered, "Don't leave me. I'll give you children, pretty children with long straight hair."

"Sit down, Carmela," he said, gently. "I'll never leave you, I'm just talking." Juan forced himself to smile, added, "What strange ideas in such a beautiful head. You'll never get rid of me." He rose, kissed her forehead, and led her to the indoor bathroom they were so proud of. "Wash up now and look lovely for me when I get back."

"W-Where are you going?"

"I've got to see Mamá Abuela to help her out with a few coins."

He left despite her complaint that she wanted to go with him, assuring her that, because of her blood loss, she was still not strong enough for the bus trip on bumpy roads and that he intended to return by evening.

In Loíza, Mamá Abuela looked near death. Fatter than ever, she wheezed every word through heaving chest, unable to gesture with her mammoth arms.

"I had a terrible vision."

"I knew you would," she gasped.

"Let me hear the whole truth."

"Can't you see I'm dying? Let me take my secrets to the grave."

"You must make your peace with me before you can make it with God." Under the shade of a small awning, he sat on the cement blocks serving as steps to the entrance of her shack and prepared to listen.

"My brother and I were very close as children," she said. "As many others, we talked about love and experimented by touching each other. When the heat of budding passion came upon us, we continued." She paused to grab his shoulder. "You must know about the heat of passion so strong you can't eat or sleep or think of anything else except satisfaction. Look how fast you married Carmela."

"She was not my sister."

"We knew it was wrong and told no one. At fifteen, I became pregnant and we found out just how wrong it was. My brother was sent away and the baby sold to some wealthy women who promised to provide well for the child. I was forbidden to seek him out, ever." Her breathing rose to a snore as her chest heaved, trying to inhale.

"Did you want to?"

"No. He was born with his eyes open and as I looked into them, I saw something I did not like."

"How could you make love to your own brother?"

"I loved him and we were just kids," she answered, whining.

"And the second time?"

"Years passed, I married and, later, my brother returned with a wife of his own. Then more years and my husband stopped relations with me because I kept getting fatter and because he was afraid of my witchcraft. I felt lonely and confided to my brother that I was still young and needed a man."

A coughing fit prevented her from continuing and alarmed Juan who thought she would die then and there. He allowed a long pause, looked up at a sky so clear and cerulean blue that he could not help snorting in disgust at the irony of such rottenness underneath its crisp, bright beauty.

With great effort she moved slowly inside the house to escape the grains of sand blowing from the nearby beach which she blamed for suffocating her. He moved into the dark interior with her and stood waiting for the end of her story.

"So he agreed knowing what happened the last time?"

"Not right away. More time passed and when he lost his wife to another man he moved in with us. As we grew older, we became closer, finally talked about the past and our youthful folly. Still, the attraction continued. He was my best friend, understood me like no other, and I loved him above anyone else. Then one day when we were alone, our pent up affection and passion, our loneliness and our needs overwhelmed us."

"How did you get away with those hidden pregnancies."

"I had always been so fat nobody could tell."

"What about your husband? Didn't Papá Abuelo care I was not his?"

"Not as long as he did not have to lie down with me."

"Why didn't you tell me before?" he asked.

"You were such a special child I thought it didn't matter."

"No, you thought it the reason I was special."

"Yes. Perhaps I should have kept my first son as a reminder never to love my brother again."

"No wonder my mind reading terrified you."

"Sometimes I felt sure you knew, then you'd ask questions about your mother and father, and after we continued the lies so long it became too complicated to tell the truth."

Shaking his head as he remembered his Uncle Moncho, now suddenly not his uncle at all but his father, Juan asked, "Why didn't you give me away too?"

"I was old when I had you and wanted a companion. Besides, you didn't have the mark."

"What mark? The mark of the devil?"

"The look of something twisted."

"Oh but now I have it just as you and your wretched family are twisted." Juan laughed. "My cousin Paula was right, you nasty, disgusting people deserve to die for what you've done to all of us." He threw some coins at her. They landed on her lap and stayed there. "I won't be coming back. Thank you for cursing me, Mother."

Mamá Abuela cried pleading that he not hate her. He said good-bye and left her gasping for breath in the steamy air.

Outside the dark little shack, after his eyes readjusted to the sunlight, he spit on the ground and left wishing he had helped Paula kill every last member of his family. Behind him, the ocean roared sending a strong wind at his back. Angry black clouds running into land from the Atlantic eclipsed the sun and vomited white lightning followed by ear-splitting booms. Juan welcomed the downpour, thick as beaded veils, drenching him. He thought he could never be clean and walked slowly trying to unravel his relationship to his bride. As his brother's daughter, was Carmela sister, niece, cousin, or all three? It was too much.

Juan rolled his wet trouser legs up to his knees as the clay roads, muddied by the torrential rain, sucked at his feet and splattered his legs with cold red earth. "Poor Carmela," he thought. *And poor me . . .* There could be no children. He felt himself to be an abomination. His tears, warm and salty, blended with cool rain dripping down his face and fell away blown by the wind.

In the fog ahead, created by the heat released from the ground, Juan saw his Congo spirit shaking its head violently.

"You are not an abomination," he said in his peculiar tongue-tied la-la-la cadence. "You are the victim of an abomination. Strike it out, strike it out, strike it out." Grass skirt awhirl, the little man danced a threat with his spear.

"Yes," Juan thought. *Stop this thing, but how?* Could he kill Rodríguez and then himself? Could he give up Carmela?

She greeted his return with concerned outcries. One look at his anxious wife filled him with a tender protective love he could not abandon. She was innocent.

"I have a cure for us, Carmela," he told her. "We must be very clean for two years." He held a finger to his lips when she began to protest. "Hush, listen to what I say. No sex, we must read the Bible, go to church, and bathe in cold water every day, including our heads. The house must be cleaned from top to bottom once a week. Do you understand?"

"Y-Yes." She seemed dubious but he knew she was grateful to have something to occupy her mind with, and he believed the two years would condition her for the rest of her life's course. Dealing with her father—the serpent, his brother, uncle, and who knew what else—was a different matter. Juan had time for that, just as he took his time finding out if he was right or if Padre Hernán was right. If only this one time he had listened to the warnings of the spirits. If only.

VII
Rafaela

Rafaela rushed to Ana Betancourt's house to tell her the latest developments in her five-year romance with Félix. Edelmira, her godchild, waited with her behind planted on the bottom step of their balcony.

"Oh, my darling," Rafaela said, scooping up the white-haired child, kissing her. "How are you my little love? Edelmira's big blue eyes shone with happiness. The five-year-old held up a tiny fat finger with a cigar band on it.

"Valdering," she said.

"What's a Valdering?" Rafaela kissed the child's finger, sat her down on her step and went in to Ana.

"What's that on her finger?" asked Rafaela.

"A paper toy one of the boys is always giving her."

"What is she doing up so early."

Ana peered out to the balcony step. "When I'm sick, I sit her outside. I'm not sure if she likes to see the train go by or if it's the two boys that play with her or both."

"I bet it's the boys." Rafaela laughed. "Speaking of boys, I'm losing my sense of humor. That damned Félix ignores me, then looks for me, then ignores me again. I don't know what to do."

Ana sat Rafaela down, served her a cup of coffee mixed with boiled milk.

"Maybe he's not the marrying type."

"Are you joking? That's all he talks about. It's always 'When I marry, my wife this and my children that' but nothing happens."

"Nothing? Where does he take you?"

"Well," Rafaela began. "He says he's not ready for a formal engagement so we should not meet in public to give anyone the wrong idea. He invites me to meet him in church but he doesn't escort me and insists we return separately. I get a ticket for a concert and he sits down after the lights go out or if we go on a real date together it's always with a crowd of people and we sometimes separate, wind up in conversation with others. Then he takes me home angry because I've embarrassed him."

"Rafaela, you don't have to answer this . . ."

"Forget about that. I know what you mean but no, we've never been alone."

Ana sighed. She was no great expert on men. Her husband left her for another woman, in spite of Ana fulfilling his desire for a child. "Then tell me what he says about marrying."

"He makes it sound like his wife should be as stiff and formal as he is. I picture him as a rooster with starched white feathers leading his henny wife, and behind them, all the children he wants to have following in a row of fluffy yellow *pollitos*. They both laughed.

"I don't want to hurt your feelings, Rafaela, except that all I can come up with is maybe he wants you to be different."

"That's crazy, nobody changes. Why fall in love with me if he wants me to be different?"

"Are you sure he's in love with you?"

"Positive. Félix is always watching to see what people think and say about him and yet doesn't realize that he stares at me like a starved dog, giving himself away."

"That's true. I remember the time you brought him around. He seemed to be smelling you." Ana laughed, leaned over her coffee cup. "Rafaela, has he never tried?"

"Where? In public he behaves as if we're just good friends and there is no private place. He still sleeps in his office, which is locked and guarded."

"Why are you in love with him?" Ana's blue eyes trapped hers.

There it was, the question Rafaela had been erasing from her mind whenever it etched itself around her consciousness.

"It's a feeling I can't help," she said. Then she smiled as if in a dream. "His eyes are dark and shiny, as beautiful as a cow's with long lashes, and his lips are so full and red they make me want to kiss them. Félix is very smart. I like that."

"You think him handsome?"

"Very."

"You believe him someone above you, someone you can't have?"

Annoyed at the implication that she only loved him because of his social standing, Rafaela remained silent. They heard a train roll by. Its clanking and the whooping cries of the boys who ran to catch it obliterated both their thoughts and conversation.

"Oh my God!" Rafaela said. "I'm going to be late for work." She had a secretarial position in San Juan. "If you think of anything or hear anything about Félix let me know, all right?" Rafaela ran out toward the gravelly bay road before Ana answered that she didn't get around much because she was sick. Edelmira waved and said, " 'Bye 'Fela."

Rafaela heard a wolf whistle, looked back at Luis Arriesgo grinning as always. "Hello gorgeous," he said.

Laughing as she went, Rafaela looked over her shoulder, said, "Flirt! You say that to all the girls."

"But it's you I love."

"Ha! Stand in line behind my many admirers."

Easy banter between them started almost as soon as he arrived in Cataño and she noticed none of the girls would talk to him. She overheard his constant teasing and, during his few unguarded moments, noticed his need of a friend.

VIII

Luis

When he first arrived, the townspeople called him the Monkey Man from Manatí. Actually, they called him the monkey because he walked on all fours but Luis added the man because they forgot that.

Emboldened by his easy laughter, they asked questions which were none of their business, questions flung through the hot dusty air like arrows to pierce his dignity and his spirit.

"How do you urinate?" "Can you have sex?" "How do you clean yourself after you, um, after you, you know?"

"With toilet paper," he replied. They laughed, relieved that in spite of their curiosity, they received an answer they would not have to envision.

Because he couldn't walk upright, his arms were more muscular, better shaped than the legs of his questioners, most of whom had legs as straight and thin as flagpoles. Luis knew that if he could stand, he would be taller than they, taller and stronger.

When they had first moved to Cataño, Luis had gone to the train tracks to watch, enviously, the schoolboys who lived between stations run and jump onto the moving train. He saw Waldemar Toledo there. Tall, happy, and everything Luis admired. He laughed a lot too, even as he chased the boys who threw rocks at Luis. Waldemar waited to jump on the train with them.

"Hey, you there," Waldemar called. "I challenge you to a race. If I win, you get away from the tracks, and if I lose, I give you two pennies."

Luis knew that Waldemar felt sorry for him, wanted to protect him, but a race? How could he win? Luis started to crawl away when he saw Waldemar remove his jacket, get down on his hands and knees then rethink it when he noticed Luis did not use his knees.

Because the gravel destroyed his pants, reducing them to tatters, Luis bent his long legs slightly at the knees, flared out his feet and used the inner sides of his shoes to propel himself, putting most of his weight on his arms. He either wrapped his hands in rags or attached wooden blocks to them.

Waldemar did the same but he had nothing to protect his hands. Already puffing, he crawled over to Luis and winked. His eyes were the light green of sugarcane.

"Ready?" Waldemar asked.

Luis had never played a game or had a friend his own age.

"Let's go," he yelled. They scampered off, raising gravel dust.

Luis won easily because Waldemar slowed whenever rocks imbedded themselves in his hands. Otherwise it was a fair race and Luis got two pennies. He proudly took them to Paula. "Look, earned without begging." It bought them a loaf of the local bread, made with lard and water. He took a bite and munched. Then he looked at its cream-colored crust and smelled its soft, fragrant dough. "I swear this tastes better than usual," he said.

After that, Luis met with Waldemar as often as he could, early mornings. Sometimes they played with white-haired baby Edelmira, bouncing her ball and tickling her chubby ribs. Waldemar usually challenged Luis to a race and Luis always won.

"Not fair," Waldemar complained. "You have the advantage, the experience."

Waldemar read to Luis out of his schoolbooks in an exaggerated imitation of his Spanish teacher's lisp.

Caribe

*"En el puenthe de Marthín Peña
matharon a Pepe Thíath
el tholthado máth bravo
que el rey de Ethpaña thenía."*

Both whooped with laughter. Waldemar was his best friend and his only same-age friend. For one full year, Luis felt happy to be part of humanity, to know companionship and to share dreams like anyone else.

One Monday morning, Waldemar jumped onto the moving train, missed his hold, and fell under the wheels. They ran over his legs and splattered everyone nearby with his blood. Before help arrived, Waldemar dragged himself away and sat down by the edge of the tracks. Pale and quiet, he trembled as he unstrung his boots, plastered flat against his broken legs. None of the school boys dared touch him including Luis who could not bear the pain straining Waldemar's face. Instead, he nudged little Edelmira back into her house with his head because she had started walking toward Waldemar.

Inside her house, he found a new problem. Mouth agape, Edelmira's mother lay sprawled on their sofa stiffening in death. Overwhelmed, Luis vented his sorrow with bitter sobs and guttural screams that frightened Edelmira into a trance.

Outside, near the train tracks, calls for help continued. Like the blur of a tornado appearing out of nowhere, Dr. Rodríguez ran toward Waldemar's side, dropped his bag, opened it, and shakily filled a syringe with morphine. As soon as he injected the boy, he picked him up, leaving his medical bag behind, and ran through the streets, sweating and yelling, "A wagon, you stupid fools. Get me a wagon!"

Loss of blood coupled with staring, hesitant neighbors who delayed obtaining transportation to a hospital allowed necrosis to set in. Dr. Figueroa, who took over from Dr. Rodríguez at the hospital, could do nothing. Waldemar died of gangrene. He was fifteen years old and left Luis with more questions. Why did this happen? What did he do to deserve this?

The Toledo family would not let Luis see Waldemar in his casket and

Luis thought they blamed him, that Waldemar's hands might have been too sore from his races with Luis to hold on to the train tightly.

As he crawled along, the tropical sun roasted his backside. In Manatí he scared away stray cows and pigs by barking. In Cataño, street dogs growled and followed him. The pebbly roads, hard and hot, scraped his hands and made them bleed until Tomás carved new wooden walking blocks for his hands. And then there were the girls.

In their blue and white school uniforms they walked along hugging books to budding breasts, talking and laughing with each other until they spotted him. Then they averted their eyes, became silent, and quickened their pace past him.

"Listen," he yelled after them. "You're all too skinny for me to fall in love with." He shifted his weight from arm to arm, angry that the girls feared he might get a crush on them and make a nuisance of himself. None of that worried Luis for long. He learned from Paula's clients that although good looks seemed to be all-important, there was usually somebody for everybody, with a little bit of compromise. That the girls never glanced at or spoke to his brother Tomás worried him.

In time, he recovered from the loss of his friend and was all right until he realized the townspeople treated Tomás and Paula as they treated him: as a household pet who has worn out its welcome, its novelty, and is now ready to be discarded. He decided to step up his begging to get Paula and Tomás as far away from him as soon as he could.

Careful not to look down at foamy green water visible between rough, wooden planks connecting dock to ferry for passengers taking the trip across the bay, he spent less time in Cataño's plaza and more time in San Juan near the fort.

Although they could never replace Waldemar, American soldiers stationed near El Morro gave Luis whole dollars and treated him like an equal. For his sixteenth birthday he had expected them to take up a collection for him so he felt disappointed when they insisted he meet them in a tavern in the old section for a drink.

"I don't touch rum or whiskey," he said. "My father was a drunkard. And he smelled just like this place."

"You can't turn it down if a special soldier's buying for you," they said.

"Really?" He perked up. "Like a general?"

"More like privates." Their laughter, overly loud and leering clued him. He followed their eyes to a curtain covering a back door. Through it, dressed in a tight uniform, a whore entered carrying a bottle of rum and two glasses. This was good, his heart beat faster, a challenge he would enjoy.

"Owwooo." He howled like a wolf to show his approval when his friends rose to leave and he trotted after her into the back room.

She drank most of the rum but she taught him a few things he had wondered about but had not dared ask Paula. Sated, he crawled outside the tavern. There, leaning against their truck, the soldiers waited.

"Gotta drive you home," they said. "Might get arrested for drunken smiling."

Unthinking, he shared the news with Paula, something that upset her.

"I didn't bring you up like that," she said.

What could he answer?

"I'm sorry," he said, not sorry at all. He liked it and would do it again. Luis did not remind Paula of her life in Manatí, amazed that in her mind she had become his mother.

Waiting for Luis to finish his beggar's rounds, Tomás, almost thirteen, stood motionless, reading under the shade of mango trees with flies buzzing around his head. Looking at him, tall, light-skinned and black-haired, Luis felt that except for the major detail of his deformity, they looked enough alike to be twins. It broke his heart to catch Tomás throwing secret glances at pretty girls who slit their eyes and turned away from him.

"Those girls had big feet, anyway," Luis said. Because Tomás ignored him, continued reading, he added, "Unless you want a wife whose shoes can serve as rowboats, ha, ha."

What had his poor brother done, wondered Luis, to deserve this. With a normal brother Tomás could live a normal life instead of being an unnaturally quiet boy with no friends, a boy who looked away whenever Luis laughed.

"And I laugh a lot," he thought. It was all so funny: the horrified faces at the sight of him, the ignorant, self-serving questions, and the hypocrisy of so-called friends whose daughters were not allowed to speak to him lest he misinterpret their courtesy and fall in love with them. *Hilarious!* His own posture when he saw himself from a distance watching himself shift his weight from arm to arm like a tired horse, showing his teeth for apples.

Prickly pears are what I get. There is no redeemer except death which I expect within three years, four at most.

"As soon as you have a trade," he told Tomás, "you must go away with the soldiers."

"Leave you and Paula to go to the States?"

"Yes. You have to go where nobody knows you. It's your only chance."

"I can work here, I don't want to leave."

"Accept the truth, Tomás, I'll not live forever and Paula will be all right but you'll never have a normal life here. They'll always remember you as the brother of the Monkey Man and wonder if your children will be like me. No girl will want to marry you."

"Then I won't marry."

"What? Then in no time at all, you'll become like your old friend from Manatí, an impregnator par excellence. Does old Dr. Rodríguez still sneak up on you when you're alone to talk to you about revolutions or about sex?"

Tomás looked at him, sad, a fuzz beginning on his upper lip, and asked, "Why do you always say things like that?"

Luis did not answer. He laughed, because he had gotten a better idea than begging as a way to make more money.

"And what an idea it was!" Luis said aloud as he remembered his days in Cataño.

"What was?" Since no one lived near his shack, the voice startled him. Because of the growing twilight, he had not seen the outline of the young man approach nor heard footsteps.

"Who are you?" Luis asked.

"A friend."

"I have no friends."

"I'm here to keep you company."

"Ah, thank you."

"I heard you talking about ideas."

"But I was thinking about money."

"Ideas are more interesting than money."

"Everybody believes they have good ideas but if those ideas don't work to fill empty stomachs they fall on deaf ears."

IX

Rodríguez

He had never been able to call one person friend although he often lied to himself and others about having been close with abolitionist Ramón Emeterio Betances, who was called the father of Puerto Rico. He often wondered what it might be like to have an intimate tie like that which had existed between Betances and Segundo Ruiz Belvis, two extremely intelligent men perfectly attuned to the goal of independence. Then he remembered Betances's painful lament when Ruiz Belvis died in South America trying to obtain support for Puerto Rican freedom from Spain and decided he had already been dealt too much frustration and pain to bother with friends who might cause more. Rodríguez did not doubt that Ruiz Belvis had been murdered by a blow, an assassination, although nothing could be proven.

One of his major consolations was the appearance on the political scene of someone he knew was not his son. A brilliant man from Ponce, Pedro Albizu Campos. A Harvard graduate who, Rodríguez believed, carried the spirit of his deceased idol.

Pedro Albizu Campos, Ponceño lawyer, orator, and radical freedom fighter advocated war against the United States as the only alternative to liberate Puerto Rico from colonialism. He believed no country used to having its hand out, no people who had accepted deep within their soul the myth that they could not survive without the crumbs thrown to them from a larger table, could ever be prepared to vote for liberty because they lived mummified in a negative illusion that their enslavement was freedom. Pedro appointed himself their liberator and preached in favor of terrorist activity against the United States.

Wagging tongues claimed that Albizu, son of an *hacendado* and a mulatta, had turned patriot only after enlisting in the United States army during World War I and having been assigned to a Negro unit. In spite of the incongruity that allowed some Puerto Ricans of mixed blood to continue their bias against blacks, Rodríguez loved Albizu Campos as fiercely as he hated the peasants who ignorantly welcomed the invading Americans in 1898 as saviors when Spain had already granted autonomy to Puerto Rico.

Pinning his hopes on Pedro, he regretted that he considered the man an ugly dwarf even as he sent him a list of the names and addresses of his offspring with an admonition.

"Here is your army," he wrote. "Visit them and speak to them, tell them to remember the words of Dr. Rafael Rodríguez."

The late arrival of love proved a second consolation. In San Juan he usually behaved with propriety so as not to give outright proof of his activities to socialite rumormongers, but he took nightly walks to remain aware of the town's pulse.

Conditioned to need little sleep from years of traveling when he had nowhere to stay, he habitually tapped his cane along the darkened cobblestones. On one of those nights he heard a whisper from an alleyway.

"Free treatment for the poor. Medicine for the sick."

He peered into shadows as a woman came forward. Using the unmistakable stance of a prostitute, she smiled with thin, wide lips painted red, showed an excess of straight, thick teeth. She was tall and her face light olive with strong, sharp features, not a little mother.

"What do you need?"

"It's what you need that concerns me."

He gasped when she came closer, rubbed full breasts against him.

"I don't carry money."

"I said free treatment for the poor."

A new experience. Never had he been sought out by a beautiful woman, even a prostitute. She glided her fingers along his jaw, down his chest and brushed his crotch.

"Hmmm," she said. "Very sick, very needy."

He laughed, feeling caught between the hope and suspicion which accompanied his every new adventure, but he allowed her to take his hand, lead him to her hovel in La Perla. She reminded him of something wild, the mountains he so loved and now suddenly longed to see again. Earthy, she emanated the scent of wet grass and plants. Picturing them walking together hand-in-hand through the rain forest, El Yungue, he imagined the scents of sage, *yerbabuena* and *anamú*, which smelled to him like a combination of human perspiration and garlic. Mixed with that were *pachulí*, the base of some exotic perfumes, and *albahaca*, sweet basil, all of which filled his mind with images of rolling naked in dense foliage.

X

Rafaela

After her visit to Ana, Rafaela considered the change in her mother's fortune astounding. For many years Doña Antonia's life had been that of a stiff and formal woman ostracized by housewives who reluctantly answered her "Good day" with tight lips and suspicious glances at their husbands, some going so far as to place themselves bodily between Doña Antonia and their men or simply crossing to the other side of the street to avoid her when they saw her coming.

A small proud soul, she juggled a meager income composed of Rafaela's salary and her own from selling her hand-crocheted tablecloths, curtains, and doilies. Overnight, she became best friend to and consoler of none other than Francisca Ferrer, the richest spinster in Cataño and sister of the recently deceased Darío. Darío the pharmacist had suffered a heart attack and left them a bigger, better house closer to the church than to the pharmacy.

During the reading of the will, Rafaela whispered in her mother's ear. "I had no idea he liked me so much. I was usually rude to him."

"It was not you he liked," Doña Antonia replied.

Rafaela bugged her eyes and dropped her jaw as far as it would stretch. "Him? *He* was my father?"

"We'll move immediately," her mother continued, "and with the money I've saved, I'll fix up the house we live in now and rent it out."

"Is that yours too?" Rafaela asked, eyes still widened.

"At the time, it was all he could give me."

"Mamá, he was a rich man."

"No, the money belongs to Francisca."

"Why didn't he marry you?"

"Francisca didn't want to be alone and did not want to share a home with another woman. She threatened to disinherit him and take away his livelihood, the pharmacy."

"What about the rent money I've been giving you?"

Doña Antonia turned her beady eyes on Rafaela, "I need it because the girls are still young." Her tone and set of lip told Rafaela the conversation was at an end.

Over the next few weeks, Rafaela basked in the luxury of her own bedroom, tiled floors, indoor plumbing, and the thought that now Félix might look at her differently, now that she bought herself stylish new clothes and her mother and Francisca Ferrer paraded up and down the streets together arm in arm as if they had always been lifetime friends instead of women who had hated and ignored each other.

"Why are you such a big friend of the woman who wouldn't let her brother marry you?"

"That's all in the past now. She's sorry."

The new odd companions, Doña Antonia's short, squat body replacing Darío's alongside the man-sized Francisca.

Each new day brought surprises so Rafaela wondered what good thing had happened next when she arrived home from work on Monday evening and found her mother and sisters dressed for church and waiting on their new spacious balcony.

"Prepare yourself for bad news," they said. Five faces furrowed their eyebrows at Rafaela.

There was that unexpected feeling again. The weighty rock plunging down her abdomen.

"What?"

Light-haired América reached down behind her, lifted Edelmira for Rafaela to see. Tears streamed down América's face.

"It's Ana. She died. Your friend Luis Arriesgo brought Edelmira over here."

"Oh, my God!" Rafaela wailed. "When did she die and how?"

"This morning, just after you left for work."

"Oh, oh, oh." Rafaela beat her head with her fists and pulled her hair. "She was sick. She told me she was sick weeks ago and I was so busy with Darío's will and this new house that I didn't go to see her. Oh, oh, oh."

"Doña Antonia stepped forward, grabbed Rafaela's shoulders and shook her.

"Get a hold of yourself and listen. You have to investigate. The Monkey Man was pale. He shivered and cried. Edelmira was splattered with blood and now she just stares."

"Did you talk to Dr. Figueroa?"

"No," América answered. "He was too busy treating Waldemar Toledo at the hospital. He had an accident."

"What about Ana?"

"I went over there," Doña Antonia said. "Ana was so skinny she looked like she died of starvation but there was no blood. We don't know how the child got splattered."

"My God, maybe Ana's not even dead." Rafaela tried to rush out but they blocked her way. That and the child's crying stopped her. Edelmira reached out for Rafaela, crying, "Mamá, mamá." Her sobs tore through Rafaela like a vengeful whip.

Europa said, "She's really dead, Rafaela. When he returned from the hospital, Dr. Figueroa sent Ana's body to the funeral parlor." Then more gently, "That's how we know when she died. Dr. Figueroa says it happened early this morning. She had cancer of the pancreas."

"Edelmira is yours now," Doña Antonia said. "Good thing there's enough room here, don't you think?" The emphasis on the last three words, the implied triumphant sarcasm in the voice enraged Rafaela. The miserable old sow was glad! She was glad that Rafaela was saddled with a child. For years she put up with Rafaela's criticism and complaints and now that she felt she had come into her own she gloated!

"Yes," Rafaela said sweetly. "Thank God that Edelmira has me, a working woman with no other obligations." She kissed Edelmira, who sighed and fell asleep on her shoulder. "Think how difficult it would have been for her if Edelmira's godmother had been an illiterate woman with illegitimate children living off the sometimes generosity of a sometimes husband." Rafaela ran into her room before any of them said a word.

She slammed her doors and fell on her bed, crying. Edelmira slept but, in the morning, stared so vacantly that Rafaela went for help.

"She's too quiet, Dr. Figueroa," Rafaela said. "Not happy like before."

Rafael examined the five-year-old by looking into her eyes, testing her reflexes, taking her pulse, and listening to her heartbeat.

"She's healthy but is suffering from mild shock," he said. "She found her mother dead, you know. Keep her fed and stimulated during the day and make sure she sleeps well. In no time at all, she'll come out of it. If not, bring her back."

Outside the house, she found Luis waiting.

"How is she?" he asked.

"She's a bit sad and acts strange but she's going to be all right."

Luis sighed and trotted away. Rafaela thought he acted strange too. No jokes, no laughing, nothing. It was not like him. Then she remembered he found Ana's body and brought Edelmira to her house. "My God," she thought. He found a dead woman and an abandoned child, no wonder he behaved so oddly. It did not occur to her to wonder why he found Ana, what he was doing in their home, and how he had managed to walk the child over to her house. What did occur to her was that she, Rafaela Moya, was now mother to Edelmira Betancourt just as if she had given birth to her. As much as she loved the child she detested the responsibility.

XI

Félix

Gloating, Félix bought back his pearls. "You won't see me again." He shook his index finger at the pawnbroker.

"That's what you said last time," Don Pancho reminded him. He was a small slim, olive-skinned man with receding black hair. "If you do, the amount of the loan goes down while the repurchase price goes up."

"No, you'll see. I own quite a few houses now." As soon as he said that, Félix regretted it. He had taken such care that no one knew how much money he saved by banking far from San Juan so his partners not be apprised and demand back his portion of setting up practice. Well, nothing to do about it now. Besides, it was only fair that he pay them back for their help.

As he expected, it did not take Don Pancho long to spread the word that Félix owned many houses or said he did.

After he paid his partners, Félix bought the biggest house in Cataño, the only one with stables in back and a large safe to hold his ledgers. He did all his own accounting, loved to watch the figures grow, and estimated he had almost as much money and real estate as Bartolomeo.

"So, are you rich yet?" Bartolomeo, fat, chomped a smelly cigar. Félix waved at the smoky air.

"Not rich but not as poor as I used to be." On weekends he had worked hard on those early houses, fixing and rebuilding himself, selling at the right time, always at a sizeable profit. His early mistakes were always buying the pearls back too soon, afraid he might never see them again but now they were safe. He had lots of money saved, two houses ready for resale, one awaiting improvement and the best one fully paid for to live in. The pearls remained in safekeeping, having served their purpose for the time being. His father had been right. If he had sold the pearls for food all he would have ended up with was the end product of eating, excrement.

Félix began to relax his quest for riches, accepted invitations to the Casino of Puerto Rico. Instead of dressing in the black suits so fashionable among the elite, he elected the style of an earlier time when land barons ruled and wore white linen. At society balls, he heard himself called Don Félix and looked at all the women, thinking about a wife. Dinner invitations from the wealthy with daughters eligible for marriage fueled his pride and his hunger for the good life. His abdomen softened and he grew a belly to match that of his hosts. Whenever he considered marriage he thought of Rafaela but there was always an obstacle.

"Damn that Edelmira," Félix thought. A whiny, snotty little girl always begging Rafaela's attention with her needy blue eyes and turned down mouth. Félix hated that Rafaela carted her everywhere she went, worse than her sisters who at least had personality. América worked as a salesgirl, took drama lessons. Europa was a problem, though. The girl smiled every tooth in her head to any man she spotted, and the twins, well, the twins were Doña Antonia's problem.

Félix invited Rafaela to his home, alone. He did not understand why he did, or rather he did not know how she would take it. On and off they had been seeing each other through the years but never alone. Félix wondered if she behaved differently when not out in public. No, he knew better. Truthfully, he was just tired of waiting, tired of wanting her and not wanting her.

She arrived laughing at him. "So, evil intentions eh?" His face reddened but she smelled so good. She still reminded him of sweet, juicy fruit. Félix knew that was as close to desire as he could get. Years of cold showers and abstinence conditioned him so that he almost never got an erection except when Rafaela touched him. If it had not been for that, he might have wondered about himself as he suspected Bartolomeo and Diego wondered about him.

"Did anyone see you?" he asked.

"Come in here?"

"Yes." He asked doubting anyone could miss noticing a flapper in a silver dress with fringes.

"Worried about my reputation? Or yours?"

"Why are you dressed like that?"

"Like it?" She danced the Charleston, swaying the fringes on her dress. "Josie's relatives sent it to me."

"I understand you're dating Claudio Blanco."

"Are you going to duel him?"

"Duel?"

"Aren't you old-fashioned enough for that?"

"Why did you come here by yourself?"

"All right, that's it!" She wrenched off a silver glove, threw it on his couch and sat down. "No more questions. We're going to have a real conversation."

"Why have you cut your hair?"

"Stop it."

He sat down beside her. "You look beautiful."

"I know. Everybody tells me."

"Does Claudio tell you?"

"What do you care?"

"I was away on business."

"Two months? With no word? We're not engaged, we're not even acknowledged formally as a couple. What do you expect? That I'll wait forever?"

"It was business," he repeated. But he thought of the interest he had taken in a landowner's daughter, a refined young lady schooled in San Germán. "Has anything happened between you and Claudio?"

"Anything like what?" When he didn't answer, she pressed. "Say it!"

"Well, did . . ."

"Ffwwapp!" The blow spun his head, stunned him, and stopped his question. She hit him smack on his cheekbone, not with open palm or the back of her hand but with her fist.

"Thank you, Félix," she said. "I've been wanting to do that for a long time and didn't know it." She jumped up from the couch, ready to fight.

"You hit me," he said stupidly, holding his cheek.

"You hit me," she mimicked, hands on hips. "I should have punched you long ago, on our first date on the beach and on every date after that, every time you scowled or cringed at anything I said or did."

"I, never."

"You didn't have to say anything. It showed. You were so ashamed of me, you made me feel I couldn't do anything right. You, you textbook."

Still sitting dumbly, he looked up at her. She struggled not to laugh. "What's so funny?" he asked.

"You're not even angry that I hit you."

"Why did you call me a textbook?"

"I knew it." She slapped her forehead, sat down next to him giggling. "All you know is studying, thinking, and analyzing—anything to avoid feeling." She softened, put her arm around him, began stroking his face with her other hand, and ignored his look of alarm. "Do you have feelings, Félix?"

"Are you going to hit me again?"

She smiled, unbuttoned his shirt and stroked his chest in circular motion with her palms. "Answer me." She breathed close, kissed his lips.

"I love you," he said. Dizzied by her scent and his growing desire, he added, "I want you."

"I know," she said, pulling away. "But you can't have me until we're friends."

"Friends?" Angered, he grabbed her arm.

"Yes." She shook him off. "Treat me with the same respect you show your dumb friends and talk to me the same way you do them."

"Bartolomeo was right. You think you're a man."

"I know as much about politics, religion, and life as any man."

"Then why aren't you better off than you are?"

"Why aren't you?"

"I am well off. I'm getting rich and, and . . ." Tricked! Manipulated into talking too much. "Damn it Rafaela, you make me furious."

"Too bad," she said, putting on her gloves. She looked around. "You buy the biggest most expensive property near the bay road, no doubt to accommodate your big head, and want people to believe you're still poor?"

"I regret it. This house is too big to handle without servants or lights."

"Miguelito needs a job. He can take care of it for you."

"So your little friend can spy on me?"

"I don't have to spy on you." She patted his face. "I can just read you my little textbook."

"You don't know everything about me."

"Nor do you know everything about me."

"I can't stand this. It's worse than hard labor in the country. At least there something grows out of the ground for one's efforts."

"We have to start over Félix. Let's begin by talking, not fighting. We'll discuss important issues, take each other seriously." She stared, awaiting his answer.

"It is true," he thought. She had a good mind, was always well informed, and had opinions, even if he did not agree with them. He would listen to these in the future. God knows, maybe it was a way out. Any and all discussions were bound to deteriorate into battle lines with fathomless trenches between them, and then he could free himself from her by sheer number of fights.

"You win. We start over. I'll call on you. You serve me coffee or tea and we'll talk about anything you wish."

Her eyes widened. "Really?" She pounced on him, her arms around his neck. "And you'll hire Miguelito?"

"I can use the kid around the house."

"You won't regret it, you'll see. His family is really bad off and he'll work hard." They kissed. It lasted too long. The hardness of his body welded her to him and the yielding softness of hers inflamed him. His hands explored her, spreading the fire. Harsh breathing filled the room until she pushed him away gasping, stared, and fled home.

Floor tiles felt cool and smooth on his bare feet as Félix walked the length of his home to his back yard to make sure Rafaela arrived at her home safely. Her silver flapper's dress shimmered as its fringes glinted in the moonlight. Another play of light, across his street, caught his eye. He looked as slits of light from partly shuttered windows narrowed and disappeared. Then he watched all nearby houses and discovered neighboring busybodies spying. He shrugged. Nothing had happened. Nothing. Still, as Rafaela turned a corner out of his sight, he wondered how many others hid to watch Rafaela tiptoe into her own home.

Three days later, Félix answered a knock on his door and found baggage at his doorstep. A distance away, Miguelito stood in whispered conversation with his mother, Tomasa the flower seller. She stared hard at her son and handed him a white carnation before she left and Miguelito turned to Félix.

Noting his pursed lips and face, Félix asked, "What's the matter?"

"Everybody's saying she's a whore because she visited here alone late at night."

"Nothing happened," Félix said. "I respect her."

"When she reached her house, neighbors saw lights and heard screaming. Now gossip against Rafaela rages like a hurricane."

"Who the hell is saying what?" Félix felt furious enough to confront the evil tongues.

"My mother first overheard the ferry man talking and laughing about it with his assistants. Then she heard the women criticizing from their balconies. It's all over the barber shops."

"There are too many stupid people on this earth. Best to ignore them rather than to give them importance."

Sour-faced, Miguelito brought in his bag, gently closed the door to Félix's big house, and inhaled deeply, eyes troubled.

XII
Juan

There was no moon that night and fog dimmed the stars.

At the stroke of midnight a small robed figure, cupping a lantern, furtively looked back through the black, deserted streets, rounded a corner, opened the gate to the Flower Street house, and tapped on a bedroom window facing the balcony.

"Psst. Let me in." The whisper was soft and low.

Juan Peña, awakened earlier by the smell of incense and candle wax, quietly unlocked the door, nodded, and stepped aside. His visitor's face hid behind the veil of a nun's habit. Through the disguise, the spirit medium recognized his caller.

"A strong love potion, please."

"For you?"

"No. Félix must marry Rafaela."

The love potion for the requested ritual would ordinarily have taken him two days of gathering certain flowers, soaking them, and reciting incantations, but he had most of the ingredients at hand already prepared so that he simply mixed them together in greater strengths.

After his client left, Juan noticed the white cloth of the nun's habit left carelessly in a heap on the floor. He rushed out the door and stopped himself before he called, "Wait! You forgot . . ."

It would not do to yell into the streets at night. Instead, he opened his Bible to read First Corinthians 13:4–7.

"Love is long-suffering and kind. Love is not jealous, it does not brag . . . get puffed up . . . behave indecently . . . look for its own inter-ests . . . become provoked . . . keep account of the injury. . . . It rejoices with the truth . . . bears all things, believes, hopes, endures all things."

Juan felt privileged to witness a real-life demonstration of the defini-tion of pure, unselfish love.

XIII
Rafaela

Rafaela and Edelmira's combined weight worried the hooks inexpertly hammered into the walls for the hammock supporting them. Barefoot, wearing a plain cotton dress, Rafaela glanced from the hooks to Edelmira, in her underwear, stretched out and snoring softly next to her. She fluffed Ede's pearly white hair.

"This is really quite comfortable," she said aloud. "And cool."

She felt air circulating beneath the sturdy netting which swayed slightly with every move she made. Once she became accustomed to the sensation of floating on tranquil waters, she relaxed, dozed, and dreamed, her subconscious comparing the revolutionary Harvard graduate with Félix.

Small and dark, the Ponceño, Pedro Albizu Campos rivalled Félix in intellect but surpassed his patriotic determination. Both lawyers, Pedro demanded violent revolt for independence, freedom now, with no compromises.

"Patriotism," he said with a poet's intensity, "means valor and sacrifice."

Félix contented himself with whatever opportunities presented immediate benefits and worked to establish himself in a comfortable niche of money and political power without responsibility to the community.

In her dream, two fish lived under the sea. Pedro, a lone, small barracuda zealously swam nonstop in murky blue waters to target and attack bigger fish invading his territory. Félix, a flat, white flounder, swam out of the way to nibble seaweed here and there, counted on getting too fat, too big to be swallowed up, hoped to become a swallower himself eventually.

Among a school of tiny fish hiding in underwater plants, she turned her head first to one, then to the other. The small man's bubbling fervor both lured and scared Rafaela. His ardent speeches incited reckless hatreds to rush, ill-prepared, into a war that endangered her situation, her family. She recoiled and drifted toward the flounder.

"You've worked so hard," Félix said. "Do you want to lose it now for who knows how many generations?"

As she swam to the safety of the flounder's shadow, Pedro disappeared in the shadow of a shark.

Rafaela opened her eyes, disgusted with herself, and looked at Edelmira still snoring softly. Keen pangs of regret assailed her that she lacked both enough talent to lead and enough hatred to follow through on revolutionary idealogy. "It's all right," she thought, "to believe in valor and sacrifice if you have enough to eat or can sustain a fighting mood far enough to sacrifice your life."

I can't do it. I just don't have the courage to martyr myself and my family to the fight for independence.

Whenever the opportunity naturally presented itself she would voice her opinions, stand up for them even, but she felt too many obligations pulling at her. She dug her fingers through her hair hard as a bit of guilt and shame struck her. She wanted a better life but she wanted it to come easily and that troubled her.

Why did Rodríguez have to enflame her with his talk? And why, for God's sake, had Albizu Campos written to her during his travels? Her life would be so much simpler if she just did not think about these impossible dreams.

"Get up," she said, to awake Edelmira. "This was a stupid experiment."

"Why? I liked sleeping like a *campesina*."

"No, you only think you like it. You don't know what you're talking about. Those poor country women work like mules their whole life for almost nothing at all and then they die young for their trouble."

"But 'Fela . . ." Ede's red-rimmed blue eyes annoyed Rafaela.

"Shut up, be good, and forgive me for filling your head with *mierda*."

Her sister América, fifteen, and Edelmira, five, silently watched her take down the hammock. América's dainty features suited her slimness.

"Don't you two have something else to take care of?" She dropped the hammock and folded it into a chest of drawers. "Why hang around watching everything I do?"

Europa came in and glanced at América who immediately took Edelmira's hand and left the bedroom.

"Do you want something or is it your turn to watch me?"

"I need some money."

"Why don't you ask your mother?"

Europa looked down, pouted her lips to cover her mouth and fidgeted. She believed her overbite marred her dark good looks.

"Don't you want to know why I need it?"

"You want to pull out your teeth and get false ones." Rafaela rasped loud unpleasant laughter, then sniffed at a pile of dirty clothes. She looked at her small-boned sister and stopped sorting her laundry. Europa's dark eyes, pained, pleaded with her. "What's wrong?"

She burst into tears. "I'm pregnant."

Rafaela knew she had not heard wrong but the words polluted her senses so that she felt blind, deaf, and unable to think for split seconds.

"Like mother, like daughter," she said, realizing the stupidity of her own words. "Go tell Mamá when she returns from church with the twins because I'm not going to do it."

"Please, Rafaela." Europa's tears streamed down her face. "I don't want to have a baby."

"What do you want me to do?"

"Take me somewhere to get rid of it."

"You think Dr. Figueroa is going to do this?"

"No, but you must know someone."

"How would I . . ." Rafaela's mouth dropped.

So. No wonder every man she met tried to sleep with her, especially Claudio Blanco. Dates with him started out badly, with his constant insinuations about the pleasures of fleshly love, and ended disastrously with him trying to force himself on her by brushing her breasts and tightening his grip on her wrists when she refused to kiss him. If her own family doubted her virtue as her sister's question about her possible association with anyone who could terminate a pregnancy implied, how could outsiders do otherwise? And Félix had asked those questions. She had slapped him for thinking what she now suspected everybody else thought. Rafaela gritted her teeth.

"You little whore." She grabbed Europa's thick curly hair, slapped her face, punched her chest, and kicked her backside. Europa covered herself, crying softly, but she did not defend herself. They stood apart panting at each other until Rafaela remembered how much she had wanted Félix and pitied her sister. "You don't even have a boyfriend. Whose is it?"

Europa covered her face. "I don't know."

"How can you not know?"

"There were many."

Despite the heat, chills made her skin crawl.

"How many? No, God, don't tell me. Any chance one will marry you?"

"Some are already married. Some are too young."

"Where? How?"

"Here. When nobody's home. You and América are working, Mamá's out with her friend Francisca, and the twins are in school."

"When did this start?"

"I began to sneak home from school after lunch when I was eleven." At Rafaela's expression, Europa lowered her head and looked at her feet. "This is the first time I've gotten caught."

Rafaela sputtered and sat on her bed atop the pile of soiled clothing.

"You've been sleeping with different men since you were eleven?"

Europa wiped her eyes and stopped crying.

"It gives me great pleasure. I love sex. I'm just not ready for children." She looked at Rafaela. "Men like it. Why not me?"

"Because you're fourteen not a thirty-year-old woman of the night. You don't want Mamá to know?"

"No. You know how she is. She thinks it was all different with her. She was in love, she stuck to one man."

"Well, I know for sure Dr. Figueroa won't help you to miscarry a child. Give me some time to think."

"I don't have much time."

Remembering the exchange of glances between her sisters and that América had taken Edelmira out of the room, she asked, "Does América know?"

"Yes, I told her."

"What did she say?"

"Nothing. She laughed."

Rafaela rose from her bed and walked through their living room to step onto the sunlit patio where América sat with Edelmira on their white metal furniture. Both ate, more like slurped, overripe mangoes. Edelmira's face shone with its sticky orange juice.

"Go wash up, Ede." The tiny little girl left to obey, holding sticky hands up in the air. América turned to face her.

"Do you know about Europa?"

"Of course. She told me, and if she hadn't, it had to happen sooner or later." América wiped her hands on her dress.

"Have you always known?"

"Everybody knows," América said, rising from under the shade of their mango tree. "I first heard about it when I was still in school. From the boys."

"And Mamá?"

"She thinks we're all like you but worries about Félix."

"What do you mean like me?" Rafaela's anger heated her face.

Her sister's delicate lips parted into a smile. "Like you, a prude." She laughed. Relief flooded Rafaela.

"I thought everybody considered me a whore."

América sobered. "They do. Everybody thinks you and Félix have made love. Everybody except me and Mamá."

Rafaela's eyes stung. She felt walloped.

"I'm a virgin."

"We know." Sweaty and smelling of sunshine, América embraced her, tried to dry Rafaela's tears with the edge of her dress. "But all your friends are men. The way you talk and dress, all give off a wrong impression."

"Then how do you know it's not true?"

"You're too clumsy about everything. Even if you did it and didn't say, I'd still be able to tell."

Rafaela ruffled América's hair and felt love for her sister.

"You're a virgin, aren't you?" Her sister did not answer. "América?"

"I'm finished," Edelmira interrupted. Her little face was still moist. They both looked down at her. "Europa's taking me to the beach."

"NO," they shouted at once, startling the child. Then they looked at each other and laughed, but Rafaela remained very quiet for the rest of the day, thinking about her dream and wondering what to do.

That evening, after dinner, she washed and dressed a very tired Edelmira and announced she was taking a walk through town and then to the plaza. Instead, she headed for Félix's house.

Miguelito opened the door, ecstatic to see her. "Miss Rafaela! Come in, come in." His white teeth shone against his sepia complexion. He was wearing oversized butler's clothes.

Rafaela cackled. "What's this?" She fingered his jacket. Pleased, the teenager turned around to show her how he looked. "Very nice but you're going to have to gain about 20 kilos before that monkey suit fits." They laughed.

"Who is that?" Félix came running downstairs wearing a smoking jacket over his pajamas. "Who are you letting into my house?"

Rafaela nudged Edelmira to step forward.

"Hello, Uncle Félix," she said, curtsying.

Félix stopped dead with his protest as Rafaela knew he would and stared at them.

"Hello, Uncle Félix," Rafaela repeated. "We were in the neighborhood and thought we'd stop by to see you. Didn't we, Ede?"

Schooled in advance, Edelmira said, "Yes, Uncle Félix, we have some-thing to tell you."

"I don't want to hear another word about the Nationalist Party and I'm not your uncle." Stricken, Edelmira threatened tears. He picked her up, kissed her, and gave her a nickel. "Look upon me as your godfather not your uncle." She kissed him back and hugged him while he glared at Rafaela. "What nerve to visit at this ungodly hour when a man is in his pajamas."

"And very elegant pajamas too," Rafaela said and sat, uninvited. "Miguelito, what long hours you work."

"Oh no, Miss Rafaela, Don Félix allows me to live here."

"Does he?" Her right eyebrow arched. "Isn't that just wonderful of Don Félix." She opened her eyes wide and emphasized the Don.

"Hummpff. He knows you got him the job." Félix sat Edelmira on a couch, gestured to Miguelito who went into the kitchen to prepare snacks, and faced Rafaela. "What are you doing here?"

"Aren't you glad to see me?"

He checked Edelmira's attentive blue eyes before he answered.

"I'm so glad you brought your chaperon or else people might get the wrong idea. Know what I mean?"

Rafaela patted her hair and fought back tears. Félix cared about her reputation. All along she had thought he did not want anyone to know they dated because he was ashamed of her background.

"Your concern touches me." She faced him. "You were right. I'm staying out of politics until I know more about it and can think with my head instead of my heart." She saw his face soften.

"And no more listening to that crazy man from Ponce?"

Unexpectedly, she felt the urge to shout, cry out that Pedro was not crazy, that Puerto Rico needed more like him, but she remembered her earlier decision and modulated her voice.

"Didn't you once want independence?"

"Yes, but now I want statehood." He waved his hands. "It's too late for independence. We can't win a war with the United States and they'll never release us voluntarily."

"They have no right here!" She screamed, chagrined that she could not totally make up her mind. Her problems forced her to lower her voice. "You're right. Nobody cares; Albizu Campos will get no support."

"Crusaders usually do not. He scares too many with his romantic notions and is more likely to get himself and his followers arrested or killed."

"Why?"

"Except for a few fanatics who will die for him, he'll probably be betrayed by those who don't want their values and beliefs changed. Even the autonomists know more about politics than he does. Their speeches support the thinking and attitudes of the majority and that's why they will be voted into office."

Closing her eyes in frustration and defeat, Rafaela said, "You're right."

"Miguelito," Félix called. "Bring us some champagne. We're celebrating."

Edelmira yawned, said, "I'm sleepy."

"Soon you can sleep," Félix told her, "but first you must be very grown up and drink some champagne."

Miguelito returned with slices of grilled beef, fried chicken, avocado slices, and chunks of soft-crust bread. Proudly, he laid the steaming, garlicky platter on the dining table, smiled, and brought out the French import.

"How do you do it?" Rafaela asked, looking at the contraband wine.

"Same way as always. Grease the right palm and all eyes look the other way. It's our history."

"You're so smart, Félix."

Puffed, Félix offered the first sip to Edelmira. "See, it tickles your nose."

"Ugh." She yawned, slumped on the couch and closed her eyes.

Rafaela watched as Félix ate with gusto. "Didn't you already have dinner?"

"Yes but this is a celebration. No arguments."

"No wonder you've gained weight. You must celebrate a lot." She turned her head. "Miguelito! You'll probably fill out that suit in no time."

The young man laughed but Félix's look told her she needed discretion. "The weight suits you. You look mature, virile."

"You can't trick me. I'm not falling for your teasing."

"I'm not teasing," she said laughing. "I think you look . . . well, you look . . ."

"Stop it!" he hissed. Miguelito quickly cleaned up and asked permission to retire to his room.

"Certainly," Félix said. "Miss Rafaela and Edelmira will be leaving soon. I'll lock up after them." Miguelito left.

"I want to be as smart as you," Rafaela said. She wanted to say, as smug as you.

"You're never like this. What do you want?"

"Why are you so suspicious?"

"I've seen that look in court. On the faces of the women who sue for breach of promise or instigate paternity suits."

It startled Rafaela that Félix had come so close to the truth of her secret.

"But we're not in court now." She moved closer.

"Get away and go home. We can talk at a more appropriate time."

"You're such a prude, Félix."

"And you're not?" He slapped away her fingers tickling his face. "Stop touching me."

"Do you know about prophylactics?"

"What?" Open-mouthed, he let his guard down and she kissed him.

"I love you," she whispered.

"You've never said that before." His face softened.

"But you know it's true." She brushed her lips against his cheek. "We love each other." His body melted and then stiffened.

"Go home. Go home right now. It's too late and we're not alone."

"I'll take Edelmira home and sneak back."

"Yes." He made a wry face. "Do that."

"I'll throw rocks up at your window."

"Right, right." He waved her away with his hand.

Because Edelmira was so petite, Rafaela easily carried her back home. She did not awaken as Rafaela removed her clothes and put her to bed. Rafaela visualized the surprise on Félix's face when she returned. She knew he only agreed so that she would leave his house. He did not believe it, did not expect her to return. She went through the motions of undressing, washing, setting up her mosquito net, and getting into bed.

Her heart beat in her ears while she watched the moon rise. She did not think it difficult to dress quietly and sneak out of the house but needed the nerve to do it. Once she got near Félix, it would be easy. She remembered the quiver that had stayed with her for days after she had refused him before. Rafaela tried to rationalize that her sister Europa needed her help, dismissed that thought, and admitted, "Why am I saving my virginity and for whom? It has always been Félix, will always be Félix, and he'll never marry anyone, sex or no sex." She sneaked out.

The sandals Rafaela chose made soft crunching sounds on the graveled streets. Félix opened the back door after the first pebble at his window. His light had been on.

He whispered. "I didn't believe you'd return."

"I know." They embraced. He picked her up and carried her up the stairs, slowly, quietly.

The size of his bedroom impressed her. A huge colonial bed with posters, three mattresses, and a customized mosquito net serving as a canopy. A matching mirrored dresser to one side and a large mahogany trunk at the foot of the bed along with a small round table and two chairs, all fit comfortably in the room.

The mosquito net was tucked in on every side except one. There, it was rolled back on itself over the top. On the table stood a second bottle of champagne and two wine glasses. In the middle of his dresser was the lamp she had seen from outside and an open law book and some papers with notations.

They kissed gently, shyly. He stroked her arms, her back, kissed her cheeks, her neck, ran his hands over her breasts. His hardness fluttered her abdomen. She moaned. Her firm flesh, warm and soft, crazed him with impatience. Their kisses became urgent, hard, and breathless. With a volition of its own, her body rubbed against his. He ripped off his pajamas, undressed her gently, but the sight of her breasts, small and full with pink tips on pointed brown nipples, roughened him. He paused, suckled her nipples, kissed her stomach, and removed her underwear.

"Wait," she said, panting. "I'm scared."

He pressed atop her, kissing her all over until he could wait no more. As quickly as he could, he pulled a rubber on his penis, parted her legs, and took her, hard. He felt a give and continued to rock against her.

She hurt but above the pain felt an urgency, her body needed and craved him. Her tension and need climbed until she experienced her first orgasm. When she whispered it in his ear, he thrust against her until he too sated his desire. They hugged and kissed, professing their love. For a long time, they did not stir. Then he moved off her and lay next to her. She tried not to notice that the first thing he did was look down at himself.

He smiled and kissed the tips of her fingers.

"My angel, my love."

"What if I hadn't been a virgin?"

"Shush." He licked her lips. "It would have been because of me." He licked her neck.

She giggled. "No wonder you're gaining weight and getting a belly. Do you think I'm food?"

"Yes." He took her again. More slowly. So slowly she was frantic by the time he entered her, and he had to put his hand over her mouth when she reached a second climax. He shuddered at the intensity of his own.

"Look at your sheets," she said.

He went to the bathroom, returned with a towel over his shoulder and a washbowl filled with water. Soap floated in the middle. She had already poured the champagne. He washed her like a baby, stopping to kiss wherever he washed.

"The sun's going to come out before you finish. Here drink this." She handed him a glass of champagne.

Félix thought it flat and warm. "Ooey," he said. "Edelmira was right."

"It's been open a long time," she said, gulping her drink. She dressed.

He dressed too, kissed her good night, and watched from his back door as she walked home.

Rafaela felt sore and swollen but she had no regrets. The revelation had come slowly but it had arrived. They had known each other too many years now for her to have any illusions. She knew Félix would not marry her no matter how much he loved her and she did not care because she knew he would never marry anyone else either. His heart belonged to her and hers to him. She tiptoed into her house, waited for her eyes to adjust to the dark. Did she hear the floorboards squeak? A shadow moved in her bedroom and fear gripped her. Her breathing accelerated and her heart throbbed in her ears at the thought of a confrontation with her mother. Paralyzed, she stood still for minutes. When nothing else moved and all she heard was soft snoring, she tiptoed into her room and climbed into her bed beside Edelmira.

Folktale III

Juan Bobo Ofendido

Simple Simon Offended

A long, long time ago there lived a simple boy. Skinny but good-looking, Juan Bobo took a wife at age eighteen. Simple but not stupid, he married by bringing the girl and her bundled belongings to his mother and saying, "Here's my wife. When do we eat?"

His mother wondered what kind of woman could accept her son as a husband and decided the young lady must be new to the area and did not know about his baby brother, the school, and much, much more, so she resolved to keep quiet and give the marriage an opportunity to succeed. To feed the extra mouth, his mother took in more laundry which the two women washed and ironed.

Juan Bobo's job was to ride a mule loaded down with a basket of the clean clothes to return them to their owners. Atop the clothes rested a piece of wood two feet wide by four feet in length just in case of thieves. While making his deliveries he spoke to everyone he met, whether he knew them or not, using his mother's phrases.

"Good morning."

"Go with God."

"Good afternoon."

"God bless you."

One day a man on horseback responded with, "Hola, guapo."

Juan Bobo scratched his head at this unfamiliar greeting and began his thinking process aloud.

"A man who calls another man handsome must be a sissy. A sissy gets called handsome by other men. That man called me a sissy."

Offended by the insult, Juan Bobo raced his mule after the man, caught up, and bashed him on the head with his two-by-four. Knocked off his horse, the man fell and lay on the ground senseless.

Abandoning the basket of clean clothes, Juan Bobo returned home with eyebrows furrowed over murderous eyes and paced back and forth flailing his arms and complaining to his wife until he told his mother what happened.

"No, child," she said. "City people use different expressions than we do. Spaniards always call each other guapo, guapa, lindo, linda, rey, or reina. Never become so offended at anything that your temper dominates you. Better to do nothing and stay quiet, or else you can hurt or even kill an innocent person."

"Say, 'Hello, handsome'," Juan Bobo told his wife.

"Hello, handsome," she repeated, blushing.

Somehow, Juan Bobo still did not like it one bit.

Part
Three

The supreme definition is under discussion: Yankee or Puerto Rican?—Pedro Albizu Campos

There were too many people seeking shelter during the storm. No one was doing anything and the situation was desperate. I took a hammer, broke open the doors and let the people in. Someone had to do it.—Felisa Rincón de Gautier, on obtaining shelter for approximately 3,000 people

Félix

Félix did not change the sheets. He laid in the smell of their love-making, suspended, neither awake nor asleep. Unaware that his mind was a blank or even that he was not sleeping, he remained open-eyed the rest of the night, perspiring under his mosquito net canopy, hearing a multitudinous chorus of Puerto Rico's tiny frogs named after the sound they make. Motionless, he listened to their loud soprano call of "*Co-quí, co-quí*" until daybreak when, abruptly, the concert of the little frogs halted.

A few hours later he giggled in his office when he realized he had forgotten to wear socks. He showed his feet to Diego. After years of playing down his relationship with Rafaela, he impulsively decided he no longer cared who knew. "Perhaps it was a good thing," he thought. They could marry after all. Instead of working on his legal papers, Félix smiled, drew lines and arrows on his note book.

"Did you swallow the moon last night?" Bartolomeo asked, blowing cigar smoke.

"W-What?" Félix stammered, dizzy, distracted.

"What's wrong with you?" Bartolomeo looked down at his doodling. "Are you in love?"

"Yes. That's it."

"Who is she?" Diego and Bartolomeo leaned forward on Félix's desk, peered into his face. "When did you meet her?"

"Rafaela." Félix giggled nervously.

"Rafaela? Are you mad?" Bartolomeo crushed out his cigar. Diego stepped back pensively. "How can you suddenly be crazy in love with your mistress?"

"Well, I, I, . . ."

"FÉLIX!" Bartolomeo grabbed him by the shoulders, shaking him. "Control yourself. She has 'given you water' and turned you into a babbling idiot."

"What? Water? N-no, it can't be. Not Rafaela." He shook his head slowly. "She wouldn't do that." Félix believed he was just having an unusual day but could not explain that to Bartolomeo because his mind felt giddy, as if he could not think or plan seriously.

"Leave him alone," Diego said. "Things change. Who cares if she doesn't come from a good family?"

Bartolomeo glared at Diego. "Our friends care. You haven't been clear-headed since your brother Waldemar died. That's understandable but we have to think now." He turned to Félix.

"Listen, you have to go see Juan the grave digger immediately. It might not be too late."

"Superstitious nonsense." Diego said.

"Your parents go to him, don't they?" Diego did not answer Bartolomeo. The entire town had seen his mother, distraught over the loss of her favorite son, go to visit Juan Peña.

"She's given you water," Bartolomeo insisted.

"All right. I'll go." Félix tried to concentrate. Yes, a woman did such things to a man if he was particularly desirable and he refused to marry her. It was a practice referred to as "giving a man water," but it was not plain water. It was specially prepared. He trembled to think that his red-cheeked Rafaela with her hazel eyes, in her impatience to marry him, might have given him tea, coffee, or lemonade voodooed after having washed her private parts with it. He woke up a bit. *The champagne!*

He went to see Juan Peña. Fear and embarrassment tortured him. The waiting room was filled with strangers. Still, Félix felt uncomfortable, believed they knew him or might know of him and would talk, tell others where they had seen him. He watched their humble faces for signs of contempt for considering himself better than them, glad he was getting his comeuppance, but no one glanced his way. Each was lost in his own problems. He fanned himself with a perfumed handkerchief, removed his Panama hat, and wiped the perspiration off his forehead and moustache until it was his turn to go into the room from where, occasionally, screams were emitted. A divider wall did not quite reach the ceiling.

Carmela motioned Félix into a side door at the front left of their waiting room. "Just in time," Félix thought. He had gone to Juan's house directly from his office, without eating, and a lingering aroma of their dinner, the spicy, starchy smell of garlicky Spanish rice and fried sweet bananas made his mouth water. As he moved his growing paunch past Carmela's scent of coconut oil, he wanted to take a bite out of her luscious brown arm.

He entered the room, closed the door behind him as the others had done, and stood still just inside until his eyes adjusted to the dimness. Two small white candles glimmered at either end of a rectangular table covered with a white tablecloth. In the middle a red rose lay tossed near a large goldfish bowl filled with clear water. Cigar smoke wafted to him. Juan Peña sat at the head of the table, visible in the dark because of his white *guayabera* and white pants.

"Sit down, Félix. There, at the opposite end of the table."

He sat not knowing what was going to happen, tried to peek under the table at Juan's feet, fascinated that the man was as comfortable walking on sun-baked gravel, sand, and rocks as on muddy roads and graves. Briefly, it occurred to him that both Diego and Bartolomeo might be hiding under the table, laughing at him.

From a rum bottle on the floor to his left Juan took a swig, swished it around in his mouth and spat into a spittoon near his right foot. Multicolored bandannas, a rosary, a crucifix, and some palm fronds lay on the table near Juan.

"Put your hands on the table," he said, "palms down, close your eyes, and meditate on your problem."

Through his daze Félix, surprised, asked, "D-Don't you want to know what it is?"

"No. The spirits will tell me."

Uneasy, Félix did as he was told, afraid that from nowhere a live chicken might suddenly come clucking and flying to peck him on the head. Or worse, that a demon might arise to skewer him like a suckling pig for what happened to his father. He tried to think quietly for a few minutes, began to fall asleep, and was startled awake by Juan Peña's spirit guide who spoke in a deep growl with an African accent.

"Let the peace of God be here," the spirit guide said. The medium waved his hands on either side of his head in a circular motion. Candle-light flickered an eerie rose color onto his glistening black face and reflected off his gold teeth. "Put your hands over the bowl of water," he said, his voice back to normal.

Félix stood, walked to the middle of the table, put both hands palms down over the bowl. Juan's face contorted as an evil spirit possessed him. It spoke in a whine.

"Why have you brought me here?" it asked. "I haven't finished my work until you're under the thumb of the woman."

Félix felt ants in his hair.

Carmela slipped quietly into the room, said, "Repent and return to your proper place with these other spirits who will show you the way to a great enlightenment."

"No," the spirit said. "I don't want to go."

"You have to," Carmela insisted. "Your place is not among the living." Félix listened, holding his breath throughout a long pause.

"I'm being told I've done wrong," the spirit said. "I've interfered in this man's life, must stop and ask forgiveness for any harm I've caused."

"Félix," Carmela commanded, "tell the spirit you forgive it."

He felt foolish but said, "I forgive you. Now go away, go away for-ever." He shooed at Juan with his hands.

"I'm going but I'm leaving a message with the medium. Good-bye, good-bye, and may God forgive me."

Juan's African spirit guide reentered him with the same fluttering hand motions to cleanse him of any lingering effects of the evil spirit, and Juan then returned to himself, puffed cigar smoke all around Félix, swished some more rum in his mouth, and spat once again into the spittoon. He said, "The love spell was very strong. Here's what you must do. . . ."

Félix left, doubtful as to how to follow the instructions Juan gave him. He felt exactly the same about Rafaela and told his partners.

"Take a trip," Bartolomeo suggested, "until your head clears. Don't write to her. Remember the last two times you went away? She dated Claudio and then she got chummy with the undesirable independence crowd."

Diego, previously scolded by Bartolomeo, said, "If you want a political career you really cannot marry Rafaela. She's unstable. You can't even take her to society functions because you can't control her ranting over freedom."

Félix stared at his partners. They were telling him what he himself knew, thought, and agreed with.

"So what," he said, rebelling. "How important are these things?"

Bartolomeo exhaled cigar smoke in Diego's direction.

"For him, not important at all." He pointed a fat finger at Félix and then at himself. "For us, very important and you know it."

Félix groaned at the many times her rude laughter embarrassed him. He could not help feeling lessened by the poor opinion of his peers and felt strongly that he would be judged by his choice just as harshly as he evaluated others by the same measure. His uncle's old injunction rang in his memory. *Tell me who you walk with and I'll tell you who you are.*

"I love Rafaela," he said, lamely.

"We don't doubt that."

"Because of our long courtship, I owe her something."

"Then give her your famous stolen pearls." Bartolomeo and Diego both guffawed. "But not a wedding band."

His face reddened but he noted they enjoyed the joke, did not hold his old ruse against him. "The hell with them," he thought. *Back to Rafaela.*

With her, the words love and marriage began a carousel in his mind. First love then marriage circled slowly, began to go round faster, alternated front and back, drew close and moved further apart but never side by side. He made up his mind. If this did not break up their relationship forever, he would, a few years hence, give her the pearls.

"I'm going to Europe on business," he told her that evening.

"Again? What about us?"

"I'll be back." He kissed her.

"Félix, can you give me a loan before you go?"

"What for?"

"Ede needs new clothes and my sisters are so jealous I can't get her anything without buying them something too. I don't have enough."

"I didn't know that," he said, indignantly. "Why didn't you tell me before?"

"Up to now, your gifts of meats and foods were shared by everybody, but now we all need something different. Ede and the twins need new clothes, América's gotten it into her head that she wants to go to New York to act, and Europa cries she'll never marry unless she fixes her teeth."

Generous, he gave her extra for herself and packed his bags feeling both relieved and surprised that she did not put up more of a fuss at his leaving so abruptly.

Instead of going directly to Europe as he told Rafaela, he crossed the island diagonally toward the southwest to reach its Caribbean side, deciding to wait for word from his colleagues at a friend's home near Phosphorescent Bay at La Parguera.

On brightly sunlit days, he feasted his eyes on the serene and multicolored water, with its changing swirls of pale green, deeper green, aqua, and, in some spots where vegetation grew underneath, lavender to purple. On cloudy nights, when moon light did not filter through, billions of microorganisms living in the water turned the calm waves of the Caribbean into a shimmering patchwork of white brilliance.

The beauty and variety of his island filled him with pride and helped him understand Rafaela's fierce protection of it. Briefly, he felt tempted to follow her lead and fantasized running for political office as a Nationalist then quickly discarded the idea as ridiculous.

The gentle, rolling murmur of the multicolored sea during daylight hours and its transformation to liquid diamonds at night soothed his anxiety and indecision about her until he received a letter on copper-colored stationery written with Bartolomeo's large, looped script.

Félix,

Sorry to tell you but Rafaela and Europa visited Dr. Rodríguez. A few days later, we saw her in San Juan and in Cataño with her sister América, in the company of some Hawaiian actors who arrived with Hilda Cray to make a movie here titled Aloha from the South Seas. *Diego saw them on another occasion walking and talking near the dock with the actors and the writer, but, as far as we know, Rafaela is not going to star in any movie.*

Yours,

In a rage, he departed to travel through Spain, Portugal, and Morocco writing only to Diego and Bartolomeo, telling them not to send more news of Rafaela.

In a Madrid cafe, he sat reading and rereading the note, which had become so soft from handling that it looked wet. Thoughtfully, Félix tore the letter into eight pieces. What did Bartolomeo mean "in the company of?"

"Bad news?"

He turned his head to a Spanish lady sitting at the next table; a sophisticated woman to judge by her hairstyle and by the cigarette she smoked from a holder. Though possessing a very high forehead, she wore her short hair in a cap of waves sculpted tightly to her head. Rising and removing his hat, he approached her table.

"At first I thought so," he said, smiling. "But now I'm not sure. While it did not exactly contain good news, it has brought me the good fortune of making your acquaintance."

Rodríguez

Ecstatic, Dr. Rodríguez prepared to meet Rafaela. His first thought when she requested to speak to him was, "She knows!" and, if she acknowledged him as her father, he prepared to write her into his will. That she arrived with a sulky toothy sister did not deter his desire to be sure.

"Rafaela!" He held out both arms to embrace her. "So good to see your lovely face again."

She smiled and patted his back as she hugged him. "Good to see you again too."

"So do you know who your father is?"

The sisters both seemed taken aback by his question.

"He's dead," Rafaela said, with a curious look on her face.

"Is that what your mother told you?"

"It's what we know. When he died, he left us a house in his will."

Annoyance prickled him. "Who?"

"Don Darío Ferrer the pharmacist from Cataño."

Darío! He remembered. That was the name of the idiot that Doña Antonia had muttered upon awakening from the drug that he had given her. Furious, Rodríguez rose to his feet.

"Why are you here?"

"My sister needs your help. I can pay generously and would consider it a great personal favor."

He looked at Europa. Yes, a little mother except with olive skin and fuller lips but the same big teeth and big nose. He laughed. "What kind of help?" He did not intend letting them round the issue discreetly.

"Elimination of a pregnancy." Rafaela stared openly into his face as she had so many times during her childhood.

Again he felt regret that she was not his, that he had been wrong. "Who knows you're here?"

"No one. We're supposed to be traveling to do Félix Cienfuegos a favor."

"Ah. All right get the little, uh, Europa into my infirmary." He led the way. Europa undressed and lay prone on the cot. "You can wait outside," he said to Rafaela.

"No, I'll wait right here, thank you. She needs my moral support."

"It's not pretty."

"You know I have a strong stomach."

"As you say." He laughed. Nobody he knew had a strong stomach least of all this young woman who thought herself tough. He chloroformed Europa. To get more information from Rafaela, he shielded her from the sights which would make her most sick.

"You now work in the capital, do you not?"

"Yes."

"Are you a good friend of Félix Cienfuegos?"

She gagged at the little she could see and did not answer for a moment. "Yes."

Rodríguez began to clean up. "And who is his father?"

"His father was a poet who died in an accident. Félix was brought up by his father's uncle."

"Is he sure who his father was?"

"You've always been interested in backgrounds, haven't you?" She cocked her head. "I remember."

"Very. Is he sure?"

"Yes. He's told me of a very strong family resemblance. Almost uncanny."

"Damn."

"What?"

"No, nothing. Everything's all right. Let her rest."

Unconcerned by wasted years, Rodríguez thought that although he was running out of time, he still had Tomás Arriesgo and the three golden ones in San Juan.

"If your sister gets pregnant again, don't bring her to me."

"What will prevent this in the future?"

"Diaphragms. In the past, they were smuggled into the United States from Germany, but all modern women use them now." Maliciously, he added, "I'll give one to each of you and demonstrate its use."

He had expected indignant protest. Instead, Rafaela held her hand out.

"Just tell us how it functions and we'll be on our way."

After he lectured with drawings, she said, "Thank you."

He wondered if she understood the rules of free care only for the very needy not for those able to travel to his office. She did. Rafaela asked, "How much Doctor?" She paid and left with Europa.

He pondered that with the phenomena of changing times, he could almost openly impregnate whomever he wished. Jazz Age women were so eager and free they needed neither chloroform nor promises of undying love, just sex and money. But there would be no more wasted trips. He prepared to headquarter in San Juan, no longer impregnate, and devote himself to two things.

One meant stopping a disturbing development among his offspring. Too many of his children had begun to meet and marry each other. That in itself would not have bothered him but these were producing Simple Simons instead of the glorious forces he had envisioned to liberate the island.

Most important for him, though, was to strictly supervise the education of his treasures: the three children of the prostitute from Old San Juan. During an accident of fate, at a time and in a place where he least

208

expected, Rodríguez had finally found the right woman, and it did not escape his sense of irony that she was not a little mother.

Beautifully olive toned and with straight, black hair from the blood of Native American ancestors imported to Puerto Rico from the mainland after the decimation of the natives, she had given him three curly-haired and good-looking children with dark olive skin. Each had sharp features and the almost maniacal eyes of the extremely intelligent or the highly creative, the three generals to lead his revolution. Time and again, he admonished his sons to work secretly until their numbers grew among the educated and powerful.

Years later, with the loss of Pedro Albizu Campos, imprisoned along with Clemente Soto Vélez—a true poet patriot—in the Atlanta Federal Penitentiary, he felt especially triumphant to know that into the void caused by their disappearance, his descendants would be ready to step in, reach out, and to carry the torch of independence.

Félix

The evening he returned from Europe, Félix, fueled with rage at the thought that Rafaela might have gone to Rodríguez to abort his child, accused her of dating other men while he was away on business. He closed his eyes and struck her nose with his fist. Blood dripped down her upper lip.

"You're insane," she screamed, punching him back.

He didn't feel her blows and kicks. Pain and regret overwhelmed him. He apologized solicitously, vowed his eternal love and devotion until she calmed down. He wiped the blood off her nose with his perfumed handkerchief, carefully folded it, returned it to his breast pocket, and gave her the rugs and laces he had brought back for her.

"If you ever do that again," she said, trembling, "you'll be a dead man." She left with her gifts, saying, "I'm accepting these because I deserve them and more, much more."

Early the next morning, he took the handkerchief to the grave digger, ready to carry out the last of Juan's instructions. "Here is her blood," Félix said, unbuttoning his pants.

With chalk, Juan drew a white circle in a portion of dirt floor, placed the handkerchief in the middle along with shavings from pieces of his secret woods from the mountains, and stepped aside while Félix urinated on the mixture. Juan poured his special alcohol on it and set it afire. As they watched, the crackling, hissing concoction turned to ashes. He collected them for Félix to throw into the ocean.

"How much do I owe you?" Félix asked.

"I don't charge. My gift was given to me free. If you want to give me something, you decide what it will be."

"Nothing," Félix said. "I decide nothing. You were the one who probably told Rafaela how to hex me in the first place. Go collect from her."

He ran from Juan's house exhilarated, happy to have outwitted the spirit medium but later became scared that the grave digger would rehex him, prejudice his cases, bring unfavorable legal decisions against his clients to ruin his career.

For weeks he shivered and ran whenever he saw Juan, but none of his fears materialized. Instead, when she was no longer angry, Félix and Rafaela continued their on again off again underground relationship—all in the name of avoiding small-town gossip—and his law practice flourished because, immediately afterwards, he handled a much publicized case.

The partners sat in their San Juan office, each at his own desk, commenting on news events, waiting for clients when Dr. Rodríguez walked in. At first glance, Félix thought it was Juan Peña, then remembered Rodríguez as the man who had stared at him, and tried to approach him long ago. He had forgotten and it was not until that moment that he understood his fear of and fascination with Juan Peña. He and Rodríguez looked alike.

"I need a lawyer," Rodríguez said. Because none of the three answered, he pointed at Félix. "You." He pulled a chair near Félix and sat down, lightly placing his medical bag on the floor next to him.

"Paternity?" Félix asked, opening a file.

"Infanticide." Diego lurched visibly, and Bartolomeo, who had been giggling, extinguished his cigar. Both got up to leave, but Rodríguez added, "Stay. You should all listen."

"Who brings the charge?"

"The church." Rodríguez removed his hat, placed it squarely atop his medical bag, removed his glasses, put them into his pocket, and crossed his legs.

"Give us the details."

"Are you taking the case?"

"Are you guilty?"

"Yes."

"Good Lord," Félix said. "What defense is possible?"

Ignoring him, Rodríguez began his recital. "I was traveling through the middle mountains on my usual rounds when one of the peasants ran after me to beg that I save a dying pregnant woman. None of the midwives had been able to turn the baby, a breach. It had gone on too long. Both mother and child were dying."

Félix began to get a bad feeling. "So what did you do?"

"I told the husband I could only save one of them. The ignoramus appeared to understand. He muttered, 'My wife, my wife,' weeping and shaking his head, so I tore pieces out of the child until the smaller limbs came out by themselves and I could smash its cranium." Rodríguez paused to blow his nose. "The mountains give me allergies."

"Has this happened before?" Félix felt nauseated.

"My allergies?" Rodríguez laughed. "Of course it has. Not to me, but to other doctors."

"And haven't they had to do something similar?"

"Some hide what they're doing, claim nature did the choosing." He paused. "Others destroy the woman by opening her up, and some, trained to save lives, can't decide which to choose and, as a result, let both die."

Félix rubbed his stomach and Bartolomeo, pale, pushed away his cigar and ashtray. Diego excused himself and left the room at a trot.

"Oh, I'm sorry," Rodríguez said. "I forgot about his brother. Sensitive isn't he?"

Bartolomeo looked at Félix. "We'll have to discuss this."

"Gentlemen," Rodríguez steepled his long, dark fingers. "I assure you on my word and years of experience, it was one or the other, and if I had understood that the husband did not know what I was asking him, I would have saved the baby, not the mother. I dislike most grown women."

"Are you shamed and remorseful then?" Félix asked.

"I am shamed only by cowardice and failure." Rodríguez spat the words out. "Such as that shown by my countrymen preferring to live on their knees with their hands out instead of acting like men and fighting for principles."

His unmoving repose and matter-of-factness angered and chilled Félix. How could this man talk about moral standards? He did not want the case. He knew no one liked Rodríguez who might get convicted on general principles. People had a way of using whatever tool presented itself to either lavish praise or to avenge their hatred even if that tool presented itself many years after the fact.

"And what a tool this is," he said, aloud.

Rodríguez and Bartolomeo misinterpreted his meaning.

"You mean to set a precedent?" Bartolomeo asked, while the doctor nodded.

Félix put his pen in his mouth, thinking. *No, the case to turn me into a laughingstock as the fool who represented, of all people, Dr. Rodríguez.*

"Are you taking the case?" Bartolomeo pressed.

"Dr. Rodríguez," Félix asked, "were there witnesses to your conversation with the husband?"

"Two midwives and an herbalist." Rodríguez chuckled. "You fine gentlemen would call him a witch doctor."

"Did they have the same understanding as you?"

"I don't presume to read minds."

Félix sighed, threw down his pen. "Doesn't the Church understand these things?"

"This time a priest witnessed the procedure. It was too much for him."

"What was he doing there?"

"Administering last rites."

Hope, a glimmer of an idea. "The priest had already given them both up for dead?" Félix asked.

"Certainly. The midwives who called me were very experienced. I was impressed with their capabilities." Rodríguez laughed. "Better than some doctors I've known. That's why I didn't bother trying to turn the infant. It would have been a waste of valuable time."

"I'll take the case." Félix smiled, planning. "We'll have to go over your defense many times before the trial but I'm confident of a favorable verdict if you can do two things."

"Which are?"

"Cry. And put drama into your voice."

"You mean like this. . . ."

To their amazement Rodríguez began a wailing lament on the inequalities of life's sufferings, the tragedies of prejudice, and misunderstanding that changed the course of history, ruining lives, and the disruption and horror of his peace of mind, of his very existence since the incident.

His speech was capable of moving the devil himself to tears and pity. Startled by witnessing this impromptu acting, they shook hands gingerly with Rodríguez and told him to return when they had finished their research.

"Why do you all look so surprised?" Rodríguez asked. "That's how I really feel all the time. Just not about this. I thought it was something everyone understood."

The doctor laughed and walked out without saying good-bye. Félix realized at that moment that this doctor was the only man he should ever fear. *That's how he feels all the time?*

Rodríguez was a bit more subdued during the trial but just as convincing in his pleas, delivered with a poet's intensity.

"As I gazed into her husband's eyes, I knew I would gladly suffer nightmares for the rest of my life if I could only save the woman he loved, so she could live to bear other children. How could I, in good conscience, give them both up for dead as the priest had done?"

The jury acquitted Rodríguez, and Félix was subsequently swamped with new clients and the request that he represent his political party in campaigns. So taken was he with his new importance that he accepted even more dinner invitations as the prize he deserved for being so brilliant, and he threw away all caution, gorging himself. His already growing paunch spread to his hips and he had to have his suits let out twice by a tailor.

IV

Juan

He bought a pistol, learned how to clean it, and practiced shooting in his patio until his neighbors complained about the noise and worried aloud that he might accidentally shoot one of them. Then he and Paula returned to Loíza Aldea during the patron saint festivals when no one objected to some practice shots at tin cans on the beach or at least could not identify the shooters disguised as *veigantes* through their gigantic garish masks and colorful costumes.

"Why do you want to do this?" Paula asked.

"The less you know the better."

"Who wronged you?"

"My family." He fired two shots, smashed both targets.

"But they're all dead." Juan did not answer. Paula pressed him. "Holy Father not Carmela?"

"Don't be ridiculous. I love my wife."

"How is it you have no children?"

"We live as sister and brother."

"By choice?"

"Because our children are freaks."

"No wonder you're crazy," Paula said, pressing her lips together and dimpling her cheeks. "Let me get you a woman."

Juan looked out to sea, lowered the pistol. He had never considered that possibility. "It would hurt Carmela."

"She doesn't have to know."

"All things come into the light sooner or later."

"You sound like old Padre Hernán."

"I would have made a good priest."

Paula rolled her eyes heavenward. "Now you sound like Luis. Come on, you've practiced enough. You never miss."

Grimly, Juan followed Paula to a prostitute in La Perla who refused to take him.

"Who are you kidding?" Paula said to the woman, misinterpreting her motives. "Your last man was not white."

"You don't understand," the woman answered. "I don't do this anymore. My boyfriend is going to buy me and my three children a house."

"Who is it?" Juan asked, suddenly alert.

"A doctor. As a matter of fact, he looks like you only much older, more respectable." The woman shook her long black hair, each straight strand thick as rope. "I've got to take advantage," she added. "He won't live much longer."

Juan's feelings exactly. "Where is this house?"

"What do you care?"

"You're lying."

"In the new section."

"Let's go, Paula."

"But, Juan."

"Never mind, I feel better already." Juan whistled back to Cataño. "Got him," he thought. *When the time comes, I'll know where to find him.* Meanwhile, he decided, Paula was right. He needed a woman.

"What was that all about?" Paula asked.

"How is Luis?" Juan wanted to change the subject.

Paula sighed. "Getting rich with his schemes."

Juan did not want to know. He already knew too much about everybody in town.

When he returned home, Carmela said, "Paula is your cousin." He prepared for the inevitable. Sexual abstinence had made her neurotic. Every session of jealous accusations followed the same pattern. First she made a statement of fact waiting for him to agree. Then she criticized that fact with innuendos and finally began accusations. "In most cases," she continued, "cousins either love each other enough to marry, or they are indifferent to each other."

"There's a third circumstance," he interrupted. "Sometimes cousins share a family secret or love each other without being in love with one another." That quieted her for a moment as she struggled for a way to continue.

"They have no right to be that close unless more is going on between them." She gathered steam. "You and Paula are too close. If you're in love with her, just tell me."

He thought the situation ridiculous. Why had he not told her the truth before? He was about to when a knock on the door interrupted him.

"Hello, Luis," he said, opening the door. "How are you?"

"Bad. I'm here for my treatment."

Carmela brought out pillows, tossed them on the floor of the waiting room. Luis crawled on top of them.

Juan put on a fresh white *guayabera* and rubbed his hands in alcohol and perfume. He floated his hands above Luis's head, moving them down the length of his deformed body and back again. As soon as his palms felt hot and his fingers cramped, he shook his hands over a bowl of water and repeated the process many times.

"Thank you," Luis said, before leaving. "It helps." The Monkey Man trotted home.

"You can't cure him," Carmela declared.

"No. I can only relieve the discomfort."

"In most cases, . . ." she stopped because Juan had his hands over his ears.

"No," he said. "Stop. I can't take it anymore. Please leave me alone."

He fled to the bathroom to shower. The water slid over his long, lean body frigid against the heat of his skin. Staying in the shower as long as he could, he wondered if he needed to find Carmela a lover for his peace of mind.

Before he fell asleep, she asked, "Will you teach me to shoot a pistol too?"

"Yes, if that's what you want." Later that night, he dreamt that she shot him as he walked down an unfamiliar alleyway in an older section of San Juan.

V

Luis

In his Manatí house of memories, Luis chuckled at the amount of money he had collected through blackmail, without getting arrested.

"Enough to apprentice my brother, Tomás, as both a machinist and a carpenter. Between those two trades, Tomás was sure to have a job always."

It had been so easy. His victims, stupid, had asked few questions and gave over the money.

Soon it became Félix's turn. Luis put it off as long as he could out of consideration for Rafaela but he had run out of victims and he was running out of time. Healing sessions with Juan Peña relieved his strained arms, relaxed the bunched up feeling of his insides and of his neck, but all they did was buy a little more time. The deadline for his life expectancy loomed dangerously close, and he had too much unfinished business.

Paula sat with a vat of dirty clothes between her brown legs, spread wide apart, grating laundry up and down a washboard. Perspiration dripped from her hairline and poured down her face as she swished a shirt in the water, wrung out soap, and scrubbed hard.

She's getting older.

"Where are the letters?" he asked. Paula perked up, wiped her brow with her wet arm.

"Again? Don't we have enough?"

"Hah, hah, enough to keep doing laundry? It doesn't suit you *mi reina negra*. You need a white maid."

She tittered. "Under my mattress. Maybe you should take Juan with you. He owns a gun."

"What? And get shot in the ass? No thanks."

He crawled to her bed. From under it, he retrieved the stack of yellowed letters, bundled them in brown wrapping paper and tied them with string. He looped the string three times and put his head through the loop to carry the letters hanging from his neck. "Must not lose these," he thought. They had provided him an adequate livelihood.

Outside, thin dark clouds spread across the sky, obscuring its blue. He trotted hurriedly to the ferry, waited patiently for the gangplank so he could catwalk into the boat.

"Thank you, thank you Sirs Walter Raleigh." The bundle thumped against his chest during the lurching of the ferry and throughout his trot to Félix's office.

From behind a murky glass door he heard a shriek. "Good," thought Luis. *Félix is alone and must have seen my shadow.*

"Open the door. It's me, Luis Arriesgo."

Wide-eyed Félix led him inside. "You scared me."

"That's obvious." He whinnied his horsy laughter. "No need for you to be afraid unless you're not ready to make restitution."

"What are you talking about?" Félix jutted out his double chin. "What do you want?" He reopened the door, looked around.

"No one saw me come in. Your secret is safe for now."

"Get to the point."

Luis removed the loop from his neck while staring at Félix's girth. "Here are some letters from my father, Cousin Félix. I would not be showing them to you after all this time if I didn't need your help."

"What the devil do you mean 'Cousin Félix'?"

"Read the letters. Your Uncle Pedro, my father, wrote these letters to my mother."

"Ridiculous."

Noting on Félix's overly round face the same pattern of disbelief mingled with loathing as all his other blackmail victims, Luis continued.

"My mother was a prostitute and your uncle her lover. I am their child, Cousin Félix." It was important to threaten these self-important *gordiflones*, with blood relation to him. "I'm not asking for much. If you give me a job, I'll be content. If not, then I'll publish them to get my share."

"If what you say is true, why didn't you come forward before?"

"At first I didn't know who wrote them and they were so tender, so full of love, I cherished them. By the time Paula found out who wrote them, we learned he had died. What did you do with the money, Cousin Félix? Spend it eating *pernil* and *pasteles?*"

Red-faced, Félix shuddered. It was always the same. The trick succeeded by a combination of outright charges and incriminating innuendo. Luis hinted at collusion, and a victim's own guilty conscience filled in whatever he did not know.

"Look at them."

Félix tore the bundle open, stacked the yellowed letters and began to read. With Félix occupied, Luis inspected the office.

"I don't believe a word. These letters are neither dated nor signed." Félix slapped his pudgy hand on his desk. "Do your worst, they will not hold up in court."

Luis collected them somberly, repackaged them and looped them around his neck again. "I'm sorry you feel that way, Cousin Félix." He saddened his eyes. "All I wanted was a job. Now I'll have to go to a newspaper. Can you open the door for me please?"

"Wait." Félix leaned his hand against the door, to keep it closed. "You are not a lawyer. I can't give you a job here."

"What about some money, then?"

"Let me think about it."

"All right, Cousin Félix. You have two days."

Before returning home, Luis stopped by El Morro to see his friends.

"Listen, Jerry. What's the name of your hometown again?"

"Birmingham, Loo-eez." Freckled-faced Jerry smiled, showing gaped teeth. "You ready to send To-más to Birmingham?"

"Not yet but soon."

"Shucks, me and my mamá'll put him up with us until he's set to go out on his own." The redhead gave him the address. "Just let me know when you're ready."

Pancho said, "Amigo, keep this too. It is my parents' address in Texas. Tomás may not do too well with the rednecks."

Jerry and Pancho laughed. Luis loved the soldiers. They never called him a monkey because he could not walk upright. It struck him suddenly that neither did Félix.

Sunset arrived in Manatí. Parrots stopped squawking and, in another couple of hours, Luis expected night to bring the symphony of tiny tree frogs and stinging mosquitoes. He sensed the young man's presence, quiet as a shadow.

"How old are you?" Luis asked.

"Fifteen."

"There's no money here."

"I know."

"Then go home."

"Can't I stay until you fall asleep?"

Luis wheezed and choked. "I took care of a grown woman and of my younger brother."

"I know."

"Then you know I don't need a caretaker."

"You can hardly breathe or talk without coughing."

It was true and the reason Luis had had to retire.

VI

Félix

Luis Arriesgo Cienfuegos? Neither Félix nor the whole town of Cataño ever thought of Luis as anything other than the Monkey Man from Manatí, a youngster so deformed that he walked on all fours, showing his horsey smile as he clanked along the ground with small blocks of wood attached to his hands like a second pair of shoes.

Félix had always avoided looking at him. Now he shuddered at the consequences to his career of either accepting or refusing the Monkey Man's demands. *God, what a bad time!* Cataño had finally become a municipality two years before and he prepared to run for office in the next elections. Remembering the bundle of papers Luis showed him, Félix double locked the door. He was glad Diego and Bartolomeo were in court and could not see his agitation. He opened the safe, removed his pearls and closed the office early. He ran to the dock, patting his breast pocket to assure the safety of the pearls.

After the afternoon blackmail attempt, the last thing Félix needed for his nerves was an inexperienced hand at the helm of the ferry taking him home. Churned by storm winds, the waters of the bay usually placid and silvery crashed against the boat with angry dull-green waves splashing him and assaulting the women passengers on the top deck with salty sprays of tepid, hostile waters, reducing their chemises to ruined hanging masses which weighed them down and marked their underwear through wet, transparent fabric.

Drenched, Félix's thick legs showed through his white trousers like long, square blocks of concrete. Just when, heart beating furiously and feeling close to drowning, he thought he was safe, the captain whammed the ferry into Cataño's dock with a thud that jolted Félix off his feet, rammed his midsection into the guard rail. With a "whmmpph," he clutched the railing and saved himself from going overboard into murky, frothy waves.

"Ridiculous," Félix thought, catching his breath. Here was this peculiar storm and Luis and the ferry boat captain acting strange. Why couldn't they leave him alone? He heard a singsong call.

"Hah, hah. Almost fell over from all those pounds you've put on, didn't you?"

Recognizing the voice, Félix bristled, turned to the grave digger who, he felt, absorbed all light. The whiteness of Juan Peña's linen suit yellowed to ivory next to his blue-black skin. Juan's ebony face swallowed up more of the rays of fading sunlight than did the gloomy clouds overhead. Out of habit, Félix stared down at the grave digger's feet. No shoes or socks, as always, his toenails hardened to wood and the blackness of his feet broken only by thick yellowed callouses on his heels.

"What the hell's so funny? And stop following me."

"Sorry, Mr. Cienfuegos, or do you prefer Don Félix?" Juan's nostrils flared slightly when he laughed. His teeth were straight and lemon yellow. He began to deny he was following him, but when he noticed Félix staring with bulged eyes at his feet, he lifted his right foot, scissoring the big and second toes in pinching motions to threaten Félix's legs. Félix backed away hating Juan, especially when disembarking townspeople laughed at them.

"Stop it!" Félix protested. "Everyone will see you acting ridiculous."

"Ha! You mean you. You're the one afraid of looking ridiculous." Juan's long, square face sobered. "Seriously, come see me for a consultation.

Communications from the other world just told me a spirit will never let you marry. I can help you with your problem. You know, like the last time."

"That was different. I have no problems now and I don't want anything to do with you. I'm not interested in the spirits."

"But they are interested in you." Amused at his discomfort, Juan tried to pinch Félix with his toes again.

"Get away, damn it, get away." Félix looked around.

The few people left on the ferry, who did not hurry home to escape the growing wind, stood motionless, staring. Félix tipped his hat at them, holding it so it would not blow away, walked a few feet away from Juan, turned back, and declared loudly, "Thank you for your concern but there is no need to trouble yourself." He then thudded down the gangplank and examined his suit for seawater stains before crunching along the bay road as fast as he could against the wind.

Galloping waves lashed up along the beach, washed across the sand, continued to the edge of the road, and tried to stream over it into the houses on the other side. Scattered palm trees bent their heads way back, whipping leafy tresses in loud commotion, and sent coconuts crashing down dangerously close to his head. A few raindrops splattered. He looked back to see if the spiritualist was following him, but Juan was still near the dock making himself look important in his white suit and bare feet by walking slowly, very straight, as if the wind could not touch him, the tall, slim master of the elements.

Félix continued past his big house thinking that few people were out in the storm and he could chance going to Rafaela's house, the one he bought her as consolation for not marrying her. He wanted to give her an additional present.

The pearls had served him more than well as tools to increase his wealth. He didn't covet them anymore and could buy six new strands whenever he wished by selling plots of his holdings, lands and homes. If someone noticed him going into her house, he could always say he was a concerned landlord. His trouble with the Monkey Man had him in an uproar of fear and he needed to talk to her to clear his mind.

Raindrops fell faster now, thick and hard, leaving large round splotches on the gravel roadway. Félix hurried along the deserted bay road ignoring the wind that pushed him back. "A terrible mistake," Félix thought. Going to see the spirit medium had been stupid, but at the time he had believed he needed help. He had been hexed. He knew it, felt it, could pinpoint the steamy Sunday night it happened.

After that, he had seen Juan occasionally, as was unavoidable in Cataño. During those times the grave digger waved, smiled and went his way, until just now, when Juan threatened his marriage prospects with a spirit. This on top of the Monkey Man's blackmail was too much for him; he had to speak to Rafaela. She knew everything that went on in town and would advise him what to do. He jumped quickly over the trough of green sewage running along the edge of the sidewalk, opened the gate, and ran up her balcony steps.

"Rafaela?" He stepped into her living room.

Out of the kitchen came not Rafaela but a short, square woman wiping her hands on an apron. Oh no, Doña Antonia, her mother. She crossed her arms between massive breasts and big belly and formed her lips into the same thin line they became whenever she saw Félix. He wondered if she had any teeth. He also wondered why she was angry that he would not marry Rafaela, she who never married but had five daughters.

"Rafaela is not home," she said. "Were you expected?"

"Well, no, but I must discuss an important matter with Rafaela." Félix stammered out the first thing that occurred to him and not knowing what to do or say next to explain his unannounced visit stood in the middle of the living room dripping water on the wood floor. He took two steps back and looked down at the wet imprints left by the soles of his shoes. "Damn that Rafaela!" he thought. She never appreciated his gifts. He had bought her beautiful rugs from Morocco, which had long since disappeared with no explanations. He would not be surprised if Doña Antonia's own house looked like a castle filled with treasures he had bought for her daughter. He vowed that the old dragon would never get her hands on the pearls—perfect, milky circles pinpointed with pastel blues

and pinks—which he was giving to Rafaela. She had earned them for her
loyalty to him.

"Surely, Don Félix, I can relay a message to my daughter."

He held up his hands in a shaking gesture. "That's very kind of you,
very kind, but, no trouble, no trouble. I shall discuss the matter with
Rafaela on another occasion."

"As you wish," Doña Antonia said. She pointed to the door and returned to the kitchen.

Disheartened, Félix turned up the lapels of his suit, went back out into
the wind and rain. He was the only one in the narrow streets, pants
flapping, jacket flying, and eyes squinting because of the tempest thickening the air with sheets of falling water and because of the steamy mist
released from the hot ground. He struggled to keep his hat, his balance.

Arriving home drenched with his black hair starched back by the
wind, he found Rafaela waiting for him.

"What are you doing here?" he demanded. Rafaela looked very attractive in royal blue voile. She and Miguelito exchanged looks.

"Miss Rafaela came in to get out of the rain." Miguelito glared.

"Who saw you? Did anyone see you?"

Rafaela puckered her pouty lips, ignored Félix, and asked Miguelito for
a brandy. Breaking into a smile, the young man ran to get it for her. She
plopped down on Félix's sofa, smoothed her sheer skirt, crossed her legs,
and patted the seat next to her.

"Get out of those wet clothes or sit down. You're blocking my view of
the walls."

It seemed to Félix that Rafaela took every opportunity to criticize the
fifty pounds his love of food had put on him just because she stayed slim
and firm. "But did anyone see you?"

She laughed the long, loud rattle that so shamed Félix, prevented him
from taking her out in public. "The whole world," she said, "knows we've
been together for years. Even before we were lovers, they thought so.
Why do you keep up the pretense?"

Without answering he stormed upstairs to his bedroom, his wet shoes
thumping and swishing as he went. Rafaela thanked Miguelito for the

brandy and laughed again, pointing out to the servant Félix's large back-side sticking out between the vents of his soaked jacket. Miguelito laughed too. He set the tray with the decanter down on a wicker table and went into the kitchen to spread sizzling noises and garlicky aromas. Rafaela sighed, leaned forward, removed her matching hat and gloves.

Félix returned in a dry suit exactly like the one he arrived in and threw himself at her feet. "I'm sorry, Rafaela." He pawed her knees and kissed the entire length of her shins, peeking at her for signs of anger. "I don't deserve you. Say you forgive me, say you love me." He watched for Miguelito.

Rafaela rolled her eyes. "Your dramas are tiresome. Just tell me what in hell's the matter with you now."

He huffed and puffed himself off the floor and onto the sofa beside her. "There's a conspiracy against me by Juan the grave digger and the Monkey Man." He saw her eyes widen. Félix beat his breast, crying, "They want to ruin me, blackmail me, take what's mine."

Rafaela's jaw sagged in mock amazement. She burst out laughing.

"You know something," he accused. "Tell me what you know."

"I know you're silly." She fingered his wet hair and puckered her lips. "Kiss me, cow eyes."

Félix kissed her, tentatively at first, looking over her shoulder to see if Miguelito was watching, then enjoying it, then forgetting what he wanted to know. Rafaela smelled of tea rose, fresh cinnamon, and brandy. His head swirled. He felt feverish. Félix sat back, smiling, with his face flushed, staring at Rafaela's earth-brown curls.

She began to giggle, lost her breath trying not to laugh, and pushed his face away with her hand. "D-Don't look at me like that Félix." She lost the battle against laughter. "Y-You've gotten so f-fat that your face looks like a big, fat baby's behind." She roared, hugging him until she could stop.

Félix sniffed, trying not to laugh himself. "Now I won't tell you that you look beautiful in that blue dress or that I wonder if it goes with these." He reached into his breast pocket, presented her with the irides-cent pearls.

"Aha!" She snatched them. "I knew it. You've been up to your old tricks, haven't you?"

"What old tricks? I like to give you things."

Her face soured. "Have you been all over the island proposing to rich, young girls you consider more suitable than me?" She played with the pearls. First she doubled the stand and draped them on her head, then she swung them from one ear, then put them across her upper lip like a moustache, and finally wrapped them around her arm like a bracelet, gauging their worth from Félix's discomfort.

Miguelito entered to announce dinner and saved Félix from a fate worse than death: going over with Rafaela the reasons why he could not marry her.

She stood up, putting on her gloves and hat. "I can't stay. My mother's visiting today."

"That's right. I forgot. I stopped by your house before coming home."

Rafaela exaggerated a gasp of horror, asked, "In broad daylight?"

"Yes, yes, I did. Your mother still hates me."

"Good! Somebody has to. You can't blame her."

"I've been very careful to protect my, uh, your reputation, my love."

"Don't be ridiculous. This is 1929, not the dark ages. Anyway, stop worrying about Luis. He's been working his swindle on every rich man in Puerto Rico, claiming to be a brother, a cousin, or an illegitimate son." Félix's mouth dropped open. "It's how he earns his livelihood," she continued. "From the bribes he receives to make him go away."

Afraid to believe it true, Félix grabbed her shoulders, asked, "Are you sure?"

"Of course. I've heard of many and you're a prime candidate for blackmail, Félix. You're rich and Luis—the whole town—knows you'd do anything to avoid talk." Rafaela raised an eyebrow. "Isn't that true?"

"He said he was my cousin, son of a sick prostitute my uncle visited in Manatí before he died."

"And I suppose he showed you love letters to prove it?"

"Yes." Félix gasped, remembering the yellowed bundle.

"Undated and unsigned?"

He lowered his head, meekly answered, "Yes."

"And you a lawyer! But Luis always counts on the fear of scandal to overpower logic."

"But my uncle did visit prostitutes and Luis didn't ask for money at first. He asked for a job which, of course, I can't give him." Félix waved at an imaginary audience. "Imagine my friends and clients' discomfort to be around a man who walks on all fours."

"Your friends and clients? Imagine Luis's suffering."

"Someone else can give him a job. Why does it have to be me?"

"Right, Félix. It doesn't have to be you, but no one wants him around either. That's why he started the confidence game. To survive. Perhaps if the townspeople had not been so condescending . . ." She paused, looked caught up in a faraway dream.

Félix frowned, remembering how so many tricked the Monkey Man into believing they liked him, were his friends, until he answered all their despicable, personal questions about his infirmity, and then ignored him. Rafaela was right. Townspeople never used his name and were stupid to feign a friendship they did not mean.

"Are you going to help him or not?"

When Félix didn't answer, Rafaela gritted her teeth and began to swing the pearls in a wide arc, like a sling. As he stared, it dawned on Félix that his gifts might have been going to the needy. He knew Rafaela capable of giving away her last cent. "Those pearls are for you, Rafaela," he said nervously. "They're very valuable. My mother gave them to me."

She tilted her head back, laughed. "Wedding bands are cheaper."

"Now, Rafaela."

"Never mind," she interrupted. "I know. You forget I can read your thoughts. You worry that the pinched noses of your right wing friends clash with my inclination to speak in favor of independence and endanger your chances of leading your party, you can't forget the time I dated Claudio, and you want me to be seen and not heard, etcetera, etcetera."

With his eyes cast down, Miguelito said, "Dinner is getting cold."

"If you don't help him, when Luis presents the letters, I'll tell everybody it's true, and you can wave good-bye to your precious reputation."

"Oh, you would not."

Not answering, Rafaela moved toward the back of the house. There was a shortcut to her house across a plot of land facing the bay road. Unfortunately, Félix's house was on a high loamy hill and the rain had turned the ground into running mud.

"Wait," Félix called. "What about Juan the grave digger and his threat that a spirit will never let me marry?"

"Oh, that's really funny. If I die before you, I'll definitely haunt you. And you'll deserve it."

"Then you never hexed me?"

"What a fool. I've heard that story too. Why should I hex you? I can haunt you in the flesh and after death." She walked back to leave through the front door. "No need to see me out, darling, someone might see you in this hurricane. Go eat."

Ignoring her sarcasm, Félix felt relieved, kissed her, told her he would take her on his next trip abroad, and, after receiving assurances she was all right, went into his dining room to eat.

Miguelito brought her an umbrella. She waved it away. Before he opened the door for her, they heard Félix shouting, "I'll give him a job." They ran into the dining room, eyes wide and asked in unison, "Will you?"

"I have the perfect job for him."

They glanced at each other, back at Félix.

"I don't know why I didn't think of it sooner." Félix paused to cut his steak. They held their breath while he gobbled spicy rice and red beans. "I'll send him to buy property for me." He pointed at them with his fork and spoke with his mouth full. "Landowners will feel sorry for him, give him the real estate cheaper than I could get it. Even with his commission, I'll still make a fortune."

Miguelito and Rafaela looked at each other again. Their shoulders slumped. Together they turned and walked back to the front door and opened it. They stood for a moment listening to the downpour drumming on neighboring metal roofs. Neither the wind nor the rain slackened, and the air was still foggy. They watched the water spill over roof tiles, stream down the sides of houses into the streets, flooding the sewer troughs and drowning the gravel road. The town was a river.

"It's sure coming down hard," Miguelito said.

"Doesn't everything?" Rafaela smiled, lifted her dress up over her head like a shawl, revealing a royal blue satin slip, and ran out into the rainstorm.

Once outdoors, Rafaela lost her hold on her dress. It swelled and flapped. Rain drops pelting her body felt like small stones as the wind roared and deafened her. She leaned forward against its force hardly able to move each leg forward and then worried she might be blown away. She strained to watch for the zinc sheeting used to brace homes in storms like these. A hurricane wind could easily send one flying to decapitate her but she did not fear. This was unusual weather but not a hurricane like the year before.

Wet, her clothes felt heavy, tore at the seams. To catch her breath, she grabbed onto one of the few telegraph poles remaining intact after last year's San Felipe hurricane. It had killed 312 people, ruined both coffee and tobacco harvests, and had cost 85 million dollars in damages, but it had helped her save face with Félix. Rafaela had blamed it for losing her job rather than to admit she had created an ugly scene in front of the Spanish American Legion.

The Puerto Rican veterans, in their stupid makeshift uniforms had paraded so proudly along with their North American counterparts. Off they marched, in shuffling missteps, to the cemeteries in San Juan and Santurce. It had been their intention to honor the fallen of both sides.

Rafaela, furious over their blindness, had other ideas. Out she leapt from behind a large white mausoleum to scream at them.

"Estúpidos!" she yelled. "You didn't fight a war. You handed over our country."

Startled, the aged veterans walking with heads held high and eyes brimming with patriotic tears halted to stare at her. Their mouths dropped open at this travesty to the memory of their dead compatriots, men they considered brave.

"What war?" she asked. "A fake! Forget the Maine. The Americans planted the bomb themselves, you fools. They just wanted Puerto Rico and Cuba."

Lorenzo Parra, a small white man, stepped forward.

"Go home, Rafaela." He spoke quietly. "Many valiant men died believing they were doing the right thing and it is them we honor."

Though bursting with much to say, their sober, saddened faces stopped her, filled her with shame. She turned and ran out of the cemetery.

She did not return to work, too embarrassed by what her employer might say, and pleaded illness until the incident could be forgotten. However, her employer sent her a note anyway.

Dear Miss Moya:

Since it is your proclivity to visit cemeteries, far be it from this office to prevent your doing so on a full-time basis.

Your services, such as they were, are no longer needed nor wanted.

Good riddance!

That had occurred in May of 1928 and she fielded Félix's questions about her job until September when San Felipe struck. She refused to admit to a stupid mistake in judgement and blamed the hurricane. Smart and with enough informants in the right places, Félix had not believed her and she knew it. To his credit, he had not nagged her about it and had, instead, surprised her with the purchase of a small house of her own.

"Watch out for stupid hurricanes," he had said. "Inside yourself."

Now, through sheets of driving rain, she spied her grouchy neighbor, Berta.

"Go home, *vieja*," she yelled.

The woman, covered in rubber sheeting, looked her up and down.

"I need milk for my grandson and I'm not going back home without it."

Rafaela steeled herself, let go of the telegraph pole, and kicked off her shoes. They blew down Barbosa Avenue. She struggled with Berta over to the general store only to find it boarded. They pounded on green painted wood with their fists until the owner opened the door to let them inside.

"Give her some damn milk and take her home." Rafaela left them to continue to her own house. "Demented old woman!" She screamed into the wind. "Making me have to take care of her too."

When Rafaela arrived home, her dress was in shreds and she could not open her fist.

"I hate everybody," she announced. "Myself most of all."

Doña Antonia, used to Rafaela's tantrums, silently picked up the heap of her discarded clothing and threw them into the garbage. They left a puddle on the living room floor. She served Rafaela a cup of tea and kneaded her hand until it released the pearls.

VII

Luis

$\mathcal{S}$topping to wheeze slowed him down even more than the thickening bones of his arms. His puny legs—lost in his trousers—served as poor, atrophied cushions while he caught his breath. Pained, Paula turned away. Tomás continued to stare, fighting back tears.

"Why do I have to go now?" Tomás asked. "Let's wait until next year."

"I'm tired of you. I don't want you around, anymore." Luis caught Paula shaking her head in denial at Tomás, who looked stricken. "It's true. I'm tired of both of you. You're both too ugly for me." He laughed and coughed. "Come on, Tomás, I don't want you to miss the boat."

Luis and Paula put Tomás on a ship bound for New York from where he would travel to Birmingham. Tears streamed out of his eyes. All the time, he stared at Luis as if he were being betrayed. Luis laughed while Paula stood waving.

"Good Luck, Tomás. You'll be all right." Tomás waved back halfheartedly, looking only at Luis. Paula added, "Look at that little ingrate. He'll miss only you."

After the ship sailed, as Luis breathed a sigh of relief, Paula said, "Good. Thank God that's over." It surprised Luis who thought himself unique in that feeling. He looked at Paula.

"She's thirty-two," he thought. Unmarried and unmarriageable because of the rumors of what she had been in Manatí. *And they don't even know what she did in Loíza Aldea.* He thought about the other sacks of money he had buried, decided one of them could buy her a husband.

"You're not glad to get rid of Tomás. You should get married and start over."

"Who's going to marry me?"

"There have been inquiries."

"Who?" It saddened him that the lie made her look animated, younger.

"Lots of men. They think I'm your son and ask permission. I thought you weren't interested so I always say no."

"You're a liar." She sniffed. "You can't play your tricks on me."

That patient hope, enduring beyond all reason in most people, Luis manipulated masterfully. He assumed his indignant pose. He stopped, furrowed his brow, and put anger in his voice.

"Oh, yes? I'm a liar? Well you can protect yourself from now on." He shook his head from side to side. "You'll be sorry, because I'm sending every man who asks about you to your doorstep. In no time at all, you'll be a bigamist. And don't walk back with me. Leave me alone." She followed him a short while. "Go away," he said. "Go home."

Reluctantly she left, saying, "When you get out of your mood, I'll be waiting."

He yelled after her, "Don't wait." Luis choked trying to stifle a cough, to catch his breath. His shoulders, chest, and arms were all that was left of his body. His legs were dangling, dainty things that resembled stretched and deflated balloons.

Arthur Brisbane, a black soldier from Atlanta, Georgia, was the first to court Paula. "Good evening, Miss Paula," he said. Her English was bad. Luis expected her to refuse him. It was all part of his plan.

"I think he has a wife back home," she said.

"I don't care." He shifted on his cot, turned his back to her. "You're on your own."

"But soldiers are handsome." She giggled like a child.

"Stupid women think so."

"It's been so long."

"Don't tell me anything. Leave me alone."

"I'm sorry. You're not a liar." When he didn't move, she tapped his back, yelled. "Talk to me!"

He rolled over, faced her. "Do I look like a matchmaker to you?"

"I never thought of being happy with a man."

"So?"

"If I ever marry, you come to live with me."

"Now I know you're crazy."

"I can't leave you." Luis endured her kisses, her stroking his hair.

"I've lived longer than anyone thought possible, even me, but now it's almost over. I can hardly breathe. Paula, be honest, if you stay because you don't want to marry, that's one thing. If you want to marry and you stay because you think you have to, then that's enslavement."

"B-But you're my baby." She began to cry.

Luis felt anxiety. "I'm not your baby." He removed her arms from around his neck. "I never was and now I'm a grown dying man. You've done more than your part. God has forgiven you, Paula. Now forgive yourself."

She dried her eyes, said, "Well I don't like the American. All that English."

Luis tried to look pensive. "There is one man but I'm not sure. He always looks like he wants to talk to me but he's slow, and when someone asks about you he stares like an idiot."

"Where is he from?"

"Santo Domingo. He has a funny last name."

"What is it?"

"Santjutze."

"What the hell is that?"

"How should I know?" Luis yawned. Paula let him go to sleep.

Two days later, a sturdy light-skinned man timidly approached Paula as she made her rounds collecting laundry.

"May I help you, Miss?" He removed his straw hat, revealed graying hair.

"I never need any help from the likes of you."

"Miss, I, I, . . ." He stepped back, mouth open and arms wide.

"Who are you?"

"My name is Pablo Santjutze Vargas." He stopped, glared at elderly eavesdroppers slowing their pace as they walked past in swishing taffeta skirts. "Your son said that I might, that I might . . ." He exhaled. "Your son said that I might call on you."

Paula turned up her nose. "I've never had children." She looked him in the eye. "I took charge of two orphans nobody wanted when I was very young. How do you know my adopted son?"

Pablo came alive. "He is my very good friend. He helped me come into some money. Now I can marry and go back to Santo Domingo."

"You mean you can go back to your home and then marry."

"No. I was born here in Bayamón. I want to marry someone from my own country but I like to live in Santo Domingo. There's more work, a bit less prejudice there." He paused, waiting for Paula to think about what he said. "Of course, if my wife prefers to stay here . . ." He looked askance at her.

She inhaled, smiled, and said, "You may carry my basket. It's not far."

Luis watched them bouncing toward the house with idiot grins on their faces. He had told Pablo how to find her.

Several weeks later they married and sailed off to Santo Domingo.

"I'll write every day," she said.

"I won't be able to read your chicken scratch." He laughed. "Send along an interpreter."

After she left, he thought: "Good. Thank God that's over."

He knew where to die. Luis dug up the two remaining bags of money, chuckling at how he got them.

For three years he had bought land and houses for Félix Cienfuegos until Félix caught him cheating. It was bound to happen. Félix was very greedy and only hired him because he knew sellers would feel sorry for Luis and give him cheaper prices. He thought Luis did not realize that when he offered to pay him only on commission. Sooner or later someone other than a distressed landowner was going to get cheated. Félix thought it was going to be Luis. Luis had other ideas.

He bargained hard, drove prices ridiculously low, and then inflated them to Félix who still believed he received a windfall. Luis insisted on delivering the papers himself, obtaining the scratchy X signature of illiterates who, ruined by 1932's hurricane San Ciprián, abandoned their devastated homes and made their way to dreams of better lives in the cities of North America. That way, Luis collected his meager commission plus the difference between what Félix paid and the real purchase price. It worked until Félix heard rumors of a Monkey Man who bought lots of property at ridiculous prices and confronted him.

"So," Félix said. "You've been cheating me and making yourself rich."

"I'm sorry Cousin Félix, but you have so much and I work so hard."

"Ha! Drop the act and that 'Cousin Félix' nonsense. Listen, no hard feelings. You can continue to work for me but I deliver the papers from now on."

Luis snorted. "And benefit from my bargaining skills while you pay me a low commission?"

Félix held his hand out to be shaken. "I'll pay you straight salary. Just name your price."

"No, thank you, Félix. I think I'll retire."

"You sure? The door stays open for you to come back anytime."

Félix's offer touched Luis, but he could not work anymore. His meager defense against robbers—strong arms, a loud voice, and the ability to crawl quickly into small, low places to hide—had disappeared. Luis crawled along too slowly now, did not laugh as much because he had trouble breathing and seeing. His eyesight had diminished at an astonishing rate, and he wanted to see his native town before he died, set his eyes one last time on the eerie karst country, an area of green and white hillocks formed by water sinking into limestone. It looked as if the hands of a divine colossus had lifted an edge of the countryside's green carpet and fluffed it so that when the land settled, air trapped underneath in pockets produced hump-backed formations with a haunting symmetry.

After getting rid of Tomás and Paula, he bought a shack that had once been the outhouse of a very rich family in Manatí, using what remained of his savings for food as he waited out his days. He regretted not getting even with the townspeople of Cataño. He should have established a big brothel, filled it with the most diseased whores he could find. It would have served the hypocrites right for making him think they were his friends until they felt lucky not to be him and turned their heads and backs. But he did not do it, prevented by warmer, kinder memories of Paula, the Figueroas, Rafaela, Waldemar Toledo, and, surprising to him, Félix who at the very end behaved decently.

Content to read from Tomás and Paula's letters that they were well, he settled down to wait until he received an answer to his long unanswered "What have I done to deserve this?"

The Manatí night turned as steamy as his memory and it buzzed with mosquitos. Luis had not realized that he had dozed off until he heard a strong baritone, the voice of the young man who had been listening to his life's story.

"Are you finished?"

Luis opened his eyes, saw him clearly. Smiling at him was Waldemar Toledo standing on strong uninjured legs.

"Get up," Waldemar said. "I'll race you."

Believing himself in a dream, Luis asked, "You'll give me two pennies if I win?"

"No, it's just for fun." Waldemar was still a fifteen-year-old schoolboy.

"But I'm, I can't . . ."

"Yes you can. Look down."

Luis looked. Marveling, he got up from his cot, stood upright, and stretched. He was a head taller than Waldemar and raced him to the clouds.

VIII
Juan

When his pistol disappeared, Juan convinced himself that it could have been stolen by any number of his clients. He told himself he did not want to bother investigating so as not to get anyone in trouble, but he really feared that Carmela had taken it to shoot him. She learned there was another woman and intimated as much every chance she got.

Juan had felt lonelier than ever when Paula left and took her advice about finding a lover. He met a dark-complected woman from a neighboring district and liked her because she looked like her father who he knew was definitely not Rodríguez. She made him feel sure there were no blood ties to him. Ecstatic that she was going to have his baby, he brought her gifts throughout her long but easy pregnancy.

The last thing Juan noticed about the child was his kinky hair. The first and second were that the child was an unnaturally pale pink and that his eyes had no color, an albino.

How could he wait any longer? He bought another pistol, kept it with him at all times, and began forays into San Juan at night, looking for the houses of any of his brother's prostitutes, trusting his inner vision to guide him. His bare feet made no sound on the cobbled streets, but his white clothing attracted the eye of more than one who tried to rob him until

242

they came close, recognized him, and backed off. He returned without accomplishing his purpose of killing Rodríguez.

"Just come from taking a long walk?" Carmela asked.

"Why ask what you know?" He headed directly to his small bedroom, and she followed him.

"There is no need for anyone to leave home every night. In most cases, a married man who goes out each night is going to see someone. You must have some whore giving you freak children."

"You know something, Carmela? Anyone can have freak children, even you." Juan was tired. It had been a mistake to wait so long to tell her. Carmela was still delicate and lovely. She could make a life with someone else if he freed her.

"I don't have to have children at all. You could wear prophylactics."

"I don't think so. You see, it's not just that."

"Are you planning to kill me?" she asked.

Juan stared at her. "Did you steal my gun because you thought I was going to shoot you?"

"If you wanted to kill me you could have done so with your bare hands. Isn't that what you did to our child?"

"You suspected that?" He sat heavily on his bed.

"Not at first." She sat next to him fanning herself. "It came to me later, all the years of not touching me. I figured it out because of that woman." Wisps of hair escaped from her braid. "There was something wrong with our baby wasn't there?"

"Yes." He sighed, too exhausted to listen to the sudden burst of spirits buzzing in his ear each at once. All morning digging graves, all afternoon helping people contact the spirits, and most of the night walking sapped him and left him so tired he could hardly talk.

"You thought it was me so you took a chance with that woman."

"Yes. No, I thought it was us with each other."

"But it is you."

"It's me. I know now that I can't escape. But it's even worse for us together." He looked hard into her eyes. "Carmela, your real father is my brother, and my father was our uncle." Juan expected Carmela to follow her usual line of argumentation: questions, denials, and insults, but he received nothing except a stare. She extended her fist, opened her hand, and held out a rubber.

"You're my husband."

"Didn't you understand what I said, what that makes us?"

"I don't want to know anything about that."

"Do you want me to treat you like a prostitute?"

"Anything is better than being treated like the Virgin Mary. What if you had never found out?"

"But I did." He looked hard at her outstretched hand. Scriptural verses condemning incest circled his mind, as did warnings against murder. Exhausted, full of pity for himself, for Carmela, for their lost years, his hand fluttered. Slowly, he reached out, closed her fingers over the condom, turned her now fisted hand over, and kissed the top of it. "No," he whispered. "No."

IX

Edelmira

Edelmira usually slept through the night if she had the nearby warmth of a body to barricade her thrashing so that she did not fall out of bed. Her nightmares had started the night she drank the champagne with Uncle Félix. Small bad dreams, in the beginning, like the one she had the first night she did not sense Rafaela in bed next to her.

Puffy white clouds followed and choked, thinned out and grabbed at her. To escape, she cycled her legs in her sleep and rolled around the bed to its edge. Her weight, though light, had almost dislodged the mosquito net tucked under the mattress when warm hands rolled her back to her proper side of the bed. Someone settled in next to her. Sleepy, she faintly registered the familiar scent of Aunt América and gave in to unconsciousness.

She slept peacefully, remembered nothing in the morning except surprise at seeing Rafaela in bed beside her instead of Aunt América. Edelmira said nothing, accepting her vague confusion as one more of many childish mistakes.

As she got older, the nightmares took on strange noises, flashes of light, and a hazy patchwork quilt of events mixed together in a jumble of puzzling times and places. They made her a bad student. Too tired from restless nights, Edelmira could not concentrate on her studies and dozed off in class.

When she was ten, Rafaela took her to Dr. Figueroa.

As usual, a majority of pregnant women filled his waiting room except for one man in the group, a lunatic named Federal. He stood stiffly, glazed eyes staring inward as he muttered aloud. Rafaela halted to listen to him.

"The world will suffer a second world war," he said, trembling. "Hurricanes will blight the earth, then great ships will dock at the ramparts. Who will be found standing after the holocaust?"

"Come on, Rafaela," Dr. Figueroa prodded. "He hasn't had his medicine and thinks he's foretelling the future."

"How can you be sure he isn't?"

"Federal is demented, ignore him. Tell me why you brought Edelmira."

"She wakes up sweating and panting as if she's run all night."

"Well there's nothing physically wrong. What is it you dream, Edelmira?"

"I don't know."

"You don't remember?"

"A big black monster, breathing clouds, screams and tries to crush me."

Dr. Figueroa looked at Rafaela's concerned face, said, "Monster dreams are common among sensitive children. Is there a lot of fighting in your house?"

Rafaela laughed. "Nobody left to fight with. América is in New York working in the theater and Europa lives near her."

"The twins? Your mother?"

"No."

"Anyone else?"

Edelmira knew who Dr. Figueroa meant. Uncle Félix and Rafaela always fought over the Nationalist Party. She remembered their most recent argument, the one that had them not speaking to each other for the past year.

The summer before, Rafaela had burst into their house with a bolt of fabric of creamy tan linen, which she measured, styled, and cut into two matching dresses. They had both worked feverishly to embroider small orange flowers with tiny green leaves along the collars, sleeves and hems. They dressed up to please Félix but when they arrived at his home, his usually pale cheeks had been puffed and splotched with red and he did not compliment them.

"What vulgarity is this?" Uncle Félix threw some papers at Rafaela. For seconds, they froze, open-mouthed at the writing sheets strewn at their feet. Edelmira, offended by his treatment, felt glad when Rafaela yelled back at him.

"Pick them up!" Rafaela commanded, pointing at the floor. "Pick them up right now and apologize." She stamped her foot, started counting, "Uno, dos, tres, . . ." Terrified, Edelmira did the same.

"Miguelito," Félix called, "show these two ladies out. And return their stupid essay."

Miguelito came into the living room, took Edelmira's hand to lead her into the kitchen. He shushed her objections with his finger to his lips and sat them both down at a mahogany table to listen to the voices in the living room. Edelmira had never heard so many forbidden words volleyed back and forth. Uncle Félix shouted first.

"Tits and Balls? Is that what your lunatic friends are teaching you?"

"It's an essay, you bastard. Did you even read it?"

"With that catchy title, how could I not?"

"Then you're too stupid to understand the symbols."

"It's a vulgar, pitiful attempt to win over the uneducated and shame the upper classes. How dare you give it to me?" Miguelito and Edelmira heard paper rustling. "Here, take it out of my house and burn it."

"You're just mad because you're a man with no balls."

"Keep talking to me like that and we're through."

"Then we're through, fucker. A woman with tits needs a man with balls."

Edelmira heard the stomping of Rafaela's heels coming her way. She looked at Miguelito. The small young man covered his eyes with his hands.

"Come on, Edelmira," Rafaela said. "Say good-bye to this useless ass forever." Rafaela grabbed Edelmira's hand and pulled her fiercely out the door. Outside, she stood fuming for a few moments and then ignored everyone she passed on the street.

At home Rafaela had thrown away her essay and said, "I'll write another and give it to someone who understands." Since then, they had not seen Uncle Félix, so there had not been any more fights.

Edelmira looked away not wanting to hear Rafaela's answer, saw Dr. Figueroa's son pass by the doorway. With his head tilted upwards, Junior Figueroa whistled as he walked past, keeping one hand in his pocket. She followed to get a better look. He was slim, his skin the gray-brown color of dried coconut.

"Hello," she said, smiling.

He turned. His eyes were light green. "Hi Blondie, are you sick?" he asked.

"No." She regretted his hair was *pasa*, ridged like raisins and plastered against his small round skull, instead of glossy mahogany. She returned to the waiting adults.

"Don't drink coffee or tea after four in the afternoon and take a warm bath before you go to bed." Rafael patted her. "Can you remember that?"

"Yes." Edelmira thought it best if she did not tell anyone about her bad dreams from then on and resolved to try harder in school.

To remain awake in class, she disregarded Dr. Figueroa's instructions and requested an extra cup of aromatic coffee, undiluted with milk, for breakfast. At lunchtime, she ran home for another cup and then drank yet another when school let out in order to be alert enough to do homework. At first she felt glad that the bitter black liquid made her lose her appetite and her roundness, but as time went by she needed more and more. Her stomach suffered a burning sensation and her breath stank. Still, she managed to graduate from high school and her nightmares stopped.

Edelmira knew Félix wanted to get rid of her, have Rafaela all to himself. He was the reason Edelmira fought with Rafaela. She had lost all respect for her godmother when Rafaela humbled herself to Félix after their big fight over her essay, saying the Great Depression forced her back to him.

At that time Rafaela had said, "He's the only wealthy person we know who helps us." With that statement, Rafaela had dressed up, taken him a gift of a special dish made with ground beef and sweet bananas, and apologized to him for allowing a bad joke to run too long.

But it was then that Edelmira began to examine Rafaela's past and future excuses for staying with Félix.

In 1928 Rafaela's excuse had been the chaos of hurricane San Felipe. In 1930 the Great Depression, in 1931 hurricane San Nicolás, in 1932 hurricane San Ciprián and the defeat of the Nationalist Party. Rafaela lost all her jobs in government, no matter how menial, by getting into political arguments with her employers. Championing the cause of independence even though it meant violent revolt scared those just starting to feel important and secure in appointed positions.

Every year it was poor Rafaela, fighter for justice and liberty, who was forced to succumb to Félix's empty promises of future marriage in order to get help to survive now. Edelmira did not think so. She believed Rafaela was all talk and no backbone just like the boys in her class who bragged about how they would grow up to free Puerto Rico but were the first to cry and inform on their friends if they were caught in some mischief at school.

And so time had passed. After a while there were no more hurricanes to blame but there was the business of Doña Antonia's funeral to arrange and that of parceling out the big house and the rented house to her sisters. Asia and África needed separate homes to live in with their husbands and children. Then Rafaela managed to find excuses for running to Félix during the 1937 Ponce massacre of nationalists and the European unrest.

Edelmira could not stand it any longer. She began to speak up.

"You're a fool," she said. Rafaela, who had never taught Edelmira to bridle her tongue, slapped her.

"You're the fool," she replied. "How do you think we'd live without Félix? Drying tobacco? Picking coffee beans? Sewing at home?" Rafaela crossed her arms and paced in front of her. "Make no mistake. I love Félix no matter how we disagree."

"He lies. He'll never marry you."

"I don't care. He'll never marry anybody else either."

Edelmira guffawed. "Except for you, everybody knows he's all over the island looking for a wife. What's going to happen to you when he finds one?"

"You don't know anything about life, love, and Félix. He's not going to find a wife because he doesn't want one, *estúpida*."

Edelmira knew her own love life would be attacked next.

"Why don't you have a boyfriend?" Rafaela asked.

"I'm young. I have plenty of time."

"You're the same age I was when I met Félix."

"Seventeen? My God, you've been with him for seventeen years?"

Rafaela threw her a warning look. "True love endures all things," she said.

"Not for me. I'm not enduring anything I don't like."

"You don't like any boy." Rafaela, thickening at the waist, put her arms on her ample hips. "That's why I worry. I know you have lots of time but you don't even want to start looking."

"Don't worry about me. I'll wait because I know exactly what I want."

"You know Dr. Figueroa was disappointed you didn't like his son."

"He would be perfect except for his hair." Edelmira's hand waved away the thought of Junior Figueroa.

"I'm trapped until you marry."

Edelmira felt trapped too. Their enslavement to Félix Cienfuegos restricted her every movement. She could not befriend just anyone or dress as she wanted because Félix might not like it, might complain and throw a tantrum, not be as generous. They were kept women.

"I know exactly what I want. And it'll never be anyone the least bit like fatso Uncle Félix."

"Who then? Another woman?"

Edelmira tasted vinegar in her mouth. Rafaela became vicious if anyone other than she attacked Félix.

Over the years, her fights with Rafaela had become so unbearable that she wanted to run away, join her Aunts América and Europa in New York. On her eighteenth birthday, she voiced her intention to leave and was not surprised by Félix's support.

"Yes, go," Félix said.

"Why should she?" Rafaela asked.

"Because she's of age now and not doing anything here," Félix replied. "There may be advantages in New York."

"So you won't feel trapped," Edelmira said, gleeful at Rafaela's ashen face.

"You've spoiled her," Félix said. "This is your reward. Let her go."

"You just want to get rid of her, you son of a bitch! Don't you realize she'll freeze in that country?"

"Your sisters didn't freeze. Neither will Edelmira."

Two months later she boarded the S.S. Puerto Rico, to New York. Félix and Rafaela waved and shouted, "Write us stories from New York." Edelmira thought them ridiculous. She might not even write them letters much less stories. She waved back glad to be rid of them, until she settled in with Aunt Europa.

Her Manhattan apartment was directly in front of the elevated platform of the 125th Street station on Broadway. A fifth-floor walkup with five roach-infested, cracker box–sized rooms with a view of the train tracks and the soot-encrusted tenements of La Salle Street and Moylan Place.

"I'm a factory forelady," Aunt Europa announced. "That's why I can afford this place." Thinner than Edelmira remembered, Aunt Europa waved her olive-skinned arms around the rooms. "Mostly Irish and Italian live here. A few Blacks and Puerto Ricans moving in, but not too many yet."

Two of the bedrooms were cold and empty. Edelmira remembered the people she saw on the street during their cab ride home and realized why they were bundled up like sacks. She wrapped her arms around herself. Her teeth chattered, making Europa laugh.

"Oh it takes a while to get used to the cold, but you will." Europa turned her around. "You're so small! I thought you'd be taller. Well, never mind. We'll fatten you up a bit."

"Why didn't Aunt América come to meet me?"

"She has problems. We'll see her tomorrow."

That first night, shivering under three thin, moth-eaten blankets, Edelmira's flesh puckered from chills that she felt when the clanking wheels of the elevated train in front of their apartment building rattled the windows and woke her. The sound of its braying and chugging reminded her of a sad old love song—filled her with lonesome yearnings and prickled her flesh with goose bumps from a sensation of déjà vu she could not identify.

"Wake up sleepyhead," Aunt Europa said in the morning.

"The sun's not out yet."

"Hah, it's not coming out today."

They took two buses to see Aunt América. The long ride took them past a nearby section where black women, resplendent in red lipstick, wore feathered hats and fur coats. That district melted into an industrial sector as the bus route followed a roadway beneath another elevated train, which unnerved Edelmira with the thought it might fall on her, until a last stop brought them to a second bus to be boarded.

"Do all the streets have lights?" she asked.

Europa laughed. "Yes, quite different, isn't it?"

"Cataño still does not have electric meters in all the homes," Edelmira said.

The new bus chugged along miles of a more rural-looking route. Finally, they reached Aunt América's tiny dollhouse, painted white, pink, and green. She opened the small front gate and ran over to them. Aunt América had shaved her eyebrows and painted on high, brown arches. She had painted pink circles on her cheeks and blood red on her mouth, overlapping her upper lip.

"Edelmira!" she exclaimed. "So good to see you again. And so grown up." América hugged her, kissed her, and whispered in her ear. "My husband understands Spanish. So be careful. Just agree with everything I say."

Edelmira noticed an automobile near the house and a man with his foot on its sideboard, a tall white man with a pink face and straw-colored hair.

"Sean, this is Edelmira. Isn't she everything I told you?" Sean smiled, shuffled, and approached, looking at Edelmira's hair.

"Real white girl, huh?"

"We Puerto Ricans come in all colors but we're not head-hunting cannibals."

Edelmira hated him and could not wait to leave. On the way home she remembered his questions with loathing. He had pointed at the lace tablecloth covering their dining room table.

"América says it's from Portugal."

"It is," Edelmira replied. "A friend of the family travels and gave it to us."

He pointed to the rugs on the floor. "Are these really from Morocco?"

"Yes. My Aunt Rafaela owns so many of these she gives them away."

"So you're all really from a good white family?"

"Are you?" Edelmira could not help herself. América and Europa gasped, but Sean was not offended.

"I'm Irish. I met América when she was ushering in the theater. Pretty girl. I went and married her." He threw his arms wide. "Now . . ."

"Aunt Europa, don't make me visit again."

Europa laughed. "Don't worry. I hate to go myself." She turned to Edelmira, showing her buck teeth. "It's hard here. Our English sounds funny to these people, and we have to make believe we don't notice that they look down on us. América was starving yet she wrote all those letters to Mamá and Rafaela saying she was a stage star." She laughed again but sobered quickly. "I bet Rafaela never believed a word. She kept sending money and gifts. It's not so bad, you'll get used to it."

"Never," Edelmira thought. "I don't have to." She could find a job and succeed. She did not care that her English sounded funny, taught to her by teachers who had never been to the states, who had taught themselves out of a textbook.

The cold shivered her flesh, trembled her insides, and settled deep inside her bones so that she never felt warm. Stinging winds bit her face, watered her eyes, and chapped her lips white.

Snow! Christmas in New York delivered a foot of plump, icelike but soft crystals catching colors as they fell until it blanketed everything in a thick white glare.

"Isn't it beautiful?" Europa asked.

"It's so cold," Edelmira replied.

"Come on let's go to Macy's. To look."

They climbed the stairs to the train platform. Edelmira, already upset that the heat of her body escaped in puffs of vapor through her mouth, shook when she saw the train tracks.

"Still cold?"

"I'm scared." She trembled.

She felt tremors under her feet, heard the rumble of a train approaching, turned to see funnels of lights like monster's eyes, and fainted. When she awoke, her body shook and rocked. She saw light and dark flash by, heard grating and screeching.

"What's happening?" Edelmira asked. Concerned passengers had placed her on a hard straw seat. She screamed until they arrived at the next station, and she ran off, clutched at a station column, and refused to let go. Forgetting the cold, she stood rooted to the spot, sweating and panting until she heard the next train arriving. Then she ran through the platform, up the stairs, and out into the snow with Europa catching up.

"You can't behave like a hick here," Europa said, panting. "This is New York."

Edelmira burst into tears. "I didn't know trains scared me," she sobbed. "Never take me on that thing again."

Europa shrugged, turned her face up, and licked at the snow. "How are you going to get to work?"

"The bus. Like when we visited Aunt América."

"It takes too long to use it for work."

For the first year her scant postcards read: "Rafaela, I'm fine. América and Europa are fine. No need to write so often. Sincerely."

Her next infrequent letters were: "Rafaela, I'm fine. We're all working and happy, no need to worry yourself over us. Sincerely." Rafaela sent money and Edelmira cried.

After that she wrote: "Dear Rafaela, how are you? It's cold here, but it gets better in summer although it doesn't last very long. We really don't need your help so stop sending money. Okay? Love, Edelmira."

Edelmira lost three factory jobs because no matter how early she left in the morning, the buses traveled so slowly she was always late. Ten tedious hours of sewing in bad light and a two-and-a-half-hour round trip looking through dirty bus windows fashioned her eyes into a kaleidoscope of red veins against the white and blue. Without the Puerto Rican sun her pearly white strands of hair turned an ugly lemon yellow that looked so artificial her coworkers asked why she dyed it that color.

"Everyone takes the train," she thought, as she brushed her hair to at least get the shine back. Each Monday morning Edelmira tried but her whole body trembled, and she saw flashes of bright lights that blinded her until she fainted. She simply could not get near the damned train tracks. She hated the buses too. Those rides were long and boring with only sad gray buildings to see.

She longed for swaying palm trees, the sound of blue and green waters with a cap of white foam roaring against brown rocks and creamy sand, for blue skies and bright sunlight to cheer her, but what could she do. She felt she had trapped herself in a hostile environment of her own free will.

"After all the things I said," she thought, "how can I ask to go back?" It reminded her of the insults she hurled at her last employer.

He had not minded her tardiness because he simply made her stay late to make up the time. She knew that what he minded was the annoyance on her face when he patted her, but she did not care and told him outright to stop.

"I mean no disrespect," he said, smiling. "I'm just demonstrative. It's my Latin half." He laughed.

For the sake of her job she put up with his touchy-feely manner of patting her head, touching her elbow, and letting his fingers linger on her hands when he showed her some new material even though she hated him. He smiled some more and nodded his head at her acceptance, but he did not stop it there. He began to pat her back with his open palm, then tried to accelerate his patting into rubbing. Anxiety prickled her at the feel of his warm moist palm and pink doughy fingers planted on her back. She wanted to scream and continue screaming, but for the sake of the job, she endured—until one day when he caught her in a bad mood.

It was hot, the bus packed, so she stood all the way, and at the factory the ancient elevator did not work so that she had to climb up five flights to a cubicle of a workroom stuffed with ten sweating women about to pass out. The sight of his smug smile and ready hands infuriated her to the point that before she could stop herself, she screamed, "*¡No me toques, so puerco!*"

Edelmira realized later that he might not have minded a simpler objection, but he was fluent in Spanish and protested, in front of his other Hispanic workers, to being called a pig. And so he fired her.

X

Félix

He drove hurriedly along the road from San Juan to Cataño willing someone to appear in his path so that he could run him down and leave him plastered on the ground as his hopes had been. On the passenger seat beside him, Rafaela sat with her arms crossed, stiffly resisting the jostle of every bump on the road. Sitting behind them, Diego and Bartolomeo crashed and smashed into each other with each jump and turn, Diego scared, Bartolomeo laughing.

"Slow down," Diego cried. "We'll all be killed."

"Not even a delegate." Félix fumed, sped up.

"We never get anywhere," Bartolomeo said. "I'm retiring from politics." He took out a cigar.

"Don't light that in here," they shouted in unison. He put it unlit into his mouth and continued speaking. "I'm going to support Muñoz Rivera's son. He's sure to become governor because of his family name. Meanwhile I have an appointment in Spain with my future sixteen-year-old bride."

Félix lightened his foot on the accelerator and the car slowed a bit. "The son is coming to his senses, like his father did."

"Yes." Diego nodded. "Did you hear him clearly say independence would not be discussed on the agenda in 1940?"

"Of course we heard him," Bartolomeo said. "That's what we were talking about. Wake up will you?"

"He's selling out to stay in power," Rafaela said. The men ignored her, continued to discuss Félix's disappointment at the tri-party union's loss of the elections.

"We should have won," Félix insisted. "Statehood's the only answer now."

"Independence," Rafaela said. "Rodríguez was right. So ignorant of history, you Simple Simons don't know who or what you are." She spoke to no one in particular, kept her eyes on the road.

Félix speeded up, roared past the shacks of Amelia, and careened into Cataño. In front of the Figueroa's house, he stepped heavily on the brakes. Their heads lurched forward and then whipped back. Diego and Bartolomeo spilled out of the car, each opening the door on his own side. Rafaela waited for Félix to open her door. When she stepped out, she smoothed the right hip of her dove grey sheath and patted her matching feathered cap.

"You look lovely, darling," Josie said. While they kissed hello, Rafael rushed out to shake hands with the men, usher them into the house, and serve them drinks. "And your hair. It's so shiny."

"It's just turning silver." She sat on the balcony. "Félix is upset that the new Popular Democratic Party won and his famous pro-statehood parties unified for nothing." She wiped her forehead. "They wound up with no delegates, and he didn't get a position." Rafaela looked at Josie, smoothed her right side again, and asked, "Can I have some morphine?"

Open-mouthed, Josie tried to turn her face into the house without taking her eyes off Rafaela and called, "Rafael, come here quick!" Josie grabbed Rafaela just as her eyes rolled up into her head and just before she fainted.

"What's wrong?" Rafael asked.

"She's feverish and has pain on her right side."

They carried her into their infirmary while Félix watched, mouth open, and trembled. Worry began like a comet burst of colors in his abdomen and spread like tentacles of fireworks throughout his entire body. He perspired yet felt cold. Rafaela was sick. *Of course!* She had not been her usual spitfire self gloating over his defeat. She had yelled no insults when Bartolomeo announced he was taking a Spanish child bride.

"How could I be so stupid?" he asked aloud.

Diego and Bartolomeo donned their hats.

"For once, she didn't complain," Bartolomeo said. "It's not your fault." He patted Félix. "She's in good hands. Let's go."

"No."

"We'll discuss our strategy some other time, Félix."

"No. I mean, yes. You two go. I'll stay."

But he could not stay long. He paced back and forth a few moments and then ran out of the Figueroa's and drove like a maniac back to San Juan, looking for Rodríguez in all his known haunts. It was not that he distrusted Rafael's abilities, it was that, well, this was Rafaela and there was just one master diagnostician on the island.

He left the motor running, stomped out of his car and banged on Rodríguez's door. "Open up! We need you."

Rodríguez, aged, peered down his balcony at Félix. "What is it?" Three young men, his sons, flanked him.

"Appendix maybe. Hurry."

In minutes, Rodríguez emerged fully dressed, carrying his medical bag. "Who is it?" he asked. "What are the symptoms?"

Félix answered his questions while he drove back, tooting his horn at pedestrians most of the way. The doctor chuckled.

"Long friendship you two have. Twenty years isn't it?" Before Félix could gulp down his astonishment, Rodríguez got out of the car, held his palm up to the Figueroas, and said, "I'm here only as a consultant and only if you permit me."

His face darkened with anger, Rafael glared at Félix but he replied in a calm tone. "Always glad to have your esteemed opinion. Please come in."

Félix did not care if he offended Dr. Figueroa and whispered to

Rodríguez, "Save her." Ignoring the contemptuous look thrown at him by both men he watched as Dr. Rodríguez, led by Rafael, went into the infirmary reciting a Simple Simon poem. He sat in the waiting room listening to their conversation.

"Must you?" Rafael asked.

"Yes, I like Simple Simon. Are your instruments sterile?"

"Yes, but . . ."

"What is her temperature?"

"104."

"What did you give her?"

"Penicillin."

"Any idea of her tolerance for pain?"

"What are you thinking?"

"That we have to go in right now."

"We? Your specialty is gynecology."

"I have many patients, including men and children. They don't all appear like walking vaginas to me."

Félix heard nothing for several minutes, then, Rafael's resignation.

"Will you be kind enough to assist me?"

"Madam!" Rodríguez called. Josie, who had been fuming at Félix, jumped up and ran into the infirmary, ran back out, and bustled about the house. She and Félix boiled water, arranged instruments, carted sheets, and prayed. He caught himself trying to finger the absent pearls, felt glad he had given them to Rafaela long ago, looked down at his empty hands, and wept.

"Control yourself, Félix," Josie said. "It's too late now for that."

When the operation was over, he rushed into the small infirmary, stroked her forehead, kissed her cheeks, and held her hands until Rodríguez said, "Is this going to go on all night? I have to get back home and it's too late for the ferry."

Ashamed, Félix got up off his knees, glanced back at Rafaela's sleeping face, and prepared to take Rodríguez home. No one said a word except for a very formal "Good night and thank you."

On the ride back to San Juan, Rodríguez turned in the passenger seat to face him.

"Your party lost in the elections."

"I'm giving my support to Muñoz Marín. He's intelligent and rational." Félix dared to glance at Rodríguez. "Not some crazy *independentista* advocating war against the United States like some mosquito challenging a behemoth."

"Ah, yes." Rodríguez chuckled. "The upstart, suspected of being a user of marijuana, plucked from U.S.A. streets, cleaned up, and brought home to Puerto Rico like a king's descendant to continue his family's dynasty."

"You're a strange man, Dr. Rodríguez. I believe you say ugly things you don't mean just to have an effect on your listeners even if your statements turn others against you."

"What a waste of intelligence you are."

No matter how Rodríguez insulted him and his politics during the drive, Félix, conditioned by learning to ignore Rafaela's ravings, remained quiet until he dropped the old doctor in front of his door where his three sons waited. Rafaela and the doctor were so much alike. Time and circumstance changed politics. Why couldn't they accept that?

The next morning, Félix could not console Rafaela.

"Now I have a scar," she screamed.

"And you'll have another," Félix said, "if you break your stitches."

She quieted, then lost herself in thought. Nothing he did or said roused any interest. She stared off into space and he knew that she did not see him. For a long time he stared at her form, tucked tightly into white sheets with a flap turned over across her breast.

Only her hair moved or seemed to as it glittered under transient flickers of sunlight filtering through the window shutters. The sound of their breathing filled the room as all three of them, Félix, Rafael, and Josie stared down at Rafaela's chiseled face and stony eyes. None knew what to say to this new sphinxlike creature. They remained suspended in a limbo of silence and uncertainty.

"Go away," Rafaela said, finally. "Everything is wonderful and everybody is so rich and happy, nobody needs you." She closed her eyes, muttered, "The hell with you, Rafaela."

Why did that sound familiar? Félix remembered Edelmira's letters and recognized Rafaela's interpretation of them, different words, same message. Infuriated at the ingratitude that saddened Rafaela, he wondered how he could snap her out of her depression.

XI

Edelmira

During her fourth bout with unemployment in as many years, Félix showed up at her door on a Sunday. Europa was at the movies with a boyfriend, and at first Edelmira thought it was the superintendent of the building who demonstrated interest in leaky faucet repairs only when Edelmira was alone in the apartment. She did not answer the knock on the door until she heard a familiar call, soft yet loud.

"Europa Moya! Edelmira Betancourt! Is anyone home? This is Félix Cienfuegos." She opened the door, wide, forgetting she still wore her pajamas and threw herself at him.

"Uncle Félix!" She hugged and kissed him.

"Here I am," he said. "To investigate all this nonsense." He walked in, surveyed the living room, and removed his hat. He was bald. "What's going on here?"

"Nothing."

"Rafaela's very unhappy. She has no spirit. I've never known her not to fight or talk."

"What's bothering her?" Edelmira asked, suddenly worried.

"You. Why are you still in your pajamas?"

"I'm fine. I don't write good letters, that's all."

"Humpff!" Félix made his famous sour face.

She hugged him again. "I'm so glad to see you."

His round face lit up pinkish and he asked, "Have you missed us?" Before she could answer, Europa returned, saw Félix, and turned back to murmur something to a dark shape in the hallway. They heard kissing noises before she entered and locked the door.

"Well hello, Félix." Affecting a model's walk, one foot in front of the other, Europa removed her coat, looked at Edelmira. "Staying with us long?"

"I'm here on business. I have a place to stay."

Europa showed her teeth. "What business? Any men you can introduce us to?"

"Humpff!" He twisted his mouth again. "Edelmira, get dressed. We're going downtown." She knew then that Europa had written about her problem.

"How are we going there?"

"By train, I want to see for myself."

"See what? See me faint?"

"Of course."

"Why?"

"So I can laugh and have an excuse to take you back."

Her mouth fell open and her eyes misted. He looked at her from one side of his face as he did whenever he tested Rafaela's reactions. "Stop looking like a stray mongrel and start packing." He stood tall, taller, she thought, than most of the men in their neighborhood and tailored better than any of her factory owners. "I'll be back to get you tomorrow at two o'clock. Are you afraid of sailing too?"

"I get seasick."

"Oh, good God!" He left, saying he had to buy some things and that there was no need for anyone to accompany him.

When Edelmira returned to Cataño shamed as a failure, her only stories were that Aunt América had never been a Broadway starlet in spite of Rafaela introducing her to Hilda Cray and the Hawaiian actors, and that América had married an American who thought her beneath him because she was Puerto Rican and that New Yorkers traveled underground in trains that resembled long, crowded coffins.

"We don't speak good English, you know. Americans laugh at us, even the friendly ones. I had to endure their corrections." Edelmira mimicked: "Chicken, not chee-ken! Wood, not 'ood! You, not ju! And all that he-she stuff." She paused. "They laughed like hyenas if I said the table she is pretty."

Edelmira studied Rafaela. "No wonder you want freedom for Puerto Rico."

"That's not the reason," Rafaela said, shaking her head. "Most nations make fun of cultural differences. We make fun of lisping Spaniards, braggart Cubans, and countrified Dominicans, don't we?" Rafaela looked at Félix who nodded.

"Human nature," he said.

"I believe we deserve our chance at self-government without exploitation from other countries whether it works in the eyes of the rest of the world or not," Rafaela said. "Just like other nations. It is a human right. Simple as that."

Safe in comfortable surroundings, Edelmira allowed Félix and Rafaela to laugh at her foolishness and to poke fun at how a choo-choo train could scare her so much.

"Whenever you fainted, you didn't fall gracefully, like a lady," Félix said. "You stiffened and crashed down with your chicken legs straight up in the air."

"How do you know?"

"My big eyes are in every place."

"There used to be a train from here to Bayamón and back," Rafaela said, thoughtfully. "But it was torn down in the twenties and you're too young to remember it. Anyway, none of that matters now." Rafaela grabbed Edelmira's winter chapped hands and looked into her eyes. "We've got to get you a career and a husband. That's what is important now."

Edelmira smiled half-heartedly. She remembered the pathetic assortment of Europa's boyfriends.

It was 1942, jobs and goods were scarce and men even more rationed. They had left in droves for the States to pursue jobs and war. Rafaela herself could not find a job after picketing against the surrender of the Casino of Puerto Rico for the sole entertainment of American troops. What was Edelmira going to do?

"Become a teacher," Rafaela said. "It only takes a year of 'normal' study at the university to qualify for the rural areas, and you'll have job security. Men love teachers, you know that."

Edelmira, who knew no such thing, had resisted the idea before. Now she had no choice.

After testing for her certification she became a rural teacher in Hato Tejas and after more study became a real teacher. Later she switched, with Félix's help, to tutoring the children of the San Juan rich.

During the next four years, she met a lot of men who thought her desirable not only because she had an education and a good job but because she was a rarity in Puerto Rico: a true blue-eyed blonde whose florid skin burned without tanning.

"Are you from Corozal?" they asked. French and German ancestry bestowed her coloring on many of the people from that area, but not too many.

"Cataño," she replied, proudly.

She began each relationship elated with hope and false love based on the most feeble of attractions—a man whose white handkerchief peeked jauntily from a pocket, another with a certain vanity in movement, or one with silky brown skin—and ended disillusioned. Early in her relationships, she found fault with them and then ran to Rafaela as if her life had ended instead of a stupid crush.

"I thought David's eyes were green," Edelmira said.

"So?" Rafaela asked.

She made a wordless sound of bother by sucking her teeth but still turned red with shame at her next words. "His eyes are hazel."

"You dropped David because his eyes are hazel, not green?" Rafaela exhaled through pouty lips, crossed her arms. "What's wrong with you, Ede? Why can't you like anyone?"

Edelmira shook her head impatiently. "I'm waiting for the right man. When he comes along, I'll know him."

"Well, all right. That was David. What's so objectionable about Manolo?"

"When he laughs, he sounds like a squawking chicken."

"So what?"

"I don't think a man who laughs like an imbecile over every simple statement I make can be very intelligent. Do you?"

"Maybe it's just nerves because he's in love."

"I don't nag you. Why do I have to marry the first *Juan Bobo* that comes along?" Edelmira felt indignant and pressured. "I'm sorry I involved you. I'm twenty-six years old, I'll tell Manolo myself that I can't marry him."

"No, Félix and I will do it." Rafaela lowered her eyes. "We'll be more kind and invent a reason he can accept. Nothing can be done if you don't love him."

Relieved, Edelmira said, "Thank you, *Madrina*." She promised Rafaela she would be more careful with her friendships in the future and got up to leave.

"Before you go, tell me who you are waiting for."

"A tall, gentle man with light brown skin, green eyes, and reddish brown wavy hair. Also with a singing voice."

"Remember this," Rafaela advised, "there are no perfect men, just men you happen to love in spite of their stupidity."

Home alone, Edelmira felt glad she had not told Rafaela how every time she got close to a man she felt he would die if she married him. The bad dreams returned as they usually did whenever she broke with a suitor.

In her dream she was back in New York waiting to board a train when she heard its engine. Excitement and power surged through her. She churned and rolled in her bed.

The train, a black blur, sped towards the platform. The urge hit her to become one with its locomotion, and Edelmira ran alongside it, heard the soft stampede of her own feet thudding on earthen ground. She felt the hot blast of air, ran with the train, smiling at the onlookers as she flew past them, feet pounding, arms pumping, every thought concentrated on beating her steely lover in the race. Ready, she jumped to embrace it and white light engulfed her. Books splattered to the ground.

Rivulets of perspiration soaked her nightgown. She awoke, heart thumping like a crazed machine, breathless. Edelmira no longer wondered what the nightmare meant, only that it would stop when there were no serious relationships to break, no disappointments to cope with. She would be more careful, not involve herself in affairs that, inexplicably, made her feel close to death.

XII
Rafaela

As years escaped her with the alarming speed of rivers flooded from burst dams, the weighty rock of accumulated disappointments sloshed deep inside her abdomen, and Rafaela also began to wake in the middle of the night from troubled sleep more and more often.

She had fallen in love with a man who did not understand himself, did not know what he really needed, and deluded himself by working toward fantasies doomed to failure. Félix amassed great riches first to prove his worth and become accepted by society, then to break into politics, then to have some grand memorial to leave to children that he never had. The elusive reality was that he did not know what to do with any of these things.

In her bed, Rafaela shifted position, pounded her fist on her pillow. With his taciturn personality, Félix snubbed members of the high society he coveted, declared them vacuous and boring, did not associate with them except at mandatory social and political functions, although at the same time he constantly worried what they thought about him. Rafaela laughed out loud.

His political aspirations, simply a vehicle, something to keep him motivated. The most fun he ever had was championing the cause of statehood against her ardent nationalism. Their arguments contented him. Talk replaced the need to take action on his convictions. Rafaela remembered the awful essay she had written long ago, giving it the vulgar title of "Tits and Balls." She giggled.

"God, I was dumb."

Of course she did it to rile him, irritate his insipid attitudes, but thinking about it now she justified the far-fetched analogies as original and relevant.

She had written about Puerto Rican women whose small breasts nonetheless provided enough milk for their many children. And about the husbands, men whose testicles fathered these offspring, and men who provided for their sons, often at the expense of their own health by toiling long hours seven days a week. She had composed the essay during the height of both her spiteful desire to embarrass Félix with vulgarity and her infatuation with militant Albizu Campos and his free Puerto Rico, but had decided, after she saw the poor following he received, that Félix might know something after all.

Even the great poet Luis Palés Matos became discouraged with freedom fighting and succumbed to the call of the arts. Palés Matos abandoned the cause of independence to celebrate negritude in his poetry, using words and rhythms reminiscent of African civilizations. If he had not been able to see a way out from under North American colonialism, what could Rafaela, with herself and a parcel of relatives to oversee, do?

The right time and the right people for independence lived and died during the late 1800s. Too few had moved then and too few had the energy and determination to move now, including Rafaela. It was too late. *Or too soon.* Years ago, the sole radical freedom fighter of her time, Albizu Campos, had been jailed in Atlanta and then exiled to New York, still an ardent patriot but a physically broken man. Rafaela shuddered at his calls for outright war and assassinations. She knew she could never approve bloodshed.

Félix's marriage and children were the biggest delusions of all. Rafaela got up out of bed, turned on the light, squinted, and looked at herself in the mirror. She was fifty-four, Félix fifty-nine. Too much silver streaked her hair. The bones of her face had hardened and she had grown jowls while he was fat and bald. She felt she had enjoyed all the benefits of marriage without the labors. He provided anything she needed without having a say about her coming and going or having a right to make demands of her in the kitchen, which she hated, or asking for children. His quest for the perfect wife to give him perfect children, another of the mysteries of Félix's active self-deception. He could not accept that he was simply one among a rare breed of confirmed bachelors who, like her, do not want children, in fact do not really like them. Caring for her sisters and raising Edelmira had proved that to both of them.

What an exasperation Edelmira turned out to be. Rafaela could not get the satisfaction of seeing her happy. She caused the senseless bachelor-hood of Junior Figueroa, who loved her, by refusing to marry and kept saying, "I'm waiting." But for what? For a man that fit peculiar specifica-tions from his hair to his voice?

Rafaela let her mind's eye travel over the faces of all the people they knew and thought of no one. Then she tried to remember trips to other parts of the island where they might have encountered someone like that. Nobody there either and yet something buried in memory wanted to surface. That description, so precise as to be impossible, nevertheless felt familiar.

Rafaela looked at herself in the mirror again. What brought all this out?

She did not deceive herself. It was the eleventh anniversary since the rise of a woman to the coveted position of mayor of San Juan. "Felisa Rincón de Gautier deserved the post," thought Rafaela, "for all her untir-ing public service." *But I helped others, why not me too?* She folded her arms across her chest, paced back and forth, looking for someone to blame.

If fat old Darío had married her mother, if she had been an only child and had attended University, if her sisters had been more independent, if she hadn't gotten Edelmira. She stopped, slapped her forehead. No, those weren't the reasons. Big mouth, losing causes, cowardice, and self-interest, she answered herself. *I compromised on issues I felt strongly about and then overreacted at the wrong times.* Her party choice, never the political favorite, made her lose jobs because of her nationalist ravings. Yet she would do it again rather than end up a total hypocrite like Félix.

Though she loved him, she never gave one inch of her personality to suit his ideal of a model wife, and, no, she had not remained faithful to him. *So there, world! Stick that up your nose.* She laughed again, loud and long, until tears ran down her face. Rafaela took out her pearls and put them on, admiring herself. She was several years younger than the mayor of San Juan. She would take better care of her skin, color her hair, be more careful how she spoke, and try again. Slowly, she removed her hands from the pearls. *Who am I deceiving? I sold out like the rest.* Valor and sacrifice led to grave discomforts.

In the end, she and Félix had both lost. Five years before, Puerto Rico had been inaugurated as a "Free Associated State," a hybrid vehicle of colonialism, neither an independent nation as she had wished nor a state as Félix had wanted.

She looked again at the pearls and thought about Felisa Rincón de Gautier's former dressmaking business and about her collection of fans. *Gifts!*

"I'll pawn these," she thought, fingering the pearls, "to open my own business before I die a complete nothing." *A gift shop will suit me.* "That's us," she thought wryly. Félix and Rafaela, the givers of worthless gifts.

XIII
Juan

This was the night of the murder. His congo spirit shook his spear, said, "He dies this evening," and darkness arrived early. The streets of old San Juan were deserted except for the tap, tap, tap of the old doctor's footsteps and muted echoes of music far away. It was October, foggy, and Juan did not encounter another soul except the old man who knew Juan followed. Rodríguez looked over his shoulder several times, threw his head back with amusement. Juan saw that Rodríguez deliberately walked down dangerous alleyways as if to lead him into a dead end, a trap.

Out of the darkness, the lady appeared in her swaying white dress to say, "You don't do it," and during the minute of confusion it took Juan to let that idea form, Rodríguez disappeared. "Damn," Juan thought. *"He knows the streets better than I do."* Where was he? Juan rushed around a corner on his left. There! Waiting, half-concealed by a darkened door frame. Juan looked around, took out his pistol. Rodríguez stepped forward to face him.

"Why have you followed me all these years?"

"To kill you."

Juan saw intensity in the old man's cloudy eyes.

"Better men than you have tried."

Juan aimed his pistol. "Say your prayers if you know any."

Dr. Rodríguez held up his hands. "Wait, your wife is my daughter."

"So, you know."

"I know all my children. Is that why?"

"I'm surprised you didn't try to sleep with her."

"Bed my own daughter? That's disgusting."

"Good-bye." Juan cocked his gun.

"Why now when I have so few years left?"

"Because I couldn't get to you before."

"Is it because I encouraged you to remain a spirit medium?" Rodríguez continued to stare at Juan, unnerving him with his probing eyes. Then the aged doctor took a deep breath and smiled sadly. "We're related aren't we?" After pausing he added, "Good God, that tremendous old woman, what was she to us?"

Juan choked on the answer, could not say or ask all he had intended to, and concentrated on keeping his hand from shaking.

"Do your worst," Rodríguez said. "In my youth, I died many times. Now it's time for the real thing but I'll live on. You can't kill a spirit, the spirit of . . ."

A shot rang out. The bullet pierced the aged man's forehead, pushed his head back. He crashed, pinned upright against a wall. Fascinated, Juan watched other bullets hit his eyes, nose, and cheeks until Rodríguez slithered down, face obliterated into a bloody mass. He lowered his undischarged pistol, turned his head to look at his brother's murderer, but she was already running away, white nun's habit flying.

"Leave that gun with me," he called. She did not stop. He put his pistol away, crouched over the body. Balcony doors opened to spill diffused light into the misty air. A presence he had not noticed before stepped closer to look. The man put his knife away, stared at Juan. Juan stared back, asked, "You saw?"

The man reached into his pocket, lit a cigarette, and said, "I saw."

Others appeared out of shadows. "What happened?"

The stranger answered, smiling. "A nun killed Rodríguez." They laughed. "Sure it was."

"It's true." A heavily painted woman stepped forward. "I did see a nun running away." Juan recognized her as someone he had healed of stomach cramps.

The police released him from the station after smelling his fully loaded pistol and after hearing eyewitnesses state that the grave digger, who was a familiar sight on the streets of San Juan, never hurt anyone and that they saw a nun shoot Rodríguez. The police left for the cathedral to investigate.

Back home Carmela waited, sweating.

"I took the habit off in a doorway, she said. "In your rowboat, I wrapped the gun in it and threw both into the bay. I don't know who saw me."

"Everybody. There were many people hiding in the shadows, and they all know who you are."

"They'll hang me."

"Not if they don't catch you. But you should have listened and left the gun with me."

"I did it because . . ."

He didn't let her finish. "It's not over. You'll have to leave before anybody talks."

"Where?"

"Santo Domingo. With Paula."

XIV
The Figueroas

Grim-faced, Dr. Figueroa returned from the morgue in a foul mood.

"I should have left the practice to Junior and retired years ago," he said. "I no longer have the stomach." He fell heavily onto his worn sofa, pressed his arthritic hands on the sagging cushions. "Josie, get new furniture. What are we, paupers?"

Gray-haired, with body straight as a telephone pole, Josie said, "Don't make my life miserable because you've gotten old. I'm old too." She sat beside him, wiped her forehead, looked at the perspiration in the palm of her hand. "I don't like it."

"Old age?" he asked. Her face was all eyes now, dull bits of green in a sea of brown wrinkles.

"The time of death," she answered. "I'm surprised he wasn't killed sooner. Why now puzzles me." Rafael stared off into space. "Why now indeed," wondered Rafael. And the way Rodríguez was murdered, his face destroyed by the pistol emptied into it.

"Juan Peña found him," he said.

"The grave digger? What irony."

"You know, I got the strangest feeling I was looking at the same man." Josie gave him a blank stare. "I had never seen them together," he explained. "Both are, or were, tall and slim with similar features and the same pattern of gray hair."

"Nappy hair." Josie said. "In your old age all Negroes look alike to you."

Rafael chuckled. "Thanks Josie. I needed a laugh." He stroked her hand absentmindedly.

"Who killed him?" she asked.

"Witnesses saw a woman running away but they claim it was too dark to see clearly."

"Did the grave digger see anything?"

"He said no. That he heard shots and almost fell over the body when he went to investigate."

"Did he have a gun?"

"Yes but it hadn't been fired."

"Strange."

"What?"

"Nothing. I don't know. Something." She crinkled her face.

"Yes," thought Rafael. Something smelled mysterious but what motive? And the people. They had glanced nervously at the grave digger and insisted the murderer was a nun. "One of his victims maybe?"

"He wasn't still at it?"

"Probably."

"Do you know how old he was?" Josie asked.

"About a thousand."

"Eighty-eight."

"That's all? Rodríguez talked about knowing Betances."

"Not a chance."

"Why not?" Rafael asked, arching his eyebrows. "They were both doctors."

"Think about this. Ramón Emeterio Betances saved people from cholera with a medicine he made himself. He not only preached against slavery, he also took advantage of a law allowing slaves to buy their freedom at the time of their baptism. He went around to churches and donated his own money to pay for it. On top of all that, he worked for independence from exile while Rodríguez did what? Try to impregnate women and brainwash frightened children?" Josie was ever the schoolteacher. "Besides, the father of our country could never associate with that awful man, even if he did know his medicine."

Rafael's ears perked up. "Josie, you said *our* country." He looked at her misty-eyed. "Is this finally your country too?"

"I have no choice. I'm too old to look for a new husband elsewhere." She unfolded her hands, put one on his shoulder. "Do you remember how he behaved the night you operated on Rafaela?"

Rafael nodded. "Brilliant doctor but peculiar man. He kept asking if I knew any Simple Simon tales because he collected them."

"Tales of poverty and death due to mental deficiency make me sick." Josie patted her stomach. "From the time I landed here, I've never understood why old-timers laugh at those tragic stories."

"Rodríguez gave me his theory."

"Well?"

"He said most countries have tales of a comical Simple Simon because the stories don't touch them but that our stories are worse, because Puerto Ricans typify their tragic lives as Simple Simon in order to cope with and laugh at their continuing hopeless dilemma." He shrugged. "It sounded profound and disturbing at the time."

"I know what you mean," Josie said. "He had a way of using the kind of logic that sounds reasonable enough to make you think it the truth even though everything moral and decent inside you rejects it. That's probably why he especially concentrated on weak women and children." Josie bit her lip and turned to face him. "He never succeeded with strong women. I know because he tried with me."

Rafael turned his face abruptly and could not speak without stammering. "You, you . . . he, he didn't."

"I can tell you now because he's dead. Once, when you were away in Manatí, he asked me to leave you and marry him."

"He was in the house?"

"Of course not!" She swatted his shoulder. "He spoke to me directly from outside the house while I sat on our balcony. When I refused him, he apologized and began to call me 'Madam.' Then as easy as you please, he turned and began to speak to a woman standing near the beach."

"My God! I wonder how many lives that man touched and ruined."

"He ruined Rafaela's by filling her head with ideas she could never be prepared to carry out."

"Maybe we too had a hand in spoiling her. She never could make up her mind which way to go."

"Don't say that!" Josie spoke too loudly. "Without our influence she would have grown up illiterate and malnourished. It was Rodríguez who made her crazy. Too bad you didn't specialize in psychiatry." Josie rose to her feet.

"Yes, think what a subject that man would have made."

"Let's go to bed," Josie said, pulling at him. "Before we get any older."

Following Josie into their bedroom, Rafael danced a waltz behind her and said, "At least Rafaela is finally a respected businesswoman."

"I have some business for you, too," Josie said, slamming their bedroom door.

XV
Edelmira

Edelmira avoided all misunderstandings. Whenever her stomach fluttered because a man's skin tanned to the warm gray-brown of dry coconuts or her knees felt weak because his hair looked a shiny mahogany, she warned him from the start.

"Accept that this is a passing fancy for me. I won't marry you, and you're wasting your time."

Because of their egos, most men did not believe she could resist their charms and continued their pursuit, supplying her with companionship until they tired of unrequited love and moved on, bitterly, to another. Not once did she feel sorry or shed a tear.

She greeted her late thirties unmarried and aging badly. Her fair skin fermented under hard, unforgiving sunlight and turned sour with premature lines and wrinkles. When striations ran across her forehead and lines etched themselves around her turned-down lips reinforcing her expression of sadness, fewer suitors approached her except for some opportunistic enough to think a well-placed older woman might gratefully shower them with gifts of gold watches and money in exchange for their company. At thirty-eight, she looked fifty and began to confine her social outings to teas with Rafaela and mutual friends, especially after Dr. Figueroa confided Rafaela's illness to her.

Today was an exception to the stay-at-home rule. Rafaela told her to be prepared to take a trip with a friend of hers who recently returned to Puerto Rico after many years in the States. It amazed Edelmira, who had few friends, that Rafaela kept in contact with almost everyone she had ever known. She almost suspected her godmother of matchmaking until she met him.

The dark-haired man, Tomás Arriesgo, tall and fair-skinned, vaguely discomfited her. He told many stories of his adventures in Alabama and Texas and insisted on visiting the grave of his brother, Luis. He drove them in a borrowed car.

In the Manatí cemetery, Tomás brought out a bottle of champagne, shed tears, and toasted, in English, saying, "To the Monkey Man, the best friend and brother a man could ever hope to have."

Rafaela joined the toast. "To the Monkey Man."

Edelmira felt brittle, breakable. *The Monkey Man?* A sudden image of herself, led by a young man who walked on all fours made her dizzy. "W-What do you mean, the Monkey Man?" she asked, nauseated.

They described Luis Arriesgo whose deformity forced him to walk on hands and feet.

"It was many years ago," Rafaela said. "He died young."

Edelmira's florid face turned white as a calla lily.

"What's the matter?" Tomás asked.

"I-I remember." Her stomach heaved.

Tomás shook his head, Rafaela smiled. "You can't remember," they said. "It was too long ago."

Edelmira felt a spray of warm liquid sprinkle her face. "It's raining blood," she said.

Tomás and Rafaela looked up at the cloudless blue sky, then at each other. Rafaela grimaced, held her hand at her right side by her rib cage. Tomás took out his handkerchief, gave it to Rafaela who used it to wipe the perspiration streaming down Edelmira's face.

"Ede, are you sick?" Rafaela asked.

"Yes." Edelmira's insides trembled and she realized she was crying.

They sat her on the bare cemetery ground, forced her knees up and her head between her legs.

Edelmira sobbed, remembered the Monkey Man's face much like Tomás's, but it was the other, the face of Luis's companion, that saddened her.

She remembered how comfortably her five-year-old backside had fit between the second and third balcony steps of the house she lived in with her mother, near the tracks of the killing train. Ede saw the boys racing and clowning around. Luis Arriesgo whinnied like a horse with his best friend, and they collapsed in giggles near her, giving her candy and bouncing her ball. She enjoyed playing with them both but she loved having Waldemar to herself better.

Ede thought him the most beautiful man she had ever seen except that he was not a man at all. He was fifteen years old and wore a schoolboy's uniform with knickers. His skin was tanned to a deep warm brown and his eyes were the light green of sugarcane.

"Hey, Blondie," Waldemar called. "Here's a present for you." He gave her a cigar band and scrunched himself down next to her. Waldemar gave her one every day but today felt different. She put it on her finger while he strapped a belt around his books, rearranged a white handkerchief in his breast pocket.

Ede watched the rising sun glint off his small, sharp nose and highlight his mahogany hair. "I love you," she said.

He laughed, loudly. "You're a baby. I'd have to wait for you to grow up, and God only knows what will happen by then." She began to cry, covering her eyes with pudgy fingers, wetting her cigar band until it broke and shredded. Waldemar hugged her. "Oh, all right. It's only fair. You wait for me every day so I'll wait for you. When you grow up, we'll get married. All right?" Ede nodded happily, heard the train whistle in the distance. Other boys joined them, other boys who took the same train by running alongside it, jumping and climbing on because they lived between train stops.

Edelmira had blocked out being sprayed with his arm, sticky blood, seeing white flashes when Waldemar fell under the train wheels, and the horrified face of the Monkey Man who trotted over to lead her, nudging her with his head, into her house only to find her mother stiffening in death. Luis's anguished, impotent howls and the discovery of her mother's open mouth and unseeing eyes had cast her into the peculiar dreamlike state she lived in for *so long* after she moved in with Rafaela.

The repressed memory was not because the death of her mother had dimmed it.

It was due to her understanding that she had killed a boy she loved. Just as he began to run, Edelmira reached out for a final, playful tug on the back of his jacket. It had been enough to break his stride, throw him off balance and ruin his timing. Later, when she heard talk that Diego Toledo's schoolboy brother died of gangrene, her child's mind made no connection. She had moved with Rafaela into a house filled with women and allowed Waldemar's features to become fuzzy, until she forgot why she had waited on a different balcony in the past.

Rafaela and Tomás stood by helplessly, startled faces gaping, as Edelmira continued to sob, not answering their inquiries of "What's wrong? What can we do to help?"

Nothing. Nothing could ever help. "All those men," Edelmira thought. All those opportunities for love, lost because their laughter was different, their eyes not as green, their skin not as dark, because she had been waiting for the return of a long-dead impossibility. She had been waiting for a ghost, for Waldemar Toledo who died at the age of fifteen under the wheels of the killing train. Her nightmares.

Finally, she calmed her weeping to a whimper. She rose from the ground, hugged Rafaela, kissed away her worry, and said, "My God, I should have been able to write you stories from New York."

When she told them, they felt astonished.

Rafaela blamed herself for not figuring it out. "Of course," she said, slapping her forehead. "Valdring! Waldemar's ring in baby talk. And your nightmares, the big black monster was the train." Rafaela stared at Luis's tombstone. "There were so many accidents, everyone felt relieved when they stopped the line."

Edelmira, filled with love for both of them, walked arm-in-arm between them back to the car. She felt newly emerged from murky waters. Now she knew how to make her beloved godmother happy before the cancer that plagued Rafaela and made her hold her side in pain conquered that indomitable spirit.

She planned to invite Junior Figueroa to dinner. Ignoring Tomás and Rafaela's alarm at her changed behavior, Edelmira laughed aloud. She imagined the surprise on Junior's face when she proposed marriage and warmed to the thought that it was never, ever too late.

XVI

Juan

"This is a strange request," he told his visitor. "She's not dead yet."

"I know but it's what I want," Miguelito said.

"Have you always loved her then?"

"From the time I was a little boy. She was so beautiful and helpful."

"Then why did you hex Félix for her and not for yourself?"

The small brown man, bald like Félix, laughed. "I didn't love her that way. I wanted her to be happy, and since she loved Félix, I wanted her to have him." He looked at his hands. "Anyway, I never got to use the potion."

"That can't be. The man was hexed."

"Not by me," Miguelito insisted. "I dropped the potion. It spilled on the kitchen floor."

"Then I'm not sure I know how to do this," Juan said, closing his eyes. Miguelito waited without moving. "Can you get me her sheets and underwear?"

"Yes, my mother helps tend her."

"Then get them for me, also a perfume he gave her, and when I give them back make sure they're on the bed the day she dies. That and the rest is going to be tricky."

Miguelito left, dressed as usual. This time he had not arrived at midnight in a nun's costume to disguise himself.

Juan pondered on a platonic love so fierce it triumphed over the tiniest bit of self-interest. With a sense of history repeating itself, he prepared to open his Bible to First Corinthian's explanation of love as he had on that night, so long ago, when they had all still been young, but he was stopped by another memory. He remembered the vision he had on an almost equally distant day when he had seen Félix on the ferry. The lady had whispered, "A spirit will never allow him to marry."

Juan chuckled. Yes, he could do this. He waited for something to occur to him and was not disappointed. Ideas, linked in a chain, flew into his mind. Beneath those ideas, the practical argument that it might be Félix's own spirit that did not allow him to marry shrank and quieted.

Miguelito returned with the sheets and pillow cases.

"I think you better hurry," he said. "She's down to skin and bones." Rafaela's faithful friend shed unabashed tears. "It hurts to look at her."

"Is there any way to get Edelmira in on this?"

"I don't want to." Miguelito said. "She's happily married now. Let's leave her alone."

"Come back in three days and follow my instructions to the letter. Write them down if you have to because I won't be able to repeat them."

The ritual completed, Juan felt satisfied it was going to work. Miguelito wrote everything down twice, giving Juan a copy.

"For someone else," he said. Miguelito paid him and left.

Juan no longer dug graves. He did not need the money, and, after Miguelito left, he resolved to stop receiving clients. He wanted to spend his days writing to Carmela in Santo Domingo, taking care of his enfeebled albino son, and thinking about Padre Hernán.

He decided to retire completely from all spiritual practices because it had been a magical week.

Juan finally found a scripture he had hunted for for decades. It was one of those verses he knew he had read but could never find again, no matter how hard he tried. Now, Ezekiel 18:27 was neatly marked and noted. Juan found and read the words aloud: "And when someone wicked turns back from his wickedness that he has committed and proceeds to execute justice and righteousness, he is the one that will preserve his own soul alive."

"I'll live with that," he thought. Had Padre Hernán won? No. No more spiritism but no church for him either. He would take his chances with kindness and prayer and leave it at that since he was still not sure there could be one true religion. Juan looked down at Miguelito's notes, tore them into small pieces, wet them with alcohol in an ashtray, and set the mixture ablaze. He stared at the burning paper as it turned black, curled, and disappeared in a thin wisp of rising smoke.

XVII

Cataño

Paved and improved somewhat by 1960, Cataño remained essentially the same town, lacking shade and charm. Crowds of tourists leaving the ferry, on their way to the Bacardi Rum factory, squinted at the never-ceasing glare of sunlight and at good-looking young girls.

On two occasions each year townspeople converged on their small beach. Once for the festival of the kites, when children demonstrated their creativity and originality by handmaking colorful banners and also proving their proficiency at making those kites fly, filling the skies on their side of the silvery bay. The other occasion was the jumping and whooping of family and friends as they screamed encouragement and approval for the boys attempting to swim from the town all the way across the bay to San Juan. Usually, the people flocked to Condado and Luquillo for entertainment, ignoring their own shrunken beach, and allowed stray dogs to take their place walking along the remaining sand near the water.

Except for those self-employed as pharmacists, mechanics, and gate builders, along with those who worked for them as assistants, jobs were few, so most who lived in Cataño emptied the town during the day to travel to San Juan and Bayamón for work in the shops.

From three schools, hordes of children of various sizes crashed out-

doors. On lunch or recess, these young people in their uniforms over-
flowed the town's streets and avenues; and today fighting his way through
their large number, Félix Cienfuegos, eminent older citizen, sweating and
gasping with mouth agape from his thundering run from the ferry down
the bay road and through Cataño's alleys to Rafaela's house, stood out.
Noting the tears running down his reddened face, a few of the retirees
turned their eyes to a For Sale sign posted on the window of the Barbosa
Avenue gift shop owned by Rafaela. They watched Félix disappear into
her house, understood that he was in mourning and removed their hats
and crossed themselves.

XVIII

Félix

While still alive, Rafaela haunted him every day of his life, hovering invisibly over his thoughts, his actions, or inactions, like a stubborn shadow unwilling to disperse even in darkness. He compared the light brown of her eyes, the sheen of her hair, and even her rude laughter to each woman he went through the motions of romancing. After she died, he no longer saw her.

She lay on his bed, ankles crossed, and her hands behind her head, yawning at his preparations.

Oblivious to her ghost, Félix took care to dress the part of a prospective bridegroom. He turned to look at his portly profile in the mirror. He was sixty-two but paid no attention to that, he believed a man like him to be always in his prime. Miguelito, noncommittal, handed Félix pieces of the custom-made white suit he intended to wear for the proposal.

"This time, Miguelito, I will bring home a bride."

Miguelito did not answer. Instead, he turned his head to see Rafaela smiling at him from sepia photographs on the dresser.

"This will be different," Félix continued, "from the many Gracielas, Isabelas, and Marianas of the past who refused me or whose parents refused me. The nerve of those people asking me if I had some prior commitment to another." His eyes strayed to the prints. "Remove

Rafaela's pictures and put them into one of the smaller, upper rooms. She's got to go before Dolores del Valle de Cienfuegos moves in." Miguelito was about to protest when Félix added, "But wait until I leave."

On impulse, he left through the servants' entrance to check his new horses, male and female thoroughbreds. Careful not to linger and catch the scent of the stables, he admired the strong, brown animals he hoped would produce foals for his future children, the ones he might sire with the tender Dolores.

He continued to the gates at the rear of his property to take the bay road. The wrought iron creaked and the ghost tapped him on the shoulder. He looked around, saw nothing, and continued into the blinding daylight.

Pausing from the crunching of his heavy steps on the sun-bleached gravel, he looked across the silver-plaited waters of the bay. Heat waves rippling the air wavered San Juan in the distance and bit through his shoes to his feet. The gravel seemed on fire.

"Good afternoon," Tomasa said. Miguelito's aged mother had had her roadside stand in the same place, under a fiery orange *flamboyán* tree, since he could remember.

"Give me a bouquet of your freshest, most fragrant flowers, please."

"Only the best for Señorita Dolores," she said. "And what a lucky girl she is." Félix heard more than a hint of sarcasm in the old flower seller's voice and attempted to feign surprise at her statement, staring at her without saying anything to put her in her place, but he remembered her friendship with Rafaela and nodded his agreement. He thought himself the lucky one. Dolores del Valle was a treasure for his old age. That she was costing him a fortune did not bother him.

During one of his many land-seeking excursions, he had found her at a debutantes ball in Ponce.

Félix feasted his eyes on one fresh young face after another until he spotted the most beautiful. He approached her father, standing to the left of the smiling child who was in pink lace and ruffles.

"My card, señor. I am Félix Cienfuegos, lawyer and landlord."

"Of course," Don Xavier said, extending his hand. He was younger than Félix. "You are well known, Don Félix. May I introduce my daughter?" Dolores's black eyes widened noticeably when the ghost pulled her hair, but she gave Félix her hand which he kissed.

"Forgive my bluntness, Don Xavier, but may we speak about the marriageability of your daughter?"

"To you?" Don Xavier looked at his wife, hesitating. She nodded imperceptibly. "I too must be blunt. We require a very large dowry."

Félix covered his shock by smiling. Other parents never took him seriously, and if they did, they promptly sent him packing to seek a woman his own age. He noted Don Xavier's frayed and shiny tuxedo and his wife's outmoded dress. Trapped, for once he felt forced to continue the pretense.

"I have more than I know how to spend and can share what I own with the parents of my future bride." They agreed.

With that, a long forsaken idea surfaced. He helped them pay off their debts and settled them in one of his houses in San Juan for the courting period, fully expecting them to run whenever an opportunity to save face presented itself. To his amazement, they stayed and the waiting was almost over.

One of the ferry man's assistants offered to help him hoist his bulk aboard for the trip. He refused. The effort made him perspire. He took out his perfumed handkerchief, wiped his face and head, and replaced his Panama hat as quickly as possible.

Immediately, his eye caught a group of young women dressed in their Sunday best. He approached them at the guard rail, his thick gray moustache twisted upwards at the corners.

"*Hola guapas,*" he said, touching his hat. They looked startled as the ghost whispered in their ears.

"Hello Grandpa," they replied, and burst into laughter.

Quickly, Félix moved to the shady side of the ferry to concentrate on important issues not on rude, ungracious women. He intended to set a marriage date today.

Rehearsing the scene in his mind's eye, he could see Dolores in her frilly lace dress sitting stiffly on her favorite chair, the pink one nearest the door, with her hands folded neatly on her lap and her eyes cast down. She was a serious child who never shook her curls at him nor laughed with her eyes. He felt sorry for her. "She is just too shy," he thought. So unlike the Rafaela he had met decades ago, during the infernal summer of 1920.

Once again, he saw Rafaela holding her finger to her cheek in thought while she decided whether or not to picnic with him, relived the night she danced the Charleston in her silver fringed dress, shuddered at the day he lost her.

He thought it impossible to believe that forty years had elapsed since their happy relationship ended. Feeling as if some monstrous joke had been played on him, he found himself unable to cope with the void and the regrets she left him. "I was supposed to die first," he thought, "and leave her all my money."

A current of wind lightly sprayed his face with seawater, waking him from his reverie, and brought him back to the reason he was on the ferry. He touched his handkerchief to his eyes and felt glad for the setting sun. His flowers were wilting. On docking in San Juan, he noticed the black-clad figure of the widow Bartolomeo. His old friend had died of a heart attack in a brothel.

"Going to the cemetery to pay your respects?"

"Once a month as always," she said. After rummaging away most of his life, Bartolomeo had married a very young woman. "But of course, you can't still know the sorrow of loss. You are to be married soon, no?" She shifted her eyes to a point behind him as if she saw someone she recognized.

"Very soon," he answered. Trying to follow her eyes but seeing nothing, Félix doubted the widow's great loss. She was still young and robust, not to mention rich. Her gleaming eyes invigorated him. When they parted, he felt like whistling. If Bartolomeo could marry a youngster, so could he.

The cobblestones tick-tacked under his heels with what he thought the comical sound of an unshod gelding, and his good humor allowed him to laugh at himself. As he approached the house, he heard voices coming from the patio. The ghost trailing behind him covered her mouth with both hands.

"I don't want to!" he heard Dolores shout. These were the loudest, most passionate words he had ever heard from her.

"You must," her mother said. "We need his money."

He paused, listened.

"Find someone else. I won't marry that old, fat pig."

Félix gasped and turned around to rush back the way he had arrived, wondering if anyone who saw him thought him foolish for tiptoeing through San Juan. He reached the town square with perspiration staining the band of his hat and the front of his shirt. Huffing and puffing and with his tie askew, he collapsed on a bench to catch his breath and to rearrange his thoughts.

Old, fat pig, she said. He shook his head in denial but could not help wondering what he had expected. He got up, not conscious of where he was headed, and walked until he reached a churchyard and continued past large stone Madonnas and angels. He stopped in front of a certain marker, offering his wilted flowers. As he saw the limp and browned bouquet, he felt ashamed of his gift, of all his gifts.

Heedless of damage to his special suit, he fell to his knees on the dirt and grass. With tears streaming down his bulging cheeks, he began, "Rafaela . . . ," but he stopped when he saw the apple green eyes of the widow Bartolomeo staring at him in shock, her fist balled to the "O" of her mouth. The ghost sat on her own tombstone, watching him.

"Wait," he thought. The widow was still in her child-bearing years and she had not lost her looks. They could form a friendship to console each other. He only had to regain his dignity by explaining away his unfortunate outburst and play on her sympathies.

The ghost slapped herself on the forehead and fell over backwards, sinking into her grave. He struggled to his feet, brushed himself off as best he could, and walked toward the widow until he noticed the pitiless look in her eyes. He stammered an apology and grimaced at the pangs in his chest. Slowly, he walked back to take the ferry home.

The bay road was empty of even the flower seller. He entered through the back gate and paused to catch his breath. Another pang hit his chest. His left arm felt heavy and pained. He banged on the back door.

"Miguelito, help me upstairs."

In bed, he said, "Go get Junior Figueroa." Miguelito tucked him into clean white sheets and put up his mosquito net. "Hurry," he gasped. "I'm having a heart attack."

"I'm going right now." Miguelito left.

His left side numbed; the weight on his chest threatened to crush him. He struggled unable to dislodge the white sheets encasing him and regretted that he sent Miguelito away, that he had not gone directly to see Junior.

Outside, the wind traveling through the fronds of the palm trees sounded like a gentle rainfall. A breeze entered the room, cooled the perspiration on his face, and billowed the canopy top of his mosquito net. Félix looked up at the white cloth and stared. Out of the corner of his eye he saw Miguelito, Edelmira, and Dr. Figueroa, Jr., approach, but he could not turn away from his mosquito net screen to flee pictures of regret nor stop his fingers from trying to grasp imaginary pearls.

Folktale IV
Juan Bobo se va para España
Simple Simon Goes to Spain

During the early days when Yunque, the god of the rain forest, still protected his people against their enemy the destructive huracán, Juan Bobo, his mother, and his wife watched as brown sparrows, busily whistling instructions to each other, flew away in a cloud of fluttering wings joined by parrots and crows. Then the frogs croaked and hopped away in a massive swirl of brown and green. Not to be left behind, the goats, cows, horses, and pigs stampeded after them.

"Where are they going?" Juan Bobo asked.

His mother looked at the last basket of laundry she and her daughter-in-law had just finished washing and ironing. Then she peered inside the tin can where she kept their pesetas. It was empty and so was their cupboard.

"To Spain to complain to the king about the lack of food."

She said this because she did not want to worry her two innocents nor did she know how to explain the approaching hurricane. "Hurry, my child," she added. "Take this last basket of laundry and return quickly with the money."

Juan Bobo set out, but before long the wind blew his hat off his head and he had to climb down into a ravine to retrieve it. While still in the pit, he heard roaring winds, looked up, and saw first his basket of laundry and then his mule fly overhead before he was buried by a mountain of falling trees. He threw himself against the ground and covered his head just in time but remained trapped for hours while his stomach grumbled.

It was a sad day for Juan Bobo when he returned to find villagers placing garlands of flowers on the pile of sticks that used to be his shack. His mother and wife were gone.

"¿Qué pasó?" he asked.

The villagers, astonished that Juan Bobo had survived a hurricane and knowing that he did not understand death, did not reply.

"Did they go to Spain?" he asked.

"Yes," they answered, relieved. "Creoles always dream of returning to Spain with fame and riches."

Juan Bobo scratched his head.

"We had no fame or riches," he said. "They must have gone for food. I too will travel to Spain. I'll speak to the king about the lack of fame and riches and food. Yes, I have many many complaints."

That same evening Juan Bobo set out on foot, with a bundle of his clothes tied to the end of a tree branch slung over his shoulders like a rifle. As the sun set, dropping like a ball and bringing night, the villagers watched his skinny legs sticking out of his shrunken pants become smaller and smaller until he had walked so far they no longer saw the bobbing of his possessions.

They believed that if he had survived a hurricane he would survive trying to reach Spain from Puerto Rico on foot and would return someday, but they waited and waited. They waited so many years, they almost forgot him. Juan Bobo was never heard from again except in legends.

Epilogue

Thirty years after his death no one mourned Félix, not even Edelmira who inherited all his money. On the thirtieth anniversary of his passing, she sat in a nursing home in Westchester, New York, remembering nothing at all. Celebrants on that occasion commemorated someone else, and their preparations had been clandestine and extensive.

First to arrive in groups of four were the priests. They attracted little attention on their planes except for those few alert airline passengers who looked past the crucifix hanging from their necks to the small flag with a lone star pinned to the soft white cloth on the right side of their tropical clerical garb. Four arrived in New York, four in Chicago, and four in New Jersey.

The Chicago faction flew in first and split up to fly to other states. More than a few of the female passengers regretted the sacrifice of eligible males as they watched the priests, tall and handsome, walk briskly to waiting cabs. Two weeks later, the preparations for the gathering concluded, the priests converged on the Marriott Marquis Hotel in New York, exchanged rooms, and put on civilian clothes.

On a raised dais in the grand ballroom, the three patriarchs sat directly in front of portraits of Betances and of Pedro Albizu Campos while they listened to *danzas* and *plenas* and stared intently at the multihued crowd of

3,000 children, grandchildren, and great-grandchildren, all in tuxedos. While the band played *"Qué bonita bandera,"* they looked for weak links.

They saw doctors, lawyers, engineers, professors, businessmen, priests, and farmers. What had they missed? There were policemen, army officers, postal workers, mechanics, and economists. When they deemed the time ripe, all would be ready and their waiting finished. Satisfied, the aged patriarchs, sons of Dr. Rafael Rodríguez, looked at one another. After a lifetime of unspoken communication, the brothers could each read the mind of the others. They smiled and looked at table three. It was filled with poets, writers, dancers, and actors.

Tapping a knife against his champagne glass, the eldest brought the crowd of relatives to silence. Immediately, those gathered hushed, stopped socializing and catching up on their lives since their last meeting, to look at their grandfathers on the platform.

With a wrinkled hand, he raised his glass of Dom Pérignon. They all raised theirs. His bald pate reflected the chandeliers as he toasted.

"Valor and sacrifice," he said.

"To our pearl in the Caribbean." They answered in unison and drained their glasses.